DAVID S.E. ZAPANTA

POSTHUMOUS

Book One of The Cadabra Rasa Series

PUBLISHED BY MELANCHOLY PRESS

A DIVISION OF THE MELANCHOLY COMPANY

PRINT EDITION: 978-0-9896647-0-7

This title is also available in a digital edition.

Cover illustration and jacket design © 2013 David S.E. Zapanta

Learn more: PosthumousTheBook.com

For my wife. For my children.
Always, always for you.

POSTHUMOUS

Pity is for the living, envy is for the dead.
—*Samuel Clemens (deceased)*

Am I dying or is this my birthday?
—*Lady Nancy Witcher Langhorne Astor (deceased)*

Early to death and early to arise,
makes a corpse healthy, wealthy and wise.
—*Benjamin Franklin (undead)*

PROLOGUE

Jesse Bettenay was a boy of twenty, bespectacled, slight, unkempt, broken-hearted. He wore a borrowed, oversized two-piece suit. The left lapel was torn, and two of the jacket's front buttons were missing. But Jesse did not care about such details as he trudged along a muddy cemetery path.

Just a week earlier, Jesse and his girlfriend, Ella, secretly consulted with a local witch doctor. Twenty-one was the legal age for rebirth in most states, and both Jesse and Ella were mere weeks away from their twenty-first birthdays. The young couple intended to die together so that they could be reborn together. But as they left the rebirth clinic they were accosted by violent Neo-Lifers; only Jesse survived the brutal attack.

Ella's parents, both staunch Burialists, steadfastly refused their daughter's dying wish to be reanimated. Like so many Neo-Lifers, all her parents knew of the undead were the ugly, brain-eating stereotypes. Jesse, a Kansas boy from a Resurrectionist upbringing, had fought stridently, futilely, to change their minds.

None of that mattered now, of course. Jesse couldn't raise enough money for the all-important talisman tax, much less pay a witch doctor to raise

Ella from the dead. No, she was truly lost to him forever. And now her body would rot beneath six feet of loam and soil, her cold flesh a feast for insatiable insects.

Jesse slogged along in the mud as his eyes smarted with a fresh wave of tears. He swiped angrily at his bruised, swollen face and berated himself with muttered recriminations. Jesse was a pauper, a nobody, powerless, his beleaguered heart pounding out a never-ending tattoo of regret.

He stumbled and fell to his knees as the deep muck shod him of his right shoe. Jesse lay prone in the mud, his suit pockets full of damp earth. He abandoned his shoe where it lay and continued on, determined to pay his last respects.

The whole of the Stony Hollow graveyard spread out below him as he crested a steep hill. Like most modern cemeteries this one was quite small, occupying less than two acres of barren land. Even so, as Jesse wandered down into the field, his mind boggled at the hundreds of pitted headstones.

Ella deserved better than this—all of these forgotten souls did. That was the beauty of rebirth—it was the ultimate second chance. *Cadabra Rasa*, the Resurrectionists called it. Jesse resolved then and there to rescue her from dark, unremarkable obscurity. But any dreams of post-mortem chivalry evaporated the moment he noticed a small crowd huddled around a nearby gravesite. No, not just any site—it was Ella's plot. Jesse knew this because he recognized Ella's parents and younger sister. He paused mid-stride and considered his sodden clothes and muddy hands. He looked as if he himself had just emerged from the very earth he so feared as a final resting place.

Jesse knew he owed it to Ella not to back down now. Even in death she was more beautiful to him than she ever was alive.

"Death is only the beginning," he whispered to himself. Jesse cautiously drew nearer, his heart beating furiously in his narrow chest. *You couldn't save her from those Neo-Lifers,* he told himself. *Rescue her now.*

It wasn't until Jesse emerged into the glen, though, that he noticed the

2

two Indiana state troopers flanking Ella's family. All of them were staring down at the gaping hole in the freshly turned soil. Jesse's eyes widened with amazement when he saw the muddy tracks that led away from Ella's empty grave.

"There, that's him," yelled Ella's father, and stabbed a finger in Jesse's direction. "That's the boyfriend!"

Ella's mother clutched weakly at her dark shawl. "You," she shrieked at Jesse. "Bring her back!" Ella's sister, Jill, tried to soothe her mother but was angrily rebuffed. "She belongs in the ground, you filthy zombie lover!"

Jesse began to back away. Thanks to a 150-year-old law known as the Reanimation Proclamation, cadaver poaching was a capital offense. The sentence was a fate worse than death to a Resurrectionist: cremation.

"I—I didn't do it," Jesse said, pushing his glasses up the bridge of his nose. "I swear to Lazarus, I didn't."

The two officers exchanged a wary glance. "Take it easy now, son," said the first trooper. He slowly reached for his holster. "We just want to talk."

But Jesse Bettenay had no intention of talking to anyone. All he wanted to do was find Ella. He turned and fled back up the path. Two shots rang out as a pair of footsteps thundered across the field. Both troopers swore as they slipped in the mud. Jesse followed Ella's trail through the damp earth as long as he could before it veered from the path and vanished in the wet grass.

One more shot rang out, closer this time.

Jesse held his breath, waiting for the final gunshot that never came. He chased his own footsteps back up the muddy path and out of the cemetery.

Over the next ten years the details of that fateful day fell prey to the usual embellishments. In one of the story's more popular iterations, the locals insist that Jesse wrested away an officer's firearm and took Ella's parents hostage. But the prevailing folklore painted Jesse as a mystic, a shaman, invoking black magic to summon an undead army to keep his would-be pursuers at bay.

Local mythology aside, a single detail emerged as irrefutable fact: No one in the little town of Stony Hollow, Indiana, ever saw Jesse Bettenay or Ella Brownstone again.

*　　*　　*

CHAPTER ONE

The first ashes of dawn fell upon Death Valley.

Murky sunlight bled across the valley floor, fleshing out dun-colored geometry from the shadows. The heavens brightened, an epiphany upon the blighted New Cali landscape, and Paradox Studios, for better or ill, was resurrected from the dense clay of life once more.

A lone figure in a baseball cap and overalls approached the studio's main gate. He noted the time on his wristwatch and settled against the iron fence. Within minutes, four men joined him. The four became six, then twenty. Several men carried homemade signs that declared BETTER DEAD THAN UNDEAD and KEEP ZOMBIE MARRIAGE _ILLEGAL_. The group continued to grow, man by man, sign by sign, until they were a mob, fifty strong. They milled about, speaking in hushed, urgent tones.

The Paradox soundstages were clearly discernible now against the grey sky. They were dwarfed only by the distant outline of the monolithic border wall known as Burly Gate. The lands to the west of the twenty-story wall, including the ruined Old Cali coastline, were known as the Havens. And the Havens, as everyone knew, was zombie country.

A murmur rippled through the crowd as a green Vista Cruiser coasted to a stop near the entrance. "It's Gleeson," said the man in the baseball cap. The father of the postwar anti-zombie movement was met with eager smiles and hearty handshakes as he emerged from the car.

George Gleeson was lean and angular, a gnarled, knotty root wrapped in leather. The crowd's enthusiasm gave him strength, invigorated him, made him forget he was a man half-past fifty. Made him forget, if only for a moment, that theirs was still an uphill battle against the undead. He limped forward and raised a scarred hand in greeting.

"Brothers," he said, his deep, gravelly voice booming. "Patriots. We can make a difference. We *will* make a difference. And that starts today, at the doorstep of the New Hollywood grey propaganda machine."

Several men nodded in agreement, yet the fear and desperation in so many of their haggard faces was new to Gleeson. Like most men of his generation, he had fought in the fabled Battle for Burly Gate, in which the might of the Living States military successfully held back the Havens' zombie hordes. But such a hard-won victory all those years ago meant little in what was fast becoming an undead-friendly world.

Gleeson hefted his megaphone as a pair of headlights twinkled in the distance. "Don't let these zombie lovers through," he shouted.

The crowd immediately converged on the dark sedan, screaming red-faced epithets and waving their signs. The driver leaned on the horn and slowly inched the sedan forward. Gleeson approached the car and pressed his megaphone against the window.

"It's bad enough we have to live alongside these abominations," he screamed, gesturing wildly at Burly Gate. "Must you entertain them, too?"

The mob, mainly veterans and unemployed blue-collar workers, were being replaced in the workforce by tireless, reanimated laborers. "Death to undeads," chanted the mob, and began to rock the car back and forth. Several large men in ghoulish deadface make-up blocked the gate as the sedan inched forward again.

"If you treat them like equals," yelled Gleeson, the tendons bulging from his wiry neck, "they will start acting like equals!" He turned back to the crowd. "Zombies may be stealing our jobs, but they will never steal our pride!"

The sedan's door flew open, knocking several surprised protesters to the ground. The passenger, a pale figure in a dark overcoat, bolted from the car. Weak sunlight glinted on a silver pendant around his neck.

"Brain-eater," someone yelled, pointing at the passenger. Gleeson caught the eye of one of the men blocking the gate. Vargas, a fellow Burly Gate veteran, quickly grabbed the figure by his thin, sinuous arm. The undead man wriggled frantically, his milky-blue eyes wide with fear.

"I'm here legally," he stammered. "I—I'm C.O.D.A.-certified!"

Gleeson cracked a wry smile as he stood over the undead worker. "Does anyone really care about your precious Coalition of Dead Actors?"

"No!" roared the mob.

"I think we need to send the almighty Coalition a little message."

The undead crew member, a gaffer renamed Rusty, turned to Gleeson. "Please," he said. "Don't do this!"

"Are you eyeballing Mr. Gleeson?" asked Vargas.

"What? No, of course not!"

"Sure looks that way to me," someone yelled.

"I—I can't help it," said Rusty. "I don't have any eyelids!"

Vargas grabbed the undead man's hand. He snapped off a bone-white pinky as if it were a piece of chalk. The crowd roared its approbation as Vargas tossed the dismembered digit over his shoulder.

"One down," Vargas said. "Nine to go."

A second pair of headlights pierced through the gloom and swept across the angry throng. A heavily armored police cruiser pulled in behind the Vista Cruiser, its blue and red lights flashing. "Release the cadaver," barked a voice from the cruiser's roof-mounted speaker.

Gleeson swore as his followers scattered, disappearing down darkened side streets and alleyways. Aside from the discarded signs in the gutter, only the men in deadface remained. They glared at the cruiser as they took their place behind Gleeson. Rusty looked stunned at his good fortune. He scrambled back into the car as it sped off onto the Paradox lot.

The officer lowered his window as Gleeson ambled up to the cruiser. "Sir, don't you have something better to do with your free time?"

Gleeson smiled as he leaned against the cruiser. At least his protests were finally attracting some attention. "We're just a group of patriots out for an early-morning stroll, officer. No harm in that, is there?"

"Watch yourself, Mr. Gleeson. The New Hollywood P.D. has zero tolerance for necrophobia."

He was flattered; they knew his name. "Is that a fact."

"That's a fact," replied the officer with a tight smile.

Behind Gleeson, the men in deadface shifted uncomfortably. "So how much are those C.O.D.A. bastards paying you to sell out your own kind?"

"This house call is free of charge, sir. Consider yourself warned."

Gleeson fumed as the patrol car roared away. He kicked at the discarded placards with a steel-toed boot. "Pick up these damn signs," he barked. "Put them in the back of my car."

By now the eastern face of Burly Gate blazed brightly in the morning light. Good men had built that wall, thought Gleeson. Strong men, full of purpose, their bodies reduced long ago to ashes and dust. He smiled and turned to the men who remained by his side.

"We're not going home until these zombie-loving propagandists have heard what the Brotherhood of Warmbloods has to say."

The zombie apocalypse was inevitable; of this, he was certain. And, warm-blooded patriots like George Gleeson, their hearts black with malice, would be ready for the undead uprising.

CHAPTER TWO

Meanwhile, on the other side of the Paradox lot, all was quiet in Viktor Vincent's large corner office. Squat and bespectacled, his brown eyes beaming from beneath a mop of grey, wavy hair, Viktor looked more like a retired school teacher than an esteemed film director.

He turned his attention to the computer in front of him. Several months ago, at the urging of a mutual friend of a friend, Viktor reluctantly consented to participate in the Legendary Filmmakers series. Now, months later, as he watched a rough cut of the documentary, he deeply regretted the decision. Staring back at him from the computer screen was a much younger, hungrier Viktor Vincent, from the set of his first film, an undead dramedy titled *Grey Matters*.

He absently rubbed his belly with both hands. "Meanwhile, thirty pounds and thirty years later..." He sighed and resumed playback of the video. The baritone-voiced narrator solemnly expounded on Viktor's career.

"That he possessed a pulse did not prevent Vincent from helming some of the century's most influential undead-themed movies. Indeed, Vincent possessed an uncanny knack for portraying undead life in a way that defied negative stereotypes."

9

Viktor buried his head in his hands. "Who on earth is *writing* this?" he groaned. The somber narration continued.

"Vincent's penchant for casting actual undead actors—at a time when other studios employed living actors in deadface make-up—certainly endeared the young director to the reanimated community. Thirty years ago, such a naturalistic approach to zombie exploitation cinema, as it was once known, was both groundbreaking and controversial."

The documentary cut to old interview footage of Viktor laughing as he said, *"Sure, let's leave exploiting the undead to pros like George Romero."*

Viktor stared blankly at the screen. His comment was taken completely out of context. The last thing he needed was an angry phone call from Romero. Since his rebirth, the *Night of the Living Dead* director was a cantankerous old corpse.

Viktor turned away from his computer. Revisiting his past was proving counter-productive; he needed to focus on the here and now. His newest project, *Reborn On the Wrong Side of the Wall*, was based on the bestselling zomance novel of the same name. The plot was simple enough: An undead heiress falls in love with a warm-blooded carpenter.

Damon Grayson, a living actor and red-carpet darling, landed the coveted role of Lucas, the lovelorn handyman. For Dawn, the undead heiress, Viktor insisted on screen legend Audrey Hepburn, who had yet to be resurrected. The producers balked, questioning if a more recent (and already reanimated) corpse couldn't be cast as Dawn. They suggested Julia Roberts, who had only passed away two years prior. But Viktor was adamant about Hepburn.

He rose from his desk and moved to the picture window. The valley spread out below him. To the east, just past Furnace Creek, lay the heart of New Hollywood. Dozens of rival studios spread out across the landscape, their myriad soundstages like a pox upon the twinkling salt plains. To the north, the outline of Cemetery Stadium was barely discernible through the mid-morning haze.

Were it not for Burly Gate, it would have been a picture-perfect view of the valley. Secretly, the director longed for the wall's demise. But even Viktor knew such a change couldn't happen overnight. The 500-mile wall housed four Living States garrisons, seven museums, and twice as many gift shops. It also hosted daily re-enactments of the Battle for Burly Gate (twice daily on Sundays). In short, the wall was Death Valley's biggest tourist draw, attracting visitors from the world over.

The Bureau of Undead Affairs declared Burly Gate an anachronistic eyesore and a tool of Living States oppression. Viktor agreed—the Cold Wars were long over, and The Battle for Burly Gate was almost thirty years ago. Since then, the living and the undead had forged an unlikely truce. Not for the first time, Viktor wondered why millions of innocent reanimates were needlessly persecuted for the actions of a few rogue shamans.

A light rap on his door interrupted the director's thoughts. He glanced at the closed door over the tops of his wire-frame glasses. Though he was unaware of it, his shoulders were perpetually hunched, causing him to har-rumph into his chest. He did so now as he addressed his undead production assistant.

"Yes, Buddy, I'm coming."

Buddy poked his pale head through the door.

"How do you always know it's me?"

"When is it not you?" Viktor paused and glanced down at his loyal P.A. "You don't have to answer that."

"I wouldn't know how to, sir."

Viktor patted Buddy on his bony shoulder. His assistant was like family to him. "What have I told you about that 'sir' nonsense?"

"Sorry sir. Force of habit I guess."

"And since when are you a Cads fan?" Viktor pointed to Buddy's brand-new Calabasas Cadavers jersey.

"Since I lost a stupid bet."

"You and your bets," Viktor chuckled. "Better luck next time."

"Second time's a charm, sir," Buddy said, referring to a well-worn un-dead platitude.

"You'd know better than most, I suppose."

Buddy shrugged. "Same shit, different life, as they say."

"So, did Damon ever receive an invitation to your weekly poker game with the crew?"

Buddy faltered as he pushed a thick pair of glasses up the nearly non-existent bridge of his nose. "No...not yet."

Damon Grayson may have been the biggest name in New Hollywood, but Buddy, like many of the undead crew members, was not among the A-list actor's biggest fans. Viktor wanted to change that; he believed a unified set was a happy set. "It would mean a lot to me if you'd reconsider."

"I—I suppose. But if half the things I've read about him lately in the 'bloids are true—"

Viktor didn't break stride. "Damon has paid his dues. He's a new man. You'll see. He doesn't have a necrophobic bone in his body."

Buddy tried to hide his dubious expression behind his clipboard. He cleared his throat again and began rattling off production details.

"Audrey's still in make-up. She doesn't look desiccated enough." Buddy glanced at Viktor. "Her words, not mine," he added quickly. "I think she looks great."

"Of course she does. The woman is still a star." He paused to pluck a loose grey hair that had fallen across his nose. He held the gossamer strand aloft in his fingertips before dispelling it with a strong breath. "Fifty years in the cold ground can't change that," he said. "She's just nervous about today's scene."

"About that, sir. Damon's not here yet." Buddy lifted a Walkie-talkie to his mouth. "Anyone have eyes on Damon yet?"

The query was quickly answered by a resounding, static-filled "No."

"He'll be here," the director replied a little too emphatically.

Buddy peered over the top of his clipboard. "He's not answering his cell phone and his manager has no idea where he is. And..." Buddy paused to clear his throat. "And Russell Mann is on the lot."

Viktor harrumphed into his sweater vest. "Very funny."

12

"I'm afraid it's true, sir. He arrived about ten minutes ago."

Viktor's plump cheeks ballooned as he harrumphed again. There was only one reason why C.O.D.A.'s undead president would deign to visit Paradox. "Damon's comment was blown way out of proportion by the 'bloids," he said more to himself than to Buddy.

"Which comment would that be, sir? It's hard to keep track."

Damon was quoted in *Reanimated Weekly* as saying that he'd 'have to be brain-dead not to act opposite undead Audrey-freaking-*Hepburn*.' Referring to the undead as brain-dead had fallen out of favor years ago. Viktor knew Russell Mann greylisted actors for far less than that during his storied career.

"I hope to Lazarus that everyone's talisman has been registered," Viktor sighed. "C.O.D.A. will be looking for any excuse to shut this production down."

Buddy tapped his pen against the page. "Already taken care of."

"You're a lifesaver, Buddy."

Buddy broke into a yellow, snaggle-toothed smile. "So I've been told, sir."

"What about the C of C?" asked Viktor, referring to C.O.D.A.'s official Code of Conduct. In light of Damon's recent gaffe, the Coalition would likely review the actor's paperwork. "Please tell me they've all been signed and returned."

Buddy sighed. "All but one."

Viktor couldn't hide his disappointment. He half-hoped his assistant had proactively forged Damon's signature, but he didn't dare ask. Instead he nodded and said, "It's fine. We'll be fine. Of course he'll sign it."

The pair finally arrived on the set. Department heads began making beelines for Viktor. "Let me know the second Damon gets here," he said. "And if anyone asks, he's in his trailer."

CHAPTER THREE

Damon Grayson's custom-built trailer, the Aspire Super Coach 5000, sported three bedrooms, two bathrooms, a rec room, and a conference room. The 100-foot long, two-story trailer also included a state-of-the-art security system that ensured its occupants remained safe from the outside world. Even so, Damon took the extra step of instructing Cornelius, his bodyguard, not to open the door to anyone, no matter who it was.

"Not even Buddy?" Cornelius asked, incredulous.

Damon studied his reflection in the glossy screen of his phone. He benefitted from good bone structure and piercing blue eyes that were usually hidden by a shock of sandy-colored hair. His near-perfect nose and strong chin, though, he owed to a surgeon's skilled hand. The cumulative effect of good genes and a scalpel yielded the sort of face that graced movie screens and magazine covers the world over.

Damon modeled various expressions as he continued to stare at himself in the shiny glass of his phone. He finally settled on what he considered his Intensity Face. He turned to Cornelius and appeared almost simian as he furrowed his brow.

"Don't tell me Buddy actually intimidates a big guy like you."

"I think Buddy can read minds," said Cornelius. "It kind of gives me the heebie-jeebies."

Damon stopped to reconsider his bodyguard. Topping out at almost seven feet, Cornelius was big even for a Samoan. His round, boyish face and kind grey eyes belied his broad-shouldered, 450-pound physique. He was no mere talent protection specialist, thought Damon; Cornelius was Burly Gate personified. And yet his bodyguard's fear of Viktor's diminutive assistant gave the actor pause. Buddy may have acted like a know-it-all, but he didn't really know everything.

"Are you kidding? Buddy's not a mind reader!" Damon hooted with laughter. "I mean, a mind-*eater*, maybe…"

Cornelius crept over to one of the tinted one-way windows. "You may want to keep it down." He crouched down and parted the satin curtains with a meaty hand. "You don't want him to catch you hiding in here."

"Neo-Lifers have put a price on my head, Neil. Believe me, I've got bigger things to worry about."

"You've gotta remember to keep it real. That's the key. Keep it real."

"Fair enough." Damon grabbed a video game controller from the couch. "We can still squeeze in one game."

Script pages for the day's scene were swept aside to make room for Cornelius. Damon pressed a button in the arm of the couch. A hidden panel in the wall slid open, revealing a gleaming flatscreen television.

"If you don't mind me saying so, you're stalling," said Cornelius.

Damon was impressed by his bodyguard's candor. His former assistant, a reedy, wide-eyed cadaver renamed Chip, never called him out on anything. Whether he was starstruck or just indifferent, one thing Chip was not was perceptive. Cornelius was right, though—Damon *was* stalling.

"It's a pretty big deal, this mixed-life kiss," Damon said.

"Miss Hepburn is quite lovely," said Cornelius. "You're the envy of New Hollywood."

"Listen, what I'm about to tell you stays between the two of us, okay, Neil?"

"Of course, Mr. Grayson," he said solemnly. "You can trust me."

Damon didn't know if he could trust anyone—but who else did he have, really? "This might sound crazy," Damon whispered, "but I've never actually kissed a cadaver before."

"Neither have I," confessed Cornelius. "But there's a first time for everything."

"I just figured the first time would be a lot different, if that makes any sense."

"You sure could do a lot worse than Miss Hepburn."

Damon smiled, more for Cornelius's benefit than his own. He was eager to change the subject. Damon picked up the second video game controller and tossed it to Cornelius.

"Come on," said Damon. "One quick game. Five minutes, I swear."

Cornelius eyed the Code of Conduct on the coffee table. "Shouldn't you at least sign that first?"

The controller sagged in Damon's hand. "You're not exactly the life of the party, are you? Don't worry, I'll get to it."

The couch creaked as it yielded to Cornelius's prodigious frame. "You're in charge," he said, and settled into the overstuffed cushions. "What're we playing?"

"Denizens of the Dark 3."

Cornelius's eyes widened. "But…the Secretary of Undead Affairs banned that game. You can't find it anywhere."

Damon scoffed. Solomon may have been powerful, but the reclusive shaman never ventured from the Havens. "It's just a game, Neil. That's all. There's nothing wrong with killing make-believe zombies."

Cornelius winced at Damon's cavalier use of the Z-word. As far as undead slurs went, it didn't get more offensive than that one. "I'm sorry. I don't feel right about this. Killing the living-challenged just seems wrong to me. Even make-believe ones." He set the controller down. "You better not let Joni catch you playing this game."

Damon was surprised Cornelius knew his undead publicist's name.

"Don't get all moral on me now," he said. "Besides, she's not my mother."

Damon bobbed and weaved on the couch as his onscreen avatar, a lantern-jawed soldier in military fatigues, ran and jumped its way across a warehouse full of undead assailants. At the press of a green button, Damon's avatar lobbed a grenade into the virtual horde. Moaning cadavers exploded like rotten tomatoes. Actual reanimated corpses were bloodless, but Damon didn't mind the game's creative license.

"I love the smell of decomp in the morning!"

Damon quickly glanced at Cornelius, whose back was turned to the television. "I am recusing myself from this potentially harmful activity."

Chip, god bless his cold, shriveled heart, would have gladly engaged in some pixelated zombie-cide. If only his assistant hadn't run off with that mystery girl from the Havens. Damon hung his head and sighed as he tossed the controller aside.

"Fine, Neil. You win."

Cornelius handed the unsigned Code of Conduct to Damon. "This is not about me. It's about the greater good. It's about—"

"Keeping it real. I understand." He quickly scribbled his signature and handed the papers back to Cornelius.

"But you didn't even read it."

Damon laughed. "Do you know how many of these things I've signed?" He cleared his throat and placed a hand over his beating heart. "Number four: 'I promise that living-challenged actors shall not be dismembered, disemboweled or in any other way be mutilated for the purpose of entertainment.'" Damon smiled. "I nailed that one, right?"

Cornelius scanned the document. "Yes, but..."

"Here's another one. Number twelve: 'I promise that living-challenged actors shall not be depicted committing acts that denigrate, debase, humiliate or otherwise portray the undead community in an unfavorable, unrealistic, or salacious manner.'" Damon paused to smooth down his hair. "In other words, no brain-eating stereotypes." He rolled his eyes back and groaned as he staggered around the trailer's lounge area.

Cornelius frowned at the Code of Conduct. "I'm not sure you should be doing that, even in private."

"C'mon, I'm just goofing around." He took the Code of Conduct and stuffed it in his back pocket. "Believe me, I don't want to wind up in Russell Mann's Black Book of Death."

The two men squinted as they emerged from the trailer into the bright sunlight. They looked toward the main gate, where a Neo-Life demonstration was in full swing.

"Zombies equal death!" they chanted. "Better dead than undead!"

If Damon felt vulnerable inside his trailer, he felt completely exposed as they crossed the lot. "Those Neo-Lifers sure know how to party," he said nervously.

Cornelius scanned the lot for anything out of the ordinary. "Just ignore them, Mr. Grayson."

Men in deadface make-up blew kisses through the gate. Damon quickly averted his face. "Kind of hard not to, Neil."

"Don't worry," said Cornelius. "If I hit someone, they have a habit of staying down."

Damon smiled, despite his worries. He was really beginning to like the big lug. He doubted the feeling was mutual.

CHAPTER FOUR

Despite her recent exhumation and resurrection, Audrey Hepburn proved to be a model cadaver. She didn't suffer from the usual post-rebirth denial or depression that accompanied many reanimations. A three-month stint in the elite charm school Erebus Academy guaranteed a smooth reintegration into everyday life. By all accounts, Audrey's rebirth couldn't have gone any better.

Of course, being an undead celebrity meant being held to a different set of standards.

Studios encouraged undead actors to both flaunt and enhance their cadaverous qualities. In Hepburn's case, an expensive maggot and leech poultice had carefully abraded what was left of her decomposed flesh. And, in addition to wearing milk-colored contact lenses (many undead suffered from a cataract-like condition known as 'milk-eye'), she also underwent extensive scar and lesion augmentation.

Now, on set, the results of her rigorous regimen were breathtaking. Adorned in nothing but a besotted black dress and a government-issued, shaman-approved talisman (cleverly disguised as a silver broach), she was the very picture of elegant, delicate decay.

Damon whistled as he strode onto the set clad in Lucas's standard-issue wardrobe—a maroon flannel shirt and ripped, faded blue jeans. "Looking good, Aud." She hid her ghastly smile behind her hand. "If I didn't know any better, I would say you're actually blushing."

"I wish I could," she said. "But excess fluid is a no-no for maintaining dry, necrotic skin."

Buddy hurried up to Damon, a scowl on his waxen face. "Where on earth have you been?" He shook the call sheet at Damon. "You should have been here two hours ago!"

Damon glanced uneasily at Cornelius, who hovered near the craft services table. "Uh, why, what have you heard?"

Buddy blocked Damon's way with his clipboard. "I need your signed C of C."

Damon pulled the rumpled papers from his leather tool belt and handed them to Buddy. Viktor, who had been chatting with Russell Mann, saw Damon and excused himself. Buddy shot Damon an angry stare before hurrying off to another part of the set.

"And here's our carpenter now," said Viktor, clapping him on the back.

"Sorry, Vik. I got tied up."

Viktor waved away the comment with a chubby hand. "You need to get into makeup."

"Already been and back," Damon replied with a lopsided grin.

"I think he looks splendid," said Audrey. "Tall, dark and brooding is just my type."

Just then the lights inside the soundstage flickered, then dimmed. The crew paused, waiting for the building's back-up generators to kick in.

"Buddy—" started Viktor, but Buddy was already on the move.

"I'm on it." Walkie-talkie in hand, he raced off to check on the emergency power.

Meanwhile, Audrey frowned as she delicately probed the semi-gelatinous surface of her eyes. She turned to Damon, her decomposed brow etched with worry. "Is it me, or—"

"No, no, it's not you," Viktor said. "There's probably a problem up at the Josiah's Bluff crematorium. Happens all the time."

Audrey's arid laughter sounded like a retching cat. "So it's not my vision? Thank goodness! But what would a crematorium have to do with losing power?"

Viktor glanced over at Russell Mann and smiled uneasily. The facility was located at the northern tip of the Havens, just beyond the Charnel Point shantytowns. The crematorium was the country's biggest and busiest, generating power to all of North America.

The lights on the soundstage flickered again but the generators still did not kick in.

"It's people!" Damon suddenly exclaimed.

"Damon," Viktor harrumphed.

"It's fueled by *people!*" Damon laughed at his own manic, wide-eyed Charlton Heston impression.

Russell Mann didn't crack a smile. He glared long and hard at Damon.

"The continued existence of that mercury-spewing power plant is no laughing matter," Mann said. "You organ donors understand nothing about the Charnel Point slums. The toxic pollution generated by Josiah's Bluff only adds to their misery."

Viktor mopped the sweat from his brow. "Can someone else find out what is happening with our *generators?*" he barked.

"Maybe the country finally ran out of Cremationists," said Damon.

Audrey's eyes grew wide. "What on earth is a Cremationist?"

Damon shrugged. "Let's just say that being undead isn't everyone's cup of tea. Some people would rather burn than return, if you know what I mean."

Viktor held his breath, but Damon did not elaborate. Cornelius watched him, closely, too.

"Well, I quite like being undead," said Audrey matter-of-factly. "Who wouldn't jump at a second chance?"

Viktor smiled grimly. "Oh, you'd be pretty surprised."

Buddy hurried back onto the set, his new Cads jersey sullied by dirty handprints. "Someone drained the gasoline from our generators," he informed Viktor. "Everything should be up and running in a minute, sir."

The soundstage was suddenly bathed in blinding light. The D.P. scrambled onto the set to double-check his light readings. Meanwhile, Viktor turned to the cast and crew and clapped his hands for attention.

"Are we ready to make movie history?" he asked with a broad smile.

"I'm breathless with anticipation." Audrey winked with a dry rustling of her remaining eyelid.

"That's the spirit," said Viktor, and escorted them towards their marks.

"They're calling this my comeback," Audrey said in a raspy voice scarcely above a whisper. "I'm a bit nervous, actually." She shook her head and fretted absently with the broach. "This still feels new to me. Everything does."

"I've seen you in action," Damon said. "You're a natural. You can do this in your sleep."

The costume designer darted in to readjust Audrey's broach. "You're kind," Audrey told Damon. "But I was told not to watch any of my old films. I'll just have to take your word for it."

"Don't let the pressure get to you," Damon said as his hairdresser ran a quick comb through his carefully tousled locks. "Rebirth is the hard part, right? Besides, it's me you should be worried about."

Audrey's ashen flesh crinkled like rice paper as she smiled. "At least, not so far. You're not as bad as they say."

"Oh, he's worse." Viktor slipped on a pair of headphones that nearly vanished within his wild mane of hair. "Way worse."

"Picture's up," warned the assistant D.P. as the camera started to roll.

Viktor glanced over at Russell Mann before turning back to his leads. "You know the drill, kids." He leaned back and watched as Damon's carefree expression magically assumed the troubled carpenter's grave demeanor.

"Remember, the world is against you," Viktor said. "They want your mixed-life romance to fail."

Viktor quietly gauged Audrey's performance as well. Half her face may have been missing, the exposed, necrotized musculature stiff and brittle, and yet, as Dawn, the Resurrectionist heiress, she was still able to articulate a surprising vulnerability.

Damon approached her now, tentatively, his face darkened by the shadow of doubt as he hit his mark. "They say you only love me for my brains," he whispered to Audrey. "But I know the truth. And the truth is, you see the love of your afterlife standing before you."

Audrey gasped, wide-eyed. Her left trapezium shredded like an old rubber band as she quickly turned her head away.

Emboldened, Damon stepped closer. "If I'm wrong..." His voice caught in his throat. "If I'm the only one who feels this way...then I may as well be cremated now. I can't live without you, Dawn, in this life or the next."

He smiled as he gingerly embraced Audrey, just as he'd done dozens of times in rehearsals. Her bony, knobby frame clattered like a paper bag of ice picks against his chest.

"It's all right," she said coyly. "I won't break."

Damon blanched as a tiny maggot poked its way out of her left nostril. "Tell me if this feels like a terrible, terrible mistake," he said uneasily as the maggot crept across her philtrum and disappeared behind a yellowed bicuspid. He quickly averted his gaze and swallowed hard. "Tell me," he said, his voice quavering, "if some things are simply not meant to be."

Viktor frowned, as did Russell and the horrified script supervisor. Damon had gone off-script. The correct line was 'tell me if things *are* simply meant to be.' This was no mere slip of the tongue. Russell scribbled furiously in a black Moleskine notebook.

"Do it." Audrey stroked his hair with chilly, mold-encrusted fingernails. "Kiss me, Lucas. Before all is lost."

Viktor quietly rose from his chair and licked his lips. The big moment was finally at hand. Viktor nodded and the camera began to track in slowly for the close-up of the fateful kiss.

Damon finally managed to meet her eye. Another maggot, this one no bigger than a sesame seed, emerged from one of her barren tear ducts. "Sorry," Damon managed to blurt, then vomited all over Audrey's little black dress. "Jesus," he croaked, his hands on his knees. He wiped his mouth with the back of his hand. "I'm, uh, having trouble finding my motivation for this scene."

The crew looked on in slack-jawed silence as Damon lifted his head and promptly vomited again on his leading lady.

Audrey didn't miss a beat. "I'm starting to take this personally," she quipped.

Russell Mann's pale eyes bulged from their sockets. He charged onto the set and stood within an inch of Damon.

"You are a discredit to your craft, Mr. Grayson."

"I'm just keeping it real," Damon replied. He flashed the crew a shaky thumbs-up.

Mann narrowed his eyes. "Can someone *please* get a damp towel for Ms. Hepburn?"

"You must find me positively repulsive," she said to Damon, her lower lip trembling.

"Hold on," he said. "I never said repulsive. Never. Listen, I'm just having a bad morning, okay? I have nothing against you people."

"You people?" said Mann, his voice climbing.

"Come on, you know what I mean," said Damon. "You're twisting my words around. Some of my best friends are zombies." He blanched a second time. "I didn't mean it that way."

Audrey slapped him hard across the face, nearly severing her withered hand in the process. "We're all just brain-eaters to you!" Her hand dangled by a single, jerky-like tendon as she stormed off the set.

"We have zero tolerance for necrophobia, Mr. Grayson," said Mann. "The undead have worked too long and too hard to make a rename for ourselves, not only in this Living-centric industry, but in the world at large. It's outdated thinking such as yours that is keeping us in the Grey Ages."

"You're laying it on a bit thick, aren't you? It's not like I'm some crazy Neo-Lifer."

"Damon," said Viktor nervously. "That's enough." He quickly turned to the crew. "Everyone, take five." But no one budged. This truly was history in the making.

"I don't have to take this," Damon said. "I've paid my dues."

"Indeed," said Mann, withdrawing the Moleskine notebook from his breast pocket. "This, coming from the man who once dispatched 256 cadavers in a single movie. Rather, 256 *living* actors in *deadface* make-up."

Damon coughed. "*Silent But Undeadly 3*. Yeah, about that—"

"That was a direct-to-video release," Viktor offered helpfully. "It was a flop, even on video. It barely made back its budget."

"You have single-handedly managed to set back undead rights by twenty years, Mr. Grayson. Have the living learned nothing from the Battle for Burly Gate?"

"I'm not responsible for the Cold Wars," said Damon. "I'm an actor, not some terrorist. I keep your people employed, Mr. Mann." He gestured to the mostly living-challenged crew. "If not for me—"

"While your handlers would lead us to believe you are the very picture of redemption, you continue to perpetuate negative stereotypes," spat Mann. "Consider yourself on notice, Mr. Grayson." He pursed his pale lips. "You may be New Hollywood's flavor of the moment, but as far as C.O.D.A. is concerned, you will *never* work in this town again."

As if on cue, Damon proceeded to vomit all over the most influential cadaver in New Hollywood.

CHAPTER FIVE

Damon was back in his Aspire Super Coach, his lanky frame slouched across a leather armchair, his head buried in his hands. Hepburn was also in her trailer, but she'd refused Damon the chance to apologize face to face for what was one of the most humiliating moments of his life. *You don't gross me out at all*, he'd shouted through her locked trailer door. But she'd remained unmoved—and her door had remained locked. So, as a form of penance, Damon was still clad in his vomit-covered flannel. Meanwhile, Cornelius stood outside his trailer, holding the throng of hungry 'bloiders at bay.

"Mr. Grayson has no comment at this time," Damon overheard him repeating to the crowd. A sudden flurry of activity was followed by a cacophony of shouted questions.

"Does Damon have a maggot phobia?"

"Does he have enough dead cred to come back from this?"

"Is it splitsville for DayBurn?"

The trailer door opened. Damon didn't bother to look up.

"You've got a good man out there," yelled Viktor from the other end of the trailer. "For a second I didn't think he'd let even me through."

"He wasn't supposed to," Damon groaned into his hands. "Remind me to fire him, please."

Viktor's feet sunk into the plush carpet as he made his way past the mahogany conference table in the middle of the trailer. "So tell me, what really happened?"

Damon stared at him from between his fingers. He wished it were as simple as nerves. "I honestly don't know, Vik. I just got queasy all of a sudden."

"Well, I'm sure your publicist will think of something. She's gotten you out of worse situations."

"Trust me, Joni's not taking any calls. I tried all morning. Her assistant said she's off chanting with monks or something in Tibet."

"She picked a hell of a time to do it," sighed Viktor. "What did Barbarelli say?"

"I—I haven't called him yet."

"Well, I suggest you do it as soon as possible," Viktor said sternly. "We need to fix this before the 'bloids blow it out of proportion."

Damon hopped up from his chair and returned with his phone. He shook the device, sprinkling the trailer's expensive decor with navy-blue water. "Here," he said, slapping the wet phone into Viktor's hand.

"Was this in your toilet?"

"It was keeping my career company." Damon sank back into the chair and resumed cradling his head in his hands. "Just watch."

Viktor said nothing as he viewed an online video clip of Damon vomiting on Audrey, followed by the on-set altercation with Russell Mann. Viktor had a reputation for running a tight ship. Nothing from his sets had ever been leaked to the 'bloids.

"Someone on the crew…?" Viktor asked.

"Does it really matter?" Damon asked. "I'd hate me, too, if I were them. Even if Joni *were* here, I don't know how she could fix this."

Viktor was suddenly a man on a mission. "Try her again," he barked from the door. "And then call Barbarelli." Red-faced, he disappeared without another word into the waiting mob's ravenous maw.

Damon sprung from his chair...and quickly sat back down. He had no intention of calling anybody. Viktor was right about Joni—his publicist had repaired his dead cred more times than he could count. Why would this time be any different? Damon wiped the water from his phone and did what any celebrity would do when faced with a crisis—he took to Flutter and declared his innocence to his million-plus followers in a series of tersely worded Beats. Within minutes his Beats Per Minute were higher than they'd ever been—higher even than Joni's at her peak—and she had close to two million followers.

I think breakfast at Tiffany's gave me food poisoning, he typed with his thumbs. Sure, it was a glib statement, but the public didn't view stars like Damon as real, flesh-and-blood people. Actors were nothing more than vapid, objectified ciphers, on-set or off. So then why risk ridicule in the 'bloidosphere for possessing even a shred of humanity?

Damon published his latest Beat and couldn't help but smile as his Flutter ranking skyrocketed predictably into the social media stratosphere. He even chuckled as he imagined Joni's face when she came back down from her mountain retreat and found she'd been dethroned from her vaunted top spot. Maybe there was an upside to this so-called scandal after all.

"Mr. Grayson, what are you doing?" Damon yelped with surprise as Cornelius towered over him. For a person of such considerable size his bodyguard was unusually light on his feet.

Damon quickly tucked his phone away in his shirt's pocket. "I'm trying to keep it real, Neil."

"By sending out a bunch of Beats?"

Damon's face grew hot. "Oh, you, uh, you follow me on Flutter?"

"So does Viktor, Mr. Grayson. He's quite upset with you."

As Damon rose from his chair he realized he was still covered in his own dried vomit. He instinctively reached for his phone to post this observation for his Flutter followers. Cornelius's expectant gaze made Damon rethink his actions. W.W.J.D. *What Would Joni Do?*

Damon changed into a fresh set of clothes. "Did anyone call my driver? Is my car ready?"

"Your driver's name is Tom. Was."

"What do you mean 'was'?"

Just then there was a quick knock at the door. Justin, the 3rd assistant director, stuck his head into the trailer. "Just thought you should know, I'm still trying to find you a car. But it looks like there's been a vote."

Damon and Cornelius exchanged a puzzled look. "I don't understand."

"You're being boycotted by the local chauffeur's union."

Damon was incredulous. "Because I accidentally vomited on Audrey Hepburn?"

"No—because you vomited on Russell Mann," Justin answered matter-of-factly. "Tough break, Mr. Grayson." A smug smile spread across the 3rd A.D.'s pale face as the door banged shut behind him.

"Okay, what about you, Neil? Let's just go in your car."

"I take the bus," said Cornelius, and fished a monthly bus pass from his wallet to prove it. "I'm trying to reduce my carbon footprint."

"Barry's gonna kill me."

"Actually, I did overhear one driver say he'd take you—but on one condition."

These sorts of disputes always came down to money. "Pay him double whatever he's asking. I'm willing to triple it, but that's it."

Cornelius's gaze dropped to the floor. "The condition was that you'd be in the back of a hearse."

Damon clapped his hands as inspiration struck. "That's perfect! Go find that guy and tell him Buddy needs a ride across town."

"I don't understand. Buddy—"

"Trust me, Neil." His phone began to beep more and more insistently as his Flutter ranking—and his BPM along with it—began a precipitous decline. "Just give me twenty minutes to get ready."

He leapt past Cornelius and out the door. His bodyguard could only watch as Damon pushed past the surprised 'bloiders and sprinted across the lot towards the make-up trailer.

CHAPTER SIX

Even on the best of days, Barry Barbarelli was not a patient man. This was not one of his best days. Nor was it Damon's. Like most people with a TV or an Internet connection, Damon's manager had watched his biggest client unload his lunch on Audrey Hepburn. Then Barbarelli watched it again. And again. He distracted himself by monitoring Damon's Q Score. It was only marginally better than the actor's plummeting dead cred.

Barbarelli jumped up from his desk and began to pace his office. "Diane!" he bellowed at the closed door. "Status!"

"Still no change," buzzed a patient but weary voice from the intercom.

Barbarelli's desk was littered with dozens of well-handled stress toys. He grabbed a rubber heart and proceeded to crush its ventricles in a vice-like grip. "As soon as you hear from him—"

"If he calls, yes, you'll be the first to know."

"The *millisecond* he calls, Diane!" He spun and hurled the toy at his computer. The heart caromed off the plasma monitor and into a wall. The monitor teetered before toppling off the desk and onto the hardwood floor with a loud clatter.

"Son of a *bitch*," he bellowed, "this new arm is a *cannon!*"

Diane appeared in the doorway. "What broke now?" She sighed as Barbarelli tugged her inside the room.

"Here, feel this." He flexed his recently acquired undead limb and nodded at the bulging, grapefruit-sized bicep. His assistant rolled her eyes and reluctantly poked his proffered prosthetic arm. "It used to belong to a college quarterback."

"Amazing."

"Well worth the quarter mil," he said of his dyborg arm. "Better than the last one."

"You need to stop punching walls."

Barbarelli's eyes darkened. "And you need to get Damon on the phone."

"Hey, hey, what's the ruckus?" Damon asked as he and Cornelius strode into the office. The actor's face and hands were hidden beneath layers of very convincing latex cadaver make-up.

"I don't even want to know," Diane said.

"The fake maggots are a nice touch." Barbarelli pointed to the white, rice-like flecks spilling from Damon's ear. "Real classy."

Damon smiled as he pecked out another Beat on his phone. "It's all about the details, Barry."

"Hey, is that a new phone?" asked Barbarelli. "Let me see it."

Damon reluctantly placed it in his manager's outstretched hand. "Don't smudge the screen."

"Don't worry, I won't." Barbarelli crushed the phone with his dyborg-enhanced strength. "This is for your own good, Damon."

"Hey, I was up to 80 BPM! You're gonna make me flatline, Barry!"

"Said the schmuck wearing deadface make-up. Are you fucking kidding me?" He turned to Cornelius and repeated the question. "Seriously, is he kidding?"

Cornelius disdained violence of any kind. "I told him it wasn't a good idea."

Barbarelli paused to squint at Cornelius. "Okay, so who the hell are you?"

"Neil's my new bodyguard."

"I'm a talent protection specialist," said Cornelius.

"Looks like you got two for the price of one," said Barbarelli.

"I'm husky," Cornelius said quietly.

Barbarelli leaned across his desk and fixed Damon with an intense look. "It's time to get serious. And you can start by taking off that ridiculous make-up. This isn't a game, Damon. Your entire career is at stake."

Damon's rosy complexion emerged bit by bit from beneath the grey, gnarled latex. "Everyone is blowing this way out of proportion, Barry." He spat a pair of stained dentures into his hand.

"Oh, yeah?" Barbarelli switched on a large flat-panel TV on the wall. Channel after channel was filled with sound bites about the incident now being referred to as AudreyGate.

Damon quickly looked away. He hated seeing himself onscreen even in the best of circumstances. "Come on, turn that off." He peeled the remaining latex and spirit gum from his face.

"Once the 'bloids name a story, it never dies," said Barbarelli.

"It's a good thing Resurrectionists believe in second chances," said Damon.

Barbarelli snorted. "You're out of second chances. If you're not careful, you won't even be able to find work doing Battle for Burly Gate reenactments."

Damon laughed as he leaned back in his seat. "We both know that'll never happen. My dead cred is through the roof."

"Sure. Try telling that to Ollie McMolley."

Damon laughed again. "Who?"

"He used to be more famous than Errol Flynn, back in the day. A living actor with dead cred to spare, just like you. The 'bloids tripped over themselves to anoint him New Hollywood's It Boy. And now, he's not even a footnote in the history books. And do you know why?"

"I have no idea, Barry. Why."

"Because he pissed off the wrong people by gadding around town in deadface make-up. Called this alter ego of his Ziggy Zombie. It was his idea of being funny. Only one up-and-coming New Hollywood cadaver didn't think rampant necrophobia was funny."

"Don't tell me," said Damon impatiently. "His name was—"

"Russell Mann!" shouted Cornelius.

"So what's your point," said Damon. "Russell has never liked me."

"My point is this, Damon: Joni is off gallivanting in Kathmandu. We can't sit on this until she decides to swoop in and rescue you from yourself."

"She's actually ascending Mt. Everest, which is in Nepal," offered Cornelius.

"What are you, the president of her fan club or something?" cracked Barbarelli.

Cornelius shifted in his chair. "She has a blog."

"I don't care who's taking care of it," Damon said impatiently. "Just tell me what I have to do. Some P.S.A.s and a late-night tour of contrition? I can do that in my sleep."

Cornelius looked up from his phone and nodded. "It worked for Tom Cruise."

"For pre-undead Cruise, sure," replied Barbarelli. "Undead Cruise, though, not so much."

"Come on, Barry. Details."

"Fine, fine. This is the deal, Damon. You must be SLS-certified before you can return to work."

"Yeah, right. There's no way I'm wasting my time with that Second Lives mumbo-jumbo! What's their motto? 'Death is only the beginning'? They're worse than the Revivologists! You can tell Russell—"

"Damon, listen to me. This was the studio's idea, not Mann's."

Cornelius nodded his approval from the corner. "That's fair."

"So you're telling me, just because someone says the word 'zombie'—"

Barbarelli pointed at him with an undead finger. "Not someone, Damon. You."

"—the whole world wants your head on a stick." Bits of deadface make-up tumbled from his lap as Damon stood up. "No way, Barry. I already passed that test once. That should be good enough for these people."

"You know the deal, Damon. There isn't a studio in town that will let you step foot on their lot without valid SLS certification. I called in a lot of favors to make this happen—all the way up to the Bureau of Undead Affairs. Believe me—you may think Russell Mann is the big bad in all of this. But the person you *should* be worried about is Solomon."

The sudden fear in his manager's voice gave Damon pause. Barry Barbarelli wasn't easily intimidated. "Fine. Fine, Barry, you win. I'll do it."

"Of course you're doing it. You're in violation of your C of C. You never had a choice." Barbarelli's smile was anything but friendly. "If you screw this up even St. Lazarus won't be able to help you."

Damon snorted and rolled his eyes. "Right. St. Lazarus. And here I thought you were a devout Cremationist, Barry."

"I don't get you," said Barbarelli. "For someone with a bug up their ass about the undead, you sure picked the wrong career path."

Damon didn't disagree. The sad truth of it was that he had been going through the motions for years, immersing himself in role after scripted role. He spoke the words of others well—well enough to garner accolades from his peers. But the unfortunate byproduct of such a lifestyle was that the 'bloids filled in the blanks of his well-protected life.

"Who knows," said Barbarelli, leaning forward. "You could have been a beautiful corpse by now. You may want to think about it. Rebirth's a great way to make the public forget a scandal. It worked for Fatty Arbuckle."

"Right," said Damon. "Keep dreaming." But what he really meant to say was, *Over my dead body.*

CHAPTER SEVEN

Russell Mann's week had been unusually busy, thanks in no small part to Damon Grayson's recent antics. Working fourteen-hour days were the norm for C.O.D.A.'s president, but lately Russell was working around the clock. Like all reanimates, he did not require sleep—but that did not mean he did not need to unwind. And unwind he did as he gratefully retired to the den of his spacious Vista del Muerte mansion with a fresh cup of tea and a copy of the *Daily Gristle*. He settled into the club chair with a raspy sigh and began perusing the paper. He skimmed the cover story, which was succinctly summed up in a terse headline: GRAYSON BURIED BY OWN NECRO-PHOBIA?

All in good time, thought Mann. His sallow cheeks crinkled like the newsprint in his shriveled fingers as he grinned. *Oh yes, all in good time.* But his smile quickly faded as he turned the page to discover a full-page advertisement assailing C.O.D.A itself.

C.O.D.A. CONDONES CENSORSHIP! declared the ad's bold-faced headline. Russell gritted his grotty teeth as he read the open letter that was directly addressed to him.

Mr. Mann:

While we applaud your dedication to undead equal rights, on behalf of all directors working within the New Hollywood studio system, we believe it is our responsibility to address the Coalition of Dead Actors' needless muzzling of artistic expression.

FACT: In a bygone era cinema's depiction of the undead was, in a word, criminal;
FACT: With the help of C.O.D.A. and partnerships with pioneering auteurs like Viktor Vincent the industry intercepted rampant necrophobia head-on;
FACT: The last decade has seen a fair and balanced portrayal of the undead in all forms of media, most especially film and television.

But, such progress begs the question: at what cost do the undead achieve their so-called 'equality of life?' At best, your Code of Conduct is nothing more than a call to censorship, Mr. Mann. At worst, it is thinly veiled anti-Living rhetoric. If left to our own devices, we believe that the entertainment industry, already more progressive than the rest of the country in its thinking, would ably self-monitor itself without C.O.D.A.'s draconian C. of C.

Russell stopped reading and withdrew his trusty Moleskine journal. He carefully recorded the list of filmmakers collectively credited with authoring the letter. Romero, Raimi, Anderson, Savini, Kirkman, Nicotero—all the usual suspects. At the top of his list he wrote GREYLISTED, and underlined the word with a dagger-like slash of his fountain pen.

He finally reached for the cup of Earl Grey and gingerly sipped the hot liquid. Just like sleep, the undead had no need for sustenance. Russell's fondness for tea was simply an affectation. Many hard-line reanimates viewed this as proof of his easternization. But Russell Mann was thick-skinned, especially for a cadaver.

Russell's rise to power from the mold-covered squalor of the Charnel Point favelas was a bona fide graveyard-to-gravy story. Such success was fodder for hate groups. Living taxpayers made such transformations possible, they insisted. And now, these very same hard-working, warm-blooded taxpayers were being usurped by government-trained undead immigrants.

Russell considered these arguments lacking in merit. "We're not the brain-dead ones," he muttered to the empty manse. He set the porcelain teacup down upon a stack of unread C.O.D.A. applications and consulted his rune-encrusted Rolex.

"Television," said Russell. The 120-inch LED screen above his mantle fluoresced to life. An infomercial for White Away, a popular undead product, loudly proclaimed the benefits of a more heavily pigmented complexion.

"Go from pale to hale," bellowed the undead host, whose treated face resembled unbrushed suede. Russell grunted his disapproval. Such reanimated remedies did nothing to bolster the confidence of the undead community. White Away was nearly as bad as Victory Veneers Press-On Teeth. Worse still was a similar copycat product, Laminated Press-On Lips.

"Darker dermis worked for me," screamed a gleeful, wide-eyed audience member.

Russell couldn't bear to hear any more. "Channel T," he said, and the *Martin Pryce Show* materialized onscreen. Russell settled into his leather club chair, a faint smile upon his gruesome lips.

Martin Pryce's call-in show was considered a cut above the usual late-night fare. Martin, who'd started out as a field reporter during the Battle for Burly Gate, eventually carved out a niche for himself in the crowded talk show landscape with conversational, in-depth interviews.

He was seated behind a glass desk, gnarled thumbs hooked through his trademark hemp suspenders. An LED-map of the 48 contiguous Living States of America twinkled on the wall behind him. Burly Gate was marked on the map by a long, crescent-shaped column of red lights that ran almost parallel to what remained of the Old Cali coastline. The Havens' familiar sickle shape was darkened on the map. Just off the coast sat Hart's Manor, the undead territory's capitol and the seat of Solomon's power. This, too, Russell noted, was conspicuously dark.

"If you're just joining us, we have Harpo-winner Damon Grayson here tonight." Martin swiveled to face his guest. Russell furrowed his brow. Why was a bone shard pinned to Damon's lapel? The pin symbolized the undead civil rights movement. That Damon was wearing it smacked of pandering mendacity.

"We're not off to a good start, Mr. Grayson," whispered Russell through his crooked teeth. "No we are not." He grabbed his journal and recorded Damon's latest transgression.

Damon leaned forward and produced a dimpled smile for the camera. "Thanks for having me, Marty. It's always a pleasure to be here."

"Too bad it couldn't be under better circumstances, eh?"

Damon's smile didn't waver. "Look, I'll be honest. I've got a big mouth."

"Earning you the nickname 'Million-Dollar Mouth.'"

Damon scratched his head. "Yeah, I've definitely paid my share of C.O.D.A. fines over the years. Some would say that my alleged necrophobia has paid for Russell Mann's mansion."

"Some would say, yes," Martin said.

"Hey, maybe he should change his name to Russell *Mansion*," Damon said.

Russell gritted his teeth hard enough to crack his remaining back molars. He jotted furiously in his notepad. "That's right," he hissed. "Keep digging your own grave, Mr. Grayson."

"Some would argue that you *are* indeed a necrophobe," said Martin. "What's your reaction to those people?"

"Well, we live in an ultra-politically correct world, Marty. It's almost impossible *not* to sound like a necrophobe if everything you say is taken out of context or picked over like a day-old carcass. Am I right?"

"Then how might you explain some of your more controversial roles? The Silent But Undeadly films, which collectively grossed over one billion dollars worldwide, are anything but P.C."

Damon's smile seemed as synthetic as a pair of press-on lips. "Wow, you don't waste any time, do you?" Damon shifted in his chair before fixing Martin with a squinty-eyed stare. "I'm a changed man, Marty. Seriously. I've moved beyond exploitation films. The undead are not props. They're actual people, like us. The *last* thing the world needs is more hurtful, demeaning stereotypes."

"I assume you're speaking specifically of undead stereotypes," Martin said as he thoughtfully perused his notes. "Because I have to tell you, Damon, they don't call you the Million-Dollar Mouth for nothing."

"I've been known to drop a few Z-bombs," Damon said. "But who hasn't? I mean, if you think about it, doesn't Cold War II seem just like yesterday?"

"It was almost fifty years ago."

Damon's face brightened. "Exactly! That's like, only one year ago in zombie years!"

Russell looked up sharply as his cell phone began to vibrate. He set down his fountain pen and hesitated before taking the call. "Good evening, sir," he said to Solomon, the Secretary of Undead Affairs. "I am taking steps to rectify the Grayson situation." He fiddled nervously with his silver cufflinks, a seventy-fifth rebirthday gift from the Secretary.

"Be sure that you do," responded the ancient, gravelly voice. "Or you'll find yourself back in the Charnel Point slums, begging for brains."

"Duly noted, sir," rasped Russell Mann. "From your lips to St. Lazarus' ears."

He slapped the phone shut and clenched it for a long minute in his cold, gnarled fist. If it were possible, Russell would have held his breath as he slowly counted to ten. But a pair of functioning lungs was a luxury he could not yet afford.

Russell pulled a second, untraceable cell phone from his vest pocket and glanced over his shoulder as he dialed.

A sullen voice answered on the third ring. "Barnabas speaking."

"Have you reconsidered my offer, Mr. Hardy?"

Barnabas Hardy's laughter was not kind. "You're a persistent son of a bitch."

"I'm used to getting what I want," Russell said. "And what I want is the corpse whisperer."

"And you figured the second time's gotta be the charm, right? The answer's still no, pal."

Russell's eyes narrowed to crusty slits. "Two million dollars says you'll change your mind."

"So now it's two million to track down this fairy tale witch doctor of yours. How much to find the Easter Bunny? Thanks but no thanks. There are plenty of other dowsers who'd gladly take your money."

Russell Mann was an ardent Resurrectionist but let the blasphemous comment slide. The corpse whisperer was a holy figure—the very embodiment of *Cadabra Rasa*.

"You're supposed to be the best fountain dowser in the world, Mr. Hardy. It is said you people can find anything."

"Sure," Hardy replied slowly. "Us 'people' can find anything. Or any-*one*."

"You found Amelia Earhart, did you not?"

Hardy chuckled. "Someone's finally doing their homework. Yeah. I found what was left of her."

Russell's ancient joints creaked and popped as he approached the bay window. From his lofty vantage point he beheld the distant, twinkling lights of Death Valley. "Like I said, Mr. Hardy, I'm used to getting what I want, no matter the cost."

"That makes two of us. Which means we're at an impasse. So I'll make this easy for you, Mr. Moneybags: Go fuck yourself. Like I told you before, I don't dowse anymore. Your precious super shaman can find himself, for all I care."

Russell fought down the panic welling up within his hollow breast. "You cross me at your own peril, Mr. Hardy."

But the line was already dead—and with it, any real hope Russell had of finding the only shaman more powerful than the mighty Solomon himself.

CHAPTER EIGHT

Myrna Thurgood's fiftieth birthday was approaching and she'd decided to acknowledge this milestone with a little cosmetic surgery. Not that she hadn't aged well, or so her friends and family insisted. But Myrna, the youngest of five siblings, knew better. Even at her age, Myrna was accustomed to being the baby of the family. The role had its share of burdens, first and foremost of which was looking the part of youth incarnate. Myrna was the first to admit that hers was a losing battle against time, against the elements, against her own biological clock. Sometimes, as she lay awake in the wee hours of the morning, she swore she could hear her clock ticking away her youth, and with it, her vanity.

Her husband Edwin, if he were still alive, would have admonished her for fretting over superficial nonsense. Edwin, who'd only just passed away earlier that year, always claimed he loved Myrna as she was, 'handcrafted by Nature's touch.' But since Edwin's passing, Myrna felt as though Nature's touch had become rather heavy-handed. Now, when Myrna looked in the mirror, she realized that her carefree countenance had become careworn.

Myrna had come into some money after Edwin's death, a bittersweet windfall from her dearly departed. With her fiftieth birthday looming—her first birthday as a widow—Myrna felt she could afford to spruce herself up. If she couldn't feel good, she thought, she should at least *look* good. The New Hollywood area was overflowing with plastic surgeons, many of them literally among the best that money could buy. One clinic in particular, in the valley, caught her fancy. *We specialize in pre-rebirth reconstruction*, the website had declared in an elegant serif font. High-profile clients included Dick Clark and undead Clara Bow. There was something about the idea of rebirth that appealed to her, even if she herself did not believe in rebirth itself. Edwin was cremated, and Myrna, too, would one day be immolated.

Without a word to anyone, Myrna drove out to the valley for a clandestine consultation with this so-called 'shaman to the stars.' Dr. Wilberforce, M.W.D. (he was a licensed medical witch doctor) welcomed Myrna with open arms into his well-appointed office. The doctor, with his easternized affectations and name, was a far cry from what Myrna expected. His only concession to his fourth-world upbringing appeared to be a burnished, silver-plated ceremonial rooster's skull worn around his neck.

"You are a beautiful woman, even for your advanced age," Wilberforce said as he scrutinized her delicate features. "Only a few wrinkles and blemishes. Your husband is a lucky man."

Myrna quietly explained that she was recently widowed. The doctor shook his head sympathetically as he gently turned her head this way and that.

"You must be very lonely," he said. "No wonder you are interested in preserving your vitality."

"My friends would laugh at me, if they knew I was here talking to a shaman."

"No shame in shamanism," the doctor joked. "No shame at all."

Myrna looked younger than ever as she blushed. "No, it's not that. My husband and I are Cremationists."

The doctor paused and sat back. "Oh. Well, that's very interesting. So what brings you here? Are you reconsidering an undead life?"

"Well I was really more interested in cosmetic surgery, to be perfectly honest. Like you said, I want to preserve my vitality."

The doctor smiled. His teeth were permanently stained a rich crimson from the blood of a thousand sacrifices. "Rebirth—or recycling, as it is also sometimes called—is the ultimate way to preserve one's vitality. Why wait for nature to take its course, wearing down your obvious physical beauty until you are nothing but a shell of your former self?"

Myrna absently primped her hair. All she'd been looking for was to get rid of some stray wrinkles and perhaps get an eye tuck. She quickly stood to leave. "I'm sorry for wasting your time, doctor."

But Wilberforce would not be deterred. He came around the desk and quickly guided her back to her chair.

"I'm not here to sell you ideology," he said. "But I do feel it's always helpful to understand what the afterworld has to offer. Cremation is indeed an honorable self-sacrifice. A cremated body can generate substantial energy—enough to provide power to the average household for a week or more. Indeed, it is the ultimate act of recycling."

Myrna was relieved. "Yes. Yes, that's exactly right. We just want to do what's right for the planet."

"Of course, of course. But when compared to one's potential usefulness as a reanimate, well, there is no comparison. The undead require no food, no sleep—making them perhaps the most ideal workforce ever imagined."

Myrna's sister Meredith, the oldest and most responsible child, was, much to her family's collective chagrin, a recent Second Lives convert. Meredith, who was past retirement age, scheduled her rebirth ceremony for the following year. She'd even put a down payment on a condo in Burlytown Heights, one of the Havens' toniest suburbs. This sudden move away from Cremationism drove a wedge between the two sisters, and, indeed, with the rest of the family. But now, Myrna wasn't so sure her sister was altogether wrong. Meredith would enjoy another full life; it was like a gift, to be granted a second chance.

"I—I need to think about this some more," said Myrna. She glanced at a veritable who's who of undead celebrities' portraits lining the office walls. One face in particular caught her eye. Gary Cooper was a favorite of Edwin's, especially during the actor's recent undead career. *Who would ever think a corpse could act like that, with such raw emotion,* Edwin had marveled. And Myrna had agreed; undead Cooper was truly inspiring.

"Take all the time you need," cooed Wilberforce. "You still have plenty of time to decide. But bear in mind that the clock is always ticking. It's simply my job to make sure you are physically stunning for your resurrection. It never hurts to be proactive." He patted her finely veined hand. "You know the old saying, 'the sooner the rebirth, the prettier the corpse.'"

Meredith said very much the same thing to her not long before they stopped talking. Myrna couldn't believe she was actually considering her own rebirth. What would Edwin think of her?

"Take your time to think it over," Wilberforce said. "I'll put you in touch with Lacy, if you like. She's a highly recommended death coach."

Myrna was in a daze. "A death coach?"

"She will shepherd you through the entire process leading up to your rebirth. She'll even help you choose what kind of resurrection is best for you. We will perform any rebirth ceremony you like—from Haitian voodoo to classic Egyptian. And I'm only one of seven doctors in the entire western hemisphere who invokes the ancient Aramaic used to resurrect St. Lazarus himself."

It all sounded quite impressive to Myrna, as was intended—even if the final outcome was always the same regardless of method. Voodoo reanimation, however, was usually the go-to method for less discerning patients.

"And before you ask, yes, it's quite true that I have amassed a particularly high body count."

Myrna grew more perplexed by the second. And here she thought rebirth was such a simple affair. It was far more complicated to come back from the dead than it looked in the movies. "A—a high body count, that's supposed to be a good thing?"

"Oh, yes, most definitely. Don't let a witch doctor with a low body count ever tell you otherwise. A shaman's magical....prowess....is directly linked to the number of resurrections performed in one's career." Wilberforce handed her a glossy pamphlet entitled *THE TRUTH ABOUT BODY COUNTS*. "Stronger magic begets a stronger, longer-lasting corpse."

"I don't know," she said. "I—I really do need to think about this a little bit more."

Myrna and the doctor were startled by a loud commotion from the clinic's parking lot. Wilberforce peered through the blinds and swore under his breath when he noticed the green Vista Cruiser idling at the curb. "These hooligans again," he muttered.

Myrna broke out in a cold sweat. "Is there something wrong?"

"No reason for alarm," the doctor replied with a tight smile. He grabbed the phone as the yelling and chanting swelled outside the window.

"Zombies equal death," cried a chorus of ragged, angry voices.

"If these traitors are too cowardly to do the right thing," someone yelled to the crowd, "we'll bring the fire to them!"

"I—I recognize that voice from the news," said Myrna. "It's that awful man, George Gleeson."

"This happens all the time," Wilberforce said, but Myrna could see he was visibly shaken by the mob's rancor.

"Resurrection is not a second chance," yelled the ex-Burly veteran. "It's a death sentence!"

Myrna tried to calm herself with thoughts of Edwin's kind face even as she reprimanded herself for being so foolish. There was a loud crash as what looked like a rock shattered the window. Myrna Thurgood and the doctor only had time to share a puzzled look as a blinding flash brought the entire building down upon them in a white-hot ball of flame.

CHAPTER NINE

The New Cali chapter of Second Lives was located in San Gabriel County. Unlike nearby La Boca Muerta, San Gabriel still had some life left to it, even if its residents were mostly grey collar workers working nightshifts in neighboring towns. Damon, like most A-list celebrities, rarely ventured beyond the tony enclaves of Vista del Muerte. The same was true for well-heeled reanimates like Russell Mann, who avoided border towns like the plague.

San Gabriel's many pawnshops, remittance centers, and Vanity Vein spas seemed almost exotic to Damon as their livery car slowly made its way downtown. Even Cornelius couldn't help but stare at the shabby ether reader salons and walk-in voodoo clinics.

Their undead driver, who was silent for most of the hour-long drive down from Vista del Muerte, observed his passengers in the rearview mirror. He grey-knuckled the steering wheel and vowed to return to charm school and make a better second life for himself. As it was, his work visa had expired months ago. It was only a matter of time before the Bureau of Undead Affairs deported him. In the meantime, he took odd jobs while he looked for a wealthy necrophile to shack up with.

The driver squinted through the windshield as the car moved at a crawl. "I know it's around here somewhere," he said, his face knotted like a rotten Danish.

"There," said Cornelius, pointing to an incongruous glass office tower that housed the Second Lives Community Outreach center.

The driver brought the car to an abrupt halt and scrambled from the front seat.

"Where's the fire?" Damon called after him.

The driver handed him a thick manila envelope. "I was hoping you might be able to read my screenplay."

Damon stared blankly at the envelope. "Oh. Uh—"

The driver spoke quickly. "It's about a vampire with a blood allergy. And—and he falls in love. With a woman. Who has a very rare blood type."

Damon handed the script back. "Not enough of a hook, sorry."

"Yes, but, it—it's the only blood type he's *not* allergic to. You'd be perfect for the part."

The car seesawed violently as Cornelius emerged from the cramped backseat. "Actually, you had me at 'blood allergy.'"

The driver quickly passed the script to Cornelius.

Damon shook his head. "Great. You read it, Neil. I don't get the whole vampire craze."

Cornelius cradled the envelope with great care. "I'd like to see what happens."

"Don't call us," Damon muttered as the driver hopped back in the car. As they waited to cross the street a woman pushing a stroller stopped dead in her tracks at the sight of Damon. The actor instinctively reached for a pen to sign a quick autograph.

"What's your name?" he asked.

"You're a terrible role model," she said with unexpected vehemence. "You treat the undead like...like *chattel!*"

"Hey lady, you don't even know me."

"Audrey Hepburn should have vomited on *you!*" she exclaimed and hurried away.

Damon turned to Cornelius. "And I thought the Neo-Lifers were the crazy ones."

But Cornelius wasn't listening. He was scanning the street for possible threats. Passers-by were already snapping pictures with their cell phones. Surely the commotion would help attract any nearby 'bloiders to their position.

"We need to get you off the street, Mr. Grayson."

Damon squared his shoulders. "Fine. Let's get this over with."

An undead security officer stopped the pair at the door. Damon wasn't expecting them to roll out the red carpet but was nonetheless surprised that they'd provided him with a security detail. The guard had not been a big man in his previous life. The subsequent centuries since his resurrection had reduced him to little more than a pile of brittle reanimated bones.

"Neil here's got my back, but thanks anyway for meeting us at the door."

The guard stared blankly at them with pale, lidless eyes as he scanned Damon with a wand.

"Whoa, what's that for?"

"Routine check for illegal weapons...sir." The guard waved Damon inside.

"You're doing a very good job," said Cornelius as the guard stood on tiptoe to pass the wand over his full height.

"You need to rethink your priorities," the guard said as he waved Cornelius through the door. "Some necrophobes earn their own fates."

Cornelius ignored the comment as he followed Damon inside.

The entrance opened into a small waiting area. The cinderblock walls, scuffed linoleum floor and flat lighting created an austere, morgue-like atmosphere. The anemic potted plants and generic paintings of dusky landscapes only heightened the funereal tone. Damon had expected something flashier from a powerful organization like Second Lives.

He stopped in front of a bulletin board overflowing with photocopied flyers, want ads, and undead personals.

"Listen to this," Damon said, tapping a pink flyer tucked away in a bottom corner of the corkboard. "'Recently rebirthed female with dark complexion seeking undead male with original teeth and minimal decomp. Must live in Valley area. No necrophiliacs.'" Damon let out a low whistle. "That's a double whammy, eh, Neil? Undead *and* single."

"It's terrible that the undead can't marry."

"Yeah, I suppose." He squinted at the personals. "Death is only the beginning of what? Eternal loneliness?" Damon shook his head. "No thanks. I'd rather be cremated than deal with undead dating."

"Some couples make pacts to find each other in the afterworld."

Damon turned away from the board. "Sounds great on paper, Neil. But if rebirth wipes your memories, what's the point of even trying?"

Cornelius believed in true love. He imagined that to confess such a thing to Damon would invite endless ridicule. "That's what those virtual memory vaults are for."

Damon laughed. "That's a good one, Neil. Have you ever tried applying for one of those vaults? You have to fill out a 500-question psych evaluation! Can you believe that?"

"You seem to know a lot about it, Mr. Grayson."

"Well, Joni told me about it."

Cornelius seemed surprised by this revelation. "What did she say, exactly?"

"Does it matter? She's still single, right? I mean, she's a great publicist, but she must be one tough girl to date."

Cornelius stared at Damon for a moment before responding. "I'm sure she's very nice."

Damon laughed again. Did Cornelius have a thing for Joni? He found the idea oddly endearing, if not completely misguided.

"She eats nice guys like you for breakfast, Neil. No offense."

Cornelius lingered for a moment to peruse the personals. "I think most women are afraid of me," he said. "On account of my being husky and all."

"Hang in there, Neil. Somewhere out there is a seven-foot gal who's dying to meet a guy like you."

They continued on past a row of faded posters advertising Kadabra-Land, a popular Havens theme park. Kenny Kadaver, the park's undead cartoon mascot, grinned broadly beneath a blood-red headline.

Damon read aloud from the poster. "KadabraLand," he intoned flatly. "Where the fun. Never. Dies."

"I've always wanted to go there," said Cornelius.

"Thanks but no thanks," Damon muttered as they approached the front desk.

The undead receptionist had been warily eyeing them from the moment they came through the door. She wore her brittle hair pulled back in a tight bun. Her prominent cheekbones made her wan, sunken face appear all the more severe. She lifted her sharp chin to greet them.

"Your new life is only a death away," she stated matter-of-factly.

"So I've heard," said Damon. "Second time's the charm, right?"

Cornelius shook his head and emitted a quiet groan. The receptionist's forehead crinkled like tissue paper as she furrowed her brow. "I'm not sure I understand."

'You know, charms, talismans—it's a play on words."

"I understand wordplay, sir," she said frostily. "What I don't understand is your needless hostility."

Damon was at a loss. He looked to Cornelius, who struggled to meet his eye. Damon was genuinely confused as he turned back to the receptionist. "I—I was just making a joke. I was trying to be funny."

"Necrophobia is no joking matter, sir."

"You can call me Damon." He leaned against the counter. "As in, Damon Grayson."

She pursed her Vinylex Life-Like Press-on Lips as she perused a list of names. "Oh, that's right. You're that...exploitation star."

"*Former* exploitation star," he said.

"Then you must be here for your SLS certification, *Mister* Grayson." She handed Damon a visitor's pass and three sharpened pencils. "It's the fourth door on the left, just past the Brain-Eaters Anonymous meeting."

Cornelius gently turned Damon away from the desk and began escorting him down the hall. "He's having a bad week," he explained over his shoulder.

The receptionist's press-on veneers gleamed as she broke into a cold smile. She bade them farewell with a well-worn reborn-again saying.

"Have a nice life, Mr. Grayson."

Damon shuffled along the corridor, an automaton guided by his bodyguard's steady hand. "Wow, that didn't go well at all. I must be losing my touch."

"You can't blame her for being offended," said Cornelius.

Damon shook his head. "Believe it or not, I wasn't trying to offend her. It just…came out all wrong."

"Maybe you can apologize to her on the way out. I think she would appreciate the gesture." Cornelius clamped a beefy hand on Damon's shoulder and shoved him into the empty classroom.

The instructor was seated behind a large metal desk. The lower half of his face from the bridge of his nose down was partially gone, exposing a cavernous nasal cavity and a gash-like smile that stretched from ear to ear. An open hardcover book lay before him; he ran a barbed fingertip across the printed page as he continued to read.

The instructor finally raised his head and leveled a sulfurous glare at Damon. He spoke carefully and deliberately, making the most of his severely compromised oral capacity. "Is something funny, Mr. Grayson?"

"No, no, I'm charmed to be here." Damon smiled uneasily as he pulled up a chair and took a seat near the back. The instructor quietly shut his book and leaned back in his seat. He coolly regarded Damon but made no effort to break the awkward silence.

"Too far back?" asked Damon. "Am I too far back? Should I switch seats?"

The instructor merely stared at Damon with a white-hot intensity that made the actor fidget in his seat. The ensuing silence was interminable;

even the sound of Damon's own breathing seemed overly vulgar in its machinations.

"You can give me the cold shoulder all you want but at some point you'll *have* to give me that exam." *An exam I already passed once before,* he thought.

More silence.

"Because if you don't, you're gonna find yourself at the end of a lawsuit."

The instructor narrowed his milky eyes but still said nothing.

"That's right, I see what's going on here. Discrimination cuts both ways, buddy. Maybe someone should make *you* take a test, too!"

The instructor cracked an ugly smile. "It's always about you, isn't it." But in his thick Havens accent it sounded more like *Itch awl aze bow chewin dit.*

Damon was so taken aback by the instructor's response that he spoke without thinking. "You say that like it's a *bad* thing."

The instructor reached into his desk and withdrew the exam booklet—it was almost as thick as a phone book. He slowly pushed back from his desk and rose to his full height of nearly seven feet.

Which NBA team did you *play for, big guy,* Damon wondered. But then Damon recognized the Havens Militia tattoo on the back of the instructor's pale hand. Damon knew military cadavers had reinforced skeletons and Kevlar-enhanced flesh. Damon also knew a military-grade corpse could easily break him in half.

He swallowed hard as the instructor finally stepped from behind his desk and shuffled towards him. He leaned down until his ruined face was just inches from Damon's chiseled features.

"One hundred years ago, one of us would have killed the other without a second thought," the instructor said slowly and with great difficulty. "If you killed me, you would be called a hero." *A hee-uh.* He leaned in even closer. "But if I killed you, Mr. Grayson," he whispered, "I would be called a murderer." *A muh-nunna.*

"I'm just here to take a stupid test," Damon said quietly. "Not to be judged for something my ancestors may have done."

The exam landed on his desk with a resounding thud. The instructor pulled up an empty chair and sat across from Damon, his thick arms folded across his chest.

"You have three hours, blood bank." *Bluh blang.*

Damon immediately raised his hand. "Is it okay to answer 'it depends' for some of these True or False questions?"

The instructor narrowed his eyes. "Chew office oh knee," he growled in his thick Havens accent. *True or false only.*

"Yeah, but, this first question—it's really vague."

The instructor bared half of his yellowed teeth as he smirked. "House oh?" *How so?*

"Well, it says 'Being undead is a choice.' Sure, it's a choice *now*. But a couple hundred years ago it wasn't."

The instructor raised his eyebrows in amusement. "Chew...office....oh knee."

"So then I have to pretend there's no such thing as the Reanimation Proclamation? Suddenly it's not a crime to raise a Burialist from the dead?"

The instructor merely shrugged before spreading his arms wide.

"Right," Damon muttered. "Chew office." He tapped his pencil on the desk and pondered his answer before reluctantly circling TRUE in the booklet. Damon could only assume there was no real right answer to what seemed like a trick question.

The second question was no better:

> *UNDEAD PERSONS WHO CONSUME HUMAN TIS-*
> *SUE AND ORGAN MEATS TO SURVIVE MUST BE*
> *REFERRED TO AS HUMANITARIANS.*

"Seriously, what's up with these weird questions? You guys don't need to eat to live. Or survive, or whatever. You know what I mean."

Damon sighed as he resumed tapping his pencil on the desk. He tried not to think of a million other things he'd rather be doing. He reluctantly circled TRUE but quickly amended his answer with a hastily written *IT DEPENDS*.

Three hours and several hundred questions later, all four of Damon's pencils were riddled with tooth marks, their erasers worn down to nubs. Damon was likewise spent, his addled mind reeling. He couldn't remember the last time he'd worked so hard on something he cared about so little.

He slammed the test booklet shut and pushed it across the desk towards the instructor. No need to check his answers. He either passed or he didn't; it made no difference to Damon. If he failed, enough money would be thrown at C.O.D.A. by the studio to ensure that he 'passed.'

Damon rose from his chair and flashed a plastic smile at the instructor. "See you around, Chuckles. It's been a real blast."

Ancient flesh creased and crinkled as what was left of the instructor's mouth twisted into a lopsided grin. "The pleasure was all mine, blood bank," he said without any trace of his Havens accent.

CHAPTER TEN

Barnabas Hardy was in a black mood as he pounded the pavement just south of Houston Street. The weather was unseasonably mild for mid-October. Heavier coats were left in closets as tourists and New Yorkers alike ventured out into the warm autumn sunshine. It was a great morning to be in New York City. Every street, every avenue offered the promise of discovery and adventure.

Nowhere else in the city was this more true than in the West Village, with its overabundance of ether reader salons, zink parlours, and voodoo apothecaries. But for all of the grittiness and bohemian earnestness, the services offered were anything but grey-collar friendly. Many a milky-eyed hipster, their collective gaze hidden behind horned-rim glasses, their decayed flesh attired in vintage fashions, effected a louche ennui in every exaggerated, shambling step down Spring Street.

Hardy thought the only thing worse than an undead hipster was a *wannabe* undead hipster. These so-called wannazees not only dyed their otherwise healthy skin a sickly grey, they also tattooed dark lesions all over their bodies to simulate decomp sores.

Hardy shook his head as he passed a crowded Frankenjoe's. It was nothing more than a glorified, overpriced den of caffeinated wannazee poseurs, their unnaturally pale heads bent over tablets and smart phones. Hardy actually knew of some wannazees who went the extra step of injecting Dotox to simulate rigor mortis. Puffer fish toxin was bad juju no matter which way you sliced it, as far as Hardy was concerned—and injecting the deadly toxin into one's joints was taking the whole zombie fetish thing a step too far. Why these wannazees didn't just undergo a bona fide resurrection was beyond Hardy.

But what would a lapsed Cremationist understand about Resurrectionism? Hardy had nothing against the undead per se—he simply didn't understand the need to reanimate a slab of meat that was no longer meant to be mobile. Or sentient. Or delinquent on a very costly talisman tax.

Hardy hustled across the cobblestone street as he reached a food cart parked near Wooster. *Buster's Last Stand* was emblazoned in blocky orange letters on the cart's dingy umbrella. Beneath the umbrella stood Buster himself.

A stooped cadaver with a shock of corn silk-like hair above each gnarled fist of an ear, Buster dutifully plied hungry tourists with steamed pretzels and boiled hot dogs from the same corner for almost eighty years. Every customer was greeted with a jaunty grin, though Buster reserved his warmest smiles for Barnabas.

"What can I do you for, old friend?" said Buster.

"You know the drill," huffed Hardy. "Not in the mood for chit chat today."

"Sure, sure. Why ruin a perfectly beautiful morning with small talk, sure."

Hardy's furrowed brow only emphasized the expanse of his broad forehead. He drummed his fingers impatiently on the warm metal countertop. "These talismans aren't gonna repo themselves."

Buster hesitated, his mouth slightly agape as he reached into his pocket. "Just remember, Barn, ole Buster is just the messenger. I don't pick the names."

"Yeah, yeah, they're given to you. This ain't my first day, Buster."
Last night's conversation with the mystery caller was still fresh in Hardy's
addled thoughts. His home phone number was unlisted; only Buster would
be stupid enough to give it to a total stranger. They may have been friends,
Buster and he, but Buster still thought with a broker's pragmatic brain.

Buster folded the slip of paper and slid it across to Hardy. "Just a messenger, Barn," he said again.

Hardy snatched the paper and opened it. He stared long and hard at the
printed name before passing it back.

"I—I'm sorry, Barn. Maybe we should let someone else—"

But Hardy was already turning away, the brim of his battered fedora
pulled down over his narrowed eyes. "I know exactly where he is."

Buster was no ether reader, but he knew what was on his old friend's
mind. "Two million bucks is a lot of money, Barn. Maybe you should reconsider the offer?"

"I know what I'm doing," Hardy growled. "I don't have time for a wild
goose chase. You an' I both know the corpse whisperer ain't real."

Buster's hunched posture worsened as he slumped in defeat. And then
he recalled a detail that suddenly bore repeating as Hardy retreated down
the street.

"I hear Silas Walker has been looking for the corpse whisperer," called
Buster. "Has been, for years."

Silas Walker was a rename Hardy hadn't heard in ages—not since he'd
given up dowsing. Like Buster, Hardy knew when it came to the undead
dowser, the crazier the rumor, the likelihood it was true. Yes, Walker was
a talented dowser—Hardy was willing to concede that much. But while
Walker enjoyed his share of front-page finds, he had always remained in
Hardy's shadow.

Buster chuckled. "Can you imagine the look on his rotten face if you
beat him to the punch? Hell, I'd pay a few million ducats just to see that!"

Buster had to be pushing 130, maybe even 150 in rebirth years. Hardy
was all too familiar with the sort of gregarious, aged cadaver who equated

longevity with wisdom. But to Hardy's mind, sometimes a pulse was a prerequisite for understanding the subtleties of what it truly meant to be alive.

"I said I know what I'm doing," replied Hardy. "I owe it to Darla to be there when she kicks the bucket. Got it?"

Buster lowered his head. He knew when he was beaten. Barnabas Hardy was nobody's fool. "Sure, Barn," he said with a sad smile. "But what if Darla—"

"Don't finish that sentence if you know what's good for you."

Luckily for both of them, Buster kept his mouth shut.

Hardy's mood worsened footstep by footstep, block by city block. The phone call, the name written on the paper, his secret vow to Darla—it all weighed him down so greatly he finally stopped short in the middle of the busy sidewalk to get his bearings.

Get it together, he thought. *You're the same damn Barnabas you were yesterday.*

Except he didn't believe that. He suddenly felt like an interloper in his own life. He rued his decision to take that late-night call. He rued his decision to become the government's patsy. And he rued the sucking sound his lack of conviction made inside his great barrel of a chest.

"Damn it, I know what I'm doing," he muttered under his breath as he navigated his way past a group of lollygagging tourists. Two meandering stragglers at the back of the group inadvertently thwarted Hardy's attempts to pass. He finally hopped the curb and began walking in the street. He caught a snippet of their conversation as he soldiered past.

"That's not what I heard at all," frowned the taller of the two stragglers, a jowly, frizzy-haired woman wearing a crisp Empire State Building sweatshirt. "I heard a zombie just brushed—" she swept her arm out as she spoke, "just like that, *brushed* up against her and *poof*—she got turned zombie."

Her companion, a fellow tourist with the sleeves of a Green Bay Packers jacket knotted around her waist, reacted with wide-eyed horror. "That's terrible. So terrible. That happened to my friend's cousin."

Hardy thought it was terrible, too. So terrible that he stopped dead in his tracks to set the record straight.

"You biddies have no idea what the hell you're talking about."

The women stood aghast, their hands clasped protectively to their chests. "Please don't hurt us," said the jowly woman.

"Becoming undead is a choice, not an accident. Got it?"

The shorter woman nodded mutely as Hardy stormed off.

Less than ten minutes later, Hardy arrived at his destination—a grungy zink parlour on St. Mark's in the East Village. He may have left the world of dowsing behind, but he still possessed a fountain dowser's keen intuition and sense of direction. The path from Buster's cart to his mark in the tattoo parlor was so clear and so obvious to Hardy that it may as well have been painted on the pavement.

Actually confronting a deadbeat who hadn't paid his talisman tax in fourteen years—that was the part that gave Hardy pause. He flashed his Talisman Reclamation badge as he pushed his way inside.

"I'm here for Moss."

"He isn't here," said Cara, the rail-thin, leather-clad cadaver who met Hardy at the door.

"Like hell he isn't." Hardy eyed the ornate designs and garish illustrations that hung on every inch of every wall. WE ALSO DO SCRIMSHAW—JUST ASK proclaimed a handwritten sign above their heads. Most people wouldn't recognize the scratchy handwriting, but Hardy knew it like the back of his hand. Knew it just as surely as he knew that Moss was in the studio apartment above the shop.

Cara rested a cold hand on Hardy's shoulder. "Maybe you and me can take a walk around the block, if you know what I mean."

"Out of my way." He headed towards the staircase at the back of the shop.

"Moss is a good guy," Cara yelled after him.

"He was one of the best," Hardy muttered under his breath. His march up the rickety stairs was fair warning to whoever waited on the other side of the door. "Repo!' yelled Hardy, then kicked the door in.

Moss, a lanky, red-haired cadaver, was sitting on a futon as *Who Are They Now?* played on a small television across the room. His eyes did not leave the screen as he smiled by way of a greeting. "I appreciate the warning, Barnabas—but I'm not going anywhere."

Hardy noticed the talisman on Moss's ring finger. "You don't think I'll do it?"

Moss patted the futon with a maggot-infested hand and motioned for Hardy to join him. "We've known each other a long time."

Hardy hadn't laid eyes on Moss in a dog's age. The years had not been kind to him. So much of his flesh had rotted away that he looked inside-out.

"This isn't a game, Moss. And this ain't a social call."

Moss never shifted his rheumy gaze from the flickering light of the TV. "Would it make a difference if I could pay you? If I had the money—right here, right now?"

"It depends." Hardy rested a calloused hand on the butt of his holstered HAMR. A Handheld Magnetic Resonator could attract a talisman from up to 100 feet away. Without the protective magic of his talisman, given his advanced state of decay, Moss wouldn't last more than a few minutes. "Do you have the money, or are you just yanking my chain?"

Moss finally looked at Hardy—looked him squarely in the eye. "I can get it, I swear I can."

Hardy slowly removed the HAMR from its holster. "I need that talisman, Moss."

"Listen, just give me a week, okay? I—I can sell something on the grey market." Moss tried unsuccessfully to stifle a nervous, high-pitched chuckle. "I mean, who needs *two* arms, right?"

What little remained of Moss's left arm was covered in tattoos; much of the ink was from his previous life. But the exposed, scrimshawed bones in his right arm, that was new to Hardy.

"No one's paying seventy grand for one of your tatted-up twigs, Moss.

It's over."

"Over? It can't be over. I just put a down payment on a Harley."

"That's not my problem, Moss."

"Sweet Lazarus, Barnabas! Can't you *make* it your problem? I'm not a deadbeat!"

"The Living States government don't see it that way. The way they see it, that there charm belongs to them. You've just been renting it."

Moss instinctively clutched the talisman in his fist. "You used to be one of us, Barnabas. You were one of the good guys. A normal joe. But then you sold out!"

"No one sold out."

Moss rose from the grungy futon, his milky eyes bright with anger. "Yes, you sold out and became The Man!"

Hardy's smile was bereft of joy. "If you can't beat 'em, join 'em, right, Mossy?"

Moss sank back onto the futon. "What happened to you, Barnabas?" he whispered. "You and Darla and me—we had such good times together, back in the day."

"Yeah, well." Hardy hefted the HAMR and reluctantly brought the humming weapon to bear on his former Best Man. "Nothing lasts forever, Mossy," he said quietly.

And then he pulled the trigger.

CHAPTER ELEVEN

The Coalition of Dead Actors was headquartered in New Hollywood proper, just a stone's throw in any direction from all of the major studios. C.O.D.A., which was located on the tenth floor of the historic Ellison building, rose above the surrounding soundstages. Russell's lofty vantage point afforded him a buzzard's-eye view of the town. And what he observed was an industry eating itself to stay alive. Russell knew C.O.D.A. was little more than a band-aid on the festering sore of New Hollywood.

Luckily for Russell, he was a shadow member of the Second Lives council. His position made him privy to many a happenstance in the undead community. If a Charnel Point corpse applied for a work visa, he was aware of it. If a local politician was secretly in the casket, he knew of that, too. And if a certain necrophobic, hate-spewing celebrity retook his S-certs, he was keenly aware of every incorrect answer on the exam.

Except in Damon's case. Russell Mann's deputy director, Charles, burst into his corner office, a printout clutched in his grey hand. "Russell," he said. "Didn't you hear me? Damon Grayson passed his certification."

Russell suppressed a smile. He had indeed heard every word of the deputy director's hysterical outburst. The surprise declaration, however, signified nothing to C.O.D.A.'s acting president.

"No," said Russell. "He did not."

Charles brandished a computer printout as proof. "He did indeed, Russell. And he didn't just squeak by, either. I don't know how he did it, but somehow he got an almost-perfect score. I mean, that's pretty amazing, isn't it?"

Russell wasn't amused by his deputy director's excitement. They weren't meant to root for their enemies, to laud their would-be oppressors for their unlikely successes.

"Amazing isn't the word for it," said Russell dryly. "Appalling, perhaps, or highly improbable. But amazing? No." Most likely Grayson had cheated. There was simply no other explanation for his anomalous grade.

"Paradox is waiting for these results. I think half the country is waiting to find out Damon's test score. I think it's great that he passed. It proves that everyone does deserve a second chance."

Russell leaned across the desk and fixed his deputy director with narrowed, milky eyes. "And I am telling you: Damon Grayson did not pass this exam. Understood?"

Charles hesitated as he looked down at the paper in his hand. "Russell, listen. I understand, but—"

"You understand *nothing*," he snapped. "Some two-bit necrophobe will not make a fool out of me."

Charles seemed to shrink within his three-button suit. His slight shoulders slumped as he stared at the ground. "This is wrong, Russell," he said quietly, shaking his head.

"You try telling that to Solomon," he whispered, his eyes bulging from their sockets. Russell angrily dismissed his deputy director; now was not the time for weakness. But all was quickly forgotten as Russell's secret cell phone vibrated with an incoming call. It was Hardy's broker, Buster.

"He'll do it," said Buster. "Ten days. No promises."

C.O.D.A.'s president smiled. In the end, Russell Mann always got his way. Always.

CHAPTER TWELVE

The Froots 'n' Veggiez Show was a beloved children's program known for its successful blend of educational songs, stories and colorful felt-faced characters. The program also had a very strong, subversive undead slant to it, which earned the long-running show a tremendous cult following on college campuses. Many a celebrity dropped by the set, whether to lampoon their onscreen personae or to serve as foils for the show's true stars, the titular Froots and Veggiez.

The former was a plucky banana that entertained dreams of becoming a world-famous wrestler. The latter was an undead carrot, who had a penchant for pratfalls and double-takes. (Veggiez was perhaps best known for the existential ode to the daily difficulties of being undead, the song 'It's Not Easy Being Grey.')

Damon was scheduled to shoot a two-minute segment for the show called 'It's Nice to Live Twice.' The purpose of the scene was to allow the actor to extol the virtues of racial sensitivity after Veggiez is teased for being undead. Damon, who grew up watching the show, jumped at the chance to appear alongside the famous pair. The show's socially conscious creators, however, were not quite so enthusiastic. A bit of behind-the-scenes arm-twisting by his manager finally landed Damon a coveted guest spot.

True to form, though, Damon seemed intent on squandering the scant goodwill afforded him by his high-placed connections. No amount of coaxing or cajoling by Cornelius could motivate the actor to arrive at the set on time.

"Let's get this show on the road," Damon declared when he finally strode onto the familiar set.

The mostly undead crew kept their distance. Only Froots, the felt-faced banana, acknowledged Damon's presence. From atop his red brick wall, he scowled down at the actor and pointed at him with a floppy arm.

"You are late," yelled Froots. "Tardiness is very, very rude!"

"Sorry, Froots. Kind of hard to get around town lately."

Froots harrumphed as he folded his arms—his trademark response whenever Veggiez said something he didn't care for. Damon couldn't help himself as he used his phone to snap a picture of Froots. "I love it when you do that!" Damon immediately posted the photo to Flutter.

Froots heaved an even louder harrumph and disappeared behind the wall.

"I think you offended him," said Cornelius.

"Yeah, but how cool is it to be here?" replied Damon. "Hey, where's Veggiez? You gotta get a picture of me with him!"

Janice, the undead show runner, finally appeared. She quickly steered Damon to a green room that was barely bigger than one of his mansion's walk-in closets. Barbarelli sat on one couch, looking simultaneously bored and furious. Becky, Joni's harried undead assistant, sat in an armchair while she pecked away on a shiny tablet. They both glared at Damon as Janice continued her tirade.

"You can't just show up late and start yelling and screaming," she said. "This is public television. We can't afford to have the crew standing idle for two hours!"

"Hey, I can explain."

"I'd like to hear this," said Barbarelli and folded his arms across his chest. This time Damon didn't snap a photo.

Becky glanced over the top of her tablet. "Yeah, me too."

"I'm not interested," Janice said with an angry wave of her hand. "You New Hollywood types think the world revolves around you. Well, it doesn't. I've worked with children who were better disciplined."

"Mr. Grayson is sorry for the inconvenience," said Cornelius.

Damon looked at his bodyguard. "Neil, what are you doing? I can speak for myself."

Barbarelli smiled. "I'm really beginning to like this guy."

"Apology accepted," said Janice, and stormed off.

"I can handle myself, Neil. I don't need a bodyguard to smooth things over with anyone."

"I'm a talent protection specialist," Cornelius replied indignantly, but it was suddenly as if he weren't even in the room.

"You need all the help you can get," Barbarelli said to Damon. "You were just arguing with a fucking *banana*."

"And what's that supposed to mean—he needs 'all the help' he can get?" demanded Becky. "Is that supposed to be another dig at my boss?"

"You're spunky," said Barbarelli in a way that sounded nothing like a compliment. "Someone has to pick up the slack around here."

Damon slumped onto the couch and reached for the bowl of candy on the coffee table. "Hey, there are red Skittles in here. My rider specifically says no red Skittles. They remind me of kidney beans."

"Ha, don't look at me," said Becky as Barbarelli rolled his eyes.

"Any word from Joni yet?" asked Damon as he carefully picked around the red Skittles.

"Nope, same as the last ten times you asked me," said Becky.

"I'm sure she's okay," said Cornelius.

Damon patted him on the leg. "She knows how to take care of herself."

"Too bad she can't take care of her own clients," said Barbarelli.

"It's not my fault she's off the grid," said Becky, her raspy voice climbing. "Joni is on a spiritual *quest*. She is trying to *find* herself!"

Barbarelli spread his mismatched arms in a grand gesture. "Client management is a 24/7 job. If you want to find yours truly, I'm right...fucking...*here*."

"And so are the red Skittles," said Damon. He had about a dozen lined up on the table. He took a picture of them and posted them to Flutter.

"I'd like to see you say that to her *face!*" snapped Becky. "She'd tie you in a knot."

Barbarelli flexed his dyborg arm. "Right. Like hell she could."

The group lapsed into an uncomfortable silence. Barbarelli and Becky glared at each other expectantly, eyebrows raised, danders up, quips at the ready. Damon was oblivious to the tension, though. He leaned back and closed his eyes.

"So how long does it take to grade a stupid test?" he asked with a bored sigh. "It's been three days."

"Four days?" volunteered Cornelius.

His comment was followed by more awkward silence. But then Becky's phone trilled with an incoming call. "Now what."

Barbarelli's phone buzzed in his hand. He stared at the caller's name. It was Viktor. Both he and Becky glanced over at Damon as his phone tweeted with the telltale sound of a plunging BPM.

Janice, the show runner, burst into the green room. "Get your sorry butt off my set," she said. "You're no longer SLS-certified, you ridiculous necrophobe."

"Very funny," said Damon. "There's no way I failed that test." But when he saw the group's disappointed faces, Damon knew something was rotten in Denmark—and it wasn't undead Olivier's recent sold-out run in the Broadway revival of *Hamlet,* either.

No, it was clear—Russell Mann was truly determined to deep-six Damon's career.

CHAPTER THIRTEEN

Hardy awoke to the scent of freshly baked bread. The fountain dowser squinted into his pillow and called out to his wife in the darkness. "Darla," he croaked. "Too early for breakfast." When she did not reply, he sat up and glanced around a bedroom he did not recognize. Then he noticed the unopened shipping box he used for a nightstand.

"Right," he said with a rueful chuckle as the reality of his new life reasserted itself.

He knew their daughter, Sofia, was having a pretty rough time of things, too. The last time she and Hardy spoke was just before she headed back to school in Ohio; it had not gone well. Hardy remembered a time not so long ago when his Sofa-Bed was a scrappy little girl with crooked pigtails. And now, his daughter tearfully, angrily, referred to her mother's impending rebirth as 'government-sanctioned suicide.' On paper, in so many words, that's exactly what it was.

Hardy left the lights off as he navigated the cluttered apartment. He cracked open a box in the living room marked BR CLOSET and began pulling on musty, rumpled clothing. Sofia had offered to help unpack his things, but in Hardy's mind the fourth-floor walk-up was only temporary. And yet, it appeared that Darla Hardy, a late-in-life convert to Resurrectionism, was bound and determined to outlast those who would miss her the most.

Buster whistled tunelessly as he lined the front of his cart with breakfast pastries and pre-wrapped bagels. He usually managed to skim some early birds before the Frankenjoe's up the block opened for the day. One of his regulars, a gangly wannazee with a Kenny Kadaver messenger bag slung over his bony shoulder, limped towards the cart.

"Morning, Buster," he said with what was meant to be a Havens accent. "The usual." *Da oozool.*

Buster smiled patiently as he bagged a cheese Danish and a banana. "Morning, Stewart. Sounds like someone's been practicing."

Stewart's eyes sparkled despite the grey contact lenses he wore. "I may be going to the Havens in December." *Un Doo-soom-boo.* He pulled a book from his bag and showed it to Buster.

The old cadaver squinted at the cover. "*Converse Like a Corpse*, eh?" He handed it back to Stewart, along with his breakfast. "Keep it up, you sound great."

He laughed. "Tell that to my girlfriend. She thinks my accent sucks." *Surks.*

"Keep practicing and you'll fit right in."

Just then a fly alighted on a large decomp sore tattooed on Stewart's cheek. He froze, a large smile plastered on his emaciated face. "Holy shit, he thinks it's *real*," Stewart whispered through clenched teeth. He gingerly pulled a smart phone from his shirt pocket and motioned for Buster to grab it.

"Do you need me to call someone?" he whispered back.

The fly began walking in circles along the raised surface of the tattoo. "No no no," Stewart whispered with great urgency. "I want you to take a picture of me with this fly on my face." In his excitement, he had abandoned all pretense of a Havens accent.

Buster held the camera at arm's length as Stewart subtly assumed a more dead-eyed expression. "Say *griiiiis*...!"

"Groooozzzzzz."

"Spoken like a true Havens native," said Buster as he handed the phone back to Stewart. The fly twitched its way across Stewart's forehead before disappearing into his tangled, greasy hair.

"I haven't washed my hair in over a month," he proudly proclaimed.

Buster responded with a crooked thumbs up as Stewart limped away.

"Christ on a cracker, I thought he'd never leave," said Hardy as he stepped out from a darkened doorway. Buster staggered back against the cart, his pale eyes wide with surprise.

"I wish you wouldn't do that."

"I didn't want to scare away one of your regulars."

Buster laughed. "He could use a good scare."

"What he needs is a good smack upside his bleached head. If you want to be a real corpse, do the deed."

Buster made no mention of the missing HAMR holster as he handed a cup of coffee to Hardy. The two men stood in silence for several minutes as Hardy carefully sipped the hot brew.

"Barn, listen," said Buster suddenly. "I know you don't want to hear this—"

"So don't say it."

"You were too good for repo work. It was killing you."

Hardy scoffed at the idea that he was too good for anything. He deserved the guilt that weighed so heavily upon his shoulders. "Killed Moss, too. He was a good guy."

"I liked Moss just fine, too, but it's time to move on. If the corpse whisperer really does exist, you're the man to find him."

"And if he don't exist, I'll be a laughingstock."

"A rich laughingstock, sure. You're doing the right thing."

Hardy downed the dregs of his coffee. "Doesn't help Moss, though, does it."

"Take it from an old cadaver. Let go of the past."

"We still talking about Moss?"

"Darla's made her choice," Buster said quietly. "She's already moved on."

"Who's her death coach? Is he a good guy?"

"She's in good hands, Barn. I promise. If she wasn't, you'd be the first to know."

"And her witch doctor?"

Buster patted Hardy on the shoulder. "You'd be the first to know, old friend. The first."

"It's a rough world out there for the undead," he said gruffly.

"Hard for the living, too."

"Yeah, well." Hardy tugged lightly on the brim of his fedora. Darla used to call him Indiana Bones, once upon a time. The memory was a bittersweet one; it brought an unexpected smile to his lips.

"It'll all be okay, Barn. You'll see."

"This conversation—"

"It stays between us," said Buster.

"Good. Now that we've got that settled I gotta see a corpse about a haircut."

Outside of the Havens, New York City boasted the highest concentration of reanimates in North America—many of them transplants from the west coast. During the first Cold War, many reanimates were spirited out of the Havens (and beneath Burly Gate) via an extensive underground network known as the Railroad Styx. Over the decades, many of these refugees wound up settling in what eventually came to be known as Little Burlytown. The undead enclave, which occupied twelve square blocks at the southwest tip of Manhattan, was a boon for dowsers like Hardy; it was a veritable fount of hard-to-come-by intel. Little Burlytown was also home to Hardy's longtime barber, a crusty, no-nonsense corpse by the rename of Louie. If the corpse whisperer did exist, Louie, a Havens ex-pat, would be able to point him in the right direction.

As Hardy walked along Little Burlytown's main drag, he passed curb-side tables laden with off-brand products and home-brewed tinctures. KENNY CADABRA ACTION KORPSE proclaimed one merchant's sign. 'SO GOOD FOR YOU' ANTI MAGGOT LOTION declared another. A cadaver came around his table to wave a small jar of coarse grey powder in Hardy's face.

"Very potent," insisted the wrinkled merchant with a sage nod. "Even just one single ounce of ground zombie testicle creates a very durable, enjoyable erection."

Hardy merely shook his head as he turned off the avenue and headed down a narrow alleyway. Aside from some rusty dumpsters and discarded boxes, there were two doors that opened into the alley. One led to an un-named 'gentlemen's spa' that specialized in formaldehyde enemas. The other door led to a hole-in-the-wall barbershop.

A homeless reanimate emerged from behind the dumpster. His meager clothes were in tatters. His pallid, necrotized flesh was even worse for wear.

"You wanna give me a piece of your mind," he asked Hardy. But his guttural Havens accent made it sound more like *yuwunnuh gimay peesore munn?* The reanimate's jaw nearly unhinged as he cackled manically, revealing molars caked in Noodle.

Hardy gave him a wide berth. "I gave at the office, pal."

A dented bell tinkled as he pulled open the door to the barbershop. Louie greeted Hardy with scaly, open arms. Paulo, the other undead barber, acknowledged him with a simple dip of his pointed chin.

"The usual for you?" Louie asked as he ushered Hardy into an empty chair.

The fountain dowser lowered his portly frame between the armrests and smiled. He knew it was cheeky for a man with advanced male-pattern baldness to waste a barber's time.

"Yeah, sure, the usual," laughed Hardy. "Why the hell not."

Sal, the reanimate sitting in the next chair over, smiled at him in the mirror. Like Hardy, he was a regular customer. He enjoyed ribbing Hardy about his well-known matrimonial woes.

"Too bad your ex got your hair in the divorce, eh?"

"Screw you Sally," he said, returning the crooked smile. "This is Mother Nature at work, not the ex."

Sal shook his surprisingly well-coiffed head. "You have the worst luck with women. The *worst*." This comment was met with friendly laughter.

"Don't I know it." Hardy sighed as he settled into the chair.

Louie leaned over him, scissors poised over his balding pate. "So, any new adventures?" he asked as he trimmed delicate wisps of hair. "You find Atlantis yet?"

Hardy snorted as curlicues of hair drifted onto the front of his smock. "I'd have better luck finding Hitler."

Sal slapped his bony kneecap and laughed, much to Paulo's chagrin.

"Keep still," he said impatiently, righting Sal's lumpy cranium. "I'm working here."

"You still looking for Hitler?" Sal cried with wide-eyed amusement. "I told you last time, if he's not in the ground, he's probably a zombie by now. And if he's a zombie—"

"I know, I know," said Hardy. "Believe me, I know. If he's a zombie, he probably doesn't remember anything about anything. He could be a freaking florist now, for all anyone knows."

Louie shook his head as he continued to prune Hardy's locks. "It's better to start clean. Start fresh. Everyone deserves a second chance. Even Hitler."

Paulo paused in mid-snip. "Says you. He killed half a million of us in 'cold blood' in the last war." He made air quotes with horribly gnarled, knotty fingers that reminded Hardy of putrefied ginger root. "Are we supposed to act like that never happened? Because I don't care what the Cremationists say, it *did* happen."

"But he wouldn't remember any of that now," said Louie. "Isn't that the point of resurrection—*Cadabra Rasa*?"

"It depends on who reanimated him in the first place," snapped Paulo.

"It isn't always just 'relive and forget,' you know."

"The hell it isn't," said Sal. "I don't remember a single thing about my old life."

Louie rolled his eyes. "Don't get him started, Sal," he said. "Please. As a personal favor to me."

Hardy quietly observed the exchange, his eyes ping-ponging between the two barbers. The fountain dowser knew a lead when he smelled one—and this one reeked of promise.

"Yeah," he said slowly. "You know Paulo and his conspiracy theories. Guy's a nut. No offense, Paulo. Besides, everyone knows not all shamans are created equal. I mean, look at how Sally here turned out."

Hardy's last comment elicited a chuckle from Louie but Paulo didn't take the bait. He merely regarded Hardy with naked skepticism. "Right," he said after a long pause. "You think I was reborn yesterday or something?"

"Aw, c'mon," said Sal. "Hardy's good people. He's paying for his wife's trans-life op, for Lazarus' sake."

"*Ex*-wife," Hardy and Louie replied together.

Paulo seemed to chew this over, his jaw cracking as it shifted from side to side. He set his scissors down on the counter and very deliberately wiped his hands on the front of his tunic. Hardy interpreted this gesture as *I wash my hands of this*. And yet, to everyone's obvious surprise, Paulo pulled up a metal folding chair and sat down.

"You didn't hear this from me," he said. "As far as you know, this is all just conjecture and speculation."

"Hearsay," said Hardy solemnly. "Got it."

Paulo stared long and hard at the empty alleyway before he continued. "Somewhere in the world is a shaman who doesn't need voodoo or a body count to raise the dead."

"No voodoo?" cried Sal. "Take it from a friend, Paulo—lay off the Green Soy."

Hardy found such a claim hard to swallow as well. What Paulo was describing wasn't possible. No voodoo meant a zombie with free will. Such an uber-shaman was too good to be true. And that's exactly who Hardy was trying to find.

"You're talking about the corpse whisperer," he said.

"Hey, keep your voices down," Louie whispered savagely. "Solomon's got ears everywhere!"

"I call shenanigans," Sal exclaimed. "That's zombie folklore. He doesn't exist. Next you'll be saying vampires are real!"

Paulo glanced again at the entrance. "That's what Solomon *wants* you to think," he whispered with a gravelly voice. "Think about it. Right now he's the most powerful shaman on the continent, if not the world. The guy's no joke. He enchanted himself with a Methuselah charm. That's top-shelf magic. His body count must be through the roof!"

"I heard he's almost 200 years old," interjected Hardy. Which meant Solomon's body count had to be in the millions. But how was he able to single-handedly perform so many resurrections? It didn't add up.

"Not bad for an organ donor," said Sal.

"I'll put it to you this way," said Paulo, dropping his voice to a near-hiss. "The crazy blood banks who put him in power are long gone. Even their *children's* children are long gone."

"So what does that have to do with the price of gris in Cali?" asked Hardy. "I mean, assuming this fairytale shaman really exists."

"Think about it," Paulo susurrated. "The corpse whisperer makes Solomon's magic look like child's play. Can you imagine Solomon being okay with that? Once you start handing out free will to us zombies, shamans can kiss their precious body counts *and* their boosted powers goodbye!"

Hardy's palms began to sweat. His heartbeat—the only one for blocks around—quickened dramatically. "So where's the proof that the guy exists?"

"Yeah," said Sal. "So far this is all just a lot of talk."

"Is it?" asked Paulo. "If you don't believe me, how do you explain that mystery resurrection in Indiana from about ten or twelve years back? Cadavers don't just spontaneously raise themselves from the dead. And from what I've heard, this miracle cadaver belonged to a Burialist."

"You know what?" Louie said thoughtfully. "I think I remember hearing about that. It was a girl, right? She crawled right up out of her grave, just like the good old days."

"What would a Burialist know about the good old days?" scoffed Sal. "Good-for-nothing grave babies don't deserve a second chance."

Hardy knew there was bad blood between the Resurrectionists and the Burialists that stretched back for centuries. Still, he never imagined an easygoing corpse like Sal would use pejorative slang like 'grave baby.'

"Still seems like a case of your basic graveyard poaching to me," insisted Hardy.

"Oh yeah?" asked Paulo. "Then explain to me why ether readers didn't find any traces of voodoo at her grave site."

"Ether readers," snorted Hardy. "Gimme a break." Ether readers passed themselves off to desperate cadavers as conduits to their past-life memories. That was their biggest offense, in Hardy's eyes. That they could 'discern' incanted magic was almost as offensive. "Buncha two-bit phonies."

"I heard the whole cemetery was paved over," said Paulo. "The graves weren't even moved—a mall was built right on top of them."

Sal chuckled. "Gotta love those crazy Burialists. It's all or nothing with them."

Hardy was still skeptical. "Sounds like an urban legend to me."

"Believe what you want," said Paulo. "But the point is, the girl left behind an empty grave to be with her boyfriend."

Sal shook his head. "Mixed-life relationships never end well. They run too hot and cold!" He barked with laughter.

Louie frowned at Hardy. "See what you started?"

"If you ask me," said Paulo, "if you find the boyfriend, you find the corpse whisperer." He leaned back with a smug smile.

Sal leaned over and smacked Hardy on the knee with the newspaper. "Finding them would be a piece of cake for someone of your alleged talent."

"Yeah, you'd think so," muttered Hardy. Assuming the young couple even existed.

Just then the bell tinkled as the door swung open. In walked a hunch-backed crone whose ancient, shrunken face was so deeply lined that Hardy was unsure if she were dead or alive. She was pushing a rickety shopping cart, from which she withdrew a clear plastic bag of what looked like pork rinds. She held up the bag and gestured to each of the men in turn, each time asking, "You like? You like some?"

"Go on, beat it," yelled Paulo. "Didn't we tell you before not to come back?"

The old woman shook the bag at him and grunted.

"Hell, screw the diet. I never say no to pork products." Hardy reached for his wallet. "How much for a bag?"

Louie touched him on the shoulder and quickly shook his head. "That's not pork."

Hardy blanched as he slowly put his money away. "I'll take your word for it."

"You're not in Kansas anymore," Paulo said solemnly. "And don't you forget it."

Louie went to the woman and gently ushered her out the door. He slipped her a five-dollar bill before sending her on her way. Louie paused a moment to glance up and down the alleyway before returning inside with a shrug.

"So, what else can you tell me about this super shaman?" asked Hardy. "Can he leap cemeteries in a single bound?"

Paulo shook his head. "Sorry. I don't know what you're talking about."

Sal, too, had moved on. He was leaning back in his chair, his chin to his concave chest, reading a dog-eared copy of *Reanimated Weekly*.

Hardy turned to Louie, appealing to him with as innocent a smile as he could muster. "Whereabouts in Indiana did you guys say that Burialist was from?"

Louie pursed his lips and switched the old radio back on. It crackled with static as he turned the silver tuning knob to an AM talk show.

"*And what I'm saying is,*" intoned an angry voice from the tinny speaker, "*is that these* greyback scabs *are stealing our* jobs!"

"Yeah, jobs you wouldn't touch with a ten-foot femur!" Sal yelled at the radio, and slapped his knee with the magazine. "Why do you think there are so many undead sewer workers?"

"Don't forget undead sanitation workers," added Paulo.

Hardy frowned. Not only were they steering clear of the Z-word, but now their Havens accents were noticeably thicker. Any thicker, and they might as well be moaning at each other.

"So that's it?" Hardy asked. "The party's over?"

Louie unclipped the smock from Hardy's thick neck. "No charge." *Naw chud.*

These guys give new meaning to the phrase 'getting the cold shoulder,' Hardy thought morosely. He reluctantly hopped from the chair and shuffled to the door. He stopped at the threshold and fought the urge to say something witty or memorable. What was the point, though? He already knew with a surprising bit of sadness that he would never be returning to this corner of Little Burlytown.

The bell over the door tinkled as he stepped outside. He was halfway down the alley when it occurred to him that Paulo was blowing smoke up his considerable ass with that whole bit about Indiana. Darla used to call him Indiana Bones, didn't she? He stopped in his tracks and groaned. How could he allow himself to be bamboozled?

"Back to square one," he mumbled. He was almost to the street when he realized he'd forgotten his hat on the counter. He squinted up at the midday sun and pondered which was more delicate—his exposed scalp, or his ego. He groaned again as he trudged back to the barbershop.

"Listen," he said, "I'm only here for my—"

Hardy stopped dead in his tracks and gasped. All that was left of Louie, Paulo and Sal were pulverized husks and jagged, exposed bones. A rotted shard of rib had been expelled with such force it was impaled in one of the mirrors. A chunk of pickled, maggot-riddled kidney sat squarely on Hardy's fedora. The old crone was standing in the middle of the room, covered in grey grit and buzzing, darting flies.

Hardy stumbled over her shopping cart as he backed away. She wasn't a wrinkled old prune; she was some sort of ghoul. She turned and glared at him through the window.

"No more talk," she spat. Her thin lips peeled back to reveal a mouth full of serrated, shark-like teeth.

"Shit," said Hardy.

Glass exploded into the alley as the crone crashed through the window and landed beside him. Hardy brought his elbow down hard on the back of her head as she lunged for him.

"Hurt you," she shrieked, and scrambled towards him on all fours.

Hardy clamped his meaty hands around her leathery neck. She began to thrash in his grasp as he bore down on her windpipe. *Do it*, he thought. *It's you or her, stupid. Do it do it do it*

"He hurt you," she croaked. She scratched at his face and tried to wrench free.

"No you don't," he grunted.

Hardy gritted his teeth and pressed his thumbs into the soft spot of her throat. He tightened his grip, relentlessly, until her trachea collapsed like a stale fortune cookie. The crone immediately deflated in his arms as a final, rank breath issued from her sagging maw.

Hot bile rose in the back of his throat as he looked down upon her prone body. He swallowed hard and braced for Round Two. But no, she laid quite still, her monstrous teeth coated with black blood and foam.

The magic is willing, thought Hardy. *But the flesh is weak.* Had she been one of Solomon's skeletal minions, Hardy knew he'd be the one laying on the ground, broken and battered and limp. He paused long enough to catch his breath and dust the remains of his friends from his clothes. Then he hotfooted it out of the alley back to the Avenue Styx.

So, he thought with grim satisfaction, *the Hoosier state it is.*

CHAPTER FOURTEEN

The morning sun shone brightly on Las Almas. Like most New Cali border towns, Las Almas had more than its share of undead residents. Las Almas, however, also had a reputation for being mixed-life friendly. Because of this, local businesses turned a blind eye to the increasing number of necrophile couples flocking to the area. Over time, this lax attitude eventually turned Las Almas into a haven for progressive thinkers and artists. Unfortunately, this also drew Neo-Lifers to the town like buzzards to carrion. This meant many mixed-life couples conducted themselves with a certain degree of caution even as they availed themselves of the trendy Las Almas vulture-culture scene.

One such couple soaking up the sights was Pam and her undead boyfriend, Clay. (His easternized name was Stephen, but she preferred his given rebirth name.) The lovers sauntered along Raven Lane, pausing every so often to duck into an art gallery or antique shop. As they rounded the corner, however, they were surprised to see the garish, neon-lit façade of a new triple X-Ray video store. Clay (nee Stephen) tut-tutted at the come-hither poster of zornography starlet Rita Rigor hanging in the blacked-out window.

"What is this neighborhood coming to, Pam?" he asked sadly and shook his lumpen head. "What's next—ether reader salons? Before you know it, this place will be another Boca Muerta!"

Pam clutched his palsied, necrotized arm a little tighter. "Clay, do you...do you think she's attractive?"

"Rita Rigor?" he said with a dry chuckle. "Naw, she's not my type. I like my women to have a pulse!" He pursed his leathery lips and pecked her delicately on the cheek. "And speaking of which—when are you going to tell your folks about us?"

A small, red insect alighted on Clay's shoulder and began inching its way along his prominent collarbone. "Soon, I promise. It's just my father—"

"Yeah, I know, I know," he said, gritting his teeth. "I'm not what he considers son-in-law material."

Pam finally noticed the insect as it neared the talisman dangling around Clay's neck. "He's very...old-fashioned."

In truth, she was truly falling in love—with a corpse she'd known for less than three months. But she was afraid to broach the subject because of the dramatic difference in their ages. Clay was nearly two centuries old, but because of a substandard resurrection he looked nearly twice his undead age.

The insect was now sitting squarely on Clay's talisman. She frowned as she tried unsuccessfully to swat it away.

"Shoo!"

"Is it another maggot? Geez, I'm sorry. I've been meaning to see my shaman about that."

The talisman suddenly vanished in a dun-colored puff of pickled flesh and bone. Clay didn't hear the distant handclap as he fell to the pavement. He clutched feebly at the smoldering, softball-sized hole in his breastbone.

"Hurts," he moaned as his skin began to shrivel. Without the magical protection afforded by his talisman, his ancient body began to decay. Oily black decomp sores exploded across his gaunt face. "Everything huh, hurts, so bad." A fly alighted on his chin before darting inside his gaping mouth.

"Clay!" His eyes began melting in their sockets. They ran down his cheeks in chunky rivulets like rancid egg yolks. Pam began to fumble inside his chest cavity for the talisman.

"Get a room," muttered a businessman as he stepped around them.

"Fuck you," Pam screamed. She searched frantically for the charm within the slushy pasta salad that used to be her boyfriend's lungs. "Someone, please! Is anyone a witch doctor!"

Meanwhile, from his distant perch atop Burly Gate, George Gleeson lowered his sniper rifle. He turned to the two-dozen men gathered around him in the abandoned, debris-strewn guard tower and smiled. Mixed in among the older Neo-Lifers were several teenaged recruits. "And that," said Gleeson, "is how it's done."

One of the younger recruits whooped as he tossed an empty beer can out over the west side of the wall. "That was freaking awesome!"

"Show-off," laughed Manny Silva, a fellow vet and Gleeson's second in command. Like Gleeson, he was badly disfigured in the Battle for Burly Gate. Now, all he had to show for his troubles was a monthly disability check from the Living States Zombie Defense Corps and a ragged stump where his right arm used to be.

"Let's see you do that with one arm tied behind your back!" Manny said and pounded Gleeson on the shoulder.

"This rifle's a beaut," he said, marveling at the military-issue hardware. "Especially the infrared scope. But I'd still choose a HAMR any day."

"Yeah, wish we had those magnetic resonators back in the day," sighed Manny. Several of the Burly vets nodded grimly. "They can strip a charm off a charging zombie faster than you can say brain-freeze!"

"Can I try," asked Calvin, the wide-eyed acolyte. "I could probably pick off my zombie neighbor in San Gabriel from up here!"

Gleeson glared at him as he handed the rifle to Manny. Even with one hand, Manny deftly disassembled the weapon. "No. Too soon for that," Gleeson said.

"You ain't even bona fide yet," laughed Manny as he snapped the metal case shut. "Don't get ahead of yourself, kid."

"You need to know the basics first," said Gleeson.

"Sure, Zombie 411, I get it," said Calvin. "So check this out. My dad is a Cremationist and his dad was a Cremationist. And my dad's dad's dad—"

Gleeson held up his scarred hand for silence. "Their sacrifices don't make you a patriot," he said, pointing at Calvin. "Do they."

"Well, I'm a Cremationist, too," he answered defensively.

"Hey, go easy on the kid," said Manny. "He climbed twenty flights just to meet you."

Gleeson paused to consider this brash recruit, the one with the arms full of tattoos and a shoulder full of chips. Neo-Lifers were getting younger every day. And dumber, too.

"Zombie 411, eh?" said Gleeson. "So tell me—why are there no sirens down there?" He pointed to the town far below, where vultures were already pecking at Clay's chunky remains.

Calvin furrowed his brow as he peered over the edge. Indeed, Burly Gate afforded the best views of Death Valley. He turned back to Gleeson and shrugged. "Dunno. Too high up to hear it?"

Gleeson glanced at Manny and shook his head. "I thought you vouched for this one."

"Better green than grey," laughed Manny. "Didn't you used to say that?"

A scrawny recruit wearing brown, oil-stained coveralls stepped forward. "My buddy is a detective with the NHPD. He says most of the force is Cremationist."

"No. That's not the answer I'm looking for." Gleeson stared across to the west side of Burly Gate. To the northwest, the distant San Lazarus Mountains were barely visible through the hazy smog and ash. Due north, beyond the mold-covered mountains, were the Charnel Point slums. Gleeson narrowed his eyes as he considered the slums, a known safe haven for Resurrectionist insurgents known as resurgents.

Beyond the Point, as every good patriot knew, was Josiah's Bluff, site of the Burly Crematorium. The wind began to howl around them, scattering debris ahead of it and ushering in a rank, throat-searing odor from deep inside the Havens.

"Jesus H, what the hell is that *smell*?" asked a lanky, knife-faced boy. His New York accent was hard to miss. "It's like a dinosaur farting barbecued garbage!" He quickly pulled the collar of his *Denizens of the Dark* T-shirt up over his nose. A few of the recruits chuckled nervously.

"That is the smell of patriotism," said Gleeson. "That is the smell of sacrifice."

Calvin looked contemptuously at the knife-faced boy. "Yeah. That's the crematorium, you idiot."

"So. The reason there are no sirens?" asked Gleeson. "It's simple. No pulse means no loss of life. And that means it's not murder to take down a zombie." He turned back to Calvin. "Zombie 101 is more like it, punk."

Manny shook his head and laughed again. "Schooled."

"Why are we standing around talking when we should be killing us some zombies?" said Calvin. "I mean, that's why we're all here, right?"

Manny cleared his throat. "Best to keep your mouth shut, Cal."

"This wall beneath our boots is the thin grey line standing between us and millions of zombies," said Gleeson. "And yet our own government has the gall to grant these brain-eaters access to *our* side of the wall in the form of work visas! Zombies do not deserve the same rights as the living!"

"Can't call 'em zombies anymore," sighed Manny. He seemed almost wistful. "Now we gotta be all politically correct. It's like the Cold Wars never happened."

The wind switched direction, bringing with it a powerful mustiness that made even Gleeson's eyes water. "And that would be La Barba Verde," Manny muttered. He coughed into the crook of his good arm. "Must be low tide."

"But isn't Burly Gate, like, a hundred feet tall?" asked Calvin. "Isn't that tall enough to keep out the brain-eaters?"

"Know your facts!" roared Gleeson. "Misinformation will get you killed!"

Calvin glanced down at the tops of his dirty, battered sneakers. Like many Neo-Life converts, Calvin's middle-class existence was being subverted by the never-ending influx of undead immigrants. Jobs for the living were becoming harder to come by. As was self-respect. If undead equality became a reality, would the Havens' sovereignty be far behind? No; it was no way to live, in the shadow of the dead.

Gleeson knew it was up to people like him to tip the scales back in their favor. And he did so by bombing rebirth centers and charm schools. But that was bush league compared to Solomon's alleged zombie mills, which cranked out thousands of walking cadavers a day. The Secretary of Undead Affairs vehemently denied their existence, but Gleeson, like many patriots, believed in rumors that cited double the daily output.

"George," said Manny, pulling Gleeson aside. "You okay?"

Gleeson patted Manny on the shoulder and turned to meet the expectant stares of the unemployed factory workers, of the disenfranchised patriots. Hollowed eyes stared back, dark with fear, with worry.

"For those wishing to become members of this brotherhood, initiation is simple. Bring me ten talismans apiece as proof of your commitment to this cause."

Calvin smirked. "I can bring you a hundred."

Gleeson smirked as well. The kid was growing on him. He was hungry, desperate for change. "Whoever brings me the most talismans first will be chosen for a very important mission."

An enthusiastic murmur rippled through the assembled men. The fear in their eyes had been replaced by something fierce, feral.

And that made George Gleeson proud to be alive.

CHAPTER FIFTEEN

The overcast sky cast its soft, steel-gray light upon the fallow land as Hardy sped through rural Pennsylvania along Interstate 80 in his ancient Peugeot 504. The gloomy horizon held little promise for the fountain dowser, and yet what lay ahead was infinitely more promising than what he had left behind in New York. He tightened his grip on the steering wheel as he mulled over what to do once he reached Indiana.

Hardy slowed the car as he neared a toll plaza. He nodded amiably at the undead attendant as he paid the toll. The attendant, who looked like he'd seen better days, stared right through Hardy. His gnarled fingertips grazed Hardy's palm as he handed back his change, causing Hardy to shudder involuntarily. The attendant read a deeper meaning into this, however, and suddenly snapped to attention. He began to spew a vile screed as the Peugeot pulled away.

"I used to be somebody!" he yelled. "I danced with Michael Jackson in the *Thriller* video! Don't judge meeee.....!"

Hardy shook his head. Why was everyone so hyper-sensitive? Dead or alive, there were no winners or losers. Existence was just one big stalemate, as far as he was concerned. All Hardy cared about was getting from point A to point B with minimal fuss or interference.

"And speaking of which," he muttered as he slowed behind a truck struggling up a particularly steep grade. The Peugeot's old diesel engine burbled as Hardy switched lanes to pass the rig. It was no big surprise to see a reanimate behind the wheel. The undead required no sleep, no nourishment, and no pit stops. Who better, then, to tackle the monotony of the open road? Surely, though, this trucker hadn't come back from the dead to drive palettes of refrigerated produce along a dusty interstate. And yet here he was, doing just that. For all Hardy knew, the driver could have been Mario Andretti in his previous life.

The truck driver cast a jaded eye down upon Hardy, who responded by flashing the peace sign. "Keep on truckin'," he said. The driver's face lit up and he happily returned the gesture.

"That's what I'm talking about," said Hardy.

After that, he drove on in relative silence, mostly because the car radio was busted, but mainly because he was still trying to piece together the scant details he had on not only the corpse whisperer, but on Hitler, too. For all he knew, they could be one and the same.

Hardy guffawed and slapped the steering wheel. "Wouldn't that be a hoot!" he yelled out the window. He laughed so hard he nearly wept. He almost ran off the road as he pushed the brimming tears from his eyes with his sleeve. He was still chuckling as he pulled into a rest area just east of the Ohio border.

He leaned back against the seat and rubbed his stubbly face. Even with his eyes closed he could still see the interstate rushing towards him. He extricated himself from the front seat and stretched his legs for a few moments. On his way to the restroom he noticed a pay phone. He stopped and rooted around in his pocket for some loose change. He absently jangled the coins in his hand as he stared long and hard at the phone.

"Aw, what the hell." He plunked several quarters into the silver slot.

His ex-wife answered on the second ring. "What?" she cried. "What do you *want* from me?"

"Darla," he said gruffly. "It's me. It's Baz. I guess you were expecting someone else. Bill collector, maybe?" But Hardy knew that wasn't the case. He was merely being kind. Even after their divorce, he still had a soft spot for the former Mrs. Hardy, the mother of his only child.

Darla sighed. "What is it, Baz? And where are you calling from?"

"It's better if you don't know that," he said softly.

A bit of kindness crept into her voice. "Are you in trouble?"

He laughed. "Ain't I always?"

Kindness quickly gave way to resentment. "Well, if you are, I can't help you."

He pressed his forehead against the cool, smooth metal of the pay phone. His bleary-eyed reflection stared back at him from the pitted chrome. "Not asking."

"So, then, why are you calling?" She tried to sound indignant, but her curiosity was obvious. It made him smile, this subterfuge. Even after two decades, they still couldn't be honest with each other.

"Just watch your back, okay?"

She laughed, not unkindly. "Oh, Baz. Fine. I'll be careful."

He wanted to know if her undead lover made her happy, but didn't ask. He wanted to know if Darla ever missed him, as he sometimes missed her. But this, too, went unasked.

"Good," he finally replied.

"How's Sofia?"

"*Please deposit one dollar for the next three minutes,*" interrupted a sterile recording, "*or your call will be terminated.*"

"What was that?" asked Darla. "Are you calling me from a pay phone?"

Hardy had tossed his cell phone and credit cards down the incinerator chute before getting out of Dodge. He was looking to secure a burner phone and a new identity from his guy in Phoenix, a retired dowser by the name of Jerky.

"Just a sec." He quickly plunked in four more quarters.

"Baz?"

"Sorry, I'm here. Sofia's tough. She's hangin' in there but she misses you."

"I wouldn't know." He could hear the pain in her voice; they'd barely spoken since the divorce. He paused, hoping his ex-wife would say something he could bring back to their daughter as a peace offering. But in his heart he knew the time for reconciliation was long in the past. Darla's resurrection was less than two weeks away, after all. Why try to mend fences now? And yet, wasn't that what he himself was trying to do at that very moment? He had to laugh at the folly of it all. One phone call did not erase twenty years of loneliness and neglect.

"Darla, listen—"

"Maybe I'll, you know, see you when I see you."

"You're sure about this whole rebirth thing, right? That witch doctor of yours, Stephens, he's a good guy?"

"You tell me, Baz. You're the one with the sixth sense."

His intuition told Hardy nothing about his ex; it never had, and it surely never would. Every dowser had a blind spot. For whatever reason, his was Darla.

"I think you know the answer to that."

Her laugh was raspy; it would grow raspier still after her rebirth. "I passed the psych test with flying colors. Dr. *DeStefano* said I'm a born cadaver." She laughed again. "I don't understand you, Baz. After all this time, after all these years—now you fucking decide to give a damn about me?"

"That ain't fair. I always gave a damn about you."

"It's not just the big things that count. The little things matter, too."

"Please deposit one dollar for the next three minutes, or your call will be terminated."

Hardy swore under his breath and searched frantically for more coins. Then he remembered the car's cupholder was brimming with change.

The recording chimed in again. *"Please deposit one dollar for the next three minutes, or your call will be terminated."*

"Darla, give me a sec, awright? I just need to run to my car for—"

"I waited long enough for you."

"I know, but—"

"It's over," she said quietly. "Take care of yourself, Baz. Have a nice life."

He couldn't bring himself to tell her goodbye. Not yet at least. "Thank you, darlin'," he said instead. "You have a nice life, too."

A dial tone blared in his ear. He reluctantly hung up the phone and sighed.

"My sweet, darlin' Darla," he said to the empty, trash-strewn parking lot.

The next few hundred miles were a blur for Hardy. The rolling Pennsylvania countryside soon gave way to the flat, arid plains of the Buckeye State. As he pulled up to the front gate at St. Joan's Chillicothe campus he realized he couldn't remember how he got there. Worse still, he couldn't account for the empty Frankenjoe's coffee cups and the Mickey Z's food wrappers littering the front seat.

He pulled into the visitor's lot and rubbed his eyes with the calloused heels of his hands. Running on autopilot was a bad sign. "C'mon, wake up, ash-hole," he moaned as a kaleidoscope of bright lights blossomed beneath his eyelids. He slapped the steering wheel and pushed himself to his feet. At least he had enough presence of mind to shove the fast food wrappers under the seat. The last thing Sofia needed to worry about was her old man's health. He brushed salt crystals and stray sesame seeds from his field jacket before setting off towards the dorms.

Hardy found her room easily enough. But Sofia's roommate, a surly Texan named Ashley, sleepily informed Hardy that his daughter was "hanging out at the quad." What her roommate had judiciously omitted was "with her new boyfriend."

Hardy tromped across the campus, marveling at the school's austere architecture. The low buildings were boxy and mostly windowless—exactly what one might expect from a predominantly Cremationist institution. Why the school was out in the middle of Ohio, in undead country, was beyond him. Such a fractious arrangement was just begging for trouble, in Hardy's opinion. But his daughter had insisted on enrolling. She wanted to become a missionary, god bless her—and St. Joan's was *the* place for aspiring emissaries.

The quad was packed with students, despite the gloomy weather. Hardy was hopeful as he scanned the young faces in the crowd. He snickered at the various displays of public affection. That is, until he discovered that one of the hormone-drunk couples included his daughter.

A look of amusement crossed the boy's face as Hardy began zigzagging through the crowd. He whispered something in Sofia's ear. She turned, a bright smile on her face that quickly faded at the sight of her father bearing down on them like a runaway freight train. Sofia broke away to meet Hardy halfway.

"Dad," she cried, and threw her arms around him. "What are you *doing* here?"

Hardy found it funny how easily his daughter made his troubles disappear. He patted her on the back and tried not to smile, if only to keep the boyfriend on his toes. "Heya, there, Sofa-Bed. I was just going to ask you the same thing."

She gave his arm a gentle squeeze. "I want you to meet Mark."

She waved Mark over, and he sheepishly complied. Mark was a gangly wisp of a boy. He was twenty pounds underweight and a few inches too tall for Hardy's taste. His pasty complexion didn't help matters. Hardy wondered if his daughter was in a mixed-life relationship, but Mark's sweaty handshake quickly dispelled that idea.

Hardy knew it was wrong, but he was mighty relieved that the boy was playing for their team. "Hullo, Mr. Hardy. 's nice to finally meet you."

Hardy narrowed his eyes. "Yeah," he said gruffly. "Same here." At least the boy had a firm handshake.

"Sofia tells me you're like a human GPS or something."

Hardy glanced sideways at his daughter. Was it meant as a compliment, or the start of the world's worst eulogy? "Yeah, something like that."

"Well, I should probably get over to the, uh, library," said Mark.

"We're still meeting for dinner, right?" asked Sofia.

Mark nervously eyed Hardy before answering. "Sure, yeah. If that's cool with everyone."

Hardy smiled. This kid knew who was boss. "Fine with me."

Mark nodded gratefully and shoved his hands deep in his pockets. He kept his head down and disappeared into the crowd.

"So how long you been dating this guy?"

"Oh, we just met," said Sofia. "Just a few minutes ago, actually. We're getting married tomorrow."

They began walking arm in arm. "Cute. You're a real gas. But I'm telling you now, little girl, if he treats you wrong, I'll make him wish he was undead."

"Come on. I know how to take of myself." What Hardy didn't realize was that she knew how to take care of him, too.

Sofia guided them to an empty bench near the edge of the quad. She took a seat but Hardy remained standing. "I been sitting for ten of the last eleven hours," he explained. "Gotta give the ole keister a break."

"So, I'm happy to see you, but why *are* you here? I figured you'd be in, like, Madagascar or something."

Hardy was still amazed by his daughter's beauty. Who would ever believe such a delicate creature could share his genes? And yet there she was, radiant and bright-eyed, just like her mother once was.

"I was in Buenos Aires last week, actually."

Sofia smiled. "Of course you were. Did you find Atlantis yet?"

Hardy smiled back and finally sat down. "Still looking."

She began picking at her chipped nail polish. "That's good." She absently tucked a blonde strand behind her ear and stared off into the distance. "So, you promised you'd talk to mom. Did you?"

Hardy sighed. "It's her body, right? Her life? Hopefully this decision will make her happy." He wanted to believe it with all his heart, but couldn't. He was on Sofia's side, but didn't dare say so, not this late in the game. Not when he had opportunities aplenty to behave like a real man, a real husband, before his marriage found its way into the crapper.

"But she won't even remember us when it's over. It's not fair." She frowned at the ground. "Rebirth is just wrong, dad. It should be illegal. No offense. I know some of your best friends are, like, zombies."

He thought of Moss, and of the dusty barbershop in Little Burlytown. "Some of them, yeah. But I think they prefer to be called living-challenged."

"What they are is brain-dead. And so are you if you don't stop mom from making the biggest mistake of her life."

"Come on. Easy now." Hardy had been around the block enough times to understand that she was really angry with him, not her mother. "To be fair, you could have at least tried calling her. Two years is a long time to bear a grudge, kiddo."

"What are you talking about? I can't tell you how many times I called, how many messages I left—" She sat back in a huff, her jaw tight with furious indignation. He tried clumsily to comfort her, but she shrugged him off. "Don't ever say I didn't try, okay?"

"I had no idea."

"What else is new. For an ether reader you're so clueless sometimes." She blinked back tears. "I'm really gonna miss her, dad."

Hardy ignored the ether reader comment. Sofia was just pressing his buttons with an obvious cheap shot like that.

"She'll still be your mom," he said, but he knew that wasn't true. He gave his daughter a squeeze. "At least you still got me, right? And that's gotta be better than nothing."

"You need to stop scaring my boyfriends away, dad."

Some of them had needed a good scare. "Yes? Is that a yes?"

She looked just like her mother as she rolled her eyes. The resemblance was uncanny. Hadn't he once seen a first rebirthday card that read, 'The undead live on in those they leave behind'?

"What a crock," he said aloud.

"Come on, dad, of course it's a yes," said his daughter, the future missionary, the redeemer of the undead. "Don't be so insecure."

"When did you become so beautiful, huh?"

"When you were off kayaking with Bigfoot." She kissed him on the cheek and stood to leave. "I gotta go. Busy busy."

Hardy grunted as he rose from the bench. "Just like that, you gotta go? I figured, I don't know, maybe we could have dinner or something."

Sofia frowned as she smiled—or maybe it was the other way around—Hardy couldn't tell which. "Dad," she said.

"You can even bring what's-his-face if you want."

"Tempting," she said. "But I suppose I should say yes since who knows when I'll see you again."

"Spoken like a true Hardy," he replied.

"Okay." She was already backing away, her face suddenly bright despite her woes. "Meet me outside my dorm around six. I know you don't need me to tell you where it is."

Hardy waved and nodded. "Sure," he said. "It's a date."

CHAPTER SIXTEEN

Hardy killed time by wandering the campus. In two hours he encountered less than a dozen reanimates (one of which was a janitor; two more were maintenance workers). Most likely the students were recent converts to Cremationism. Who better than an undead missionary to convert the undead?

"And around and around we go," Hardy said wearily.

With an hour left to kill before dinner, he decided to conduct more research online. As he changed course for the campus library Hardy encountered a small clique of undead students (bringing the tally up to fifteen). Ever vigilant, he noticed they were all toting the same thick *Undead Mythology & Folklore* textbooks under their bony arms.

"Excuse me, who teaches that course?" he asked. The students exchanged a puzzled look. "I'm thinkin' of auditing the class."

"His rename is Professor Forrest," one of them replied. "He's the reanimate in residence."

In other words, thought Hardy, he was the school's token undead professor, a necessary evil to qualify for federal funding.

"Do you know where his office is?" asked one of the students.

Hardy smiled. "I think I can manage."

Professor Forrest's office was located in the sub-basement of the Cultural Studies building, down the hall from the boiler room and right next to a supply closet. The door to his office was closed but the light was on. Hardy rapped lightly on the door.

"Come back tomorrow," Forrest called from inside. "Office hours are over."

"My name is Barnabas Hardy. I'm a fountain dowser. I just need a few minutes of your time, professor."

Hardy heard the clang of a metal drawer and the squeak of cheap chair castors. The door opened a crack but no one was there.

"Did you say fountain dowser?" The voice came from near the floor.

Hardy jumped back. "Hey, you're a little guy."

"I'm a little person, yes."

And a living-challenged one to boot, Hardy thought. He pretended not to notice the discarded Press-On Lips packaging in the professor's wastebasket. "Shoot. Yeah, sorry about that."

Forrest regarded him with translucent, crust-rimmed eyes as he tried discreetly to adjust his misshapen mouth. "I expected you to be taller," he said finally.

Hardy smiled. He didn't know why, but he liked this guy already. "So, ever heard of the corpse whisperer?"

As it turned out, Professor Forrest knew a great deal about voodoo-free resurrections. He'd written a book on the subject, but both the L.S. government and Solomon had it banned.

"They destroyed literally every copy they could find, the philistines," said Forrest. "They actually burned them in the Josiah's Bluff crematorium, if you can believe it."

Hardy laughed. "So what yer saying is, they cremated a book about Resurrectionism? That's rich. You're lucky they didn't roast your marshmallows, too."

Forrest grinned. "'The resurrection will not be televised,' as the old saying goes. But what would you expect? Our worlds are culturally bankrupt. We no longer revel in our shared pasts. Now, on the other hand, if I were to vomit on a beloved movie icon, well, you'd never hear the end of it."

Hardy scratched his head thoughtfully.

"Can't argue with you there."

"And then there are people like you, Mr. Hardy. Anthropological pirates who pillage and exploit history for their own personal gain."

"Guilty as charged, professor. Fountain dowsing pays the bills."

Dusty gris-gris bags, primitive Loa totems and ceremonial candles lined the shelves of the cinderblock office. Stacked in a corner were several well-worn ceremonial drums. What impressed Hardy, though, was the professor's extensive collection of rare and unusual Resurrectionist artifacts. Normally such pieces could only be found in the oldest undead communities, like Carrion Flats, or in voodoo museums. There were several teak wood cruciforms, used by shamans in the reading of first rites. There was also a chalice made of hammered gold, its rim stained crimson with sacrificial blood.

Forrest even had an extremely rare, centuries-old lead crystal decanter in his collection. These decanters, normally carved from limestone, were used to hold the Tears of Life. Ornate decanters, such as Forrest's, were typically used in the resurrection of ancient monarchs, including Alexander the Great. There were only three such lead decanters in existence that Hardy knew of—he'd personally tracked down two of them.

Hardy suspected his rival, the undead dowser Silas Walker, had beaten him to the punch. If that was the case, many of Forrest's artifacts were likely recovered with the aid of voodoo. Dowsing wasn't easy, but a gifted dowser, like Hardy, made it look easy. (Perhaps *too* easy; fellow dowsers, like Walker, viewed Hardy's intuition as nothing more than a 'glorified autopilot.')

"You got a lot of valuable paraphernalia here," said Hardy. "I'm sure that stuff didn't just find itself."

Forrest's grin, while genuine, was tempered by the weak adhesive on his synthetic lips. He cleared his throat and tried to act as if half his mouth wasn't drooping. "Point taken, sir."

"You could use these voodoo relics to raise quite the army all by your lonesome," Hardy mused. Having spoken extemporaneously, he suddenly considered the diminutive professor in a different light. Was it possible that Forrest had once been Napoleon Bonaparte? On the face of it, such suppositions seemed ridiculous, but one such hunch had led Hardy directly to the elusive D.B. Cooper. (The infamous hijacker, now undead, was selling dinette sets in a strip mall in Rochester, NY.) In Forrest's case, his advanced decomp led Hardy to peg the professor's physical age at around 250, maybe 275. *Definitely old enough to be Bonaparte*, thought Hardy.

"I suppose I could become quite the tyrant, yes," said Forrest, derailing the fountain dowser's train of thought. "That is, if I were a shaman. Sadly, though, my kind is not predisposed to magic." Forrest tapped a yellow fingernail on his desk blotter. He inched his chair closer to Hardy. "With one exception. Which brings us to the reason for your visit."

"I don't follow you. Unless..." The professor urged Hardy on with raised eyebrows. "Are you tellin' me that the corpse whisperer...is a corpse?"

"In so many words, yes."

Hardy's skin began to crawl. They may have been two floors underground, but he suddenly felt exposed, vulnerable. "I don't think we should be talkin' so nonchalantly about this. You could get yourself in a lot of trouble for sayin' stuff like that."

"I've spoken and written things far worse than that, I assure you. And yet Solomon's Gestapo has not come for me in the night."

Hardy had heard plenty of chilling stories about the reanimated skeletons known as the Scrimshaw Collective. "Even so, you never know who might be listening in."

There was a loud rattle outside the door, followed by a deafening hum.

Hardy jumped to his feet as the walls began to vibrate. He grabbed the professor and hefted him over his shoulder. "Hold on," he yelled. "I'll get us out of here!"

To his surprise, Forrest wasn't panicked. Just the opposite. The professor was laughing so hard his vinyl lips had fallen onto Hardy's shoulder. Forrest noticed this, and laughed even harder. If it were possible, he would have shed tears.

"The boiler, it's the boiler," Forrest explained between spastic fits of laughter.

"Oh." He sheepishly put Forrest down. "Right." He plucked the lips from his shoulder and ceremoniously handed them to Forrest. "Normally I'm not so skittish."

"I haven't laughed that hard in a long, long time, Mr. Hardy. I think I may have literally split my side." Forrest pressed the lips against his mouth and beckoned him closer. Hardy obliged by assuming a crouch beside the professor. Forrest cupped a hand to Hardy's ear. "Go to Stony Hollow, Indiana," he whispered over the din of the boiler. "Ask for a witch doctor named Baptiste."

Hardy's intuition immediately recalibrated itself to this new bit of intel. "Baptiste," he whispered back. "Got it."

"Tell him I sent you." Forrest reached into his desk and pulled out a small sandstone cruciform hanging from a woven hemp cord. He dangled it in front of the fountain dowser before solemnly placing the gritty rock in his hand. "And show him this as proof that you and I spoke."

"Why are you doing this? You don't know me from Adam."

"*Veritas numquam perit*, Mr. Hardy. 'Truth never perishes.'"

The fountain dowser grinned widely. "I can dig it."

The sound of the cast iron boiler was deafening as Hardy stepped into the hallway. As he exited the building he discovered he'd lost track of time; night had fallen while he was underground.

"This campus is like a casino," he grumbled to a moth fluttering in the weak glow of an incandescent bulb. "No windows."

He allowed his natural sense of direction to guide him back to his car on the other side of the campus. It wasn't until he passed the dining hall that Hardy remembered his dinner date with Sofia. He instinctively reached for his cell phone, but his building's incinerator had reduced it to a lump of melted plastic.

"Classic," muttered Hardy. He didn't even know what time it was and didn't want to find out. Five minutes or an hour late—it wouldn't matter to Sofia.

Hardy took a detour over to his daughter's dorm, but she'd left no note. Not surprisingly, her room was empty. Hardy knew this because he'd picked the lock and peeked inside. The radioactive glare of the bedside clock was hard to miss in the dark. He grimaced as he noted the time; he'd missed dinner by almost two hours. Hardy sat on the edge of Sofia's bed and buried his head in his hands. *What's done is done*, he thought. He reached into his coat pocket and withdrew a sealed envelope containing several hundred dollars in cash. He left it under her pillow, but pulled it back out to scribble a last-minute note.

Your mother wanted you to have this, he wrote in his blocky scrawl.

So what if it was a lie? Better that his two girls smoothed things over while they still could. Hardy had the rest of his natural lifetime to reconcile things with Sofia.

That is, assuming he ever discovered a way to cast a Methuselah charm on himself.

* * *

CHAPTER SEVENTEEN

Maya felt conspicuous in her brand-new dress suit and heels as she rode the elevator to the eighth floor of her new job. *No more begging in the streets for you*, she told herself as she slowly counted the floors. No more scraping by in the Charnel Point slums, either, where whatever wasn't covered in mud or mold was buzzing with black flies. Even now, as she rose through the center of the downtown Albuquerque office building, Maya had to tell herself that this was really happening, that her relife really did have meaning.

The elevator doors whispered open on the eighth floor, revealing a brightly lit waiting room. Maya smiled at the receptionist but panicked as she struggled to remember the woman's name. Was it Mandy? Candy?

The receptionist, plump and ruddy-cheeked, returned the smile. "It's Maya, right?"

"And you're *Sandy*," Maya replied, relieved. She clutched the handle of her empty briefcase with both hands.

"It only gets easier, hon," said Sandy, causing Maya to like her immediately and immensely. Where was the rampant necrophobia she had been warned about? So far, Maya had been treated with nothing but kindness.

Her friends back in the Havens were wrong about this side of the wall—not all warm-blooded people were Neo-Lifers.

"It's that obvious?"

"Like a deer in headlights," said Sandy with a good-natured chuckle. "You're the third cubicle on the right." She rose partway from her desk chair to point the way with a green highlighter.

Maya was too excited to speak. She'd never had her own desk, much less her own telephone *and* her very own computer. She set her briefcase down and took a minute to bask in such unexpected euphoria. She hadn't been so elated since she'd been granted the work visa two months ago.

"You earned this," she whispered.

As she pulled up to her desk in her fancy desk chair she noticed the welcome packet from Grey Skies Ahead. The federally funded program gave thousands of cadavers like Maya a chance at a better existence. Grey Skies' motto was *Don't Just Survive, Thrive.* At that very moment, Maya felt all things were possible.

Yet as she turned on her computer and listened to the quiet hum of its hard drive, she was struck by a very intense tingling in her left hand. Her ring finger, specifically. The strange buzzing sensation traveled up her arm like a swarm of angry flies. Her first instinct was to remove her talisman, but to do so was akin to kissing her new relife goodbye. She'd worked too long and too hard to ever let that happen.

So Maya endured the intense tingling as it radiated from her talisman and spread throughout her body. She forced herself to smile when Petra, another plump, ruddy-faced coworker, stopped by Maya's cubicle to introduce herself. By now the pain had spread to her neck and face. Maya tried to focus on the woman's dangling turquoise and silver earrings.

"So nice to meet you," Maya said, but it sounded more like *suh nigh tomb eat chew*.

Petra frowned as she leaned in closer to Maya. "Are you okay? You don't look so good."

Maya struggled to speak clearly, coherently. She knew she was the only undead employee in the company—so far. She desperately wanted to prove that the undead were just as capable and responsible as the living. But what escaped her cold lips was "Um fun." *I'm fine.* Maya started to panic in earnest.

"Do you need to lie down?" asked Petra. She turned to Sandy and waved her over. "I think Maya might be sick."

Maya nodded vigorously. Yes, that was it—she was ill. Why else was she suddenly craving raw organ meat? She desperately banished the terrible thought from her mind. No, she was better than that; she did not consume the living, no matter how warm or fleshy their entrails were rumored to be.

Sandy chuckled as she ambled down the carpeted hallway. "It's just first-day jitters."

Teeth bared, Maya suddenly rose from her chair and lunged at Petra.

"Nuh, um nuh dune sis," she cried as Sandy tried to pull her off. "Cand stobmuh sev!"

Maya sunk her yellow teeth into the soft flesh of Petra's neck. Blood sprayed the walls of the cubicle in a hot arterial spray as she gnawed her way through muscle and sinew and tendons. Horrified and helpless, her gaping mouth full of thick blood and viscera, Maya shut her eyes as the rest of her body performed an irresistible, autonomous pantomime of wanton, sense-less carnage.

"We repeat: two people are dead in Albuquerque's Plaza District after a reanimated cadaver brutally murdered her coworkers in what witnesses described as an unprovoked attack. The undead employee, who was reborn in the Havens, surrendered earlier today to local law enforcement. She denied responsibility for her colleagues' grisly deaths, insisting, and I quote, 'My shaman made me do it.'

"A statement released by a group of rogue shamans known as the Seattle Six claimed responsibility for the Albuquerque attacks, as well as similar attacks in cities throughout the Midwest. The group also stated that the random repossessions of cadavers will continue until the Living States government withdraws its bid to impose a strict 'death cap' on all shamans who perform resurrections. It is believed that such a restriction would severely limit a shaman's potential magical abilities. The so-called 'death ceiling' would limit individual voodoo practitioners to only 500 total resurrections. Currently there is no limit to the number of rebirths that can be performed.

"President Hammond was quick to condemn the rogue shamans, but insisted that the proposed death cap was vital to the safety and longevity of the Living States. 'We will continue to welcome the oppressed, living or dead, into our borders,' he said, 'but we cannot, and we will not, grant shamans on either side of Burly Gate free reign to amass potentially dangerous body counts.'

"President Hammond was also quick to say that 'the mass repossessions that led to the Battle for Burly Gate will never happen again in our lifetimes, or in our children's lifetimes.'

"The usually reclusive Secretary of Undead Affairs also spoke out against today's deaths, describing 'any senseless death as a wasted second chance.'

"It is widely believed that the Secretary's personal body count is in the tens of thousands, leading many to question what sort of threat he might pose to national security.

"Many radical Neo-Life groups insist the proposed Death Cap bill does not go far enough, and have called for even tighter rebirth restrictions.

"More on the tragedy in Albuquerque as it develops. We now return you to a very special episode of *Who Are They Now,* which is already in progress."

*　　*　　*

CHAPTER EIGHTEEN

The early shift was ending down at the talisman production plant just south of Boca Muerta. Plant #41 was among the oldest in the country, producing on average 5,000 ring-shaped talismans a day. All talismans were fabricated to strict Living States Government specs and shipped from the plant to undisclosed locations around the country. Many believed the Boca Muerta talismans to be among the best though in truth no one talisman was better than another. Any shaman worth his gris-gris bags knew that it was the quality of spells and high body counts that boosted a talisman's power.

None of this mattered to the plant's undead workers, however. So crushed was their collective spirit by the drudgery of their jobs that they may as well have been producing paperclips. Like many of their grey-collar brethren, the workers at plant #41 were undocumented aliens who toiled for less than a living wage. Even so, none complained. Boca Muerta's squalor was more preferable than the untamed wilds of the Havens.

The early shift began its mass exodus from the guts of the factory. The sound of slow, uneven shuffling was borne aloft by two hundred pairs of flaking, necrotic feet. Soon, the streets of Boca Muerta teemed with dead-eyed, slack-jawed workers, their talismans twinkling in the weak moonlight.

For many, their chief concern was simply putting one foot in front of the other. For some, scoring their next hit of Noodle was first and foremost in their dulled minds. Only a select few dared dream of making it big in nearby New Hollywood.

Every step away from the factory was another imagined step towards freedom and prosperity. A chorus of ragged moans rose up from barren throats. And yet jaundiced eyes widened with surprise as black cargo vans emerged from the shadows, from alleyways, engines revving, heavy metal doors sliding open. Reanimated skeletons lunged into the moonlight, revealing bleached skulls and mirthless grins.

The hapless cadavers were corralled in the span of a few heartbeats. The corpse-laden vans sped off, bound for the mold-covered lands beyond Burly Gate.

Meanwhile, just one block away, a Death Valley squad car sat parked by the side of the road. The two on-duty officers had witnessed everything in shocked silence.

The officer behind the wheel put the car into gear and glanced over at his partner. "Those....those were Solomon's minions, right?" He swallowed hard; he'd heard that they couldn't be stopped by bullets—or much else. "We, uh, we should follow them, right?"

His partner took a sip of tepid coffee and set it on the dash. "Why? I didn't see anything—did you?"

The officer behind the wheel paused; his hand was still on the gearshift. "My old lady's sister is undead, Marv. I mean, if it could happen to those workers, it could happen to her, right?"

"But it didn't happen to her." He took another sip of coffee. "Stand down, cubby. Most of these deadbacks are illegals anyway. Plus there's no way just the two of us could take down a bunch of minions."

"I—I guess you're right."

His partner smirked. "Of course I am. No skin off our noses."

By now the vans were long gone. Emboldened, the young officer cleared his throat and turned to his partner. "It's true they were in *Jason and the*

Argonauts before they worked for Solomon, right? The minions, I mean."

"You ask too many questions, you know that?"

"That movie really scared me when I was a kid. I've hated skeletons ever since."

Marv snorted. "You're *still* a kid. Now let's get the hell out of here before more of those things show up."

The squad car slowly pulled away from the curb. It made a wide U-turn and headed away from Burly Gate. The officers didn't even glance twice at the idling midnight-blue Cutlass Supreme parked further up the road.

Manny drummed his fingers impatiently on the steering wheel. He always got antsy on stakeouts. He grew antsier still knowing that someone else had beaten the Brotherhood to the punch with one fell swoop. He turned to Gleeson, who was slouched in the passenger seat.

Gleeson, too, was growing impatient. The latest batch of recruits was failing to deliver on the simple task of ten talismans apiece. That is, except for Calvin. He'd come through with a hundred talismans, just as he said he would. But a handful of charms was chump change compared to the millions of talismans still in circulation. Gleeson knew they needed to take their activism to the next level. If not, it was only a matter of time before the country's liberal, zombie-loving politicians had Cold War III—and the blood of honest Americans—on their hands.

The two Burly Gate veterans exchanged a knowing look. "Follow those vans," Gleeson said.

"Great minds think alike," said Manny. He stomped the gas pedal to the floor and the Cutlass revved off into the night. The sheer face of Burly Gate rose up before them, blotting out twinkling constellations. The terrain became more and more desolate as the pair continued west past abandoned, weed-choked lots.

"North," said Gleeson, and Manny took a hard right onto Burly Boulevard. Gleeson leaned forward and squinted through the windshield. "There," he said, pointing to a line of vans in the distance.

"See 'em," said Manny. His knee steadied the wheel for the split-second his hand left the wheel to slap at the gearshift.

"Not too close," warned Gleeson. The Boca Muerta checkpoint was now miles behind them to the south. The San Gabriel border crossing, the only other checkpoint, was over 200 miles to the north.

"I don't get it, George. Where the hell are they headed?" whispered Manny.

"I don't know," replied Gleeson. "It can't be this easy."

Manny hunched over the wheel as they slowly closed the gap with the speeding caravan. "Think it's a trap?"

Half a mile up, three more vans merged onto the boulevard from a side street. Gleeson broke into a smile. "Probably."

"Am I missing something?"

Two more black cargo vans merged onto the boulevard. Unlike the other vans, these were not low to the ground. "They're empty," Gleeson said. He directed Manny to get off the boulevard.

Manny shook his head. "Knew it couldn't be that easy."

"If we do this, we do it on our terms, not his."

"You talking about who I think you're talking about?"

If they were indeed heading into an ambush, it only meant the Brotherhood had finally caught Solomon's eye. They couldn't afford to grow careless now.

"I have a plan," said Gleeson. "It's time to find out how committed to the cause this Calvin kid really is."

CHAPTER NINETEEN

The video clip of Damon vomiting on Audrey Hepburn continued to drive the worst of Damon's negative press. The original clip quickly went viral, but subsequent, altered videos achieved true meme status. One such doctored clip showed Damon vomiting not on Hepburn, but on various heads of state, from a reanimated Winston Churchill to the Secretary of Undead Affairs himself.

Damon's inner circle decided his dead cred could be salvaged, but only if they acted quickly. Damon and his manager were summoned to the Paradox lot for what Viktor hoped would be a civilized discussion. But what his inner circle was asking of him was simply too much for Damon to bear with good grace.

"You're all crazy," he declared. "There's absolutely no way I'd even *consider* working at KadabraLand!"

"You're doing it," yelled Barbarelli. His eyes bulged as he leaned forward across Viktor's desk. "Or we'll freaking *make* you do it you ridiculous little turd!"

"There's no way *anyone* is making me work in some rinky-dink theme park for one *day,* let alone for one *week!*" Damon yelled back.

"Have you ever actually been to a KadabraLand?" asked Buddy. "They're actually pretty nice."

"So why don't you go live there," snapped Damon. "And while you're at it, *you* can dress up like Kenny Kadaver because *I'm* not doing it."

"Just hear us out," said Viktor.

"It's demeaning!" said Damon. "I'm a Harpo award-winner!"

Cornelius had to physically restrain Barbarelli, who lunged at Damon with his dyborg arm. "Who do you think made that happen, those Harpos?" he cried. "Do you think you actually deserved them? We made you!"

"None of my acting has ever been Show-Tuned," Damon said of the software used by directors to amp up on-camera performances. "Never."

"Not that *you* know of," scoffed Barbarelli.

"I believe you, Mr. Grayson," said Cornelius. "I think you're a very good actor."

Viktor had heard stories about Barbarelli's temper, but the truth was far worse. Not for the first time, he missed Joni's comparative finesse. "Barry," he said calmly. "You're not helping."

Viktor motioned for Cornelius to drop Barbarelli into a nearby chair. Cornelius was only too happy to oblige. Damon's manager tumbled unceremoniously onto his backside with a loud grunt.

"Watch the coccyx, you big ape," groused Barbarelli. "It's not paid for yet."

"Damon listen," said Viktor. "Trust me. It's the only way to make things right."

"I'm telling you, Russell Mann must have screwed with the results," said Damon. "There's just no way I could have failed."

Buddy paused to raise his hand. "I checked the results myself. Twice. No offense, Damon," he said with obvious disdain, "but it's like you weren't even trying."

"No offense, *Buddy*, but for all we know you could be in Russell's pocket." Everyone stared at Damon. Viktor was especially dumbfounded.

"You'll say anything, won't you," Viktor said angrily. "I looked over your S-certs, too. Some of your answers defied logic."

Now it was Damon who was angry. His heart had been in the right place even if his score proved otherwise. He glanced at Cornelius, who offered a small smile of encouragement in return.

"Flunking some stupid test doesn't make you a bad person," said Damon.

"No, but flunking *this* test makes you look like a racist necrophobe," said Barbarelli. "It doesn't matter if Russell *did* screw with your results—perception is everything in this town, Damon."

"So now you guys think I'm going to start bombing rebirth clinics?"

"You would never do that," Cornelius said quietly.

Viktor pinched his eyes shut and quietly kneaded the bridge of his nose. They hadn't even gotten to the worst part of this bargain. "Damon," he sighed.

"Come on, at least tell me it's the park in France. I could use a week's vacation."

"Please, let me tell him," Barbarelli said.

"Tell me what," said Damon. "It's not the one in Albany, is it? I hear that one is a real hole."

Viktor reached into his desk and took a hearty swig from a silver flask. "It's Cadabra City," he harrumphed. "In the Havens."

This time it was Damon that Cornelius was forced to hold at bay. "No way," he yelled, straining with all his might against his bodyguard's iron grasp. "Screw you, Viktor. Screw all of you!"

He bit Cornelius on the arm but he would have had better luck biting a lamppost. Cornelius didn't flinch, though his feelings were badly bruised. He tightened his grip incrementally, just enough to leave Damon gasping for air.

"This can't be happening," he wheezed. "All I did was puke on Audrey Hepburn—"

"And don't forget Russell. You did vomit on him, too," Buddy added.

Damon cast a dark look at Buddy. "Should that really make me public enemy number one?"

"It's never about you, is it," said Viktor. "I don't understand you sometimes, Damon. You seem so intent on squandering your talent. It's like you have a death wish."

Damon made a half-hearted attempt to free himself from Cornelius's grasp but quickly gave up. "So what is this now, an intervention or something?"

"We're trying to help you," said Viktor. "We're trying to salvage what's left of your career."

"It can't be that bad," Damon said limply. But he could see the truth reflected in their stony faces. It *was* that bad. Why else would dressing up like a theme park mascot be on the table? "So what if I say no?" asked Damon. "What's the worst that can happen?"

"The studio sues you for breach of contract," Barbarelli answered matter-of-factly.

"This can't be happening," Damon muttered.

Viktor saw a glimmer at the end of the tunnel. "It's just one week."

Damon buried his head in his hands. "Right. One week—in the Havens. Jesus, Vik."

"For the record, the park's Kadabra Estates is a four-star resort," said Buddy. "It's on par with any New Cali resort this side of the wall."

"We could go with you," Viktor said, his eyes twinkling behind his glasses. "Sure. We could spin this into something you want to do voluntarily. You know, spend a week living among the undead to better understand them."

"It worked for undead Pacino," said Barbarelli. "Won himself a Harpo *and* a Humanitarian after he lived a month in the Charnel Point slums. Claimed it was research for a role but I heard he was actually in rehab for Green Soy addiction."

"The point is," said Viktor, "we can turn this to your advantage—to our advantage, really. We bring a camera and tell the 'bloids that we're shooting a behind-the-scenes doc for the home market."

"That's brilliant," whispered Buddy. "I want to go with you." Buddy had been reborn in the Havens but was whisked away by Viktor to an elite New Cali charm school. Venturing past Burly Gate was the perfect opportunity to discover more about his undead roots. Maybe he'd even track down his shaman.

"Me too," said Cornelius. His head nearly brushed the ceiling as he rose to his full height. "Mr. Grayson will need protection."

Damon, too, was slowly warming up to the idea. No doubt about it, Viktor was a genius. "It would be like our own *Hearts of Darkness*."

Viktor laughed. "Let's hope it's not quite that harrowing." He turned to Damon's manager. "How about you, Barry? Up for a little adventure?"

"I can't. I'm having some work done," Barbarelli said.

"What about Joni?" Damon asked. He assumed there was a good reason her assistant hadn't been invited to the meeting. "Shouldn't we wait for her to get back?"

"According to her Sherpa's blog they're still two days from Everest's summit," offered Cornelius. "She might not be back for a while."

Viktor set the empty flask down on the corner of the desk with a hollow clink. "Listen, Damon. It's true—Russell probably *is* out to get you. Once you make it into that notebook of his the writing is all but on the wall."

"But in my case the wall had to be Burly Gate, right?"

"I'll put it this way," said Viktor. "If you don't follow through on this, there's no shaman in the world powerful enough to resurrect your career."

How could Damon possibly say no to these people who were willing to put so much on the line for him? Of course, if he *didn't* do this, he'd find himself permanently bumped from the A-list to the Z-list.

Damon smiled, despite his lingering reservations. "Abra cadabra," he said.

CHAPTER TWENTY

Darla Hardy knew she had not been herself lately. She blamed Barnabas for this. Rather, she blamed his absence for her addled state of mind. Darla was no stranger to solitude; Barnabas was always on the go, traipsing the globe in search of expensive bric-a-brac for bored socialites. *Dowsing pays the bills, darlin'*, he used to say. He repeated it often enough that Darla wanted to tattoo the words across his fat forehead.

And yet, even back in their salad days she realized it was the only life he knew, dowsing. And he was damn good at it, too—even she knew that about him way back when. His freakish intuition was glamorous and mysterious. Barnabas had a way of understanding the hows and whys of a person, understood motivations and ramifications simply by observing even the minutest of details. Barnabas called this sixth sense his gift, and indeed it was. And, it did pay well. Very well. Truly, Darla was never left wanting for anything her heart allegedly desired. But Darla did not crave material possessions; she never had. Her heart's desire was always Barnabas.

For all his formidable intuition, why couldn't he understand something so fundamental, so elemental about her?

Of course, being as taciturn as her ex-husband merely exacerbated her emotional isolation. Ultimately, it was to their mutual detriment that they kept their true feelings buried. As for her undead lover, Lydia was warm, and kind. She openly cared for Darla in a way that Barnabas never could. In other words, Lydia was a breath of fresh air. Were it not for her, Darla would never have embraced Resurrectionism. Nor would she have a fancy-shmancy witch doctor in Westchester County.

Darla's friends joked that she was in the midst of a mid-life crisis. Perhaps she was. Being faced by one's own mortality certainly drove many people towards the extended longevity offered by rebirth. Many more, however, were attracted to the Resurrectionist concept of *nepenthe*—the act of overcoming one's grief simply by erasing it from memory.

Jonas, her death coach, was a soft-spoken man with dark, close-set eyes and a bushy beard that reminded Darla of Charles Dickens. Jonas had a knack for reading Darla's many moods. He also had a knack for keeping her on course towards her rebirth.

"The trepidation you're feeling is quite normal," he said as they sat side by side on her old couch. He patted her hand and smiled. Lydia sat across from them in an armchair, the *New York Times Magazine* open upon her lap.

"I keep telling her that," Lydia said without looking up from the crossword puzzle. "Every day."

"Lydia had her share of reservations as well, on the eve of her own rebirth," said Jonas. "The single most important thing you must do—that we must all do—is to let go of the past. Only in this way can any of us move forward."

"I'm doing my best," said Darla.

"You still have that box of photo albums," said Lydia. "How is that letting go of your past?"

Darla understood how difficult it was for Lydia to accept that she had once been married, that she had a daughter. A beautiful daughter. Headstrong, like her father. "It's not my past yet," she said quietly. *Shit or get off the pot,* Barnabas would have told her gruffly. And he was right.

Jonas leaned in and looked Darla in the eye. "There it is again," he said.

"That kernel of doubt."

It was more than just a kernel. "If I could just talk to Sofia one last time—"

"She calls at least once a day," said Lydia. She closed the magazine. "At least."

"We've talked about this before, Darla. In just one week, none of this will matter. *Cadabra Rasa.*"

Lydia rose from her chair and crossed the room to Darla. She knelt down and took her warm hands into hers. "Yes. *Cadabra Rasa,*" she said.

Jonas watched her expectantly, his dark eyes stern. "Say the words that will set you free."

In one week, there would be no more Sofia, no more Barnabas, and, more importantly, no more Darla Hardy. And that, she reminded herself, was supposed to be a good thing. She clutched Lydia's cold hands as the phone began to ring.

"Say the words, Darla," said Jonas. "Ignore the phone. It is just a distraction. Exist in this moment. Say the words."

Lydia tightened her grasp as the phone continued to ring. "Jonas is only trying to help you, sweetie. He's only trying to help *us.*"

Darla counted the rings. She knew it was Sofia. It had to be. "She needs closure."

"We do not speak for the living," Jonas reminded her. "We do not think for the living."

"We die for ourselves. Death is only the beginning," Darla said blankly, completing the scripture verse. She looked towards the phone, imagined herself running across the room to answer it. The phone fell silent after the sixth ring—as it always did.

"There, that wasn't so hard, was it?" asked Jonas. "Now, say the words."

Darla willed the phone to ring again, but knew the time for miracles was long past. She smiled for Lydia's benefit, though she felt dead inside.

One week. Nepenthe. And then, no more Darla Hardy.

"Cadabra Rasa."

*   *   *

Meanwhile, halfway around the world in Nepal, a small mountain-climbing expedition was setting up camp. After six days on Everest, the small party was still at least two days from reaching the summit. The group was comprised of wealthy undead singles, one of which was Damon's publicist.

Tall, fit and bright-eyed, Joni was the sort of well-kept cadaver who could easily pass for being alive. Unlike many reanimated corpses, she did not revel in decay's effects on a post-death body. Instead, she celebrated her second life by obtaining the finest body upgrades money could buy.

Out of habit, Joni reached for her powered-down phone. She knew there was no signal all the way up in the Himalayas, but the temptation to turn on her phone was almost too strong to bear. Instead, she found comfort in the touch of its smooth glass against her hand; it was a compromise she could live with, for now.

In the meantime, Joni reminded herself that she'd climbed to the top of the world for a reason—to escape the never-ending stress of her daily life. At least, that's what her therapist back in New Hollywood had told her. *You need some perspective,* she'd explained. So climb Joni did, unmindful of the extreme cold and thinning air. Only their guide, an ancient Sherpa shrouded in pelts, was affected by the adverse weather. If not for his warm-blooded limitations, the small group of undead adventurers—many of them surgically enhanced, like Joni—would still be ascending Everest.

Joni tapped the blank screen before shoving the phone back in her pocket. She needed to remind herself that the world wasn't falling apart without her, that her clients could babysit themselves for several days. As for her Beats Per Minute—Joni assumed she'd flatlined the moment she left the base camp. All she needed was a signal and a few hours to revive her Flutter ranking. She paused to laugh at how beholden to social media she was—even when the world in its entirety was literally spread out before her.

One of her fellow climbers trudged towards her through the knee-deep

118

snowdrift, a wide smile on his narrow face. She couldn't remember his re-name—it was Dan, or Stan. Either way, Joni didn't care. The man may have been wealthy (almost as wealthy as she was), and he may have been blandly handsome the way most fine-tuned New Hollywood corpses were, but his clumsy advances did not warm the cockles of her dead heart.

"Hard to resist, no?" he said as he drew up alongside her.

Joni almost laughed in his face until she noticed he was looking at the top of her phone protruding from her coat pocket.

"It's not that hard," she said with a sly smile of her own.

"So why do you look so...tense?"

He placed his hand on her shoulder and flashed a mouthful of perfectly aligned, post-rebirth enhanced veneers. Joni flashed a smile of her own as she placed her hand atop his— and crushed it in a vise-like grip. A tooth upgrade was nice, but Joni preferred post-life strength to beauty.

"Touch me again," she said, "and I'll rip your puny arm out of its socket."

She tightened her grip for emphasis. Dan/Stan quickly nodded, and gratefully removed his hand as Joni relinquished her iron grip.

"I—I should see what the others are up to," he said quickly.

"Yeah, you do that," she replied as he trundled off through the snow. Joni knew her actions would make her the group pariah, but she didn't care. Better to be alone than settle for Mr. Rotten.

She returned her gaze to the seemingly endless frozen expanse of the Himalayas and couldn't help but wonder where all the good men were—because none of them were here with her at the top of the world.

Joni turned at the sound of someone struggling through the snow behind her. "Listen Dan, or Stan, or whatever the hell your stupid rename is—"

It was their group's Sherpa, and he was holding what looked like a giant Walkie-talkie. A fierce, brittle wind lashed around them as he placed the bulky satellite phone into her hands.

"Call for you."

"For *me*?"

"Very urgent." He burrowed deeper into his furs as he followed his tracks back to camp.

"It's not my fault," said her assistant, Becky. "I was intentionally left out of the loop—it was all Barry Barbarelli's idea!" She was speaking so fast that Joni could barely understand her. Is that what she herself sounded like in her daily life—so rushed, frantic?

"Becky, slow down. Just take a deep breath—"

"Take a deep *breath*?" She was bordering on hysterical.

"Becky. Calm down. Please."

"Okay. Calming down."

"Now, start from the beginning."

Her assistant did as she was told. Joni quickly learned about Audrey-Gate and everything that followed. The more she heard, the less she missed about New Hollywood. And yet Joni understood it was exactly where she was meant to be.

CHAPTER TWENTY-ONE

Dr. Baptiste was getting on in years, despite outward appearances. He may have looked like a man in his early fifties, but the voodoo practitioner was nearly a century old. One of the perks of being a shaman was the ability to retard the aging process with spells and incantations, but enchantments could only do so much. This was especially true with the limited resources available to him in his little corner of Indiana. He had long since stopped lamenting the dearth of ingredients in Stony Hollow needed for conducting proper voodoo ceremonies. A truly gifted witch doctor could make do with very little, and luckily for his patients, Dr. Baptiste was one such medicine man.

While he was not a miracle worker per se, he still possessed a high enough body count to perform a moderately advanced spell like the Messiah Touch. In other words, he could heal most undead ailments with a simple touch and a brief incantation. The drawn-out ceremonies, which included herbs and animal sacrifices, were mostly just that—elaborate displays for the sake of his undead patients. Baptiste believed a connection to old-world rituals aided in the healing process, especially when what ailed his patients was more mental than physical. Considering the number of bias attacks that occurred in their sleepy corner of the world, bolstering his patients' self-worth seemed mandatory. So it was that Baptiste was not just a local witch doctor, but something of a spiritual adviser, too.

This philosophy was in stark contrast to that of Solomon's fundamental belief that a shaman should view his charges as nothing more than golems requiring occasional maintenance. Baptiste had heard the rumors, of course—of mass resurrections performed in the Havens' La Barba Verde archipelago. Their sole purpose was not to further the cause of Resurrectionism but to bolster Solomon's already impressive body count. How else was he capable of such high-level magic, if not for the allegedly millions of ill-gotten talismans under his control? Indeed, if the stories were true, Solomon was somehow amassing a secret army for himself.

As the rumors persisted, and as Solomon grew more and more powerful, Baptiste realized it was time for him to continue his work with the undead elsewhere. He eventually chose a small town in flyover country to settle down, far enough from both coasts to avoid the politics of Burly Gate, the power plant, and everything else that might detract from his work as a magic practitioner. Politics, by its very nature, was fractious; Baptiste's credo was 'mend, don't offend.' Such an outlook had served him well over the last thirty years as the local medicine man, and he wasn't about to change.

He was sipping his morning coffee—a dark roast from the Frankenjoe's on the corner—and completing the cryptoquote in the *Hoosier Hoot*, when he heard a car pull into the gravel lot. His first appointment of the day, a re-animate renamed Mudge, was scheduled for an 8:30 visit. Baptiste glanced over the top of his paper at the clock on the wall.

"Well, he's early today," he muttered into the steam rising from his coffee. He continued working on the *Hoot*'s word puzzle, determined to finish it before Mudge tried the front door. Finding it locked was just the sort of thing that a regular patient like Mudge would take as a personal affront. The spirits were out to get him, or so he believed. Why else did he suffer so greatly, and so frequently, with all manner of undead ailments big and small? His staff thought Mudge a hypochondriac, and had jokingly dubbed him Job for his ceaseless troubles. But Baptiste understood what his patient really needed above all else was a sympathetic ear to bend.

As he finished his coffee Baptiste realized that Mudge had been waiting quietly for almost fifteen minutes. The doctor took this as a sign that Mudge's anxiety was finally improving. He grabbed Mudge's thick file from the table to remind himself what the purpose of today's visit was.

"That's right," he mumbled thoughtfully, tapping the manila folder with his pencil. *Patient complaining of impaired speech, uncontrollable moaning*, one of his nurses had scribbled in the file. "Goat throat."

As far as afflictions went, this one was as common as any other affecting the undead, second only to decomp. A simple incantation and a sprinkling of Holy water (no matter that it was simply distilled water purchased from Valu-Mart, and not the real thing) would probably do the trick. Such simple remedies always sufficed with Mudge.

Baptiste switched the lights on as he moved through the clinic to unlock the door. Only, it wasn't Mudge. In place of a stooped cadaver stood a burly man in a rumpled overcoat. He was, Baptiste noted, most very certainly not dead. If anything, he looked quite hale, despite the dark circles under his deep-set eyes.

"This is the undead clinic," said Baptiste through the window. "You want Dr. Thompson. He's a few miles down the road, just past the post office."

The man's haggard face lit up with a strange smile. "No, I got the right place," he said. "You're Baptiste, right?"

Baptiste took a step back from the door, convinced that Solomon was looking to finally settle old scores. He always knew the day would come, and yet, the good shaman was not ready for his day of reckoning. What would his patients do without him?

"You've got the wrong man," he said.

"That's what they always say," replied the stranger. He reached into his pocket.

Baptiste fell to the ground and shielded his head with the fat file. "I have no regrets!" he yelled from beneath the manila folder, and braced for the gunshot. When none came, he cautiously peered out from behind the file and noticed the sandstone cruciform dangling from the man's outstretched fist.

"The name's Barnabas Hardy."

Baptiste quickly hopped to his feet. "*The* Barnabas Hardy, the fountain dowser?"

He glanced over his shoulder at the empty parking lot. "Well, it depends on what you've heard."

"You're the one who finally tracked down Jimmy Hoffa."

Some of the weariness left his eyes as he broke into a smile. "The one and the same. Now, before you ask, yer pal Professor Forrest sent me."

Baptiste's hands trembled as he fumbled with the keys. *That's just the caffeine hitting you*, he thought. But he knew the truth. And the truth, as Forrest knew, never perished.

"*Veritas numquam perit,*" said Baptiste aloud, echoing the sentiment.

"Damn skippy," replied Hardy, and quickly followed the befuddled medicine man inside.

"So let me understand this," said Baptiste. "You're a fountain dowser but you don't believe the corpse whisperer exists?" Baptiste was seated behind his gunmetal gray desk, his elbows resting on a stack of paperwork. Hardy was seated in the chair usually reserved for patient consultations. He was gulping down water from a floral-patterned Dixie cup.

Hardy reached over and refilled the cup to the brim with distilled water from a plastic gallon jug. "A healthy bit of skepticism never hurt anyone, doc." He tilted his head and threw back another shot of not-so-Holy water. "Except when it does. Hurt someone, I mean."

Like most people who encountered him for the first time, Baptiste immediately liked Hardy (once he realized the man wasn't an assassin). Why that was so, he wasn't quite sure. Perhaps outsized charisma was a quality innate to individuals in Hardy's line of work. What better way to pry information from strangers than with an uncommonly strong duende?

"It's better if you tell me what you know," said Baptiste. He and people like Professor Forrest belonged to a lesser-known sect of Resurrectionism known as the Savane. Savanes believed in the concept of life after undeath. This was the very same immaculate resurrection that Russell Mann so desperately craved.

"I gotta tell ya, it's not much. The corpse whisperer is a corpse." He shrugged. "And…that there was a mystery resurrection a few years back, right here in your neck of the woods."

"Professor Forrest told you all of that?"

"Well, no. I already knew some of that goin' in. But that's about it."

Baptiste knew that such knowledge of the corpse whisperer—even what precious little Hardy already knew—was enough to make anyone a marked man. And yet, the old witch doctor recognized the importance of unearthing the truth about the world's most powerful shaman.

"If this guy is real—and I'm not saying he ain't—wouldn't you be out of a job if he showed up?"

"Worse things have happened, Mr. Hardy." For some reason, this made Baptiste think of patients like Mudge. Which is when he realized—where *was* Mudge? He was almost 45 minutes late. Perhaps he was scared off when he saw Hardy in the parking lot? He buzzed the nurse's station. "Has Mr. Mudge arrived yet?"

Sisely, who was part of the morning staff, buzzed back. "I actually just tried calling him at home and at work. No one has seen him since the end of yesterday's night shift."

"Got a missing person?" asked Hardy with raised, bushy eyebrows.

"You could set a clock by this patient," Baptiste explained to Hardy. "For him not to show up, well, it's just very odd. But it's probably nothing."

"Listen, just say the word, doc, and I'll find him." He took another swig of the faux Holy water. "It's what I do."

CHAPTER TWENTY-TWO

Hardy headed off in the Peugeot. He didn't have a map. He didn't even have directions to Mudge's house. *Don't need 'em,* he'd told the doctor. *Just point me in the general direction.* When it came to dowsing, Hardy knew he was one of the best in the Western Hemisphere, if not the world. Finding a reanimate in a Podunk town of less than 300 people was child's play. He expected to return with Baptiste's patient before the doctor could finish the rest of his little word jumble.

The doctor had promised to tell Hardy whatever he wanted to know about the corpse whisperer—assuming he returned with Mudge. Hardy thought it was a fair arrangement. The doctor had suggested several places Hardy might want to try first, including Mudge's apartment over Jansen's Hardware, and the public library, where Mudge often went to research the latest advances in undead medical treatments. But Hardy had a hunch, and he was currently following it out to the other side of town. He slowed as he neared the old meat grinder factory where Mudge was employed, but something didn't sit right with Hardy. He knew in his bones that the reanimate wasn't there. And his hunch had nothing to do with the angry picketers yelling at passing traffic.

"Go back to the Havens, you deadback scab!" yelled one red-faced, overall-clad factory worker as Hardy slowly drove past. Hardy consulted his reflection in the rearview mirror and was surprised to see how haggard he looked. He chalked it up to his family woes. Between Darla and Sofia, he barely had time to think about himself. He'd been on autopilot since before Chillicothe. That was no way for a man to live—especially not someone in his line of work.

"Snap out of it," he barked, and slapped himself in the face to drive the point home. He blinked and focused his attention on what lay ahead on the winding road. And it was literally *a head*. Its yellow eyes flitted open as the car screeched to a stop.

Hardy left the engine running as he scrambled out of the front seat. "Mudge," he said. "Mudge, you okay?"

The head heaved a mighty sigh. "I've been better," he said matter-of-factly. It was a miracle that he wasn't being consumed by advanced decomp.

That Baptiste must be one hell of a shaman, thought Hardy with genuine admiration. Clearly, his body count had to be in the thousands. Even so, Mudge had become a bit ripe from sitting out in the sun. Hardy swatted away several persistent black flies and quickly scooped him up from the pavement. Unsure of the proper etiquette for carrying a disembodied head, he carefully cradled Mudge's head like a football.

"Let's get you over to Baptiste."

"What time is it anyway?" asked Mudge. "I have an 8:30 appointment."

"First things first. We gotta find the rest of you before we go anywhere."

"I'm afraid that could take a while."

Hardy switched Mudge to the crook of his arm, Emily Post-Life be damned. "Then let's get cracking."

It was close to ten o'clock by the time Hardy tracked down all but Mudge's right hand and left big toe. The rest of his pruny remains were piled in the trunk of the Peugeot. For lack of a better plan, Hardy had propped Mudge's head in the passenger seat, atop his balled-up overcoat. His talisman, still caked in mud, dangled from his right ear.

"That Baptiste sure knows how to cast a spell, don't he," said Hardy.

Mudge would have nodded if his head were still attached to his body. He settled for raising his eyebrows.

More picketers were outside the factory, and they were even rowdier. As Hardy came down the hill towards the protest he watched one of the workers lob a softball-sized rock at a passing minivan's window. The rock glanced off the roof before coming to rest on the side of the road.

Mudge looked at Hardy with alarm as the Peugeot slowed. "What are you doing? This is the factory, right? You can't stop here! Keep going!"

Hardy glanced sideways at the head in his front seat. "I figured as much," he grunted. He put the car into park and left the engine running. "Be back inna minute."

"At least put me on the dash so I can see," Mudge yelped, but Hardy was already striding across the parking lot towards the line of angry men.

"Hey, what's your beef, mister?" asked the stringy-haired worker who'd thrown the rock. The name 'Kurtis' was stitched on his denim work shirt. He nudged one of his companions and pointed to the New York plates on the Peugeot. "You lost or something, Mr. Empire State?"

"Any of you mugs know where I can find a zombie by the rename o' Mudge?"

"Sure do," said Kurtis, and a group of workers joined him in laughter. "I'd start a mile up the road, and then take your first left, and then another left—"

Hardy shut him up with a powerful jab to the bridge of his nose. Blood cascaded down his face and soaked his starched collar. Hardy pulled a blackjack from his back pocket and whacked Kurtis's companion in the mouth. Cavity-riddled teeth scattered in a wide arc before clattering to the cold pavement like so many uncultured pearls.

"He broge by fugkin *node*," wailed Kurtis. But his friends, despite outnumbering Hardy eight to one, were already backing away from the wide-eyed madman. Hardy took a step towards them. He thought of Darla, and the dangerous prejudice that awaited her at every turn.

Her choice, he thought, gnashing his teeth. *And this here is* my *choice.* Blood roared in his ears as he lunged for the nearest body. He didn't feel their blows raining down upon him. "We're just getting started boys," he bellowed. And then he showed them how a real man brawled.

CHAPTER TWENTY-THREE

The town's sole police car was just pulling out of the lot as Hardy was pulling in. He waved and smiled despite his split lower lip. Perhaps it was only Hardy's imagination, but he could have sworn Mudge had somehow managed to inch away from him. Being covered in his coworkers' blood probably had something to do with Mudge's discomfort, but Hardy didn't care.

Baptiste ran out to meet the car. He gasped when he saw Hardy's bloody clothes. "What on earth—?"

"Long story short," said Hardy wearily, "I found Mudge." He hooked a bloodied thumb back towards the Peugeot. "His head's in the front, the rest of 'im is in the back."

Five minutes later Mudge was in one examination room, and Hardy in the other. He was leaning with his back against the wall as Tina, one of the younger nurses, patched him up.

"I won't say those boys didn't have it coming," she said as she applied a salve to Hardy's lip. "But you're lucky they didn't bust you up worse'n this."

The clear balm turned pink as Hardy smiled, splitting his swollen lip anew. "You should see *them*. They're the ones that need a doctor." He closed his eyes and replayed the fight in his mind. He forgot how good it felt to mix it up like that. "And maybe a good dentist."

"Well, normally we don't treat the living here at the clinic, but..." She threw her hands up. "Doctor's orders."

"Baptiste's a good guy."

Tina nodded as she applied an ice pack to a contusion on Hardy's forearm. "We like him just fine around here. This town would be lost without him, really."

Hardy knew it was only a matter of time before they heard the wail of approaching sirens. "And speaking of which, I need to talk to him before I hit the bricks."

As petite as she was (she couldn't have weighed more than a hundred pounds, he thought), Tina held Hardy at bay with a light touch to his shoulder. The baleful look she gave him from beneath her poufy bangs suggested she was no pushover.

"Stay here. Mr. Mudge is a tough cookie. He has so many high-level enchantments that he'll keep for another few minutes."

"You're the boss," he said as she left the room. Baptiste entered less than a minute later.

"Mr. Hardy—as much as I appreciate what you—"

"Just tell me what you can and I'll be on my way."

The doctor seemed to mull over the request before locking the door. He pulled up a chair and sighed as he sat across from Hardy. "A deal's a deal," said Baptiste. "So this is what I know. The Burialist was a local girl. She went to school right here in Clay County. As the story goes, she was out of town visiting her Resurrectionist boyfriend when they were attacked by Neo-Lifers."

Hardy's flesh began to crawl as he remembered what Paulo said to him that day in the barbershop: *You're not in Kansas anymore. And don't you forget it.*

"Kansas," said Hardy.

"Yes, her boyfriend was from Kansas. How on earth did you know that?"

"Call it a hunch, doc."

"That's amazing."

"You resurrect corpses for a living and you think a dowser's intuition is something special? Doc, please, it hurts too much to laugh."

"The girl's name was Brownstone. Ella Brownstone. Her family left the area soon after she disappeared."

You mean after she crawled out of the ground, thought Hardy. "What about the Resurrectionist boyfriend? What happened to him?"

Baptiste leaned back in the chair. "Oh. Well, he survived the attack. He didn't have any real kin to speak of. From what I recall he grew up in a foster home. She was his only family, really."

There was a light knock at the door. Baptiste unlocked the door and Sisely stepped into the room. "Okay, I know it's none of my business...."

Baptiste frowned at her. "What have I told you about eavesdropping?"

Sisely didn't just hear things through the grapevine—she *was* the grapevine. If something happened in Clay County, no matter how trivial, she made it her business to know about it. Being only one of three ether readers in the entire state allowed her to keep close tabs on the undead community as well.

"Pish tosh." Plastic bangles clattered on her birdlike wrist as she waved her hand. "That Brownstone girl was just the sweetest thing. She used to babysit my niece. Really, just such a nice girl. It's a shame what happened to her."

"So let me get this straight," said Hardy. "We got a young girl, a Burialist, who is attacked and killed while visiting her Resurrectionist boyfriend."

"Jesse," interjected Sisely. "His name was Jesse Bettenay."

Hardy laughed. "Jesse Bettenay?" he exclaimed. "Are you pulling my leg? There's gotta be at least a million Jesse Bettenays in the phone book."

"At the very least, yes," agreed Baptiste.

"He might as well be named John Smith, for crying out loud."

Hardy paused, waiting for his intuition to kick into high gear. But what he was hearing simply wasn't adding up.

"The parents approved of this relationship?"

"Oh, no, they were very strict, very devout," Sisely quickly replied. "But their relationship was the worst-kept secret."

"Any chance the girl's parents tried to take out the boyfriend?" A botched rubout was entirely plausible.

Baptiste looked horrified. "By hiring Neo-Lifers? You can't be serious."

Hardy shrugged. Nine times out of ten his wild hunches paid off. "Hey, I'm not judging. Just figured I'd ask an obvious question. Burialists aren't exactly the most tolerant people in the world—especially when it comes to rebirth."

Sisely squared her narrow shoulders. "I assure you, *Mister* Hardy, that the Brownstones are good, earth-fearing people. Besides, didn't you hear what the doctor said? Ella was murdered."

Hardy ran the tip of his tongue along his swollen lip. "Hate makes people do crazy things. Can't imagine there are a whole bunch of hate crimes in Kansas, though."

"Not undead-related ones, no," said Baptiste. "But that's because there aren't many Resurrectionists in those parts."

Hardy nodded thoughtfully as he mulled over the details. What was he missing? "There something you ain't telling me?"

"That Bettenay boy had powers," Sisely whispered. "Dark powers."

Baptiste admonished her with a stern look. "You know better than that."

"He's wanted for graveyard poaching," Sisely whispered dramatically. "That's a capital offense!"

"Assuming he resurrected her," said Hardy.

"Of course he did," insisted Sisely. "I heard he drove all night from Wichita to stop her burial. He only missed it by a few hours."

Hardy thought again of Darla, and wondered why he'd given up so easily on working things out with her. As far as grand gestures went, this boyfriend had him beat, hands down. Assuming any of it really happened, of course.

"Were there any witnesses when she was attacked? Or when she died?" Hardy looked from Baptiste to Sisely. "What about when she crawled out of the ground? Did anyone see *that*? 'Cause if you want my professional opinion, doc, this all still sounds really sketchy to me. Unless..."

Baptiste leaned forward. "Yes?"

Hardy glanced out the window. If there were any bloodthirsty ghouls lurking in the bushes, he didn't see them. Not yet, at least. If there *were* witnesses, perhaps they were too afraid to come forward.

"Maybe we shouldn't be talking about this," said Hardy. "You never know who might be listening in."

Baptiste merely laughed. "The entire clinic is enchanted by a myriad of protective spells, Mr. Hardy. For all intents and purposes we are invisible to the outside world."

"I found you easy enough, though," said Hardy.

"Dowsers have a way of seeing things that defies magic," said Baptiste. "Why this is, I've never been able to understand."

Hardy nodded approvingly. He didn't understand how his gift worked, either. At least dowsing wasn't powered by body counts.

"You know your way around some pretty powerful spells," said Hardy. "But Solomon is no slouch in the magic department."

"Dr. Baptiste could give that wrinkled warlock a run for his money any old day," replied Sisely. "Why else do you think Undead Affairs ran him out of the Havens on a rail?"

This was news to Hardy. He barely suppressed a smile as he regarded the old witch doctor in a whole new light. Very few people crossed Solomon and lived to tell the tale. Baptiste was Hardy's kind of people. "Do tell, doc."

"I think you should check in on Mr. Mudge," Baptiste said to Sisely. "We wouldn't want our patient putrefying, would we?"

"Oh. Of course, doctor." She blushed and quickly excused herself from the room.

"She means well," remarked Baptiste after a long pause. "But sometimes she tends towards hyperbole."

"That why you ain't looking me in the eye, doc—hyperbole?" Hardy chuckled as he hopped down from the examination table. "Exaggeration is an ether reader's bread and butter."

"How—how did you know...?"

"That she was part of the sisterhood?" Hardy chuckled again. He could spot an ether reader from a mile away. He'd pegged Sisely as one from the second he'd laid eyes on her. "I've met my fair share of 'em, doc. Let's just leave it at that."

Hardy realized they had gotten off the subject at hand. It was time to put Clay County behind him.

"Listen, about this whole corpse whisperer thing," he said. "I know how much you want this Jesse Bettenay to be the real deal."

"He's real enough to folks in these parts," said Baptiste. "He gives the undead hope."

Hardy heard what the doctor wasn't saying. In other words, this Jesse Bettenay was as commonplace as his name. So then why was Hardy so disappointed by the truth?

"Sure. Fair enough."

Baptiste may not have been as intuitive as a fountain dowser, but he still understood people. And the change he noticed in Hardy was both immediate and obvious. The doctor gave him an avuncular pat on the shoulder and smiled as he said, "*Amor vincit omnia.*"

"C'mon, doc. I'm not exactly up on my undead languages."

Baptiste realized he was taking a giant leap of faith simply by talking to Hardy. But he trusted Professor Forrest. Members of the Savane understood what was at stake.

"It's Latin. It means 'love conquers all,' Mr. Hardy. It's a very engaging sentiment."

"If you say so, doc."

Hardy suddenly heard Darla's impatient voice in his head, upbraiding him with an emotional urgency that was conspicuously absent from their lackluster marriage.

Some people are willing to die for love, the voice said. *Are you?*

Hardy winced as he imagined Darla laid out on a table in a sterile, nondescript room of a rebirth clinic. The thought of her surrendering her soul to ancient alchemies filled him with a deep and unabiding sadness. Darla and Sofia needed him. What good was he to either of them if he was off chasing phantoms?

The two men were silent as they crunched their way across the gravel lot. Neither took notice of the bright, clear sky or the intensity of the changing foliage. They were too burdened by their own thoughts, their own secrets.

Hardy groaned as he lowered himself into the front seat of his car. "Thanks for patching me up, doc. I guess I'm getting a bit long in the tooth. Can't mix it up like I useta."

Baptiste chuckled. "From what I understand it was ten against one."

"Yeah, something like that."

"I hope you discover the truth about whatever it is you seek from this life."

Hardy narrowed his tired, red-rimmed eyes. "You're still holdin' out on me, doc."

The old witch doctor smiled. "Perhaps. What does your dowser's intuition tell you?"

The Peugeot's diesel engine rattled to life. "It's telling me that I need a stiff drink and eight hours of sack time."

"Is it true you found D. B. Cooper?"

Hardy cracked a weary smile. "Being a dowser had nuthin' to do with it. It's all a big game of hide-and-seek. Sometimes people are just ready to be found, doc."

Baptiste knew the feeling well. He patted the hood of the car. "Take care of yourself, Mr. Hardy. The undead need more men like you."

If only, thought Hardy. But he knew the truth. The undead needed *less* selfish louts like him, and a hell of a lot more caring witch doctors like Baptiste.

Hardy pulled out of the lot and slowly headed south toward where he expected to find the cemetery. It didn't take a Burialist to know that a grave-yard was a good place to do some digging.

Ten minutes later, though, what Hardy found was not a field full of headstones but the site of the Stony Hollow Mall—just as Paulo had said. He stared at the mostly empty parking lot and tried to imagine the worm-food smorgasbord that once occupied the land. He realized, reluctantly, that he would have to take a bunch of ether readers at their word.

"No magic," he said, recalling what Louie had said. "But it still don't add up." He hopped back into the Peugeot with a grunt and a sigh. He turned the car around and headed northeast toward the state line. If he really pushed himself he could make it back to New York in less than eighteen hours.

But as he neared the outskirts of town the world's best fountain dowser began to question his judgment. Just because he wanted to see Darla didn't mean she wanted to see *him*. The truth was she was hitting the reset button on her life. In other words, Sofia was right. She and Hardy meant squat to her.

"Less than squat," he said, and shook his head.

And yet, something was telling Hardy that going to Darla now was the only possible option. Intuition had nothing to do with it; for the first time in his life, Hardy was following his heart. He gripped the wheel, and swore to finally do right by the only woman who had ever tolerated his never-ending buffet of bullshit.

But when Hardy saw the Stony Hollow patrol car in his rearview mirror, his heart sank. It was no hunch—his ultimate act of chivalry was clearly not meant to be.

CHAPTER TWENTY-FOUR

The patrol car's dome light remained dark as it maintained a respectable distance behind the Peugeot. Hardy watched the miles tick by on the odometer. At the ten-mile mark, he'd had enough.

"C'mon, c'mon, shit or get off the pot," he muttered.

It wasn't until both cars were in the middle of nowhere that the patrol car flashed its lights. They pulled to the side of the road just opposite a greasy spoon called Digg's Diner. Hardy's prodigious belly rumbled as the car filled with the artery-hardening aroma of fried oil and pork products.

Hardy drummed his fingers on the wheel and waited patiently for the hammer to drop. *Let's do this*, he thought. He figured he might have to spend a night in a Clay County jail. That still left him two full days to get back before Darla's rebirth.

The cop ambled up to the Peugeot and leaned in through the window. The local law enforcement was a gun-toting cadaver, much to Hardy's surprise.

"Officer," he said with a quick salute. "What can I do you for?"

"I take it you're the out-of-towner who had a run-in with some of our workers down at the plant?"

"Guilty as charged."

The officer tipped his hat back on his ashy forehead. "You don't exactly sound all that...apologetic about it."

Hardy took note of the rename stitched on the well-pressed uniform: Sergeant Birch. "Can't say that I'm too busted up about what I did, no."

Birch's crooked smile was polite at best. "Dr. Baptiste? Down at the clinic? He tells me you're a fountain blood, or some such?"

Hardy hadn't been called a fountain blood in ages. This Sergeant Birch knew a thing or two about a thing or two.

"Yeah, something like that," said Hardy.

"We don't have many magical fountains around here," he said. "Least-ways, none that I know of."

Something about their little exchange felt off to Hardy. And it wasn't the slight trace of a Carrion Flats accent he heard in the sergeant's voice, either.

"You're a long way from the Havens, aintcha?"

Birch narrowed his pale, yellow eyes. "And you're a long way from New York...*aintcha*." He leaned further into the car. "Listen. Mudge is a good friend of mine, which means I'm willing to cut you a break. So when I tell you to stop digging, I mean it. We don't need any more trouble here in Stony Hollow from Undead Affairs."

"Hold on a sec. You tellin' me I'm not the only one looking for—"

Birch held up a leather glove-clad hand. "You don't get it, do you?"

"Are you running me out of town, Sergeant Birch? 'Cause if you are, I was heading back east anyways."

"That right? Well, I suggest you sample our fine local cuisine first, courtesy of Digg's."

All thoughts of Darla receded as Hardy's intuition finally flared to life. "Maybe I'll do that, sure."

"Ask for Sally. I hear tell she pours a mean cup of joe."

Hardy suddenly saw Sergeant Birch in a different light. They weren't just shooting the breeze here. Hardy all but licked his bruised lips as he savored the moment.

"Sally. Joe. Got it."

Birch pulled the brim of his hat down over his hollow, deep-set eyes. "You have a good day, sir. *Veritas numquam perit.*"

Hardy felt like he was finally firing on all cylinders as he entered the diner. He knew without a doubt that he was meant to be there at that exact moment in time. And, more importantly, he also knew he was meant to order up a double helping of eggs over-easy with hash browns and thick-cut bacon on the side.

And, of course, a steaming-hot cup of joe.

The waitress was seated at the far end of the counter, head in hand as she lazily flipped through a Sears catalog. She smiled wearily at Hardy as she shuffled over to his booth, pad and pencil at the ready.

"Heya, sweetie, what can I get for ya?"

Hardy's stomach rumbled greedily. But business came first. "I'm looking for Sally. I hear tell she pours a mean cup of joe. But..." He paused and studied the waitress, who likewise studied him back. "But you ain't her."

"Nope. At least, not since the last time I checked." She cackled with a smoker's raspy, throat-clearing laugh. "I'm Bess. Sally's out back."

Hardy ignored his hunger pangs as he rose from the booth. "I gotta talk to her."

"Sit," she said. "Eat. Sally'll still be there when you're done. I promise."

Hardy had no reason to doubt her; in fact, he felt oddly carefree as he ordered his breakfast. But he immediately lost himself in thought as he recounted what he'd learned that morning. The facts—assuming what Baptiste told him was true—simply weren't adding up. Finding Amelia Earhart had been child's play compared to this. Some crucial piece of the puzzle was definitely missing.

He continued to noodle over the details after his breakfast was brought to the table. Four runny egg yolks and three cups of coffee later, Hardy decided it was time to move on.

Bess was ready for him. She shuffled back to the table with the check as Hardy fished for his wallet. She placed the bill face down on the table amidst the crumbs and coffee rings.

"It's on the house," she said with a wink.

Puzzled, Hardy flipped the bill over. Mixed in with his itemized breakfast was a cryptic line item: *RR 7, Harper County*. Hardy nodded. He knew a backwater address when he saw one. The mystery address begat a route upon a mental map; it coalesced from the ether upon a grey ribbon of flat prairie highway.

Hardy smiled as he rose from the cramped booth. "Let's get this show on the road."

"You and Miss Sally are gonna get along just fine."

She gestured for Hardy to follow her. They exited the diner through a back door that led to an empty lot. Aside from some brown weeds and discarded cigarette butts there wasn't much to see.

"She's around the side," said Bess.

They continued past a row of metal garbage cans towards a large shed behind a copse of pine trees. She hunched over and fiddled with a rusty combination lock on the door.

"Waitasec," said Hardy. "You keep her locked up?" For a chilling moment Hardy thought he'd walked into an ambush. But then the shed door opened with a rusty creak to reveal a tarp-covered car. Bess pulled the dusty tarp back to reveal a yellow, mint-condition 1969 Ford Mustang.

"And this would be Sally," said Hardy with a boyish grin. His pulse quickened as he took notice of the car's Kansas plates. "But what's this car gotta do with me?"

"If someone told you about Sally, there's probably a good reason for you to be driving it."

"I like my car just fine, thanks. She's never let me down."

Bess's face lit up with a crooked smile. "Yeah, but can she go from zero to 60 in less than six seconds?"

Hardy, too, smiled. He had a much better shot of making it back for Darla's rebirth in the Mustang. "Looks like me and Sally have ourselves a date."

"Dr. Baptiste said you were a smart cookie." She handed him a set of keys. One belonged to the Mustang. The other was an old skeleton key. "We been waiting a long time for you to show up, make things right."

Hardy doubted the diner was enchanted with protective spells. He suddenly felt like a sitting duck, talking out in the open. "Well, I appreciate the vote of confidence."

"There's one of them GPS thingies in the glove box if you need it."

He slid behind the wheel and nodded approvingly. "I guess Baptiste didn't tell you everything."

He was itching to get going, but first things first. He pulled around front and grabbed his things from the Peugeot.

"You been real good to me," he said gruffly as he patted the dashboard. "Real good. So try not to take this personally, okay?"

He gave the grey interior of the car the once-over before flipping down the visor to reveal an old picture of Darla and Sofia he'd tucked away. He shoved it into his pocket and hopped back in the Mustang, grim-faced, his hands tight on the unfamiliar wheel as the road rose up to meet him.

CHAPTER TWENTY-FIVE

At Viktor's urging, Damon was sequestered in a no-name motel far from New Hollywood. The dingy accommodations were a far cry from the opulence to which Damon was accustomed. Had Viktor and Barbarelli not expressly forbid him from all forms of social media, Damon would have surely uploaded pictures of his miserable surroundings. When cell phone pictures of Damon leaving the Paradox lot in deadface hit the 'bloidosphere, though, the beleaguered actor finally appreciated the merits of keeping a low profile.

Variety's succinct analysis of the ensuing firestorm cut to the heart of the matter:

> *'The outcome of Grayson's self-imposed exile will likely determine the future relevance of not only Paradox Studios, but New Hollywood's opportunistic, dysfunctional love affair with all things undead. With the Battle for Burly Gate still fresh in the nation's collective consciousness, Damon Grayson is nothing more than collateral damage.'*

Damon had remained atypically mum during much of the media's pillorying of his character. He'd even suffered through jokes made at his expense by late-night hosts. But, after being hounded mercilessly by 'bloiders, reporters, paparazzi and Second Lives leaders, and despite the death threats, hate mail and constant harassment by rabid right-wing groups, the piece in *Variety* was what finally broke his spirit. Luckily for Damon, he still had Viktor on his side. The studio, too, remained supportive, albeit from a small remove. But even a tenuous bond was better than none at all.

It was Cornelius who emerged as Damon's most stalwart supporter. While the studio secured the necessary visas and other logistical details, Cornelius dutifully boned up on undead culture west of Burly Gate. In the course of his research his worst suspicions about the Havens were confirmed. He felt it was his responsibility to warn Damon that conditions on the other side of the wall could be harsh, even by undead standards.

"How bad could it be, really?" asked Damon. "I hear Cadabra City's not so bad. And Burlytown Heights is just some big retirement community, isn't it?" Damon sat up and assumed Solomon's stiff, wide-eyed expression. "'Welcome to the Havens, the State of Rest,'" he said, quoting a slogan from the ubiquitous tourism ads.

"No," said Cornelius. "I meant the other wall."

"What other wall are you talking about?"

Cornelius sighed. Even a fourth-grader knew about the second wall. "Never mind," he said. "It's not important."

"Come on, don't treat me like I'm stupid," said Damon impatiently. "It's not my fault that you're, like, a walking Wiki."

"I like to read," he said with a shrug. "A lot."

"So what about this other wall?"

"Well, Burlytown Heights is pretty exclusive. It's basically a gated community."

"So you're telling me that zom—I mean, the undead built their own wall? Who the heck are *they* trying to keep out?"

"Carrion Flats is a rough place. So are the Charnel Point slums."

Damon stared blankly at his bodyguard. "Wow. I guess I should have paid more attention in school."

Cornelius slipped on a pair of small spectacles and read aloud from one of the travel books. "'One does not need to stray far from family-friendly KadabraLand and the bustling Burlytown Heights night-life before Carrion Flats' fourth-world conditions become readily apparent. Travelers should be aware that unlike Cadabra City, in Carrion Flats proper there is little infrastructure to speak of, which means no landlines, electricity or plumbing.'"

"Anything else?"

Cornelius hadn't even begun to cover the various old-world ailments like Black Death and Green Decomp that ran rampant through the poorer slums. Then he remembered that Viktor had asked everyone to avoid discussing the less glamorous details with Damon. But Cornelius truly believed that a first-time visitor had a right to know what awaited him beyond Burly Gate. There were constant bomb threats from Resurrectionist insurgents, and up in the San Lazarus Mountains, exiled witch doctors, leper colonies and roving bands of brain-eaters.

"Yes, there's more," Cornelius replied after a considerable pause. "A lot more."

"Thanks anyway, Neil. I have no intention of straying too far from my suite at Kadabra Estates."

"But this is the perfect opportunity to experience a different culture. Do you really want to stay in Cadabra City the whole time?"

"Sure," snorted Damon. "If I can help it."

"Aren't you even a little bit curious about Burlytown Heights? I hear it has a pretty active art scene."

"We'll see, Neil. Maybe we can get in a little sightseeing, soak up some of the local color." And by that he meant drinking himself unconscious in one of the Estate's Michelin-rated restaurants. Damon had had enough of the undead culture to last a lifetime. And no one, not even Cornelius, could convince him otherwise.

Later that night, however, Damon was huddled over his tablet's glowing screen as he explored various tourism websites. He had never paid much mind to what lay beyond Burly Gate, but something in Cornelius's cautionary tone had suddenly piqued his curiosity.

Many of the websites provided little in the way of any practical information, aimed as they were at families or college students looking for spring break alternatives. The other sites catered mainly to out-of-towners seeking 'mettle-testing extreme retreats' where one 'truly had to tough it out in harsh fourth-world conditions.'

Damon's interest in the Havens eventually waned. He decided to spend a few minutes Ogling himself online before resting his eyes. He typed his name into the search bar, and the Ogle search engine turned up almost one million results in a matter of seconds. Many of the websites contained links to the Audrey Hepburn video, while other links included images of Damon wearing deadface make-up.

"Why do I even bother," he muttered. Two hours and several hundred websites later, though, he was still Ogling himself. *One more link*, he kept telling himself. He was an Internet junkie, addicted not so much to himself as he was to the world's perception of him, filtered through hundreds of thousands of online news sites, fan blogs and user forums. It was a masochistic pastime for a digital, post-zombie age.

Damon leaned back and rubbed his bleary eyes. He realized he was not so much an individual as he was an amalgam of smartly crafted parts and perceptions. In a sense, he was a patchwork person, assembled to fulfill a specific role in the cultural zeitgeist. And, he had allowed it to happen. People like Barbarelli and Joni—they were nothing more than enabling Igors to the dysfunctional mad scientist that was New Hollywood. Somehow, somewhere, amidst the whirlwind of his success, he had surrendered any vestige of himself that was uniquely his. He used to harbor simple desires, but now...now he could never go back to who he was before.

He gladly powered down his tablet. But that did not stop the parade of anonymous online comments from chipping away at his well-hidden core. He considered going across the hall to shanghai Cornelius, maybe watch a little bit of the Cads game together. Damon rose from his chair to do just that, then thought better of it. Who was he kidding? Cornelius was too nice to ever say no to anything. He slumped back in his chair and grabbed the remote, but then paused when he saw his reflection in the blank screen. He looked tired and lonely and small.

Just then there was a quick succession of four quick knocks at the door. Damon bounded from the chair, glad for the distraction. Cornelius filled the doorway, his phone in one hand, his wallet in the other. Seeing Damon so pensive made him frown.

"Are you well, Mr. Grayson?"

"Never better, why?"

"Your eyes are all bloodshot."

"I was Ogling myself," he replied sheepishly.

Cornelius consulted his watch. "This whole time?"

"You make that sound like a bad thing, Neil."

"It's not a good thing, that's for sure." Cornelius glanced down at his wallet. "So, I was just wondering if you needed anything from outside. I can run to Frankenjoe's if you want."

"Sure," said Damon with a lopsided grin. "How about a new life?"

Cornelius frowned. "Are you sure you're all right?"

So many people relied on Damon for their livelihood—from Viktor to Cornelius. "I'm fine. It's just been a rough couple of weeks."

"That's why you have me, Mr. Grayson."

"You're an entourage of one, Neil."

"I'm just keeping it real. That's how I roll."

Damon glanced back at the television's blank screen. Celebrity was a lonely life sometimes, but it didn't have to be. "Listen, don't feel like you have to say yes, okay?" Damon was amazed by how afraid of rejection he really was. But for the last several years, all he ever heard was what people thought he wanted to hear. Damon took a deep breath and pretended the outcome didn't matter.

"So," he said. "Wanna watch the Cads game with me?"

Cornelius pushed past Damon and grabbed the remote from the night-stand. "I think the game just started," he said, and plunked down on the foot of Damon's bed. "Gomez is finally off the DL but Franco has been pretty good at first base." He turned to Damon and smiled. "But that's just me."

Damon realized he wouldn't change a thing about his life. Let the 'bloi-ders kick him around all they wanted. The Neo-Lifers, too, with their vendetta against him, would have to wait. This unexpected moment would never become just another result on Ogle, to be scrutinized and dissected by the faceless masses.

No, the moment was his; he seized it.

CHAPTER TWENTY-SIX

Back east, in Chillicothe, Ohio, Sofia Hardy paced the floor of her dorm room. She clutched a phone in one hand, a torn sheet of paper in the other. Sofia paused as she looked from the number written on the paper to the phone. She pinched her eyes shut, almost as if willing the number to dial itself. She finally opened her eyes and exhaled as she resumed her pacing. She didn't look up as her roommate bustled into the room.

"Oh my god," Ashley said. She hurled a laundry bag onto her cluttered twin bed. "Are you *serious*, Sofia?"

"I know, I know."

"You said you were gonna call, like, over an *hour* ago."

Sofia stopped pacing and plopped down onto the foot of her own bed. "What's the point? It's not like she'll remember me a week from now."

"You know I don't condone what your mom is doing, but, you'll totally regret this if you don't try one last time."

"Right," Sofia said softly. "Shit." She didn't protest as Ashley held out her hand for the phone. If anything, Sofia was glad to be rid of it. She held onto the dog-eared slip of paper, though. She shoved it into her pocket and laughed uneasily.

"You okay?"

Sofia shooed the question away with an impatient wave of her hand. "I'm awesome."

"I think you need some fresh air. It's not too late for you to come with us to that death cap rally."

Sofia never shied away from a good cause. But as much as she believed in imposing limits on a shaman's potential power, deep down, she felt like her parents would disapprove of her social activism.

"Maybe I'll meet you there. I need to stop by the Cultural Studies building first."

Ashley wrinkled her nose. "Why would you want to go there?"

The truth was that Sofia didn't know why, either. She simply had a strong feeling she was supposed to go. "Mark asked me to meet him."

"Whatever. That's so random."

Sofia hated lying, especially to Ashley. Right now, it felt like her roommate was the only family she had left. Even so, she had to make sure certain things remained between the two of them.

"Hey, you haven't told anyone about my mom...right?"

Ashley scowled. "I promised I wouldn't."

"Because I could lose my scholarship if—"

"No one is going to find out. Relax." Ashley threw on her coat and gestured to the door. "You sure you don't want to come?"

"I'll meet you later."

Ashley flexed her hands into a pair of wool gloves. "Well, if you try calling her again, good luck."

Sofia's eyes suddenly brimmed with tears. She wanted to say thank you, but managed a quick nod instead. She remained sitting for several minutes more before removing the paper from her pocket. She knew the phone number by heart now, she'd dialed it so many times over the last few months. But something about cradling the paper in her hand brought her comfort; in some small yet significant way it represented a tangible link to her mother.

"Why do you have to be so *stubborn*," she muttered under her breath. The comment was directed at her mother, but she realized the same could be said of the Hardys in general.

She held her breath and counted to three before dialing the number. It was a ritual of hers, this futile, little-girl belief that a repeated act might finally align the stars in her favor. And, as always, she would hang up after the sixth ring. *This time*, she thought, *this time will be different.*

It has *to be.*

And, this time, the outcome was indeed different.

"Hello," said a raspy voice.

A single, spoken word unfurled a tightly clenched fist from around her heart. There was still time to save her mother—from the Resurrectionists, and from herself.

"Mom," she said. "It's me." The silence on the other end of the line was unexpected, dumbfounding. "It's me," she said quietly. "It's Sofia."

"Sofia, listen. This is your mother's friend, Lydia."

Sofia fought the urge to smash the phone against the wall.

"Lydia, listen," she said. "This is your 'friend's' daughter, and I really need to speak to her. Okay?"

"Your mother's death coach has advised her to sever all ties with family and friends. I'm sorry."

But she didn't sound sorry in the least. "I want her to tell me that. I want to hear *her* say it."

"You won't change her mind, Sofie. No one will."

"My name is *Sofia*, you home-wrecking bitch!"

"Have a nice life," Lydia said coldly, and hung up.

Sofia clutched the phone to her chest and stared blankly at the wall. "I can't believe I just did that," she said to the empty room. "Oh, my god. I can't fucking believe it."

Her first instinct was to call her dad. But she quickly realized he was M.I.A. He could be gone for weeks. Months. He could be in Guam, or Budapest, for all she knew.

He could even be dead.

Sofia buckled under the crushing weight of her deepest fear. She looked around the small room and realized she needed to be outside. The halls were empty, the dorm rooms silent. Everyone was at the rally, of course. It was all anyone on campus could talk about, this death cap.

The futility of their protest only angered Sofia. There was nothing any of them in their tiny, self-contained corner of Ohio could do to quell the siren's call of Resurrectionism. She couldn't even save her own mother. How could she ever hope to be a missionary?

She paused as she neared the dark outline of the Cultural Studies building. Now that she was standing there, she couldn't fathom why it seemed so important that she be there at all. But then she noticed a spidery figure approaching the side of the building. He was clad in a mud-colored long coat, like a character out of Colonial Williamsburg. A pair of dark sunglasses ruined the illusion, but Sofia was convinced he was much older than he looked.

He suddenly stopped mid-stride and glanced in her direction. Sofia, who was standing in the shadows, was almost certain she was hidden from view. She remained quite still nonetheless, for as long as he stared her way. The longer she looked at him, the more she thought of her father. Her father's presence became so palpable to her she swore the air was tinged with his minty aftershave.

And then someone tapped Sofia's shoulder from behind. She yelped and whirled around, hand outstretched, clipping Mark in the ear with her fist.

He cupped his ear but merely laughed away his obvious surprise. "Whoa, you nearly took my head off!"

Sofia silenced him with a savage shush and tugged him down behind a bench. "He'll see you," she whispered angrily.

Mark poked his head over the top of the bench. "Who will?"

"That creepy guy." She peered through the slats of the bench. Her face flushed when she realized the man was gone.

"There's no one there, Sofia," Mark whispered back, his own eyes wider than hers.

She punched him in the arm, then shoved him away. "Don't make fun of me, you jerk. I know what I saw, okay?"

"Okay," said Mark, laughing again.

"I said *okay*?"

"Man you are really feisty tonight."

"Don't call me that." She stood up and brushed the dirt from her jeans.

"Come on, you know I'm just joking around."

Deep down Sofia understood it wasn't Mark she was really mad at. She couldn't tell him that of course. It was bad enough she'd confided in Ashley about her mother. As for Mark—he was a staunch Cremationist. When it came to the undead, he firmly believed that zombies were wasteful, selfish and stupid. They were, in his words, the worst kind of traitors. What would her own boyfriend think of her, if he knew her mother was a reborn-again Resurrectionist?

Rather than apologize for lashing out at him, Sofia instead sighed and said with a scowl, "I'm just not in the mood right now, okay?"

To his credit, Mark kissed her on the cheek and asked if she wanted to skip the rally. "We can just chill out and split some cheese fries at Mack's," he said.

Mack's wasn't far from the rally, but cheese fries were exactly what she wanted. For once, it was a relief to be understood. She took his hand in hers and gave it a gentle squeeze.

"Your treat, right?"

"I'd be stupid to say no," he said with a quick laugh. They headed towards the parking lot, where his so-called Shitbox Chevette was parked. As they hopped in the car, the spidery figure in the moldy colonial garb was all but forgotten.

Meanwhile, in the sub-basement of the Cultural Studies building, St. Joan's sole undead faculty member was spending another late night alone.

Professor Forrest wasn't bothered that his fellow instructors rarely fraternized with him. Nor was he bothered that his office was a glorified utility closet. No, what upset Forrest was his students' lackadaisical attitude towards his course.

He sighed as he shuffled through a stack of typo-riddled, intellectually barren essays. Not for the first time he questioned why he continued to teach when it brought him nothing but disappointment. The thought had crossed his mind that perhaps he was not the eloquent educator he considered himself to be. But if that were so, how did one explain the brilliance of his undead students on the other side of the wall? Despite his past scholastic successes (and what such success bespoke about his own academic abilities), Forrest knew that his Undead Myths & Folklore syllabus was hardly taken seriously by the few students who deigned to attend.

Forrest shoved the rest of the ungraded papers into his battered briefcase. His idealism, like his once-pristine leather case, had since become scuffed and marred beyond repair. He raked the briefcase's zipper closed with an angry flourish. Rising from his chair he paused to administer a gentle double-tap to his Press-On lips.

Just as he reached for the light switch there came a loud knock at his office door. He froze, willing whomever it was to go away. There was a second, louder knock. The professor pursed his Press-Ons, a curt dismissal ready upon his synthetic lips as he threw open the door. "Come back in the mor—"

Silas Walker, the undead fountain dowser, was standing in the hall. That he should appear only days after Barnabas Hardy, a rival dowser, was certainly no coincidence.

"Professor," said Walker. He removed his sunglasses and revealed an empty eye socket limned with jagged grooves. He tucked the dark glasses away in a pocket of his peat-colored regiment coat. "I had a feeling I'd find you here." He clicked a barbed fingernail thoughtfully on one of the coat's many pewter buttons as he quietly surveyed the room.

"Of course," muttered Forrest as he observed Walker in turn. The dowser was clearly using the narcotic Green Soy. The lower half of Walker's craggy countenance was covered in a furry, moss-like mold—a telltale sign of his heavy drug use.

"Word on the street is that St. Joan's received a very special visitor this week." ❢

Forrest realized there was no point in asking how he came by the information. Dowsers routinely spun logic-defying guesses into tangible leads. Forrest wondered what else Silas Walker knew.

"St. Joan's attracts all types, Silas. Our missionary program is world-renowned."

Walker scoffed. "The undead do not require the living to save us. We were doing just fine before our land was stolen out from under us."

The dowser narrowed his yellow, deep-set eye as he studied the artifact-crammed bookcases. He grabbed a Loa totem from a listing shelf and hefted it in his hand for a long moment.

"I found this in the Czech Republic of all places," he said. "Budapest is definitely not the first place one would think to look for something indigenous to Haiti." He placed it with great care back on the shelf.

"It was in a dirty burlap sack, in a muddy, dung-filled ditch, discarded like so much refuse. And yet it called out to me, Professor. From half a world away, your precious voodoo totem called to me. It called to me day and night, beckoning me. Summoning me. I had no choice but to find it, lest its incessant chatter inside my head drive me to mental ruin. But such is the dowser's dilemma."

He pushed past Forrest and dropped like the leathery bag of bones he was into the desk chair. "And track it I did, professor. I searched for twelve days before I found it along that lonely stretch of winding, forgotten road. I knew it was there, though, knew I was close. And yet dowsing can be a tricky business. It can be fickle. Inexact. A dowser cannot navigate on signals from the ether alone."

Forrest knew this, of course. He did not need nor appreciate the lecture. Nor did he need Walker's services any longer. He had all but exhausted his modest savings in rescuing undead artifacts from the metaphorical road-sides of the world.

"You are certainly one of the best," he said.

The undead dowser's smile grew wider, revealing molars caked in the grey grit of Peruvian Noodle. It was a filthy, dangerous drug, Noodle. It was also incredibly expensive. Heavy users eventually craved Noodle in its raw, unprocessed form. It was far more powerful—and addictive—than Green Soy.

"I am second to no one," said Walker, his brittle voice climbing. "Just look around this room. What other proof do you *need*?"

Forrest glanced at his desk, where a fully charged HAMR sat in the locked bottom drawer. The only thing standing in the way of accessing it was Walker himself. No, Forrest's best chance of survival was getting outside.

"Why don't we continue this conversation aboveground?" he asked. He started for the door.

"I'm pretty comfortable right here, professor." He spun slowly in the chair until he was facing the desk. He drummed his gnarled fingers upon the vinyl blotter.

"Well, I was just on my way out for the evening."

"He's a hack, you know. A phony."

Forrest nervously licked his prosthetic lips. "Who is?"

"He does not find his quarry so much as it finds him. They're attracted to him, like scavengers drawn to carrion. That's not skill, in my book. The man is a walking magnet, nothing more. And yet—!" Papers and crusty skin scattered as Walker slammed his hands against the desk. He glared at Forrest. "And yet," he hissed, "he is considered the best of our kind. It's appalling."

Forrest was not qualified to judge—or begrudge—the way in which Hardy's gift manifested itself. "He struck me as a decent man."

"Barnabas Hardy? Decent? You're more ignorant than I gave you cred-it for, professor."

Forrest bristled at the remark. "I've had quite enough of you," he snapped.

Walker lunged from the chair. He closed the distance between them in a single stride of his spidery legs. He sank into a crouch and gently cupped Forrest's chin in his calloused palm.

"Silas Walker will tell you when you've had enough, little man. Now, we've known each other a long, long time. Why don't you tell your dear old friend Silas the truth. What did Barnabas Hardy want with a Havens reject like you?"

Forrest tightened his grip on the briefcase as the enormous cast-iron boiler roared to life. Silas Walker's friendship came at a steep price. But the old professor knew Hardy's quest for the corpse whisperer was more important to the Savane than his own life.

"He didn't say," Forrest replied after a long pause. "And I didn't ask."

Walker pursed his brittle lips and unfolded his sinewy frame to its full six feet. He turned in a slow circle as he once more scrutinized the crowded shelves. Walker's moral compass may have been faulty, thought Forrest, but his dowser's intuition was not. Forrest prayed to Lazarus that one missing artifact in particular would somehow escape his notice.

"The Savane are a funny lot," Walker quietly mused. He paused and turned to the professor. "I imagine that a learned cadaver like yourself would be inclined to agree." A maggot emerged from a mossy patch of mold on his chin as he cocked his head and smiled.

Were he still living, the blood would have surely drained from Forrest's face. He had never given any indication that he was a member of the Savane. Not to anyone outside the secret society, and certainly not to a Noodle-addled mercenary like Silas Walker.

"The Savane have their share of peculiarities, yes." He again eyed the drawer that hid the HAMR. "But I'm at a loss as to how the Savane are germane to this discussion."

"Obfuscation is not your strong suit, professor. Nor is lying."

"If you have something to say, then out with it already."

Walker leaned in closer until their exposed nasal cavities were mere inches apart. "The sandstone cruciform. The one that cost me this—!" He jammed a finger into his empty eye socket. "Where *is* it?"

Forrest's synthetic lips peeled away from his mouth as he broke into a wide, nervous grin. "That cruciform is one of my most cherished possessions. I keep it in my desk under lock and key."

He set his briefcase down and fished a key ring from his trouser pocket. He jangled it in his hand as he approached his desk.

"Here," he said. "I'll show you."

Walker folded his arms impatiently across his chest as Forrest fumbled with the key.

"Ah," muttered the professor as he clasped his hand around the HAMR's cold, smooth handle. "Here it is."

Walker's eye widened as Forrest brought the humming weapon to bear on the talisman dangling from the dowser's gaunt neck. The silver medallion and several of his coat's metal buttons were drawn into the HAMR's chamber with a loud *zink*. Walker gasped as he pawed at his neck. He staggered towards Forrest, slack-jawed, before falling to one knee.

Forrest knew Walker's resurrection predated his own by at least sixty years, making him well over 200. After so much drug use, physically his body looked almost double that. The dowser would be reduced to a rancid pile of decomp within minutes. No cadaver should ever endure such a fate, this sudden, catastrophic decomposition—even a Noodle head like Silas Walker.

Such cruelty simply wasn't the Resurrectionist way.

As the dowser writhed on the cement floor Forrest paused in the doorway to unload the HAMR's chamber. He took the talisman and flung it into a corner of the room. Forrest would be long gone by the time Walker retrieved it—if he did at all.

But as he turned to leave Walker rolled towards the door and pinned it shut with his shoulder. The professor gasped as Walker leapt to his feet and easily snatched the HAMR away. Why was he unaffected by the loss of his talisman?

"You really are more ignorant than I thought, professor," he said.

"It—it was self-defense! You left me no choice!"

Walker shook his head as he turned the HAMR over in his hands. "What galls me the most is that you would seek to effect my demise with a tool created by our living oppressor's military-industrial complex. Have you no pride?"

Forrest was too stunned to speak.

"You're nothing more than a self-loathing grey colonial," said Walker. "And before you declare me a hypocrite, for my own colonist's attire, know this: Just because I have donned the dress of my oppressor does not mean I have *become* my oppressor."

He reached for Forrest's hand and clasped it gingerly in his own. He studied the ring-shaped talisman on Forrest's ring finger before meeting the teacher's panicked stare.

"It's such a shame, really," said Walker. "You're ignorant, yes, but you're not stupid."

"We all deserve a suh, second chance," said Forrest.

"No," Walker replied flatly as he prised the talisman from Forrest's finger. "We do not."

Forrest's rigor mortis was immediate, crippling, a supernova of blinding pain. His brittle patellae shattered as he toppled to his knees. His reality, his corporeal identity, what was left of it, was reduced to the cold cement floor beneath his prone, stiffening body. Valor, bravery, honor—these high ideals were the furthest things from what was left of Professor's Forrest's mind. Only an end to his excruciating pain mattered.

"Anything," he cried as weeping decomp sores blossomed across his back and arms. "Tell you anything to make it stop."

Walker was still not suffering any deleterious effects from the prolonged absence of his own talisman. He sucked at the remaining granules of Noodle lodged in his rotted molars.

"You know what I want." The talisman gleamed as he held it in front of his empty eye socket. "I suggest you cut to the chase."

It felt as though a fist had been rammed down Forrest's throat. He struggled to articulate the words that would stop his body's merciless putrefaction.

"Cus...cus puh-ruh," he moaned. The room grew dark as his milky eyes began to shrivel in their sockets. "Cupsss hiss-purrr."

Walker slid the talisman back onto Forrest's gnarled finger. The rampant decay immediately stopped—but the agonizing pain did not. "Speak it again."

Forrest whimpered as he lay in a pile of his own crusty, necrotic flesh. "Swee...sweed Lat-ruzz fo-gimm-mee."

Silas Walker was out of patience. He leaned down and snapped off one of Forrest's thumbs. "Say it again. What is Barnabas Hardy looking for?"

Forrest grimaced as he tried desperately to manipulate what was left of his tongue. "Corrr....corrrrpzz wizz...wizz-perrr..."

"The corpse whisperer?" This time it was the undead dowser who was stunned into silence. Under less dire circumstances, Walker would have dismissed such a statement as ill-conceived folly. He stepped back from the professor as carrion-hungry blow flies began to alight on Forrest's badly desiccated body. Silas Walker knew with dreaded certainty that if the mythical super shaman did exist, it was only a matter of time before Hardy found him.

"Where is Hardy now?" he growled.

The preservative powers of Forrest's talisman were no match for his advanced state of decomp. Now, his charm merely prolonged his suffering. "Tay...giddoff," he pleaded from beneath a blanket of buzzing, darting flies. "Rring. Tayg...iddoff."

"Where is he!"

Forrest knew now there was no light at the end of the tunnel, no requiem of solace to be found in the ether. He yearned for the void, for a cessation of his tiny, painful universe. "Bap-teez."

Walker brightened. He knew of the disgraced witch doctor Baptiste.

He was powerful and scrupulous. An odd combination, to be sure. The last he'd heard, Baptiste's body count was second only to Solomon's.

"Huh, hurds," moaned Forrest. Flies began to boil from his mouth, his sinuses. Walker swatted the red-eyed flies from his own face. If he wasn't careful, he could come down with a chronic case of the Buzz. He stepped over Forrest and quickly shut the office door behind him.

Walker knew Hardy was a moving target. He sensed his trajectory, knew he was heading west. Baptiste, on the other hand, would be easy to find. His was a bright light on the dark horizon. It was so bright, and so obvious, that Walker all but ignored a lesser spark on the periphery of his field of inner vision. It was an anomaly, this random blip, this...sofa bed? It was about ten miles away, in Chillicothe proper. Most likely it was a ruse, a red herring left behind by Hardy to throw other dowsers off his trail. Walker himself had engineered such boondoggles in his time.

"Silas Walker wasn't reborn yesterday, Mr. Hardy," he whispered.

The undead dowser knew if he had any chance of finding the corpse whisperer first, he could ill afford to chase down phantom leads. The next leg of his journey clearly led to Baptiste.

Walker smiled as he distilled a destination from the all-powerful ether. It formed a name upon his brittle, Noodle-dusted lips:

"Stony Hollow."

CHAPTER TWENTY-SEVEN

Cornelius found himself in high spirits.

Watching the Cads game with Damon was a real watershed moment for their nascent friendship. It was nice to think that Damon was starting to see Cornelius not as his talent protection specialist, but as someone with whom he could enjoy the smaller things in life—even if the Cads ultimately lost in extra innings. For the first time, it felt like he and Damon were experiencing a genuine camaraderie. It would be the first real friendship for Cornelius, period.

The truth was that although Cornelius was built like Burly Gate, he was no one's rock. Not yet, at least. It pleased him greatly to think that perhaps one day he might become a permanent, positive influence in the troubled actor's life.

Cornelius decided a proper celebration was in order. He quickly withdrew a thick tome from his luggage. *Only Humans,* the bestselling biography by Mary Shelley, was an intimate look at the undead actor Boris. He was one of the country's most infamous—and misunderstood—reanimates ever to be reborn.

Cornelius smiled as he studied the gaunt, greenish-grey portrait on the book jacket. Everything about Boris's face was iconic—from the jagged scar that traversed his pronounced forehead to the twin bolts that jutted from his neck.

Damon's publicist, Joni, had reviewed the book on her blog, describing it as honest and insightful. Her few words of praise were enough for Cornelius. (Her last recommendation, *Our Corpses, Our Selves*, was one of Cornelius's favorite reads.)

He eyed the room's oil-stained, fiber-filled lump of a recliner with equal parts disdain and distrust. Even if he could wedge himself into it, Cornelius knew such a dubious-looking chair couldn't support someone even half his weight. As any avid reader knew, a good read deserved a good seat.

And you, sir, he thought, *are not a good seat.*

He pushed aside the pressed-board dresser and sat directly on the floor. The brown, threadbare carpet provided very little padding, but Cornelius didn't mind. He plucked his trusty reading glasses from his shirt pocket and perched them on his nose.

Next, he opened the book and savored the delicate crackle of its pristine spine. Before long, he found himself immersed in the early life of the man who would be known as Witch Doctor Frankenstein's monster. Page turn by page turn, Mary Shelley carefully unearthed the man behind the mythology.

But even as Cornelius delved deeper into the mysteries behind Boris's reconstruction and eventual rebirth, his thoughts returned to Joni and her blog. To think that she had read the same elegiac prose he now beheld with such quiet awe made his heart sing. The unexpected sound of multiple footsteps outside his room, however, cut his reverie short. As a safety precaution, the entire motel was blocked out by Paradox. There was no reason anyone should be wandering the halls—especially at three o'clock in the morning.

Cornelius quickly turned off the light and crept to the window. The sight of a dark sedan idling in the otherwise empty lot made him frown. There was no one to blame but himself for his lack of vigilance.

So much for keeping it real, he thought.

There were more footsteps, followed by a hushed, urgent exchange. Cornelius assumed that he might be dealing with three, maybe four individuals. That they were armed was a given.

Cornelius sidled up to his side of the door and peered through the peephole. His suspicions were confirmed: three men were huddled together in the middle of the darkened corridor.

"I'm tellin' you, he's here," said the first man. "I'd bet my freakin' life on it."

"Three fleabags later, and you're still swearing on your worthless life," said the second man. He ran a gloved hand over his bald head. It came away darkened with sweat. "That's priceless."

"Are you sure you got the right room?" asked the third man, a stocky, pug-nosed bruiser wielding what looked like an aluminum baseball bat. Cornelius pressed his face against the peephole to get a better look.

The men froze, casting furtive glances in every direction. "Let's get this over with," grumbled the man with the bat.

"That's Grayson's room," said the first man, pointing at Cornelius's room. Cornelius grinned as he stepped back from the door and girded himself for the altercation.

A key slid into the lock. Tumblers clicked into place, and the doorknob slowly turned. Despite standing in the shadows, Cornelius would be impossible to miss. He had a second, maybe two at most, to leverage the element of surprise.

The door yawned open, and the man with the baseball bat was the first to enter. He was also the first to notice Cornelius as he emerged from the shadows.

"Jesus Christ," the man yelled, his eyes wide, "it's the wrong roo—"

Cornelius silenced him with a quick elbow jab to the larynx. The man dropped the bat and fell to his knees. His throat rattled wetly as he gasped for breath. "Brad," he coughed, "Brad, don't—"

"Tom? Brad poked his bald head into the room. Perspiration ran down his forehead in shiny little rivulets. Cornelius threw his substantial weight against the door, pinning Brad's head against the jamb. Brad panicked, flailing his arms uselessly against the door. He peered up at Cornelius through beet-red eyes.

"Pweeze," he pleaded. "Can't bweeve."

Cornelius noticed Brad was clutching a digital SLR camera in his damp hands. "You're 'bloiders," he growled, narrowing his eyes to slits.

"No no no um a junnowist! Pwess! *PWESS!*"

Cornelius shrugged. "If you say so." He pressed just hard enough on the door to dislocate Brad's jaw. The 'bloider cried out and slumped to the floor in a sweaty, unconscious heap.

Cornelius charged from the room just as an access door at the end of the hall banged shut. A flurry of footsteps followed as the last man fled down the stairwell. A man of Cornelius's size knew better than to chase someone down four flights of stairs. Instead he picked up the fallen baseball bat and waited patiently at the window.

A service exit banged open as the man bolted into the parking lot. The set of keys jangled in his hand as he made a beeline for the idling car. "Holy shit holy shit holy shit," he babbled, his eyes wild. "Gonna kill us!"

"Hey," Cornelius yelled out the window. The man froze, and looked back towards the service door. *Definitely amateurs*, he thought, then hurled the bat at the car like a javelin. The sedan's windshield imploded in a cloud of tempered glass.

Seeing this, the man fell to his knees in the parking lot. "I surrender!" he bawled. "Please stop *hurting* us!"

Cornelius rounded up the man's two friends and flung one over each shoulder. He trudged down the hall and summoned the elevator. After pressing the button for the lobby he dropped both limp men on the ground like so much dirty laundry.

"Tell your friend I want his keys."

Tom, whose neck was starting to bruise, nodded vigorously. "Eddyfing you wad," he croaked through a mouthful of mucous-infused blood.

"What I want," growled Cornelius, "is for you 'bloiders to leave Damon

Grayson alone." Tom responded with another emphatic nod.

The descent to the lobby was mercifully short. Tom nudged his companion, but he was still out cold. Cornelius leaned down and tested Brad's dislocated jaw with the tip of his index finger. It flopped open, spilling blood and saliva down his chin and onto his polo shirt.

"If I see any of you again," Cornelius said, "I won't hold back."

Tom coughed as he bent down and began to tug Brad's prone body from the elevator. Cornelius, who was two steps behind them, did not offer any assistance.

"I want those keys," he said to Tom. "Leave your friend behind as collateral." Tom nodded obediently and scurried out to the parking lot.

The desk clerk, a skittish, bug-eyed reanimate, was hoisting up his slacks as he emerged from the back office. "What's with all the noise," he demanded. "You know what time it is, mister?"

Cornelius turned and grabbed him by the collar. "I gave you explicit instructions not to let anyone upstairs."

"An' I *didn't*," he spat.

"You expect me to believe you fell asleep on the job?"

The desk clerk managed a smile, despite missing most of his teeth. "I been in bed tonight," he replied, glancing back at the office door. "But that don't mean I was *sleeping*." He slapped the desk with his pruny hand. "Gotta love them necrophiliacs!"

Cornelius turned away in disgust as Tom returned. He held out the keys as if they were radioactive. "Here. Take 'em!" He flinched as Cornelius grabbed the keychain.

"Lose anything important?" Cornelius asked the desk clerk.

"Don't look at me. I still got my keys on me." He pulled a set of keys from his pocket and showed them to Cornelius. "See?"

By now all three men were piled into the sedan, their frightened faces clearly visible through what was left of the windshield. Broken glass crunched under the tires as the car sped out of the parking lot.

"I shoulda figgered you husky types like it rough," said the desk clerk.

Cornelius narrowed his eyes. "Being husky has nothing to do with it. Those men were 'bloiders."

"Sure they were," said the desk clerk with a wink. "Gotcha, boss."

Cornelius was only too happy to return to his room. There was hardly any evidence of a scuffle, save for some oily, face-sized smears on the front of the door. That, and the abandoned digital camera.

"The 'bloider's weapon of choice," he muttered sadly as he scooped it up from the carpet. He erased the memory card before cracking the camera in half like a boiled lobster. He dumped the pieces in the wastebasket and walked across the hall.

He paused and knocked lightly on Damon's door. "Mr. Grayson, it's me. It's Cornelius. I just want to make sure you're okay."

He paused for a reply before knocking again. Then he overheard angry voices coming from inside Damon's room. He quickly used the extra key to open the door.

"Mr. Grayson?"

Cornelius was relieved to see that Damon had fallen asleep with the television on. Cornelius shut the set off and turned to leave. He hesitated as Damon stirred.

"But what if she doesn't know the real me?" he murmured and burrowed deeper into the starchy blankets.

The worry in Damon's voice was unexpected, heartbreaking. Cornelius removed his spectacles and stared quietly at the floor for a long moment.

Who *was* the real Damon Grayson, he wondered.

Book in hand, he crept from the room and plopped down on the cheap hallway carpet. He doubted the 'bloiders would return, but he suddenly felt protective of Damon—not as a bodyguard, but as something more. Something, someone, like a friend.

Damon's plaintive question echoed in the stillness of the empty night. *What if she doesn't know the real me?* It was a question Cornelius had asked himself in those long, lonely hours when a certain publicist's witty blog posts entertained and enthralled his curious, hungry mind.

Cornelius considered the heavy book in his hands, idly turning it this way and that. He finally cracked it open but stared blankly at the words on the page.

He liked Joni, yes, but it was the lesser of two secrets that burdened his heart. Cornelius understood that he lacked a certain kind of courage to be truly honest with Damon. And honesty, he believed, should be the cornerstone of any great friendship.

He shut the book and laid his head against the wall. Cornelius did not sleep, but he nonetheless closed his eyes and wondered how much longer he could live a lie.

CHAPTER TWENTY-EIGHT

Once upon a time, long before the Great Quake, the California coastline was revered for its scenic vistas and beautiful beaches. Many a coastal town was the provenance of the wealthy, enjoyed by many but owned by only a select few. In this same once-upon-a-time, before two Cold Wars divided the land, the undead were scattered far and wide across the country, enjoying the sorts of freedoms no one considered until such liberties were suddenly snatched away.

The Great Quake shattered Old Cali and allowed the cold, contaminated waters of the Pacific to obliterate much of the coast in a tidal surge that killed millions. The shattered tectonic plates allowed the ocean waters to rise until even the San Lazarus mountain range was nothing more than a mold-covered archipelago. Eventually the waters receded, but what remained of the ruined Old Cali landscape was all but uninhabitable—for those with a pulse. It wasn't until the advent of the first Cold War, and the outbreak of the undead malady known as Leper's Lament, that the Living States government began rounding up the undead for what it called 'the greater good of those whose hearts still beat within their breasts.' Cadavers afflicted with Leper's Lament were to be relocated to a 'safe haven' within the protective confines afforded by Burly Gate. The quarantine was meant to be temporary. But as the first Cold War raged on, the so-called safe haven became less of a short-term solution for containing the millions of infected cadavers. The undead, detained against their will, were held on 'their' side of the wall by force.

As the undead population west of the wall grew, so, too, did their resentment grow. Many interred in this safe haven believed that Leper's Lament was engineered by the Living States government as a way of ridding the country of its undead brethren. The rumors quickly fueled anti-living sentiment until it reached a fever pitch. The undead lashed out time and again at their oppressors, to no avail.

Then-president Ulysses S. Grant appointed a young Living States shaman named Samuel Solomon to head up the newly formed 'Bureau of Indigenous Zombie Affairs.' Solomon's mandate was simple: monitor the activities of the undead sequestered in Old Cali, and 'to use various black magicks known for keeping ambulatory cadavers well-behaved and in a docile state.'

The effects of the Bureau's influence were not immediate, but they were long-lasting. Soon, the undead population came to see Solomon, through his many gestures of goodwill and fair treatment, as their advocate. This odd dynamic evolved until the Bureau was viewed by the undead as the balm for their social ills.

Rutherford B. Hayes, Grant's successor, said at the time of Secretary Solomon, 'The Bureau has contained the zombie menace to the satisfaction of many in the capitol, due in no small part to the sympathetic actions and palliative magicks of its acting Secretary.'

It was in this manner that Solomon entrenched himself in Old Cali and eventually outlasted even his staunchest supporters. The Havens was his and his alone to rule. He continued in this fashion for decades until the damage was too late to repair without engendering an undead uprising that would eventually ignite another Cold War. Solomon, no longer a callow shaman, was now a cunning mystic. The Havens was his to lose; he had no plans of relinquishing his power to those in the east who viewed the undead and their magical keepers as less important than the living.

His theurgistic reign continued long after his official capacity as secretary of Undead Affairs was rescinded. It may have been a token gesture, but it spoke volumes about Solomon's threat to the Living States. He was disavowed, but his absolute influence could not be undone. The undead were his to control, their Leper's Lament music to his wizened ears.

President Arthur Hammond sat at the head of the mahogany conference table, his angular, media-friendly face grim as he considered the details of Solomon's rise to power. He was mindful of how previous administrations had been lulled into a misguided sense of security, not only by the presence of Burly Gate, but by Solomon's conspicuous reclusiveness as well. Not for the first time, Hammond wondered if Solomon worked a strange alchemy on the men of this office. Even now, was he himself somehow, unwittingly, under the shaman's spell?

To Hammond's right sat Vice President Anne Landis. She took in the whole of the dark war room in a single, piercing glance. She had little patience for the retinue of advisors and their soft stance on the Havens. She was not opposed to the idea of undead equal rights—but she strongly believed those rights should not come at the expense of the living. She was more than happy to be the administration's so-called bad cop.

To Hammond's left sat Defense Secretary Dennis Noyse. He was military for life, a man perpetually at attention. His look was grave, his thin lips fixed in a permanent grimace. Like Landis, his was a more hawkish stance on Solomon. The shaman was a threat, plain and simple.

In front of each of them sat a thick mission brief detailing the specifics of Operation Hocus-Pocus. First put into motion by F.D.R.'s administration, the carefully considered plan had spent years in preparation. The nation had since weathered two wars and lost countless good men and women to the undead menace.

While Hammond himself was not opposed to the idea of rebirth, publicly he maintained a tough anti-Resurrection stance. It wasn't right for him personally, this absolute morality, but it was certainly right for the country.

"What is the status of our man on the ground?" Hammond asked as he thumbed through the thick mission brief.

Defense Secretary Noyse leaned forward and locked eyes with Hammond. "The key operative is still in play, Mr. President."

"Has he crossed the border yet?"

"Still on Living States soil but he should reach the Havens within the next 18 hours."

"Given all present circumstances, what is our current chance for success? Is our man committed to this for the long haul?"

Noyse glanced around the room. It was no secret that he had been opposed to the death cap. He considered it an impotent, half-baked measure; there simply weren't enough boots on the ground to enforce such a law. And the idea of a self-policing honor system was simply too ludicrous to even consider.

On the other hand, cutting off shamans' access to the Tears of Life in the last war had been instrumental in crippling Solomon's ability to perform resurrections. By infiltrating the Havens to destroy dozens of Tears-producing fountains at their source allowed the Living States to deal a crushing blow to the undead militia. But Noyse knew that Hammond would never stoop to something he perceived as unethical—no matter how decisive a strategy it was proven to be. The vice president, however, would require far less convincing.

"To indirectly answer your question, Mr. President, we were hoping to limit the impact of shamans loyal to Solomon's cause by imposing the so-called death cap."

"And if you were to directly answer my question?"

Noyse licked his lips. "The proposed bill has...exacerbated the situation."

"Putting our operative at substantial risk," added Landis. "But he will do whatever it takes to achieve mission success."

Like Baptiste and Gleeson, the president had heard disturbing rumors regarding the nature of Solomon's mounting body count. "Do we really believe that Solomon is somehow performing mass resurrections somewhere in the Havens?"

"Our intel would suggest so, yes, Mr. President. This base of operations is located just south of Bloodstone Basin," said Noyse.

"Putting it somewhere in the San Lazarus Mountains," said Hammond.

The existence of secret resurrection mills was the sort of thing that kept Hammond up at night. What was their purpose, if not for Solomon to fortify an already sizable army? Hammond knew they could ill afford another Battle for Burly Gate.

"So, chance for mission success—"

Noyse shook his head. "Very hard to say."

Hammond clasped his hands behind his head and he leaned back in his chair. "What do the e-readers say?"

Landis and Noyse exchanged a concerned glance. Hammond's reliance on mystics did not sit well with the American public. Nor did it sit well with either of them.

"Mr. President—"

"What. Do they. *Say*."

Landis cleared her throat. "The ether readers see...all-out war if the mission fails. But, of course, any pronouncement must be taken with the usual grain of salt."

"Obviously," said Hammond dryly. "But, if we take the e-readers at their word, it's clear that there is simply no margin for error. Which means we cannot fail in this endeavor. Every day we wait is another day that Solomon amasses a higher body count. If the e-readers are correct, we are left with only one, true option." He met each of their expectant looks in turn and told them exactly what they needed to hear.

"Solomon cannot be allowed to exist another day upon God's green earth."

CHAPTER TWENTY-NINE

Located five miles north of the 160, Crystal Springs was accessible only by a narrow dirt road. Hardy had no conscious knowledge of this, had never driven through Kansas, much less Harper County, and yet he easily navigated his way past field after field, pasture after pasture. After a brief pit stop in Missouri, he'd been behind the wheel for eight straight hours. Now, finally, his back aching, his neck stiff, he knew he was quickly closing in on his destination.

But just as he was about to turn off the highway onto the dirt lane he noticed a pair of headlights twinkling in his rearview mirror. If Bettenay were the real deal, he didn't want to lead Solomon's minions right to the poor kid's doorstep.

His first instinct was to floor it and double back later, but the need to turn off the interstate was building to a fever pitch. The headlights grew larger in the mirror as Hardy eased up on the gas. There was nothing but barren farmland in either direction. *Turn north, turn turn turn turn.* It was now or never.

"Screw it." The seat belt bit into his waist as he pulled sharply over to the side of the road and waited for the inevitable clash.

Within seconds a lime green Lamborghini with Kansas plates roared down the interstate. It slowed as it neared the Mustang. Hardy ignored the pins and needles in his legs as he stepped awkwardly onto the shoulder of the road.

The Lamborghini's driver rolled down the passenger side window. "Car trouble?"

Hardy did a double-take at the sight of the undead, overalls-clad bumpkin behind the wheel. "Just stretching my legs," he answered slowly.

"Sure, yah. Important to keep blood flowing, sure."

Said the corpse, thought Hardy.

"Just passing through?"

Hardy glanced back east along the dusty interstate as the Lamborghini idled alongside the Mustang. Despite the intense need to oblige his inner compass, Hardy realized the incongruity of Farmer Bob behind the wheel of a quarter-million-dollar sports car. "Aren't we all?"

Hardy shook the pins and needles from his leg as he approached the Lamborghini. "That's one he'll of a fine automobile yer driving there, pal."

"It gets me to where I need to go, sure," replied Farmer Bob. "Your vehicle ain't none too shabby, neither."

Hardy hesitated as he reached for the brim of the fedora he'd left behind in the Little Burlytown barbershop. It was a shoot-the-shit move, the cocking of the hat, an affectation. But such aw-shucks, everyman gestures were part of Hardy's repertoire for endearing himself to locals.

"Lamborghinis don't come cheap," said Hardy as he leaned into the open window. The interior smelled of musk—the cheap, synthetic kind you'd find in a drug store. It didn't add up. "So, you win the lottery or something?"

"Sure, yah, something like that, sure. Well, I best be on my way." Hardy stepped back as the Lamborghini abruptly roared away.

"Was it something I said?" he asked with a smirk as he returned to his car.

He turned off the 160 and quickly left it behind. He followed a dirt lane that the surrounding prairie and the elements had all but reclaimed. Within minutes the highway was a thin grey line in his rearview mirror. Hardy persevered, chasing what remained of the trail towards a copse of trees on the horizon.

The fountain dowser had been down this metaphorical road before. His senses were pinging, electrified by the nearness of his quarry. He didn't give two figs for what such a discovery might mean for the world. Immortality was overrated, as far as he was concerned. Hardy had enough problems as it was; living forever sounded like a death sentence for someone with his practical sensibilities. And, up until recently, he thought Darla and he were of the same mind.

Nope, he thought. *Wrong again, you clueless, brain-dead bastard.*

As if to underscore his cluelessness, what Hardy found at the end of the dirt path was the last thing he expected.

CHAPTER THIRTY

The dusty Mustang emerged from the woods and rolled to a halt at the edge of the overgrown town square. Crystal Springs, all six buildings of it, had been ravaged by a long-ago fire. What remained were cinders and ash. Only two buildings were remotely identifiable: the Immaculate Reconception church and the Harper Home for Wayward Children.

The church, a one-story clapboard affair, had collapsed in on itself. The steeple was toppled onto the building beside it, caving in the roof of what might have been a library. The orphanage, however, seemed slightly more intact. The earth around it was scorched, but the two-story building was still standing.

"This don't feel right," muttered Hardy. He glanced back the way he came. It was clear from the freshly trampled undergrowth that no one had been through those woods in a very long time. He turned back and took in the ruined town in a single glance. Then he turned until he was facing northwest towards a distant ridge about 1,500 yards beyond the edge of town.

First things first, thought Hardy. *What happens in Crystal Springs, stays in Crystal Springs.*

A flock of finches darted from a broken second-floor window as Hardy made his noisy approach through the debris and dry brush. As he neared the orphanage he noticed what looked like partially buried bones.

"That's 'cause they *are* bones," Hardy said to the empty square. He began to brush away the loose dirt with his hands. Within minutes he had unearthed the remains of at least three human skeletons. He carefully turned over a skull with the edge of his shoe. What remained of the cranium was etched with scrimshawed patterns.

"Minions," he whispered. Which meant that Jesse Bettenay could already be long dead. But something about that didn't sit right with Hardy. He picked up a steel spike-studded femur and saw no bullet holes or signs of blunt force. Hardy scoured the earth around the skeletons but found no spent bullet casings or bone fragments.

"How could a bunch of hayseeds hold back even one minion without weapons," Hardy wondered aloud. Only a shaman with a seriously high body count could hope to repel anything enchanted with Solomon's magic. *Someone like Bettenay?*

Hardy glanced back towards the distant ridge before returning his attention to the orphanage. He didn't know what he was looking for as he stepped over the charred threshold. The fountain dowser simply existed in the moment and listened to the growing hum in his ears.

"Gettin' warmer," he whispered.

The weakened floor beams creaked under his weight as he slowly made his way past the bottom of a crooked staircase. A moldy, ash-covered couch lay on its side, the ripped chenille pillows spread out like stepping stones across the ruined carpet. He paused in the middle of the room and turned in a slow circle. There wasn't much to see in the blackened ruins—just molting wallpaper and the stiffened bodies of vermin in varying states of decay. And yet his intuition was pinging loudly.

"Yeah, yeah," he muttered under his breath. "I'm working on it."

He continued his slow pirouette until it occurred to him to look up. The hum grew louder as he glanced at the sagging, water-stained ceiling.

I can take a hint. Upstairs it is.

Hardy stood at the foot of the stairs and stared up at what was left of the second floor. Ten years and thirty pounds ago he would have bounded up the rickety steps like a champion. But now he merely gritted his teeth and made his way upstairs, gingerly, like the tired old man he was.

The stairs moaned before buckling beneath his weight. He grabbed for the banister and ripped it free from the wall in a shower of moldy plaster. He swore as he stumbled, swore again as he somehow righted himself without falling ass over teapot down the stairs. He took the last few steps in an awkward bound. As he leaned against a wall to catch his breath he pretended the hammering in his chest was from exertion.

Here lies Indiana Bones, the Human GPS, he thought grimly.

The rooms—what remained of them—were clearly bedrooms. He counted nine rooms in all, four rooms on each side of the hall and one at the end of the corridor.

No chance of anonymity here, Hardy thought. *Not in a place this small.*

Without further ado he approached the third door on the right. He had no doubt in his mind that it once belonged to Jesse. He didn't expect to find anything except the detritus of a forgotten, lonely life. But as Hardy reached for the door Darla's face leapt from the recesses of his mind. Her eyes were so clear and perfect Hardy almost believed she was somehow standing beside him.

Barnabas, said the apparition.

He laughed uneasily as he rubbed his eyes with the calloused heels of his hands. Clearly he was hallucinating. What was next—dancing pink elephants?

Darla's visage vanished as Hardy pushed the door open. In that same instant, the pinging in his ears became a loud, angry buzz that made the fountain dowser grimace in pain.

And then, silence. Even the hum of his intuition had been quelled. Hardy blinked as he glanced long and hard at his strange surroundings. He had no recollection of where he was, much less how he'd gotten there. All he saw was an open door before him.

Puzzled, Hardy walked through it.

The first thing he noticed was the faded movie poster taped to the wall above a cluttered desk. "The Whispering Corpse," said Hardy as he read the movie's title aloud. "Come on now. Come *on*. Are you fucking *kidding* me."

He ripped the dusty poster from the wall and crumpled it into a ball. Then he turned and kicked the desk chair for good measure. A boondoggle. How could he have fallen for the cheapest trick in the book? It had to be Silas Walker. But how? No one could out-dowse Hardy when he was on top of his game. But that was the problem. He *wasn't* on top of his game, and hadn't been, not since Moss. Even so, he'd never gotten his signals so crossed before.

Hardy paused to wipe soot and ash from his hands. *Okay, just hold on a sec. Think this through. Look again.* Then he noticed a muddy, threadbare suit stuffed behind the mattress.

He ignored the dangerously unstable floorboards as he crossed the room and laid the suit on the bed. One of the trouser pockets yielded a folded piece of mud-stained notebook paper. Chunks of grey dirt spilled onto the floorboards as he unfolded the paper.

His voice was thick, hoarse; it filled the room as he read the carefully written words upon the page. "'*Tecum vivere amem, tecum obeam libens,*'" he said as he struggled with what was probably Latin. Was Jesse Bettenay a member of the Savane, too? An egghead like Forrest would surely know.

Hardy read the translation that was scribbled below the incantation: *I want to live and to die with you.*

Hardy rooted through the other pockets and came up empty. He quickly turned to a soot-covered bookshelf above a tiny desk in the corner. The books, bloated and water-stained, reeked of mildew. Hardy left those volumes alone. The book he was interested in was lying under the desk.

It was a self-help book titled *Undead Like Me*, by Alistair Moon. Hardy knew the book well. It was no surprise that a Resurrectionist like Bettenay would own a copy of it. It was also no surprise that various passages were underlined, or that handwritten notes had been jotted in the margins. Bettenay was certainly no dilettante in the resurrection department—but that didn't necessarily mean he was the corpse whisperer.

As Hardy continued to flip through the book two handwritten notes jumped out from the margins. AUDITION WED. 7PM HARPER CTY PLAYHOUSE read one in slanting lowercase. CALL P. FOGARTY, WICHITA WIRE read the second note in sloppy cursive. *One book, two readers,* thought Hardy. Were the two notes unrelated?

Hardy tucked the folded notepaper between the pages of the book and shoved it in his pocket. As he resumed his search of the room he had to wonder why Bettenay's belongings had not been packed away to make room for another boy. Perhaps the fire that leveled the town had occurred soon after Bettenay's disappearance. Or maybe Bettenay had set the fires himself?

The room overlooked the square. Hardy leaned out the window and considered the pile of scrimshawed bones that littered the square. From two floors up, the skeletons' placement directly outside the orphanage seemed convenient. *No, not convenient,* he thought, smiling slyly. The word he was looking for was contrived. The remains of an unlikely battle were meant to scare away less inquisitive types. Hardy quickly descended the rickety staircase and headed back outside. He immediately grabbed one of the longer bones. It broke easily over his knee like a stick of chalk.

"Hollow," he said matter-of-factly to the arid town square. He picked up one of the skulls and brushed away the dirt. What had looked like etched filigree was merely finely painted lines. Such simple trickery would easily fool someone sitting in the cheap seats.

Hardy frowned as he gazed once more toward the distant ridge. *I can take a hint*, he thought, and climbed back into the Mustang. Hardy quickly left Crystal Springs behind in a thick cloud of prairie dust.

CHAPTER THIRTY-ONE

Darla's witch doctor, the shaman DeStefano, was not happy with his staff of death coaches. He was especially displeased with Jonas, who was normally his top recruiter. Not so this month; the reanimated death coach was well below his quota. As passage of the controversial Death Cap bill loomed, such a shortfall was unacceptable.

Jonas was well aware of his low numbers, but many of his recruits were either delaying their rebirths or canceling them altogether. It wasn't that resurrection was suddenly on the wane—far from it. But in the rush to push through as many rebirths as possible ahead of the death cap, corners had to be cut. In many cases, this meant fudging psych evaluations—even if it meant passing candidates ill-suited for reanimation. Darla Hardy was one such candidate, despite being a willing convert to Resurrectionism. Jonas had certainly spent enough time counseling her over the last few months to understand that what truly motivated Darla was not love, as she repeatedly claimed, but fear. Specifically, it was a fear of dying alone, unloved and unmourned.

But DeStefano was indifferent to the many nuances that influenced a candidate's decision to seek rebirth, be it the honorable pursuit of *Cadabra*

Rasa or the need to escape a terminal illness. At the end of the day, Jonas knew all of his patients were nothing more than bodies to the wealthy witch doctor. A high body count was not a means to offering better or stronger magic. No, what DeStefano saw in confused, skittish patients like Darla Hardy was a chance for better bragging rights, and nothing more.

And Jonas, who once cared so deeply about his job, felt as soulless as the Neo-Lifers claimed all cadavers to be. Now, when his cell phone rang, it was with dread that he took the calls of his would-be charges, and assuaged their fears in hopes of meeting his quotas.

And for this crime, Jonas, once considered by his peers to be among the most compassionate of their profession, wished he himself had never been reborn. Now, cell phone in hand, he preemptively reached out to Darla Hardy.

"Hi, it's me," he said, his rigid smile buried beneath his tufted beard. "Great news—I was able to move your appointment up."

"Are you sure I'm really ready for this? I—I still have so many questions."

"And rebirth, Darla," he said gently, "is the only answer you need." His smile faded as the line grew silent. "Whatever your doubts are...soon they will be irrelevant."

"Lydia," she said. "We've been fighting so much lately."

Jonas paused at a busy street corner and watched patiently as traffic whizzed past. He knew he was invisible to these distracted drivers, so reckless were they as their minds wandered. All it would take was a single step—a single, careless step off the curb—to reshape one unlucky driver's day, if not their entire life. Jonas knew he could survive a collision—his talisman all but guaranteed it. But such a gesture was not about his survival; no, his 'accident' might send a message to his charges, awaken them to the many benefits of life on both sides of the grave. Doubters, like Darla Hardy, might finally be able to decide for themselves what path was best for them.

Or such an act, with its false sense of sacrifice, could all be in vain.

"Jonas, are you still there?"

Jonas stepped back from the rushing traffic. "Yes. I'm still here," he said quietly.

"You said you moved up my appointment?"

"Yes," said Jonas, her trusted death coach. "You're in luck, Darla. For you, *Cadabra Rasa* begins tomorrow."

"Tomorrow. That...that's so soon. My family—"

Jonas found it difficult to remain firm. "Your family is dead to you."

Darla's heartbreak was both obvious and contagious. "No," she said in a voice so small it was all but drowned out by the traffic. "I'll be dead to them."

Jonas clutched the phone in his cold hand. DeStefano was a man without a real care in the world. And yet, if Jonas failed again to meet his quota, the witch doctor would surely make an example out of him.

"So you've made your decision, then? Are you worthy of a fresh start, Darla? Do you deserve this second chance?"

"Yes, Jonas. I'm ready to die."

Jonas closed his yellow eyes and smiled. Then he removed his talisman and stepped off the curb and into sweet oblivion.

CHAPTER THIRTY-TWO

What Hardy found beyond the burnt-out remains of Crystal Springs was another small town. It was very well hidden; if not for sunlight glinting off a distant satellite dish, a less intuitive person would never have discovered the private development. Unlike Crystal Springs, this town appeared to be the very model of extravagance. From his vantage point atop the ridge, Hardy counted fourteen mansions. From the look of them, they appeared to be relatively new construction—probably built within the last eight or ten years. In almost every driveway sat a luxury car; Hardy was willing to bet his left nut that not a single vehicle was worth less than a hundred grand.

Just like Farmer Bob's Lamborghini, thought Hardy.

He decided it was time for a closer look at this millionaire's prairie utopia. He began to work his way around the town's perimeter. Hardy knew he'd have better luck if he came in through the main road—if there was one. To come skulking in from the shadows, uninvited, unannounced, would only spell trouble for him in the long run.

Even if it would be faster just to sneak in the back way, he thought as he trudged on foot through thick underbrush. That a town with so many wealthy residents did not hide itself behind a wall meant it felt no threat from the outside world. Which meant Hardy's plan to waltz into town on the main road wasn't enough of a plan.

After walking for a few minutes more Hardy stopped to inspect what looked like a shallow, dried-up pond bed. "Now what the hell is *this* doing here?" He crouched down and ran his hands over the cracked, barren soil. Then he tentatively licked the silt from his calloused fingertips. "How is this even possible?" But it was true—Hardy had dowsed his way to an old fountain. And not just any fountain; this one had once been flush with the Tears of Life.

Hardy stood and brushed the dust from his clothes. There was no doubt about it—he was getting rusty. Back in the day, he would have made a bee-line straight to this arid patch of earth from half a world away. And now, his discovery of the well was pure happenstance. Hardy moved on, determined to see this quest through to the bitter end.

Hardy found the road into town easily enough. The well-maintained road snaked its way through the woods in one direction. The other direction led straight into the center of town, past a gleaming volunteer fire department. Two firemen stood alongside a fire truck, chatting amiably until they noticed the dirty, unkempt stranger strolling down Main Street. The smaller of the two men quickly headed back inside. The larger man—a well-groomed bruiser with a movie-star smile, met Hardy at the foot of the driveway. He extended his hand by way of a greeting.

"We don't get many visitors around here," he said.

Hardy was sweating despite the chill in the air. He wiped his brow with the back of his arm before accepting the proffered hand. "Yeah, ran into some car trouble back onna interstate."

"But that's over eight miles away. How the heck did you wind up all the way out here?"

"Poor sense of direction, I guess," answered Hardy. "And dumb luck."

"Looks like you ran into a bit of trouble yourself," he said, indicating Hardy's split lip.

The fireman's tone was friendly enough. But Hardy sensed he was being sized up. Like the man said, they didn't get many visitors in these parts. "I feel a lot worse than I look."

This comment elicited its intended chuckle from the fireman. "Then you must feel pretty rotten."

Hardy glanced up the street. The town, such as it was, didn't offer much in the way of amenities. The fire department was certainly an oddity—as was the steel and glass movie theater up the street. It was as big and modern as any theater in a big city. So what was it doing out here in the sticks? The theater made the main street convenience store look more rinky-dink than it actually was.

"Mackenzie Cross," Hardy said, squinting to read the theater's marquee. "That's that kid actor who went all squirrely, right?"

"Squirrely."

"My daughter loved that one movie of his, the one where he's defending his house against that gang of undead crooks."

"He was exploited," said the fireman. "He hasn't been the same since."

"Sure, he was exploited all the way to the bank." Hardy fell silent as he pondered the movie theater. Why did he have the strange feeling that its screen was dark, its stadium seats empty?

"You look a bit perplexed, friend."

"Yer reading me like a book," said Hardy. "Is there a phone in town I can use? Mine died way back in Missouri."

"There's a pay phone just up the street at the All-Around," he said, pointing the way past the super-sized supermarket to the convenience store. "I'm heading that way myself."

I bet you are, thought Hardy. "So what do you do for fun all the way out here? Besides goin' to the movies, of course."

"I didn't catch where you're from," the fireman said.

"Back east."

"And where exactly are you headed?"

Hardy smiled. "Wherever the road takes me. Assuming I can get my car running again."

"Right. Your car." They stopped in the middle of the road. "So why are you really here, friend?"

Hardy hadn't come all this way, and risked so much, to beat around the bush. But he wasn't looking for another fight, either—especially with a younger man nearly twice his size.

"I'm looking for someone. Maybe you know her. Ella Brownstone."

The fireman's movie-star smile did not falter. Hardy surmised this fighter of fires had to be one hell of a poker player. "No one by that rename here, friend."

The pause that followed his reply lasted only a split second. But in that conversational hiccup was Hardy's obvious, unspoken thought: *Rename? Who said she was undead?*

Hardy was wise enough not to point out the gaffe, but he did capitalize on it. "Yeah, figured it was kind of a long shot. I know her boyfriend was from this neck of the woods. Seemed like a good enough place to start looking."

The fireman squinted at Hardy. "Her boyfriend."

Hardy chuckled. "Jesse Bettenay, yeah. Any idea where I might find him?"

The distant rumbling of a truck on the interstate could be heard in the ensuing, leaden silence.

"You sure you got the right Jesse? It's a very common name."

Hardy looked him squarely in the eye. "I'm pretty sure I got the right Jesse."

"I hate to be the bearer of bad news friend, but Jesse Bettenay is dead."

"No kidding."

"He died almost twelve years ago to the day in a tragic fire."

Hardy glanced down the street towards the fancy fire station but kept mum as the fireman continued. "He left behind no family to speak of. Only memories."

Something about the fireman's little speech felt canned, rehearsed. Like he was reading from a script. It made the entire town seem somehow artificial, almost like a big stage play. So who was directing this show?

It has to be Bettenay, thought Hardy. He was so certain of it he could feel it in his bones. But how could an orphan on the lam for graveyard poaching bankroll a whole town? It didn't seem possible—unless Jesse Bettenay had assumed a new identity in the last twelve years. Hardy finally realized he needed to stop looking for the love-struck kid who owned that muddy suit. The firefighter was right—*that* Jesse Bettenay was dead and gone. The Jesse Bettenay for whom money was no object—that was the man Hardy was determined to find.

Hardy was so lost in his labyrinthine thought process that he didn't notice the four large cadavers shambling towards him until it was too late. The retired Havens militiamen easily dwarfed the firefighter. They quickly closed ranks around the fountain dowser.

Then they showed him how real men brawled.

*　　*　　*

Hours later, Hardy awoke in the back seat of the Mustang. He sat up with a loud groan and dully inventoried his injuries. Aside from a throbbing headache and a lot of nasty bruises in some tender spots, he seemed to be more or less intact. He was well aware they'd gone easy on him; their intent hadn't been to kill so much as to maim. No doubt he'd been spared by whatever parameters had been established by their benefactor.

Hardy laughed at himself. Here he was, covered in his own coagulated blood—and he was *still* trying to crack the damn case. If this little setback didn't stop him, nothing would. He ignored the shooting pains in his shoulder and lower back as he climbed out of the parked car. Even in the near-pitch black night he could tell he was on the side of a highway—most likely the 160, judging from the lay of the land.

He contemplated his next move as a cool, dry wind swept across the desolate prairie. Going back the way he came wasn't an option. No, Hardy knew he needed to keep heading west, even if the people he most cared about were in the opposite direction.

Hardy slid in behind the wheel and started the car. He noticed the gas tank was full—which meant he had to be within several miles of a gas station. In the absence of any concrete leads, splashing some cold water on his face and stocking up on supplies for the road ahead seemed as good a plan as any.

The gas station, a one-pump affair named Pip's, was about fifteen miles further down the road. The cashier, a bespectacled kid barely older than Sofia, was slouched behind the register, an issue of *Juggs* facedown on the counter. The *Late Show* played on a muted TV bolted to the wall. David Letterman, a child himself of the heartland, smiled and shrugged his way through the silent monologue.

Local boy makes good, thought Hardy. *Just like Jesse Bettenay.* The fountain dowser stopped dead in his tracks and stared long and hard at the television. Could the corpse whisperer be a former weatherman?

"Boy, someone did a number on you, boss," the cashier said.

"A bunch of someones," said Hardy as he limped around the shop. He grabbed a bottle of extra-strength aspirin and a yellowed box of Band-Aids from a shelf and tossed them onto the counter. An economy-sized package of beef jerky, a box of chocolate-covered donut holes, and a six-pack of cherry Shasta were added to the growing stockpile.

"Is all this for you?" asked the kid.

"Well, it ain't for the pope," cracked Hardy. He returned his attention to the television. *No, can't be Letterman,* he realized. *He's an Indiana boy.* Plus, he was way too old to be Bettenay. But Hardy knew he was finally on to something with this train of thought.

The cashier noticed how transfixed Hardy was by the program. "Hold on, I'll turn it up for ya." He picked up a blue ballpoint pen and poked at the TV's broken volume button.

The aspirin bottle opened with a satisfying *pop* in Hardy's hands. He tossed back four of the pills and washed them down with a donut hole and a hearty swig of cherry Shasta. "Help yourself," he burped, and tossed a twenty onto the counter.

The cashier gave the volume button a few more pokes with the pen as Letterman launched into the evening's Top Ten list. "'Ten Things Damon Grayson Shouldn't Do at KadabraLand,'" the cashier echoed blankly. He stuffed an entire donut hole in his mouth and turned to Hardy. "Guy's a dingleberry if you ask me."

Hardy tore into the package of beef jerky and reveled in the saltiness of the cured meat. "Who, Grayson? He just needs to get his head outta his ass and his foot outta his mouth."

"Guy's a zombie lover."

Hardy glanced at the kid from the corner of his eye. *You're just passing through,* he reminded himself. *No reason to start trouble with the locals over a bit of necrophobia.* Then he realized that he himself could be considered a zombie lover. He still loved Darla—whether or not she had a pulse. And that's where he had Jesse Bettenay beat; Hardy had no intention of abandoning his soon-to-be dead wife. If the firefighter was to be believed (and Hardy did believe him), Ella Brownstone was the corpse that got away.

"Number five," Letterman yelled with a gleeful, gap-toothed smile. "Don't vomit on co-star Sindy Sinew!" He clutched the sides of his face in mock terror. The studio audience roared with laughter.

Hardy recognized the pose made so famous by a young Mackenzie Cross. "I was just talking about that kid," he said.

"Did you ever notice that Sindy Sinew's hair is made of maggots?" asked the cashier.

Hardy stared at the boy. "Maggots."

"Yeah. How gross is that?"

A new pathway coalesced upon the ethereal landscape. The route zigged where Hardy expected it to zag. The clarity of the vision left him shaking his head in disbelief.

"I'm a friggin' idiot," Hardy said. He left everything on the counter and bolted for the door.

"You left your holes," the cashier yelled after the fountain dowser.

But Hardy was already behind the wheel of the Mustang, his foot pressed hard against the gas pedal.

CHAPTER THIRTY-THREE

Ashland Heights was a southeastern New Cali city known more for its high crime rate than it was for its lackluster views of Burly Gate. Located less than five miles east of the wall, the city had yet to experience the sort of gentrification that caused property values to skyrocket in nearby Las Almas. Those in Ashland Heights who wanted a cup of Frankenjoe's coffee had to drive at least fifteen miles in any direction to satisfy their craving. Rebirth centers were even harder to come by; the nearest one was nearly an hour's drive away.

Local politicians argued that the area was a magnet for lowlifes and malcontents, intent on sowing necrophobia throughout much of SoNewCali. Indeed, many considered Ashland Heights, with its concentration of Burly Gate veterans, to be the birthplace of the postwar Neo-Life movement. Recent rebirth center bombings and undead bias crimes all seemingly pointed back to one Ashland Heights resident: George Gleeson. Whether or not there was any truth to this did not matter to Gleeson. He eagerly fostered these rumors; they lent him a sort of credibility that further legitimized the dangerous Neo-Life agenda.

But such thoughts were pushed to the back of Gleeson's mind as he paced back and forth across his apartment building's tarpaper roof. He watched as the weak western sun slowly vanished behind Burly Gate. The wall cast its long shadow across the valley; soon, Ashland Heights would succumb to an all-encompassing darkness. George Gleeson crossed the roof to the large telescope set up on a tripod beneath a metal awning. From atop his five-story perch, Gleeson beheld a nearly uninterrupted 90-mile stretch of Burly Gate. Boca Muerta was thirty miles to the south of Ashland Heights. It was there that Gleeson first pointed the telescope. Over the next twenty minutes he performed a careful sweep of the top of the wall. Illegal incursions by deadbacks were at their highest after dusk. He waited patiently, a two-way radio in hand, as he continued to monitor the wall. After a few minutes he switched the scope to night-vision mode.

"Come on, come on," he muttered. "Where are you, you brain-eating bastards?"

The distant warning lights of the Burly Gate HAMR towers fluoresced brightly against the lunar-like blacks and greys created by the low-light scope. Gleeson turned his attention north towards a point along the wall known as Leper's Leap. The higher ground elevation in that area made it a popular spot for assailing the wall. Those who were able to scale the granite face from the Havens side were aided by a dense line of trees on the Living States side of the wall. It was here that Gleeson's men spent the most time, patrolling the area in cars or on foot.

"Patrol Alpha," crackled a voice over the two-way. "All clear so far." Patrol Beta reported back in kind. Gleeson smiled at the obvious disappointment in their voices. Unlike Calvin, many of his followers had yet to make their modest quota of ten talismans. Many of them, desperate for Gleeson's taciturn approval, had foolishly tried to supplement their numbers with easily detected fakes. Which meant many of his potential recruits simply didn't possess the sort of ruthlessness that came so easily to Calvin. A boy like Calvin could do a lot of good in the Zombie Defense Corps—which is why Gleeson was so keen on bringing him into his more radical fold. Neo-Lifers were not restricted by the sort of social and ethical mores (and their attendant, manufactured dilemmas) that the government imposed upon its military. In Gleeson's mind, all bets were off for real patriots; the Living States borders demanded protection no matter the cost to so-called civil liberties.

Gleeson checked his watch. Manny would be arriving with the boy in a matter of minutes. He peered again through the scope towards Leper's Leap. He, too, was disappointed by the lack of turnout by even one tenacious cadaver. Perhaps their nightly vigils were finally curbing illegal entries over the wall.

"Or maybe not," he muttered. He easily picked out two dark specks breaching the top of the wall—their exposed bones shined brightly against the dark, ashy landscape. But it was the telltale glow on their ring fingers in the night vision that truly gave them away. Gleeson quickly raised the radio to his mouth. "Patrol Beta. Two DB's inbound less than half a klick north from your current position."

"Copy that," came the reply. "ETA two minutes."

Gleeson kept the channel open and watched patiently through the scope. The two figures made it past the concertina wire that topped the wall and began their descent down Burly Gate's granite face. Gleeson knew that even at that height the fall wouldn't outright kill a zombie; there was always some no-good shaman willing to put the pieces back together again—and boost their precious body count in the process.

"Patrol Beta, status."

"We have eyes on the prize, over. No joy—both targets out of HAMR range."

"Let them come to you," said Gleeson. He peered through the scope. The deadbacks were still at least 100 feet above Living States soil—almost within range of the Magnetic Resonators.

The radio crackled in Gleeson's hand. "Got 'em, we got 'em!" Gleeson overheard the telltale *ZINK* of a talisman being drawn into a HAMR's chamber. A second muffled *ZINK* quickly followed. Gleeson smiled as both deadbacks lost their grip and plummeted out of view behind the trees.

"It's maggot central over here," came the update over the radio. "Jesus, what a mess!"

"Resume your patrol, Beta team! The night is young and the wall is long."

"Words to live by," responded Manny over the radio. "You're a poet, George. Who knew you had it in you."

Gleeson peered over the edge of the roof as the old Cutlass chugged up the deserted, trash-strewn street.

"Bring him to the bunker," said Gleeson. 'You never know who might be watching."

George Gleeson's decommissioned apocalypse bunker was a steel-reinforced concrete structure located directly beneath the apartment building. It had none of the trappings of home but was as fortified as any citadel. The bunker, which measured roughly 20 by 30 feet, was crammed with everything from MREs to batteries to mag-frag grenades. It also included quite an arsenal—with enough firearms and ammunition to outfit an entire squad.

The six-inch thick Kevlar-enhanced steel door opened with a loud clang as Manny ushered Calvin into the windowless bunker. The young recruit, who had been quiet on the ride from San Gabriel, was suitably impressed by the zombie-proofed room.

"This...this is the coolest thing I have ever seen in my entire life," whispered Calvin. He quickly turned to Gleeson, who was hunched over a disassembled RAMR. "Whoa—is that a HAMR rifle?"

"It sure is," said Manny, who'd recently scored it on the black market. "Has three times the range of a regular Resonator sidearm. A brain-eater couldn't get within 300 feet of you with one of those babies pointed at it."

"You guys have the coolest shit ever."

Gleeson deftly assembled the RAMR as he spoke. "You need to respect your munitions. Don't dishonor them with petty words."

Calvin was already lost. He looked to Manny for help, who in turn shrugged. The fact that Manny had known Gleeson for the better part of three decades accounted for nothing. George was the boss, plain and simple.

"Sorry," said Calvin. "I didn't mean to offend you or your...stuff."

Gleeson sighted down the thick barrel of the assembled RAMR before returning it to the munitions locker. When he finally turned to face them, he somehow seemed more imposing than Calvin remembered. Maybe it was an illusion created by the cramped confines of the dark bunker. Or maybe it was because George Gleeson appeared larger than life to those who lacked true heroism in their own hearts.

"I asked Manny to bring you here because I was impressed by your commitment—both to me and to what our patriotic struggle represents."

"I just like killing zombies is all," said Calvin. He reached into his pants pocket and withdrew a clinking handful of ring-shaped talismans. "Here. Twelve more. You can count them if you want."

"Hey, you didn't tell me about those!" Manny patted Calvin on the back. "You are on a roll!"

"If you give me a RAMR of my own I could totally do some serious damage."

Gleeson knew the boy spoke the truth—at least a version of the truth that he himself believed. "I'm impressed. You're a born soldier, Calvin."

"George don't impress so easy," said Manny. "You oughta be proud of yourself, Cal."

Calvin lowered his head in what seemed like an uncharacteristic moment of modesty. "Thank you, sir," he said, clearing his throat. "That means a lot, coming from you."

"Cal and his dad don't exactly see eye to eye on everything," said Manny.

"Is that right," said Gleeson. He approached Calvin and looked him directly in the eye. It was easy to see the tow-headed, buck-toothed little boy he once was. Even at twenty he still had long blonde lashes and a trace of baby fat around the jaw and neckline. But Gleeson could also see in him the man Calvin wanted to become.

"Is that who you're running from, your father?"

"I'm not afraid of him."

Not anymore, thought Gleeson. "No. Of course not."

"I'm like a zombie to him," said Calvin in a tone of barely suppressed anger. "Like a...a *thing*...that isn't even alive."

Burly Gate veterans like Gleeson and Manny were all too familiar with the same sort of unsolicited contempt. Their only crime had been serving their country in what turned out to be an unpopular war; Gleeson could only guess at Calvin's sins.

"We're the only family you'll ever need," he said. "All I ask for in return is your unwavering loyalty."

"You don't have to ask me twice, sir," Calvin said with a big grin.

Calvin's young life was something Gleeson was willing to gamble with if it meant keeping the country safe.

"Are you ready to defend the sanctity of our borders, no matter what the cost?"

"You can count on me, Mr. Gleeson."

He draped an arm around the boy's shoulder. "Good. Because what I'm going to ask of you is above and beyond bringing me a handful of talismans. You'll be deep undercover, and you'll be alone. So, can I still count on you, Calvin?"

Calvin glanced around the apocalypse bunker and greatly coveted all that he saw before him. But what he prized above all else was unconditional acceptance.

"Like you said, Mr. Gleeson, the night is young, and the wall is long."

Gleeson smiled. "Please," he said. "Call me George."

CHAPTER THIRTY-FOUR

Cornelius had not budged from his spot on the motel's grungy hallway carpet since scaring off the 'bloiders.

After reading through the night he had completed all but thirty pages of the 532-page tome, *Only Humans*. He pinched the remaining chapters' pages delicately between his fingers and sighed. He always hated reaching the end of a good book. At least he had packed more books for the trip.

Cornelius looked up sharply as the elevator at the end of the hall clattered open—and out stepped Joni. Joni, who was supposed to be on the side of Everest. Cornelius recoiled as if struck at the sight of Damon's publicist.

"You," she said, pointing at Cornelius as she charged up the hall. "You're his bodyguard."

"You—you remember who I am?"

This stopped Joni in her tracks. "Are you trying to distract me? Is that his room behind you?"

Cornelius nodded but did not move from the doorway.

"I need to get in there before he crawls out a window."

"Mr. Grayson wouldn't do something like that."

Joni laughed. "Believe me, it wouldn't be the first time." She tried to push past Cornelius but he dutifully blocked her way.

"He—he might be indecent."

"So help me Lazarus, if you don't let me in there—" The change in her demeanor was just as sudden and unexpected as her arrival. "I love that book," she said, pointing to Cornelius's copy of *Only Humans*. "Did you read the part yet where Boris punched that 'bloider in the face—"

"—then made him dinner in the Universal commissary? Yeah, he was a good person." Cornelius had never known the kind of happiness he felt at that very moment.

"Listen, this is great and all—"

"Cornelius."

"—Cornelius, right. But if you don't let me see my client, I will hurt you."

He could suddenly understand why Damon might climb out a window. He reluctantly stepped aside to let her pass. "He tries to be a good person."

"I know." She poked the book jacket. "We already established that."

"No, I—I meant Damon. I mean, Mr. Grayson."

Joni smiled as she looked Cornelius in the eye. "Do I make you nervous?"

"A little bit."

She patted him on the shoulder. "Good."

He was keenly aware that her cold hand was still resting on his shoulder. "Try to go easy on him."

An edge crept into her smile. "Don't worry. I won't try too hard."

Damon slept fitfully, beneath the imagined weight of cold, unyielding soil. He awoke with a start, desperately gulping for air.

"Did it work," he croaked, "am I undead?" He sat up, disoriented, as the murky hotel room swam into focus. He rubbed his bleary eyes with the heels of his hands. "Son of a gun," he said with a nervous laugh. He fell back against the pillow, embarrassed and relieved.

"So now you're a closet Resurrectionist?" asked an impatient voice.

Damon nearly fell out of bed. "Jesus Christ!"

Joni was standing at the foot of his bed, her arms folded expectantly across her chest. With her dun-colored complexion, she'd been easy to miss in the dark room. She tossed him a scruffy, starched robe from the closet. "Cornelius let me in a few minutes ago. I have to say, he's a bit more...*robust* than I remember."

"That's one way of putting it," said Damon as he climbed out of bed. "So aren't you supposed to be off the grid somewhere in The Himalayas?"

"Up until twenty hours ago I *was* off the grid," she said angrily. "But then I made the mistake of turning on my phone."

"Yeah, that probably wasn't such a great idea."

"You think? Can you imagine how surprised I was to see over 3,000 unread messages?"

"That's one heck of a data plan you have," Damon muttered.

Joni's refurbished musculature shifted beneath her taut, synthetic flesh as she advanced on him. If she'd wanted to, she could have easily put Damon through a wall.

"What is *wrong* with you? Can't I leave town for two weeks without you doing something stupid?"

Damon laughed nervously as her sky-blue dyborg eyes bore into him. "It's not like I did it on purpose."

"Yeah, that's the problem. You seem to have the worst instincts for self-preservation."

"That's why I have you."

Joni narrowed her eyes. "Is that supposed to be funny?"

Damon sighed. He knew the truth: he needed Joni more than she needed him. "Don't you know me by now?"

She jabbed a cold finger into his shoulder. "If it weren't for me, you'd be known as the *Billion*-Dollar mouth."

"Okay, fine. So what are we supposed to do? How do we fix this? Going to KadabraLand is a terrible idea."

Joni smiled. "It's not great, no. But it's not terrible. You could stand to be knocked down a few pegs."

"This is a lot more than a few pegs!"

"Your dead cred is in the toilet and you're not even SLS-certified. Good job on screwing *that* up, by the way. Really classy. No one has failed that exam in over fifty years."

Damon frowned. Wasn't she supposed to be on *his* side? "Listen, I'm not as bad as everyone thinks I am."

Joni folded her chiseled arms across her chest. "Then prove it, Damon. Stop behaving like a colossal ass and *prove* it."

Just then there was a knock at the door. Cornelius stood in the doorway, a large suitcase in tow. In the last few minutes he had changed into a blue button-down shirt.

"Car's downstairs," he said, eyeing Joni suspiciously. "Am I...interrupting something?"

"Please. Don't be ridiculous," she said.

"Yeah," said Damon as he pulled on a pair of battered designer jeans. "Seriously, Neil."

No matter what the 'bloids said about him, Damon definitely did not have a 'bones jones' for any undead actress, no matter who she was. And he definitely wasn't attracted to Joni. She scared him, frankly. But Damon suspected that Cornelius's tastes were not quite so discerning when it came to his publicist. If not for the whole undead thing, she would have been very attractive.

Damon threw on a black T-shirt and grabbed his suitcase. Unlike Cornelius, he was traveling light. This wasn't a vacation after all; it was just another job, albeit one that would make or break his career. He patted Cornelius on the arm in an avuncular fashion. "Why don't I bring our stuff down to the car so the two of you can chat?"

Cornelius looked mortified, but Joni seemed strangely amused. She smiled at Cornelius and patted the bed next to her. "I won't bite," she said.

"Come on, big guy, now's your chance," whispered Damon as he pried Cornelius's white-knuckled hand from the suitcase handle. "You can thank me later." Damon grunted as he gave his bodyguard a final, friendly shove towards the bed.

"I meant to tell you earlier—sorry about your ascent," Cornelius said, emphasizing the first syllable. Damon quietly shook his head.

Joni, though, looked surprised. "You didn't tell me you read my blog," she said to Cornelius.

"That's why I'm reading *Only Humans*—because of your review."

"Are you two playing a joke on me," Joni asked Damon. "Because if you are, someone is going to find themselves in the ground."

"My forum name is huskyboy625," Cornelius said shyly.

"That's *you*?" said Joni. Her features softened. She touched Cornelius on the arm. "Oh, my god," she whispered. "That's you."

Damon quietly shut the door behind him. He tarried in the hall and listened to their hushed susurrations. A sudden burst of muted laughter followed him all the way down the hall.

The undead driver was leaning against the black Town Car, the *Gristle Gazette* sports section spread open across the hood. He barely acknowledged Damon as the actor approached the car. He continued to ignore Damon as he struggled to lift Cornelius's suitcase into the trunk of the car.

"Can you give me a hand here, pal?" asked Damon, trying hard to sound civil.

The driver responded with a thousand-year stare. His bored indifference was magnified, literally, by a very thick pair of black-framed glasses. He very deliberately—and needlessly—licked the tip of his fingers and flipped a page of the newspaper.

"Okay, fine," said Damon. "I get it." He resumed his struggle with Cornelius's suitcase. He could barely lift it above the bumper. "Thing weighs a ton," he grunted. He dropped it back to the pavement with a loud thud. He leaned on it as he caught his breath. "Seriously now," said Damon. "A little help here, guy? I don't want to blow a disc."

The driver yawned. Damon had been receiving the same cold shoulder from undead workers since the Hepburn incident. It was mildly irritating before, but now it seemed vindictive.

"Listen buddy, you don't even know me."

"No," the driver said calmly, "but I know your type."

Damon gritted his teeth. He was tired of being judged, especially when there were worse people out there bombing clinics and killing innocent people.

"Okay, seriously now. I could really use some help here, Z."

The driver glanced up sharply and turned on Damon. "I'm not your Z."

"Jesus. Relax. I didn't mean it like that. How dumb do you think I am?"

The pungent stench of formaldehyde wafted off the driver as he removed his blazer and tossed it in the front seat. He was painfully thin—literally just taut skin wrapped around a clattering collection of bones. Dark, shiny grey lesions spread across the driver's neck, face and arms. Such advanced decomp in a reanimated cadaver pointed to weak voodoo, chronic negligence, or both. Either way, the driver was most likely a Burialist resurrected against his will. Damon guessed he had to be at least a hundred in rebirth years, if not more. Who knew how long he was in the ground before that, thought Damon. Decades, probably.

The driver removed his glasses and placed them neatly in his shirt pocket. "You think you're better than us," he said, squinting at Damon. "You're a bunch of thieves. You stole our land and then imprisoned us behind that stupid wall."

"Hey, listen, that was way before my time. I read about it in the history books, just like you."

The driver cracked his knuckles. The sound was crisp, like a piece of Styrofoam being snapped in two. Damon inadvertently laughed as he realized what the driver intended to do. He had never struck an undead person before, aside from undead stunt actors. But they were rigged to fall apart upon impact, like a breakaway table in a fight scene. Even so, Damon knew that the average reanimate couldn't really take a punch. The driver had to know this, too. As it was, he barely came up to Damon's chin. Damon suddenly felt guilty for laughing.

"Listen, I'm sorry. I honestly didn't mean to offend you." He held out his hand but the driver swatted it away.

"You want a piece of me?"

If he'd really wanted to, Damon could easily snap off the driver's index finger. "Hey, I already said I was sorry."

The driver glared up at him for a long beat before abruptly turning away.

"It's a good thing I need this job," he said as he pushed his glasses onto his wrinkled face. "Or you'd be in big trouble."

"I don't doubt it."

The driver's heavy spectacles nearly flew off as he wheeled on Damon again. "Don't patronize me. You're lucky I showed up at all. No one else wanted this gig. I'm getting paid triple overtime just to drive your privileged, pampered butt."

"Fine. So will you help me with this suitcase?"

The driver donned his blazer and resumed reading the paper. It was as if the altercation never happened. "Nope," he said.

Damon wondered if this was how B-list actors got treated. He shuddered to think about the shoddy treatment C-listers must receive. Damon comforted himself by considering he probably made more money in five minutes than the driver made in an entire month. *So be it*, he thought, and resigned himself to waiting for Cornelius.

Ten minutes later, Damon was still waiting. He could only imagine what was happening back at the room. Then he realized he didn't want to know. Cornelius didn't strike Damon as the lothario type. Big as he was, though, Joni could easily have her way with him, no matter how 'husky' he was.

Cornelius emerged from the lobby just as Damon was heading back inside. He looked perplexed.

"I was getting worried about you, Neil." He punched him playfully on the arm. "I figured, you know, I needed to step up and guard my bodyguard."

"That's pretty funny," Cornelius replied absently. He picked up his suitcase and easily flipped it into the trunk of the car.

"Uh, you okay, big guy?"

Cornelius looked down at Damon as if he'd somehow materialized beside him. "Joni's nice," he said.

"She has her moments."

"Actually...." Cornelius began to fret with the hem of his dress shirt. "I hope you don't mind, but...I think I'd like to ask her out. On a date."

Damon was truly dumbfounded. Not because he disliked his publicist. He just didn't understand the whole mixed-life angle. "Joni? *My* Joni?"

"She showed me her pancreas," sighed Cornelius.

Damon pictured Joni in her rebirthday suit and nearly gagged. "Neil, please—"

"It was a picture of the pancreas she wants to buy." He sighed again and stared, moony-eyed, at Damon.

Joni could be very charismatic when she wanted to be. It's what made her a good publicist; she came across as everyone's BFF. As earnest and likable as his bodyguard was, Cornelius wasn't Joni's type at all. She tended towards alpha-male reanimates with prominent cheek bones and vacation homes in Aspen. Then again, ever since that last transplant, she did have a big heart. Bigger, at least, than the previous one.

"I hate to ask this," said Damon, and took a deep breath. "Are you sure the feeling is mutual?"

Cornelius looked stricken, as if the thought hadn't even occurred to him. "We've been chatting online for months, Mr. Grayson."

"She didn't even know it was you, though!"

"But I knew it was her. And today, well, she let me hold her hand."

Damon's heart went out to him. Sure, he was smitten, but it wouldn't last; they simply didn't have enough in common. Besides, if zomance novels like *Born on the Wrong Side of the Wall* were to be believed, mixed-life relationships never ended well for their protagonists.

"Well, good for you, Neil." Damon tried to pat him on the shoulder but came up short by a good two feet. He settled for patting Cornelius on the shoulder blade instead. "Just…try not to take things too fast."

Just then, Joni came strolling out to the car. She was all smiles as she tossed Damon his Kevlar vest.

"A lot of people will be out of work if you go and get yourself killed," she said.

Damon was stunned. He'd never seen her look so rejuvenated. He and the driver looked on in amazement as Joni stood on tiptoe and tilted her angular face to meet Cornelius's expectant gaze.

"You have my private number. I know there's no phone service out there so call me when you get back. Promise me, Cornelius."

His eyes widened. "Of course I promise, Eartha."

"Try to keep that other promise, too," she whispered. "You owe it to yourself."

Cornelius glanced nervously at Damon. "I'll try."

Damon and the driver exchanged incredulous looks. "Some bones get all the breaks," said the driver disgustedly.

"Good luck with your new pancreas," said Cornelius as Joni climbed into her Lexus. He seemed to deflate as he watched her speed out of the parking lot. It was another minute before he turned back to Damon.

"Eartha?" asked Damon. "Really?"

"It's her rebirth name."

"I know it is, I just can't believe she told you. She hates that rename."

Cornelius shrugged. "We really connected."

And without another word he began to wedge his massive frame into the back seat of the Town Car. The chassis creaked and moaned as he shifted to and fro in the cabin. Somehow, he was able to fasten his seatbelt, but only just barely. He leaned over and patted the seat beside him.

"Plenty of room," he said.

Damon still had lingering misgivings about the entire endeavor, but it was too late now to turn back. "I guess that makes me Jell-O." He barely had the door closed before the driver put the car into gear.

"Next stop, Boca Muerta," said Cornelius. He took out his camera and snapped a picture of the driver. "The journey begins."

The driver glared at them in the rearview mirror and shook his grey, scaly head. "Tourists," he muttered.

CHAPTER THIRTY-FIVE

Nestled in the Las Almas foothills, the Elysian Fieldhouse was Vista del Muerte's oldest country club. Its membership was reserved for New Hollywood's undead elite. Power players like Robert DeNiro and Meryl Streep were literally dying to gain entry into its exclusive, reanimates-only ranks.

It was no surprise that C.O.D.A.'s president was one of Elysian Fieldhouse's most esteemed members.

Russell was seated in his usual corner booth as he conducted Coalition-related business. At the moment, he was being pitched a remake of *Casablanca*—to be shot with its original stars. Russell merely hummed noncommittally as he took small sips of his Earl Gray.

"I just need you to greenlight Bogart's resurrection," said Mathias Matthews, the studio head of Arrival Media. "Paradox got to resurrect Hepburn, right? So fair's fair, right?"

"Miss Hepburn was an exception."

"You have to be regretting that now, though, right?"

Russell merely bared his teeth in a crusty grin. "The Reanimation Proclamation clearly states–"

Mathias held up his veiny hand before leaning in close. "Which is why

I came to you, Russell. You've got powerful friends. And I need two dead-and-buried movie stars for my picture."

"You're free to submit a reanimation application."

"But that will take months!" Silverware rattled as Mathias pounded the table with his fist. "Listen, Russell, I have it on good authority that Paradox has a three-picture deal with Chaplin—and the little bastard's carcass is still in the fucking *ground*!"

Russell continued to quietly sip his tea. "You have an odd way of groveling," he remarked.

"I shouldn't have to, all right? I play by your rules, Russell. I follow your stinking C of C to the *letter*. That's got to count for something to the great and powerful Russell Mann!"

Hugo, Russell's broad-shouldered bodyguard, approached the booth. "Time's up," he said, stabbing a thick finger at Matthews.

Matthews swatted his large hand away. "No way. I waited seven goddamn months for this face-to-face. I'm not going anywhere until I have my two leads!"

Russell nodded to Hugo, who quickly reached across the table and hoisted Matthews into the air by his arm. "Mr. Mann's time is very valuable—and right now you're wasting it." Russell downed the last of his Earl Gray as Hugo unceremoniously carried Matthews kicking and screaming from the club.

The waiter quickly approached the table with a porcelain tea pot. "Would Mr. Mann like a fresh tea towel as well?" asked the waiter. Russell rose to his feet as the club's newest towel girl, a comely blonde cadaver named Reese, replaced the tea-soaked towel on his chair with a new one.

She smiled at Russell as she worried the soiled towel with her fragile, bird-like hands. "It's an honor to finally meet you," said the former rom-com darling. Soon, like Hepburn before her, little Reese, with her quick eyes and sharp smile, would find herself back on the silver screen. Her time as an Elysian Fieldhouse towel girl was merely the first step in her second career. There were hundreds of unemployed actors—thousands—who would jump at the chance to know C.O.D.A.'s president in such an intimate manner.

"That will be all, Miss Reese," he said.

He turned his attention to the sidewalk outside, where Hugo waved away a throng of undead panhandlers. Normally the entire perimeter of the club was kept free of vagrants, but today seemed to prove the exception. Russell whipped out his Moleskine journal and jotted a quick note about this unfortunate oversight. He tore the page from his notebook and slipped it to the waiter.

"Give this to the manager immediately," he said. "And have my car brought around."

Ten minutes later, as Russell departed the club, he was chagrined to find that not only was his car not waiting for him, but there also seemed to be even more homeless cadavers milling about.

"Utterly disgraceful," he rasped. But before he could head back into the clubhouse he was accosted by a group of persistent undead beggars. From their tattered clothing, to the terrible freezer burned-like condition of their pallid flesh, their very appearance was an affront to Russell's refined tastes. He covered his face and swatted blindly with his briefcase at the accompanying black cloud of flies. But the panhandlers, all of them unemployed actors, were desperate for work. That the coalition's strict Code of Conduct had made it increasingly more difficult for the undead to find legitimate work in the absence of exploitation movies was of little consequence to Russell.

"Neeeed aaaaa jooooooooob, Missssssterrrr Maaannnnn.....!" they moaned.

"Anything, even jusssst a two-liiiine paaaarrrrrt......" they groaned.

"Willl wooorkkk for scaaaaallle.....!" they intoned.

Mann yelled for Hugo as the fly-ridden mob closed in around him. "Fight them off!" he yelled.

Brittle bones snapped like dry kindling as Hugo reluctantly began battling back the homeless cadavers. But he, too, was quickly overwhelmed as the cadavers redoubled their efforts. Their crusty talons found purchase in Hugo's fleshy arms and face. Blinded by pain, he lashed out at the mob, rending rotted limbs with reckless abandon. Russell, meanwhile, had fallen back out of the fray. He took a moment to smooth down his stiff hair and adjust his torn suit jacket. The garment could be repaired easily enough; not so the newly torn flesh of his forearm. He made a futile attempt to piece together the ripped skin with just his fingers. Russell Mann may have been undead, but he was no zombie; he resolved to have the damage repaired that afternoon.

Meanwhile, the vagrants' offensive continued, despite Hugo's best efforts to contain it. Russell respected brute force, but he understood that sometimes a sharp tongue was the mightiest weapon. He brought his finest vitriol to bear on the mewling horde.

"Just look at the lot of you," he seethed. "When was the last time any of you saw the inside of a witch doctor's office? When was the last time you took any pride in your appearance?" Many of the vagrants fell silent even as many more arrived on the scene, hell-bent for leather as they beseeched Russell for gainful employment. He took them all in with a sweeping wave of his cold, grey hand.

"You represent all that is wrong with the undead," cried Russell. "Your sorry existence, eked out in the gutters, sucking down Noodle, is why we struggle for equality in the world of the living!"

Hugo stood panting beside Russell, an unlucky vagrant's arm clutched in his meaty hands. He wielded it like a club to keep the more tenacious beggars at bay.

"If you would like to discuss employment options with Mr. Mann you must go through the proper channels," yelled Hugo above the din.

Just as Russell sized up the ragged crowd he noticed with a bit of alarm that a minion was coolly observing them from across the boulevard. Russell knew that Solomon saw what his minions saw—which meant he had witnessed the sidewalk altercation in its incriminating entirety.

Time stopped for Russell as the minion slowly shook its hollow, scrimshawed skull in his direction.

"I am not the one who should be judged!" shouted Russell. Hugo looked from Russell to the minion across the street—and immediately stood down from his defense of the coalition president.

"Mr. Mann—I don't think you should be—"

An overwhelming panic wrapped itself around Russell. The more he struggled against it, the more he found himself bound by its crushing embrace.

"Do not dare to tell me what to think!"

Traffic in both directions screeched to a halt as the minion began its slow, clattering march across the boulevard. The cadavers fled at the sight of their skeletal protector, leaving behind rent limbs and hunks of sloughed-off viscera. Russell, though, stubbornly stood his ground as the minion towered over him.

"I run this town," hissed Russell.

"Mr. Mann, I—I can't take this guy. He'll rip both of us apart."

Russell experienced an odd moment of calm as he stared up into the minion's impassive, implacable face. He couldn't help but marvel at the intricate, crimson-stained patterns etched into the paper-white skull.

"Beneath this rotten flesh, we are made of the same stuff, the same marrow, you and I," he whispered. "We are brothers."

The minion was incapable of speech. It merely regarded Russell with its vacant eye sockets, consumed his courage, devoured it with a simple tilt of its great skull.

"I—I was simply defending our honor," Russell said to the minion, but he was really addressing Solomon. "Mustn't we be judged by our greatest accomplishments, rather than our occasional failures?"

"Mr. Mann," warned Hugo as a dark grey Bentley with Havens plates pulled up to the curb. "You really need to stop talking, like, right now."

"Your concern is noted," said Russell quietly.

"But that—that's you-know-who's car!"

"Indeed it is, Hugo."

The minion's enchanted vertebrae creaked as it raised a slender, spike-studded arm. It silently pointed to one of the many phrases inscribed in its bones. First he tapped the words *HEARD YOU*. Then he tapped a second, cryptic phrase: *ALWAYS WATCHING*. The minion lowered its arm and slowly beckoned for Russell to get into the empty sedan. At least Solomon had respected him enough not to send one of his black cargo vans. If this was to be a one-way trip, why not do it with some *savoir faire*?

"Mr. Mann," said Hugo, "What...what should I do?"

Russell knew, once Solomon's Scrimshaw Collective came calling, escape was no longer an option. He once again stared deeply into the skull's empty eye sockets before turning to his hapless bodyguard.

"You do nothing, Hugo," he said. "You do...nothing."

CHAPTER THIRTY-SIX

Damon Grayson was growing restless. Their car hadn't made any progress since leaving the motel two hours earlier. Indeed, the Town Car was mired in the usual mid-morning gridlock that plagued the Valley. Damon didn't enjoy being idle. It gave him too much time to ponder what he was heading into.

If not for their driver, Damon might have confided in Cornelius about his many, many reservations—about venturing into the Havens, and especially about himself. But just to look at Cornelius, it was obvious he was on an entirely different, blissful plane. His bodyguard's dopey expression said it all: he was in love. Damon still had his doubts about Joni's intentions. He quickly pecked out a text message to her on his phone.

Are you 2 for real? he wrote, and hit the send button.

Damon's phone buzzed almost immediately with her reply. *He gets me u big jerk*, read Joni's text. *U better not mess this up 4 me.*

The driver locked the car doors as they neared Two-Timers Town. He honked the horn impatiently as a homeless reanimate in a Havens Militia jacket shambled in and out of the crawling traffic. Cornelius winced as the beggar ripped of his middle finger and hurled it at their car. It broke apart like a clod of dirt against the windshield.

"Get a job," the driver muttered.

Damon peered out the window as they continued to inch along. The undead driver in the car beside them was applying liberal amounts of White Away to her pallid features. In another car, Damon saw a rather decrepit reanimate trying desperately to attach a floppy pair of vinyl lips to what was left of his mouth. The driver was so focused on the task that he rear-ended the SUV in front of him.

They turned onto Romero Boulevard and the sheer stone face of Burly Gate rose up before them through the mid-morning haze. Cornelius rolled down his window and began snapping pictures.

"Hey," barked the driver. "Shut the window before someone steals that camera!"

Chastened, Cornelius reluctantly complied. The landscape became increasingly bleak and desolate as they neared the border. Abandoned brownstones gave way to dilapidated factories and weed-choked lots. Damon had never been this far west before, but he'd heard plenty of stories of roving bands of undead gangs. He knew, too, that many of the vacant factories teemed with undead squatters.

Cornelius shook his head at the unrelenting blight. "This must be paradise, compared to Charnel Point," he said.

"Charnel Point's a rough place," confirmed the driver. "You couldn't pay me to ever go back there."

"That's mighty encouraging," Damon muttered.

The driver grinned at Damon's obvious discomfort. "It's especially tough for the living. No matter how big or how rich you are on this side of the wall means nothing on the other side. To the undead, you're nothing more than fresh meat."

"Good thing we're staying at Kadabra Estates," Damon said.

Cornelius frowned. "The Havens can't really be so bad, Mr. Grayson. You'll see."

"What now," the driver said as the car slowed to a crawl. A crowd of wide-eyed reanimates stood by the side of the road, chanting and waving signs that read BRING BURLY DOWN!

"That wall is going nowhere fast," said the driver. "What makes these hippies think they can make a difference?"

"Burly's in pretty bad shape," Cornelius said. "Engineers say another quake could bring the whole thing down."

Damon smiled to himself. What the protestors, politicians and Mother Nature could not accomplish, many a New Hollywood blockbuster had wrought on the silver screen. Damon himself had starred in one such disaster movie, *Bury My Ashes at Burly Gate*. Despite the pro-war sentiment, undead audiences cheered every time the wall fell. But that jubilation was nowhere to be found in this demonstration.

A young woman—she must have only been in her early twenties before her rebirth—stepped up to the car and smacked Damon's tinted window with her open palm. Damon jumped as if she'd smacked him directly. He hoped Cornelius hadn't seen him flinch.

"This wall must fall," she cried through the glass. "Burly bricks make you sick!"

"What the heck is she talking about?" asked Damon.

"I just watched a really interesting documentary about the wall," said Cornelius.

"Of course you did," said Damon.

"Scientists think that the wall's granite slabs emit dangerous levels of radon. They think the radon is responsible for health issues in border towns on both sides of the wall."

"Health issues," echoed Damon. "Yeah? Like what?"

"Cancer in the living, severe decomp in the undead." Cornelius shook his head. "It's really sad."

"Man, talk about propaganda. People will say *anything* to bring this wall down."

"They shouldn't have to," Cornelius said quietly.

"It's not like there aren't other walls like Burly in the world, Neil. I mean, seriously, China's wall can be seen from *space*."

"Yes," said Cornelius. "But in China the living and the undead coexist peacefully. It took centuries, but it does prove such a thing is possible, Mr. Grayson."

"I suppose."

Damon glanced out the window and realized they were nearing the border crossing. The razor-wire fence atop Burly Gate glinted like diamonds in the hazy sunlight. Somehow, some enterprising vandals had found a way to spray-paint graffiti along the top of the wall:

GO WEST, YOUNG CORPSE!
CHARM SCHOOL DROPOUT
JESUS IS MY CO-SHAMAN
BETTER DEAD THAN UNDEAD!

The Town Car slowly turned onto a ten-lane road and merged with a long convoy of tour buses and taxis. The roadway was flanked by two massive structures just inside of the wall. On the south side of the road was Fort Burly, an imposing stone and steel structure. On the north side of the roadway was the massive terminal where thousands of travelers crossed the border on foot.

Opportunistic entrepreneurs wandered between the lanes of traffic, hawking items like bottled water, Fly-B-Gon spray, and KadabraLand maps. Signs and billboards, promoting everything from four-star dining at Kadabra Estates to low-end reanimate remedies, peppered the roadside. One billboard in particular, however, caught Damon's eye. It was an advertisement for his film, *Open Wounds 2,* which was newly released on video. As they passed under the billboard Damon noticed a vandal had spray-painted ZOMBIE LOVER on his forehead.

"That's not very nice," said Cornelius. Even so, he slyly snapped a picture of the billboard as the car inched below it.

Just then a military truck honked as it lumbered past the Town Car. A

Zombie Defense corpsman seated in the back of the truck stared at them dispassionately. The truck veered off towards Fort Burly. The military base, with its modified Z198 155mm Howitzers and HAMR towers, stood in stark contrast to the tourist-friendly terminal, with banks of LED signs maniacally proclaiming SHOPPING! EATING! EXTRA PARKING!

"'Bring 'em back alive,'" Damon read from a recruitment billboard posted outside the fort. *Works for me*, he thought grimly.

The driver sighed as the traffic moved at a snail's pace. "This is worse than usual," he muttered.

"You can't be too careful," said Cornelius. As a well-trained protection specialist, he was ever mindful of safety concerns. He knew that border security had been tightened after a recent bombing attempt. He wasn't surprised to see zedheads wielding modified metal detectors scanning vehicles and their occupants not only for contraband talismans but explosives, too.

The driver began nosing the front bumper into the next lane. The terminal's drop-off point was only a few hundred feet away. It may as well have been a few hundred miles. The Town Car made small, lurching gains that left it straddling two lanes.

"We're going to be here for a few hours," the driver said over his shoulder. "I'm supposed to bring you to Departures, but you'll get there way faster if you get out here."

Damon wasn't in any hurry to cross the border but the thought of being cooped up in the car for even five more minutes made his head spin. The sooner they checked into Kadabra Estates the better, as far as he was concerned.

"What the hell. Let's go for it," he said. "Maybe I can squeeze in some last-minute shopping along the way."

"I think we're safer if we stay in the car for now," Cornelius said.

The driver didn't wait for Damon's reply. He threw his door open and scrambled from the front seat. Damon gagged as a strong westerly breeze filled the car with a caustic, throat-searing mustiness.

"What the hell is that *smell?*" he asked. He pulled the collar of his shirt up over his nose.

"That would be Charnel Point," said the driver with a wicked smile. "I hope no one has mold allergies."

"But those slums are nowhere near here," said Damon.

"Mr. Grayson," admonished Cornelius. "You shouldn't call them slums."

"They sure aren't," the driver said happily. The favelas were located high up in the mold-covered San Lazarus Mountains, which were almost fifty miles to the north. "Must be low tide."

"All right, you guys got me," said Damon with a good-natured laugh as he searched the backseat for hidden cameras. "Good one."

"We should go," Cornelius said uneasily. Standing in the middle of traffic was not the best idea. "Viktor is probably already at the hotel."

A deep despair welled up within Damon. The whole endeavor was a mistake; he could feel it in his bones. "I don't care, I'm not going."

Cornelius slowly untangled himself from the backseat. "We can't turn back now."

This was no jaunt. They were heading straight into bona fide zombie country. The undead would literally tear apart a necrophobe like him. How had he allowed himself to be talked into such a stupid idea?

"The hell we can't," said Damon. "Do me a favor, send my regards to Kenny Kadaver."

Cornelius heaved a mighty sigh. "This is for your own good," he said. "Please don't take this personally." He glanced around for possible 'bloiders. It was hard to tell, but it seemed like no one was watching. He quickly reached down under the chassis and tilted the Town Car onto its side.

"What the hell—" blurted Damon as he slid across the slippery leather upholstery. He managed to land on his feet as he tumbled onto the pavement.

Cornelius quickly reached down to pull him up but Damon swatted his large hand away. "I don't need your help. You and Joni and everyone else can go screw themselves. I'm done."

Cornelius cracked his knuckles as he rose to his full height. "I'll carry you across the border if I have to."

"The hell you will," said Damon, backing away. "You work for me, remember?"

"Actually, I've been off the clock since last week."

Damon gaped at him, incredulous. "I don't understand. Why would you do that?"

Cornelius shrugged. "I like you."

The driver's sunken eyes rasped like Velcro as they rolled in their sockets. "Oh, for the love of Lazarus." He heaved Damon's bag onto the road.

He disappeared up to his waist in the trunk of the car to retrieve Cornelius's suitcase. Suddenly, there was a loud, dry crunch and the driver toppled backwards onto the sidewalk. His hands, however, were still locked like talons around the suitcase handle.

"Need a hand?" asked Damon, and reached down to assist the driver.

"Not from you, blood bank," he said, and waved him away with a rotten stump.

Cornelius apologized profusely as he lifted the driver to his feet. "Please," he said, "let me pay to have them reattached. Or buy you new ones. Better ones. It's the least I could do."

Damon swore under his breath as the honking continued all around them. To make matters worse, a crowd was quickly forming on the side of the roadway. He scrutinized the onlookers' curious faces for 'bloiders. People in the crowd raised their camera phones as if making a toast. Damon instinctively averted his face.

"Neil," he said testily. "Time to amscray."

"But how is he going to drive without hands?" Cornelius asked.

The driver hopped into the front seat. "I may be living-challenged but I'm not brain dead!"

Cornelius stepped back as the Town Car lunged from the curb and promptly rear-ended an idling charter bus. The crowd turned its attention from a figurative car wreck to gawk at a literal one. In the blink of a milky eye, Damon had become yesterday's news. He quickly grabbed his bag and began to hotfoot it between the lanes of stalled traffic.

It wasn't until Damon was inside the terminal that he realized Cornelius wasn't right behind him. There was no way he was going back out there— the 'bloids would surely blame him for the fender-bender.

He swore under his breath and kept moving

Cornelius, meanwhile, was completely out of sorts. Luggage in hand, he glanced back at the Town Car. Not only had the collision snapped the driver's neck, it had dislodged one of his yellow eyes and sent it rolling down the congested roadway. Cornelius chased it down between the stalled lanes of traffic, barking in triumph as he snatched the eyeball from the ground.

"Found it," he yelled, bearing the eye aloft like a giddy gold miner. He quickly handed it back to the driver, who merely grunted his thanks. It was only then that Cornelius realized Damon had left his line of vision.

He ignored the muted cheers of onlookers as he quickly weaved his way through the lanes of traffic. "It's okay," Cornelius whispered. "He couldn't have gotten very far."

As Cornelius neared the terminal entrance a pair of smiling, grey-skinned reborn-agains approached him. They both wore identical chalk-white robes tied back with crude hemp belts. The shorter of the two men sported a round lapel pin that read *WWLD?* He threw open his bony arms to greet Cornelius.

"Brother," he said, "have you found St. Lazarus yet?"

"I'm not your brother," Cornelius said testily as he scanned the crowd.

The shorter reborn-again's crooked, yellow smile did not waver. "But death is only the beginning."

His companion, lanky and mostly fleshless beneath his long robes, wore a lapel pin that read *GOD IS UNDEAD*. He sized up Cornelius and tried a different approach.

"Perhaps we can interest you in some death insurance? Second Living Liability policies offer generous coverage in the event of accidental dismemberment."

Cornelius checked his phone. The interference caused by Burly's powerful HAMR towers disrupted cell phone service for miles around. There was no way for him to call Damon.

"You're talking to the wrong person," Cornelius said uneasily.

"We also cover lost or stolen talismans."

"Excuse me, please," Cornelius said and resumed walking. "I really need to find my friend."

"Have a nice life," the shorter one said earnestly.

"No one lives forever," the lanky one called after Cornelius as he ducked inside. "Not even the undead!"

Cornelius was immediately overwhelmed by the sheer size of the complex. It was easy to believe how the Boca Muerta border crossing processed over 100,000 travelers a day. Its proximity to KadabraLand and New Hollywood made it a popular hub with tourists from all over the world. It also made it an attractive target for Neo-Lifers and radical Resurrectionists. Cornelius knew that if he had any hope of finding Damon he had to act quickly.

He was distracted by a commotion in a nearby Frankenjoe's. A security guard was hauling a homeless reanimate out of the trendy coffee house by his collar.

"This is racial profiling," cried the beggar as he thrashed his pale, spindly limbs. "I ain't no terrorist! I used to be Isaac Newton!"

"Right, sure you were," said the guard. "And I used to be Betty Boop. Keep it moving, pal, before I get the ZDC over here. These nice people want to enjoy their lattes in peace."

"You're all fascists," declared the beggar. "Every last one of you!" A small glassine bag fell from his wretched clothes as he squirmed free of the guard's grasp. Grey, ash-like powder spilled across the tops of his sandals.

"This just keeps getting better," said the guard. "I assume you know Noodle possession is a felony in the state of New California."

"Narc!" yelled the beggar.

The Frankenjoe's patrons looked on with bored indifference as the beggar turned and fled. Cornelius was about to intervene when the guard brought the beggar down with a HAMR blast. The guard scooped up the talisman and stowed it in his pocket.

"All right, come with me, Einstein."

The beggar curled into a ball and clutched his head. Without his talisman, there was nothing to stop his rampant decomposition. His eyes bulged in their sockets as his skin shrink-wrapped his skull.

Cornelius set his suitcase down with a heavy thud. The security guard turned to him and smiled. "Best part of the job," he said.

"He needs his talisman," said Cornelius. "He won't last without it."

The guard chuckled. "Sure he will. He's so high on Noodle it would take days for the decomp to kill him."

Harried travelers stepped around the beggar without a second glance. "But he's suffering."

"And you're trying my patience," snapped the guard. "I don't care how big you are. I suggest you mind your own business, friend."

"It—it hurts," gasped the beggar. "My skin huh-hurts!" He started to claw at the rapidly decaying flesh on his arms.

"That talisman is government property," said Cornelius. "You have no right to withhold it from this man."

"I warned you," snarled the guard. Cornelius didn't flinch as the guard landed a solid punch to his jaw.

"And I'm warning *you*," growled Cornelius. "If you do that again, I may have to hurt you."

The guard responded with a right hook that Cornelius easily stopped with his massive hand. He considered how the guard's fist seemed no bigger than a tennis ball against the expanse of his own palm. He narrowed his eyes at the sight of the Neo-Life tattoo—a heart consumed by flames—on the man's wrist.

"Wait, wait a second," pleaded the guard as his hand was swallowed up within Cornelius's grasp. "I'm just doing my job."

"That depends on who you're working for," said Cornelius. The guard howled in pain as Cornelius tightened his grip infinitesimally. "The talisman, please."

"Hey, way to stick it to that rent-a-cop," jeered a long-haired reanimate in a tie-dyed Grateful Undead tour shirt.

"Mind your fucking business, rent-a-life!" yelled the guard. He reached for his HAMR.

Cornelius didn't bat an eyelash as he snapped the guard's wrist like a stale breadstick. The HAMR clattered to the floor. Cornelius gingerly nudged the gun away with the edge of his foot. He knew it was only a matter of time before their difference of opinion escalated into something worse.

"The talisman," he said again, ignoring the horrified stares of onlookers. "Please."

"Yeah, bring Burly down, man," shouted the deadhead. "Reanimates live!"

The color had drained from the security guard's face. He thrust his free hand deep into his pocket and withdrew a handful of talismans. He tossed them at the beggar like so much loose change.

Cornelius relinquished his grip and the guard immediately fell to his knees. "I'm sorry I had to do that to you," he said.

The deadhead's stringy locks fell into his wan face as he nodded vigorously. "Dude, that was so awesome. Can I get your autograph or something?"

Cornelius knelt down and began pawing through the discarded talismans. He had no idea which one belonged to the beggar. "What's your rebirthday," he asked.

The beggar sat up, wild-eyed, and pushed Cornelius away. "Don't touch those, don't!"

"But—"

"Kill you," he hissed. "I'll eat your heart!"

The security guard's laughter was almost a cackle. "Do it," he gasped as his eyes welled with tears. "Come on, Einstein!"

One of the Frankenjoe's patrons looked up from his laptop and spoke to

Cornelius. "You should get out of here before the real cops show up."

"Don't worry," said his wannazee friend as he sipped an iced coffee. "I was live-blogging the whole thing. I'll totally cover for you."

Cornelius didn't need to be told twice. He grabbed his suitcase and quickly disappeared into the bustling crowd.

Damon was halfway across the large terminal before it occurred to him that finding Cornelius wasn't going to be as easy as he thought. He scanned the crowded terminal but there were simply too many people. And some of them were beginning to stare. One person in particular, an elderly member of an Asian tour group, pointed Damon out to her companions. A chorus of oohs and ahhs was followed by a blinding onslaught of camera flashes.

Damon pulled the brim of his Cads hat over his eyes and quickly detoured into a nearby gift shop. He ignored the shelves of cheap New Hollywood souvenirs and ducked behind a rack of spy novels. He peered out from between two adjacent jargon-laden thrillers and watched the tour group pause every few seconds to snap pictures of whatever crossed their path.

I've seen glaciers move faster than this bunch, he thought.

Just then two men paused outside the gift shop. One wore a ZDC puce-and-grey necroflage jacket, the other a grease-stained denim vest. Stubble and grit covered their faces to varying degrees. Both men were lean, as if they hadn't eaten a decent meal in weeks. They couldn't have been more conspicuous if they'd tried.

"You sure he went this way?" asked the man in the army jacket. He sounded more desperate than he looked. "How do you know it was even him? This place is crawling with fucking celebrities."

"My buddy down at Paradox knows what he's talking about. I'm telling you, that was Grayson. Just trust me, okay? That reward money is as good as ours."

Reward money? thought Damon. How much was his life worth to these people?

The man in the denim vest scrutinized the faces swirling around them.

As he turned back to his partner Damon noticed the burning heart tattoo on the back of his neck. Suddenly 'bloiders didn't seem so bad.

Great, thought Damon. *Neo-Lifers. This keeps getting better and better.*

He tried his cell phone again with no success. Just as he was trying to formulate a plan a little girl wandered behind the book display. She held a resin reproduction of Burly Gate in one hand, and a grape lollipop in the other. She was equally captivated by both—until she noticed Damon.

"Are you playing hide and seek?" she asked.

Damon was never crazy about kids—as costars or otherwise. And this girl in the oversized Froots 'n' Veggiez shirt was definitely not an exception. He couldn't hope to guess at her age—she could have been three or eight—he had no idea.

"You could say that," whispered Damon after a pause.

She grew bored of the Burly Gate replica and handed it to Damon.

"Gross. Why is this so sticky?"

"You live in my TV," she said matter-of-factly.

By now a few customers were staring their way. He peeked through the paperbacks. The two Neo-Lifers were still standing outside the gift shop.

"I'm just really screwed if I don't get this money," insisted the man in the army jacket. Damon wondered if the man was ex-ZDC. If so, he'd have to take out the man in the denim vest first. It wasn't much of a plan, but it was a start. In truth, he hoped he could just out-wait them both.

"Listen," said the man in the denim vest, "once we pull this off, you'll have enough dough for a whole new house and then some, okay? So quit fucking worrying."

An employee came from behind the register and approached Damon. He saw her face brighten the instant she recognized him. He quickly put a finger to his lips. She nodded enthusiastically and gave him a silent thumbs-up as she tiptoed back to the register.

"My dad says you're good at catching phrases," said the little girl.

Damon stared blankly at her. "What?"

She stamped her foot and folded her arms. "I *said*, my dad says you're good at catching *phrases*."

Damon ducked down as the man in the denim vest glanced their way. He started into the gift shop but his friend tugged him back by the sleeve. "Give me your phone," he said gruffly. "I can't get a fucking signal to save my life."

"Who you calling, huh? I told you, I don't want to split this five ways. Got it?"

The man in the army jacket didn't look convinced. "Better five ways than no ways, Frank."

The man in the denim vest checked his watch and swore. "We already wasted enough time. Let's go."

"Okay, okay. But maybe we should check some of these shops for Grayson. You never know—we could get lucky."

"Fine, make it quick. I'll check some of the shops on the other side. We can still get him at the gate if we really have to."

"You should probably get out of here," Damon whispered to the little girl. "You might get hurt."

She responded by picking her nose, zealously.

W.C. Fields knew what the heck he was talking about, Damon thought ruefully. *I'll have to let the ol' corpse know next time I see him. If I see him.*

The man in the army jacket wandered around near the front. He fingered a few sweatshirts on the rack and lifted a hat or two off the shelf. Each time he checked the price tag he reacted as if stung.

"Seriously," Damon whispered to the girl. "Time for you to take the show on the road." But the unabashed nasal exploratory continued unabated.

The man in the army jacket proceeded to wander down the aisle towards them. He paused every few seconds to paw over the worthless, touristy bric-a-brac. As he leaned over a display of Kenny Kadaver keychains, Damon noticed the butt of a handgun sticking out of his waistband. He was now only ten feet away and closing in. Damon reached for a Cemetery

Stadium paperweight and hefted it in his hand. Anything could be used as a weapon. Anything. Even touristy bric-a-brac.

Six feet now. His friend in the denim vest returned and entered the shop. All that stood between them was a flimsy wooden rack and some pocket-sized bricks of bound paper.

Four feet. The man was close enough that Damon smelled the cigarette smoke and fried food in his grungy clothing. Damon knew by the sudden change in the girl's expression that she smelled it, too—even with a finger jammed up one side of her nose.

Two feet. All the man had to do was turn his head several degrees to the left and it would all be over. Damon gripped the paperweight so hard his knuckles were bone white.

And then Damon's heart stopped as the girl stepped from behind the display. She didn't bother to remove the finger from her nose as she addressed Damon's would-be assassin.

"Ew," she said. "You smell like my Grandma Gussie."

His face darkened at the sound of her voice. He whirled on her angrily, but stopped dead in his tracks when he saw what she was doing.

"Jesus Christ, kid, that's disgusting."

The girl took a step towards him and stamped her foot. "You said a swear."

"You better watch your mouth, kid."

The man in the denim vest grabbed his friend by the arm. "What the hell are you doing back here? You're fighting with a fucking kid? Come on, we gotta jet."

The girl grunted and stamped her foot again. The two men left without looking back. Damon was so flabbergasted that he didn't know what to do. He looked down at the paperweight and sighed with relief. He turned it over in his hand and noticed a gold sticker on the felt bottom that read *Made in the Havens*. He gratefully dusted it off and returned it to its empty spot on the shelf.

"Thank you very, very much," he said to the girl. "If you ever need a job as a bodyguard, let me know."

She nodded with wide-eyed sincerity. "Okay, I will."

At that moment, in her child-like innocence, she reminded him very much of Cornelius. Damon laughed at the thought of this, and felt glad that Cornelius was part of his modest entourage, such as it was.

On the way out of the store Damon paused to sign an autograph for the cashier. He also plucked a hundred-dollar bill from his wallet and slid it across the counter.

"Whatever that little nose-picker in the Froots 'n' Veggiez shirt wants, it's on me."

He turned to leave but paused as he was struck by inspiration. Damon went over to the clothing racks and began assembling an off-the-rack ensemble. *Camouflage is more like it*, he thought. He returned to the register after a few minutes, his arms loaded up with the tackiest clothes he could find.

"Will you need a gift receipt?" asked the perplexed cashier.

"Nope. These are all keepers."

Damon saw no sign of either man as he left the store. He didn't see Cornelius, either. Which meant Damon was on his own for the time being. He entertained the notion of simply exiting the terminal and not looking back. But if he did something so cowardly, so selfish, how could he ever look anyone in the eye again? He'd be laughed out of New Hollywood for sure.

If he were stripped of his career, Damon Grayson would be stripped of the comfort and security he so desperately relied on. So, new clothing in hand, he headed to the nearest restroom. If he didn't want to live like the common man, he could at least dress like one to save his skin.

CHAPTER THIRTY-SEVEN

Meanwhile, on the north side of the busy terminal, Viktor Vincent and Buddy had already fallen into a very long line for the checkpoint. Like Damon and Cornelius, the pair opted to cross the border on foot. A small HD video camera in hand, Viktor catalogued random faces of the living and the dead alike as they swarmed through the terminal. From chatty missionaries to wide-eyed Second Lives acolytes to slack-jawed grey-collar workers, every traveler was a story waiting to be told.

Viktor finally trained the camera on Buddy, whose cold, grey face was buried in the pages of his notebook. "I really feel like we forgot something," Buddy said as he ran down his checklist for the umpteenth time. He pulled out their itinerary and quickly frowned through his thick glasses. "We were supposed to be in Cadabra City by now."

Viktor patted his undead assistant on the shoulder. "You'll enjoy yourself more if you put that notebook away."

"We've already been on this line for half an hour," Buddy fretted. As the line inched forward they reached a posted sign that read, YOUR WAIT TIME: 1 HOUR. Viktor slow-panned from his assistant's worried face to the sign before putting the camera away. Seeing him without a viewfinder between them, the director finally understood what weighed so heavily on his undead friend's mind.

"You have just as much right to the Havens as the next cadaver," said Viktor. "Try to think of this as a homecoming."

Buddy pushed his glasses up what was left of his nose. "I suppose I'm having a bit of an identity crisis." he said with a nervous laugh. He'd worked so hard to lose his Havens accent—and now he was going to sound like just another tourist. The guilt this caused only confused him more. But he didn't expect Viktor to understand. Despite the director's obvious empathy, Buddy's dilemma was uniquely an undead one.

"I expect we'll both learn something about ourselves on this trip—and we have Damon to thank for that."

It was one thing to work with the living, thought Buddy. But what did it say about him to be associated with a notorious necrophobe like Damon? To Buddy, this was not a simple matter of loyalty—it was about integrity. And at that very moment, as Buddy waited in line to visit his homeland, he wrestled with the reality of Viktor's observation: were it not for Damon's many gaffes, would Buddy have found the courage to make such an important trip on his own? Did it even matter? He turned to Viktor, who had an expectant look on his plump face.

"I'll thank him when I see him," said Buddy. *If I see him.*

Though neither one would admit it, both men had their doubts that Damon would honor his part of the deal. It was up to Joni and Barry now, as far as Buddy was concerned. He'd given up on the troubled actor after he'd failed his S-certs.

The line inched forward again. Buddy stood on tiptoe to get a better look at the checkpoint. He noticed a small group of well-kept reanimates easily pass through customs on the Havens side. Buddy, with his bad teeth and exposed nasal cavity, suddenly felt very self-conscious as the surprisingly photogenic cadavers sauntered past, their designer luggage in tow. He quickly lowered his head and wished to be anywhere else in the world. That they snickered at his own garish appearance had to be a trick of his imagination. But Viktor's sympathetic, well-intentioned smile told Buddy all he needed to know.

"They're not fit enough to carry your casket," said Viktor.

Buddy couldn't help but smile at the corniness of such an outdated undead sentiment. "If you say so, sir."

"I know so." He grabbed Buddy's suitcase as the line inched forward. "Allow me, old friend."

For once, Buddy didn't feel quite so alone, or quite so unworthy of the relife he'd created for himself. *It's good to be dead,* he thought. *Quite good.* But when Viktor was spotted by prowling news crews, he quickly set Buddy's suitcase down.

"It was only a matter of time," sighed the director.

Yes, Buddy knew Damon's publicist had tipped off several 'bloids that Viktor would be at Boca Muerta. Still, he had held out hope that he could have left this world for the next before the 'bloiders ever tracked him down.

Viktor quickly became the center of attention as lights and boom mics were thrust in his direction. He had no trouble producing a camera-ready smile as his face was broadcast onto countless TVs, computer screens, and smart phones around the world.

As for Buddy—once again the slight, wall-eyed corpse in the Calabasas Cadavers jersey was all but invisible to the world. It was as if he didn't exist. As if he had never been reborn at all.

CHAPTER THIRTY-EIGHT

When Damon finally emerged from the Mickey Z's restroom he was clad in the latest *tourist chic*: a baggy yellow KadabraLand sweatshirt with a lime green pair of official Calabasas Cadavers sweatpants. The outfit was topped off with a faux-distressed *Property of the ZDC* mesh trucker hat.

He'd also purchased a Crazy-Sized Mediocre Meal at Mickey Z's after his costume change. Damon was happy to blend in with the crowd as he sauntered through the terminal munching on french fries. He adjusted his pair of ten-dollar sunglasses as he walked past several 'bloiders. Then he spotted Cornelius. The look of concern on his bodyguard's face as he scanned the crowd gave Damon pause. The big guy seemed truly worried about him in a way that Barbarelli or Joni never could be. Damon needed these people in his life, yes—but Cornelius needed him, too. Humbled, Damon strode over to him. Cornelius, though, was distracted by his cell phone. He brought it to his ear before frowning down at the small screen.

"Fancy meeting *you* here," Damon said, and coquettishly fiddled with the Kenny Kadaver misting fan around his neck.

Cornelius slowly lowered his phone and turned to Damon, wide-eyed. "Thank goodness you're all right. But what happened to your clothes?"

"Camouflage."

Cornelius smiled. "Well, you certainly fooled *me*, Mr. Grayson."

"Have a french fry, please, before I eat the whole bag. My trainer's gonna kill me."

Cornelius made a face. "I'd really rather not, if that's okay."

Damon gestured with a soggy french fry towards the checkpoint. "Let's get this over with, right?"

The long approach to the gate was lined on both sides by ten-foot signs. ATTENTION CITIZENS, YOU ARE NOW LEAVING LIVING STATES SOIL AT YOUR OWN RISK, stated one. THE L.S. GOVT IS NO LONGER RESPONSIBLE FOR YOUR WELFARE BEYOND THIS POINT, stated another. Cornelius paused and dutifully snapped photographs of both signs.

"Wait, what about that one," said Damon, pointing to another sign that read, ALL DYBORG LIMBS MUST BE DECLARED. ANY UNREGISTERED DYBORG LIMBS WILL BE CONFISCATED—NO EXCEPTIONS.

Cornelius wrinkled his nose. "That's distasteful," he said.

"Sure," said Damon, but it's kind of funny, too. We live in a very strange world, Neil."

"Too strange." Cornelius glanced over his shoulder as they fell into line.

The queue inched its way forward until finally they were next. The customs agent didn't look twice at Damon until he noticed the name on the passport.

"Holy smokes, you're him," said the agent. "You're that guy!"

Damon ducked his head and hoped that no one was looking their way. "That guy, yeah," he responded with a nervous chuckle.

The agent glanced excitedly from the passport to Damon. "I mean, the way you're dressed—I didn't even recognize you!"

"Yeah, that's kind of the point," he whispered. "I'm traveling incognito."

"I have that same exact pair of sweatpants at home!"

"Imagine that," Damon replied nervously. "Well, I don't want to hold up all these nice people waiting behind me."

"It would really make my day if you said it."

Damon tried to hide his impatience. "Say what?"

"You know," the agent said with an expectant grin. "That one line—from *Bury My Ashes at Burly Gate*. It's one of my all-time favorite movies."

Damon cleared his throat as people turned to stare. "Well, ah, it's always nice to meet a fan," he said flatly.

"I must have watched it at least a hundred times," said the customs agent. "I know *every* line by heart."

Damon was finally won over by the agent's enthusiasm. A little bona fide adulation was gratifying after being worked over by the 'bloids for so long. "I bet I know which line is your favorite."

Damon squared his shoulders and easily assumed the role of a military man whose troops were desperately low on morale and even lower on ammunition. The line was from a pivotal moment in the movie—when the undead forces were minutes from breaching the wall.

"Don't fire until you see the whites of their bones," growled Damon as he clutched the Kenny Kadaver misting fan in his trembling fist.

"You have a good day," the agent said with a bright smile as he handed Damon his passport. "Stay safe." The agent's smile quickly faded, however, as he sized up Cornelius.

"Aren't *you* a husky one." It wasn't so much a rhetorical question as it was an accusation. "You probably eat people like me for breakfast."

Cornelius tried to sound pleasant. "I'm on a very restrictive diet."

"How do you sleep at night?" snapped the agent.

Cornelius shifted uncomfortably. "Well, to be honest, I never gave it much thought."

Damon hitched up his sweatpants and doubled back to see what was delaying Cornelius. He gave the agent a friendly pat on the shoulder.

"Is there a problem?" he asked.

"This doesn't concern you, sir," the agent said crossly. "Please, move along."

"Yeah, well, the big guy's with me. He's my bodyguard."

"Actually, technically speaking, I'm a talent protection specialist," said Cornelius.

"Right. Let's see what's in your suitcase. It looks mighty heavy."

Damon shook his head as Cornelius opened his luggage. Inside the suitcase were several days' worth of clothes, plus close to two-dozen hardcover books. The agent picked up one of the thicker tomes, *An Annotated History of the Cold Wars, Volume I*. Cornelius bristled as the guard carelessly riffled through the autographed first edition as if it were a bargain-bin book. Cornelius bristled again as the guard slammed the book shut and tossed the 1,200-page volume back into the suitcase.

"You always bring a library with you when you travel?"

Cornelius shrugged. "Doesn't everybody?"

"I didn't notice any books on Cremationism in there. I suppose you're not in favor of the Burly Crematorium?"

Cornelius scowled at the agent. "Meaning *what*, exactly?"

"I think you know what I mean," answered the customs agent. "I think you know *exactly* what I mean."

"I suggest you stop harassing this man and let him through." It was the undead beggar from Frankenjoe's—except now a transit police badge dangled from a lanyard around his scrawny neck.

"I'm just doing my job, Phil," the agent remarked with obvious impatience. "That crematorium is property of the Living States government."

Damon stepped closer. He didn't understand why the guard was harping on Cremationism. Cornelius could be a Wiccan, for all Damon cared. "Listen, this big lug wouldn't harm a fly. He's your basic gentle giant."

"I *am* husky," agreed Cornelius.

"In my experience," said the agent, "the bigger they are, the longer they burn."

"You're profiling him, is what you're doing," Phil angrily replied. "This guy just saved my relife. I'm vouching for him. Let him pass."

Damon stepped closer. "I'm vouching for him, too."

It was clear from the agent's disdainful expression that their opinion mattered little to him. But he seemed especially disappointed with Damon. "You need to keep better company." He reluctantly stamped Cornelius's passport and stood aside to let him pass.

"Thanks for sticking up for me," Cornelius said to Damon. "It means a lot to me."

"No sweat. You're a good guy, Neil."

And with that Damon and Cornelius began walking toward the light at the end of the tunnel. Damon wrinkled his nose at the musty stench that grew stronger with every step. As they neared the end of American soil, Damon faltered. The land of living death awaited them.

Come on, he told himself as he watched hundreds of travelers cross the border without hesitation. *You can do this. This isn't the end, it's just the start of Act 2.* And yet as Damon took another step forward, he paused at the scuffed white line on the pavement that indicated the actual border. His mind went to dark places as he considered the tons of granite just a few feet over their heads.

This whole wall could come down at any moment. You'd be buried alive.

"Or not," he said aloud. He defiantly straddled the border and smiled smugly. "I don't know if I'm half dead or half alive."

Cornelius stood with his back to Damon. He was staring at a group of tourists posing happily alongside a large bronze plaque that commemorated the Battle for Burly Gate.

"So many people died right here, right where we're standing," said Cornelius. He turned to Damon, the camera held limply in his large hand. "It doesn't seem right to take a vacation picture in this place."

"People die all the time, Neil. Sometimes they come back, sometimes they don't."

Cornelius furrowed his brow; he was still standing on the Living States side. "Mr. Grayson, I need to say something."

"Am I being insensitive again?" He looked down at his feet before meeting Cornelius's expectant gaze. "I was talking about my career, Neil. I know, not very funny, I guess." He continued to straddle the border. "I sure could use some of your optimism. This will all work out, right? In the end, we all live happily ever after?"

Cornelius shrugged. "Being dead's not so bad. Joni seems to be pretty content."

That's because, somehow, you make that sourpuss happy, Damon thought. *Because, in you, she found a deep vein of gold.* He looked at Cornelius and wished he could say such unscripted things aloud to someone he considered to be not just *a* friend, but his *only* friend. Instead he smiled tightly, and finally brought both feet down in the Havens.

"Welcome to the afterworld," he said as he spread his arms wide. He took a deep breath and coughed. "Just smell that musty air."

Cornelius sniffed, as if sampling the aroma of freshly baked bread. "Smells okay to me."

Damon was skeptical as he slowly considered his surroundings. Aside from the San Lazarus Mountains that loomed in the hazy distance, everything looked the same, felt the same, so far. And yet Damon couldn't shake the feeling that *he* was somehow different, just by sheer dint of geography. That, and he couldn't shake the eerie sensation that they were being watched. And not by 'bloiders, or paparazzi. No, this was different. He shivered involuntarily, despite the balmy temperature.

"Feels like someone's standing on my grave." His laughter lacked conviction, heart.

"It's not as bad as you think," said Cornelius.

"What's not?"

"Hey, I think that might be our car over there," he said quickly.

They began walking towards the old Cadillac El Dorado that had pulled to the curb. The side panels were riddled with rust and its bald, whitewall tires needed air. A handwritten sign that read HARRY BEARD—Damon's alias when he traveled—was attached to the inside of the window with what looked like strips of black electrical tape. It looked to be the same tape that was holding the cracked sideview mirror in place.

"What a piece of junk," said Damon. "There's no way I'm riding in that thing."

"It might be very nice inside," offered Cornelius. "And it sure beats taking the bus any old day."

"I have standards, Neil. I can't be seen in a clunker like that."

Travelers continued to emerge from the dark tunnel. Like Damon, they shielded their eyes from the sun's hazy glare. Among those squinting in the bright sunlight were the Neo-Lifers from the gift shop.

Damon swore under his breath. Had they recognized him? Damon quickly grabbed his bags. "C'mon. Let's get the hell out of here, Neil."

The driver emerged from the El Dorado as they quickly approached the car. He was a small, balding man with droopy eyes. He sported a robust salt-and-pepper mustache that made his weak chin seem all the weaker. He tried to compensate for it by wearing a large bowtie. What caught Damon's eye, though, was the man's healthy pallor.

"Mr. Beard, I presume," the driver asked.

"You're not dead," said Damon. Cornelius bowed his head in embarrassment. "I'm sorry, I didn't mean it that way."

"No, no, of course not," laughed the driver as he took their bags. "No, it's just like that gentleman from that Monty Python movie—'I'm not dead yet.'"

The tail end of the car sagged under the combined weight of their luggage. Damon was dubious that the old Caddie's suspension could bear the weight of passengers—especially Cornelius. Cornelius got in first, and the car leaned perilously to one side.

"You're a husky one!" laughed the driver.

"It's in the genes," Cornelius said uneasily.

"I'm sure it is, my friend," said the driver with another good-natured laugh. Damon liked this guy already. The difference between him and their other driver was like night and day.

"Buckle up," advised the driver.

He leaned over and turned up the car's air conditioner. Cool air slowly wheezed through the vents but barely reached the backseat. The driver licked his fingertips and smoothed down his bushy eyebrows.

"Have faith," he said as the car coughed and spluttered. "Come hell or high water, we'll arrive in one piece."

CHAPTER THIRTY-NINE

The old Cadillac did not disappoint; once in motion, it offered an unusually smooth ride. This was due in part to Cadabra City's well-maintained main thoroughfare. Contrary to what many people believed, there was no lingering damage from the Great Quake. Damon was a little disappointed by the lack of a dystopian, rubble-strewn landscape. What was Cadabra City's draw, he wondered. Why were its resort hotels, high-end boutiques and nightclubs different from similar offerings east of the wall?

Aside from the persistent moldy smell, which was quite strong on the western side of the wall, he found it easy to imagine they were cruising the Vegas strip. For all its outward glitz and vitality, downtown Cadabra exuded a seediness, an artificiality that only accentuated the lifelessness behind the neon façades. Burly Gate, too, felt less substantial, as if it were part of a large set on a New Hollywood soundstage. Just the thought of it made Damon long for the Paradox lot. He missed being in front of the cameras, doing what he excelled at—pretending to be something, someone, he wasn't.

It's only seven days, Damon reminded himself. *And then it's back to your old life, your old ways.*

"First-timers?" asked the driver, interrupting Damon's thoughts.

"Well, we're not *two*-timers, if that's what you mean," Damon said quickly.

Cornelius fell silent at the utterance of the slur.

"Of course, of course," the driver said. "No insinuations here. I just meant you two were fourth world first-timers."

"First-and-last-timers," said Damon. "We're here for the week and then it's back to the states for us."

"That's too bad. You'll miss the Day of the Undead festivities. This year's parade promises to be one of its best."

Cornelius looked genuinely disappointed. "It really is a once-in-a-life-time opportunity."

"No thanks," said Damon under his breath. His support of grey pride on the *Martin Pryce Show* was a means to an end. He had no idea why the caged buzzard sang and, quite frankly, he really didn't care.

He leaned back and idly began reading the billboards that peppered downtown Cadabra. There were hundreds of them, a dense, geometric scourge that infiltrated the landscape. Even architecture wasn't immune; billboards covered façades and sprouted, fungus-like, from crowded roof-tops.

Damon marveled at ads for undead products he'd never heard of (and he thought he knew them all). What was Rapid Redux Relief, and why was a stern, sallow-faced Jean Claude Van Damme endorsing its effectiveness? Buddy would know. Buddy knew everything. Damon made a mental note to ask him about it.

"My wife is quite excited for your new picture," the driver confessed. "She's an avid fan of the book. Her book club read it a few months back."

"My cover is blown," laughed Damon. In truth, he would have been a little offended if the driver hadn't recognized him.

"Oh, we've already met. We actually worked together on one of your earlier pictures."

Damon wracked his brains but could not conjure a name to go with the unfamiliar face. "I'm sorry," he finally said, "I don't remember you."

"I wouldn't expect you to," he said with a casual wave. "It was a long time ago. Another lifetime. I used to have a lot more hair. I was the head of special effects down at Schism House, back in the day. I actually did your prosthetics for..." He paused and snapped his fingers. "Gimme a minute, it'll come to me, just a second." He frowned as he stared through the windshield at some point in the past. "*Bokor Bob's Revenge*," he cried out triumphantly. "Yes!"

"Oh my god—Walter? Walter *Vine*?"

He laughed. "The one and only, I'm afraid. I'm all that's left of Schism."

"What the heck are you doing here? You were the best deadface man in the business."

Walter smiled at them in his rearview. "You mean why am I driving a livery cab in the fourth world? Ah, well, you know, New Hollywood found its conscience and men like me became obsolete. "C'est la vie," he said with a toss of his soft, freckled hand. "I did some consulting work in the video game industry for a little while after that. Zombie games like *Denizens of the Dark* are big business."

"He knows," said Cornelius crossly. "Those games are not very nice. They're worse than the old exploitation movies ever were."

"Walter's a good guy, Neil," Damon said sternly enough to make Cornelius look away. He immediately felt a sting of guilt—Damon hadn't meant it as a rebuke. And yet, who was Cornelius to judge?

"No, I agree, not very nice," said Walter. "Something a bit too mean-spirited about it even for my old blood. It's one thing to watch simulated violence, quite another to actually perpetrate it."

The Cadillac slowed to a stop at a busy intersection. Damon was relieved to see a road sign that read KADABRA ESTATES, 2 MILES. He longed for a good night's sleep. *The sleep of the dead*, he thought, and immediately banished the idea from his tired, addled mind. But before he could close his eyes a horde of moaning, undead beggars seemingly appeared out of nowhere and began to swarm the vehicle.

Damon instinctively, discreetly, checked his door to make sure it was locked. Then he steeled his exhausted body as unwanted adrenaline surged through his veins. He was ready for anything.

"Pleassse," they hissed, baring crooked teeth as they pressed their scaly faces against the windows. "Braiiinsss…We need braaaiiinnsss…." Cracked fingernails scrabbled quietly against the other side of the glass.

"At least they asked politely," observed Cornelius.

"Sorry," Damon yelled through the closed window. "No brains here!" He pointed to his head and shook it for added emphasis. "No! No brains!"

A silver-haired beggar, his face a wretched Rorschach of black decomp, a pickled eye dangling from its socket, gawked at the traffic light, which was about to turn green. He began to pound on Damon's window, his mouth open so wide his shriveled tonsils were visible.

"Pleassse," he moaned.

Mercifully, the light turned green and their car left the intersection. Damon watched as the beggars swarmed over the car behind them. Its driver honked, to no avail.

They continued on a northwest course through the city. The skyline became more modest, the buildings more ramshackle and homely. Fine dining and high-end retail gave way to fast-food chains and dodgy souvenir shops. Every so often a calling center appeared, boasting LANDLINES! OUTGOING CALLS ONLY $3.99/MINUTE. At one point they even passed a Havens Militia recruitment office. ARMED & CHARMED declared a banner hanging in the grimy window.

The congestion on the well-tended road began to ease somewhat as they neared the Burlytown Heights border. Even the crowds had thinned. The pedestrians, tourists mostly, did not stroll so much as proceed briskly, their heads bowed to avoid eye contact with the living-challenged locals. Damon noticed that the undead, their bony shoulders hunched, their milky eyes furtive, mostly kept to themselves, too.

"They're all dressed the same," Damon observed of the locals.

"Park employees," said Walter. "It's the only game in town, really. The factories up north in Bloodstone Basin have great benefits, but the pay is terrible. Plus, the water ferries can be very expensive if you use them every day. Dangerous, too."

Cornelius held his camera at the ready as they entered the sprawling KadabraLand park. He eagerly snapped pictures of the Gaudi-designed Kadabra Kastle as it slowly came into view above the surrounding trees.

"I read that the Havens Militia occupied the castle during Cold War II," Cornelius said to no one in particular.

"Yeah, and I heard they promoted Kenny Kadaver to Major," said Damon with a roll of his eyes.

"Ah, here we are," Walter declared as the Cadillac pulled into the long Kadabra Estates driveway. "Home sweet home, Mr. Beard. For the next week, at least."

The old car escaped the notice of the 'bloiders camped outside the entrance. Instead they descended on a sleek Bentley that pulled up behind the Cadillac. "Frankie," they yelled as camera flashes blinded the large, grey-skinned passenger emerging from the Bentley.

Cornelius glanced up with a start as Boris, history's most infamous dyborg, paused to shake hands in the quickly forming crowd. Cornelius reached for his own camera but hesitated as the ruckus reached a fever pitch.

"Don't tell me you actually like that pompous jerk, Neil."

Cornelius was about to reply when he noticed a bellhop manhandling their luggage into the lobby. "Excuse me, Mr. Grayson." He hurried after the bellhop. "Please be careful with those suitcases," he said. "Some of those books are first editions!"

"He's been acting weird all day," Damon said to Walter as he shook the older man's wrinkled hand.

"He's a husky one, isn't he?"

Damon laughed even as he considered Boris from the corner of his eye. "Yeah, he's one heck of a healthy eater."

Walter studied Damon for a moment. He began to say something, then seemed to think better of it. Instead he handed Damon his business card. "Should you need a tour guide—or even just a familiar ear to bend—I'm your man. Any time, day or night."

The two men shook hands again before Damon followed Cornelius inside. Damon paused to marvel at the inlaid marble floor and mahogany-paneled walls. White satin panels cascaded gracefully from the vaulted ceiling. They undulated gently in the putrid breeze.

Damon braced for the usual stares and finger-pointing as he walked to the front desk, but was surprised that no one paid him any mind. Then he remembered he didn't exactly look the part of a celebrity, thanks to the cheap gift shop garb. He was just another anonymous traveler with questionable fashion sense.

"Ah, there you are, Mr. Beard," said the manager, a well-kept man in a brown four-button suit. "We've been expecting you." He wore an enameled KadabraLand logo on his lapel, which complemented his Kenny Kadaver tie. Damon was a bit surprised to see that the manager was not undead.

"There's a problem with your reservation," said Cornelius.

Damon rubbed his eyes. "Of course there is." He didn't want to create a scene in front of everyone. The last thing he wanted was to wind up in a viral video wearing a pair of green Cads sweatpants. He'd never live that down. Never. "So is there a suite for me or not?"

"Not exactly," said the manager. "As you'll be working for the park, even on a transient basis, resort regulations clearly state that all park employees must reside in employee housing."

"Employee housing," Damon said flatly. "Do you know who the hell I even am?"

"Yes. I'm familiar with your considerable body of work. But I assure you, our employee housing is quite adequate and very private."

Private sounded good to Damon. He knew it was better just to settle in and make Barry fix everything in the morning. "Tell me it's at least a double."

The manager smiled. "You could say that, yes."

CHAPTER FORTY

The hotel manager personally led them down a narrow, winding utility stair-well. As they descended the two flights Damon kept thinking *this is not a good sign.* And then, finally, they reached the bottom of the stairs. It was the end of the line, literally.

"Why the hell are we in the basement?" asked Damon. The question sounded harsh as it echoed in the musty stairwell.

The manager ignored the question and led them down a long corridor lit by flickering fluorescents. It occurred to Damon that the manager was prob-ably trying to do them a favor by keeping mum about his stay at the resort, which made sense. They probably didn't want 'bloiders stirring up trouble and upsetting the other guests.

Damon finally relaxed, and even managed to laugh at himself. *Nice way to keep it real*, he thought. But then the manager paused at the end of the hall. The words RESTRICTED ACCESS: PARK ACTORS ONLY was stenciled on the set of double doors. The manager punched a five-digit code into the keypad on the wall. A green light flashed as the lock released with a loud *CHACK*.

The manager turned to Damon. "Don't worry. I'll make sure you have the access code. It changes daily."

Cornelius nodded his approval. "Smart," he said. He looked at Damon, and was surprised by his disgusted expression. "It *is* smart," he insisted. "Safe, too. Safer than that motel."

They passed through a second set of doors before coming to a stop in front of a door labeled DORM. Someone had hung a novelty sign alongside the entrance. It featured a cartoon corpse happily declaring YOU DON'T NEED TO BE DEAD TO WORK HERE—BUT IT SURE HELPS! The plastic sign still had a gift shop price tag on it.

Damon frowned at the hackneyed, dime-store sentiment. He'd seen it hundreds of times before. It was older than mold, as the saying went. It brought to mind an old schoolyard taunt: *Your mother's so old she's covered in mold!*

"Ah, here we are, the Carrion Flats room," said the manager. He opened the metal door with a grand flourish. "A double, just like you requested, Mr. Beard."

The accommodations, such as they were, could have fit inside Damon's trailer with room to spare. Damon silently cursed Russell Mann and his precious SLS certification.

"*Bunk beds.*" Damon made the statement sound like an epithet. "Are you *kidding* me."

Cornelius poked his head into the room. "I call the bottom."

Aside from the beds, the room contained a five-drawer melamine dresser and matching nightstand. A metal floor lamp with a crooked plastic shade was pushed into the corner. Damon observed that there was no television. Instead, there was a radio alarm clock, its display flashing a pale green *12:00.*

"There's no jacuzzi," said Damon.

"That is correct, Mr. Beard."

"And there's no bathroom."

The manager fiddled with his Kenny Kadaver tie pin. "Indeed not, Mr. Beard."

Damon narrowed his eyes as he opened the empty drawers one by one. "So where's the mini-bar?"

"I'm afraid this accommodation does not include that particular amenity."

Damon struggled to remain calm. "How am I supposed to call room service if there's no *phone* in here?"

"Park employees generally are not allowed to place outgoing phone calls," explained the manager. "But I will arrange for maintenance to bring a landline telephone down for your convenience."

"That's very thoughtful, thank you," said Cornelius.

"Don't thank him, we're not staying here," Damon snapped.

"The entire resort is booked, I'm afraid," the manager quickly replied.

"No, I mean we're not staying at Kadabra Estates. This room of yours? It's a tomb, not a room. This place is a joke. This whole *thing* is a bad joke."

"I doubt you'll be able to find a room anywhere in the city. There's a NANA convention in town."

Damon was growing testier by the minute. "Who the hell is Nana?"

The hotel manager cleared his throat. "It's, ah, the North American Necrophilia Association."

"Right, of course. How could I forget." Damon noticed another novelty sign. It was hanging on the wall behind him. This one was covered with little red devils and read THIS IS _NOT_ A GOOD SIGN!

"We can try to find another hotel tomorrow," suggested Cornelius. "Or maybe we can stay with Viktor."

Damon was too tired to argue. The stress of the past week was catching up to him. They may have surmounted the fourth wall, but now he was hitting a wall of his own.

"Fine," he said finally. "I don't care anymore."

The manager handed the room key to Damon and then turned to Cornelius. "Now, if you'll follow me, sir, I'll show you to your room."

"I don't understand," said Cornelius. "I thought this *was* my room."

The manager laughed. "Don't be ridiculous. You're not employed by the park. Besides, we can't let a local hero stay in employee housing."

Cornelius glanced nervously at Damon. "No, that's okay. I'd rather stay here. Or maybe we could just switch rooms?"

"Nonsense," said the manager, as if offended by the very idea of it. "You have been invited to stay in the Asphodel Suite at the behest of the Secretary of Undead Affairs himself."

Cornelius strenuously avoided making eye contact with Damon. He scratched his head and smiled uneasily. "Wow, that's…that's quite an honor."

"Yeah," said Damon flatly. "Sure is."

"Your friend is an inspiration to the living-challenged," the manager said to Damon. "You should be proud of his heroism."

"Wait a sec, you lost me," said Damon. "What do the living-challenged have to do with it?"

The color drained from the manager's cheeks. He turned to Cornelius, who had a large hand over his face. "I—I'm so sorry," he stammered, mortified by his tremendous faux pas. "I just assumed—" The manager's face was beginning to turn a deep shade of crimson.

Despite his own terrible embarrassment, Cornelius's pallor remained unchanged. "Mr. Grayson," he said uneasily. "There's something I need to tell you."

The manager quickly excused himself. Damon waited patiently, his arms folded across his baggy KadabraLand sweatshirt. "I hope this is good, Neil."

Cornelius's expression was grave. His tongue was like sandpaper as he licked his dry lips. "You should probably sit down, Mr. Grayson."

"Should I." He considered Cornelius for a long, tense moment. Damon realized he'd never seen him look so nervous. The bottom bunk's cheap bedsprings creaked as he reluctantly sat down on the thin mattress. "Okay, fire away, Neil."

"Well, I'm husky, Mr. Grayson."

Damon's smile was not kind. "Yes, we've already established that. Numerous times."

Cornelius closed his eyes and continued. "No, I mean, I'm a *HUSK-E.*"

"I don't understand."

"It's an acronym. It stands for Human Skills Emulator."

"Which means what, Neil? What's the big deal?"

"I'm what the media might call a designer corpse. But what I really am is a dyborg. You know, like…like Frankenstein's monster."

Damon stood up so fast he smashed his head on the overhead bunk. He fell back onto the bottom bunk, clutching the top of his head. He didn't know whether to laugh or to cry. He heard what Cornelius was saying, but he didn't understand *why* he was saying it. He gingerly touched the lump that was forming on his crown. His fingers came away tinged with blood. "Great," he muttered.

"Mr. Grayson, are you okay?"

"That depends, Neil. Are you telling me…" He grimaced as he struggled to form the words he didn't want to say aloud. "Did you just come out of the casket? You're a freaking *zombie?*"

"That's not a very nice word, Mr. Grayson."

"Jesus, Neil. So you've been lying to me this whole time?"

"I meant to tell you sooner. I wanted to. You have to believe that."

Damon glared at Cornelius as he stood to open the door. "You may think I'm a necrophobe, but at least I'm not a liar."

Cornelius hung his head and reluctantly turned to leave. He paused in the doorway, his large hand trembling where it rested on the doorknob. "I've always had your best interests at heart, Mr. Grayson. You're the only real friend I've ever had."

He caught Damon off guard with a quick but heartfelt hug.

"Please be careful, Mr. Grayson."

It was with a bitter heart and a troubled mind that Damon looked away. But when he willed himself to turn back and meet Cornelius's eye, the doorway was empty.

Far underground, in a room fit for a Burialist's corpse, Damon found no solace in the sudden loneliness masquerading itself as solitude. He closed his eyes and struggled with an unexpected, gut-wrenching remorse that left him gasping for breath.

CHAPTER FORTY-ONE

It was no secret that the Bureau of Undead Affairs monitored the rebirth rates on both sides of the wall. A recent study conducted by the bureau found that a resurrection occurred every four minutes in the Living States. It was an impressive figure until one considered that a rebirth occurred every sixteen seconds in the Havens.

What was lesser known, though, was the fact that Solomon skimmed from many a rebirth center's output. Witch doctors on both sides of Burly Gate were forced to tithe a percentage of their overall resurrections to him—which effectively kept their body counts low while at the same time boosting his.

Some doctors—like Baptiste, in Stony Hollow—eked out livings in clinics so small that they seemed to escape Solomon's notice. But then there were shamans like Darla Hardy's DeStefano, who became more careless as their practices grew. His resurrection ceremonies were as sloppy as his psych evaluations were shoddy. Many of his patients went on to become charm-school dropouts. Or worse, Noodle addicts.

What was more egregious, at least in Solomon's eyes, was that DeStefano's tithing did not reflect his clinic's actual output. The Westchester witch doctor's biggest miscalculation, however, was believing in his own seeming invulnerability. Which was why he was woefully ignorant of Undead Affairs' supernatural surveillance. Had he been more observant, and less concerned with ramping up his body count, he might have noticed the black vans patrolling his sleepy Westchester town. On the day of Darla Hardy's fateful rebirth, DeStefano ignored the dangerous signs that his thriving practice was at its end.

Darla, too, was unaware of the violence that awaited DeStefano and his faithful staff. As she drove down the clinic's shady street, she was too consumed by her last living hours to realize the significance of a black van parked around the corner, its engine idling, the driver invisible behind deeply tinted windows.

Darla Hardy likewise knew nothing of the freight trains bound for Solomon's secret mills in the Havens, their boxcars laden with undead cargo. Each cadaver on that train counted as one body. And each body represented another talisman's power that could be usurped by Solomon.

Darla paused on the front steps of the clinic, and inhaled deeply of the damp, earthy scent of a beautiful Northeast autumn. She did not cry at the thought of all she would miss as a newly-minted cadaver. What was the point of dwelling on such things?

She lingered a moment longer, suddenly overcome by the distinct feeling she was being watched. She glanced around nervously, hopefully, but did not see a familiar grey Peugeot in the packed parking lot.

Darla finally headed inside. Soon, very soon, Solomon's scrimshawed minions would storm the clinic. But until then, it would be business as usual—for the well-heeled voodoo practitioner and his trusting clients.

The receptionist smiled and directed Darla to take a seat in the overcrowded waiting room. She perched herself on the edge of her chair and waited anxiously to be called for her procedure. She reassured herself that moving her appointment up was the right thing to do. The sooner she left her old life behind, the better. What was the point in delaying the glory of one's rebirth?

At least, that's what she kept telling herself, until the words sounded like hollow nonsense inside her head.

After a few minutes a nurse appeared, chart in hand. A wrinkled, silver-haired question mark of a man rose unsteadily to his feet. His family members—all fifteen of them—quickly followed suit.

"Looks like the whole brood showed up for your big day!" crowed the nurse.

"It's my grampa's rebirthday today," whispered a wide-eyed, towheaded girl.

"It sure is," said the nurse as she efficiently ushered them from the room.

Darla stared at the vacant chair beside her and wished that Lydia and she had not fought so horribly the night before. But, like Lydia, Darla had her pride. She did not need her motives for rebirth called into question, especially in light of Jonas's suicide. Lydia had made it abundantly clear to Darla that moving the date up was a mistake.

It's like you're running from something, she'd said, *including me.* Darla insisted it simply wasn't true; she was ready for *nepenthe*—end of story.

And the end of me, too, she thought now. The *verboten* photos of Barnabas and Sofia she'd kept in her wallet were the real reason for their argument. (Darla had stashed them before Lydia forced her to throw out her remaining photo albums.) She carefully removed the photos from her wallet and held them in her trembling hand.

"No photographs allowed!" admonished a redheaded woman with wide-set eyes and too-thin lips. "You have no business being reborn if you can't let go of your past."

"Why don't you mind your own business," said Darla, but she tucked the pictures away just the same. She knew that when she awoke in her new life, the faces of her family would be that of strangers to her.

The nurse appeared again and called Darla's name. The former Mrs. Hardy arose, alone, and fought back unexpected tears as she followed the nurse to one of the rebirth rooms.

The two women made small talk as Darla was prepped for her procedure. She distracted herself by thinking of the letter she'd written in the wee hours of the morning. She almost hadn't mailed it, had feared it was too revealing, too earnest. But in the end she hoped it transcended her own limitations as someone who was grossly unaccustomed to emotional honesty:

> *Dear Baz,*
>
> *I want you to know that I am sorry for so many things. We all make mistakes. My mistake was being afraid to admit what makes me happy.*
>
> *What I wish for as I write this letter is to hear you call me darling the way you do just one more time. It always made me smile because it made me feel so safe...*
>
> *Please tell Sofia I will always be her mother, no matter what. Death won't change that. She is my only child and I love her.*
>
> *Baz I know now that you and Sofia are the ones who make me happy. I know it is too little too late to tell you this but it is the truth....*
>
> *I love you. Goodbye my lovely one, my man, my Barnabas. Signed...your darling Darla*

DeStefano entered the room, wearing a white coat and a friendly smile. "And on the third day, she rose," he said pleasantly. "Are we ready for our first rites, or would you like to wait a few minutes for latecomers to share this special experience with you?"

Darla wiped away her foolish tears. *Looks like we're finally out of time, Barnabas*, she thought. "No. I'm fine," she said hoarsely.

"I can call the nurse in, if you'd like someone else in the room with you."

No, damn it. I don't want your lousy pity. "Yes, please," she replied, and was instantly ashamed by the desperate quaver in her voice. "That would be very nice."

"Great, she's already on her way back in."

Screw you. Screw your charity. "Thank you." Darla couldn't stop the tears anymore. She didn't try.

"Resurrection is not the end, Mrs. Hardy. It is the beginning of something beautiful. It is the ultimate second chance. I promise you, I've performed hundreds of rebirths. Thousands. You won't remember a thing."

The nurse entered the room bearing a chalice containing the Tears of Life. DeStefano was already holding the cruciform over Darla's heart. He began his chant, a mystical amalgam of Latin and Fons, Langaj and Aramaic.

"Any last words, Mrs. Hardy?" asked the nurse with a bored, polite smile.

"Sofia," she said, as her breath slipped away. "Barnabas," she said. Her consciousness started to recede like the hissing tide. Something raw and vital stirred within her breast. It spun, a vortex of white-hot light, pulling, tugging at the fading thoughts inside her thoughts.

Her lungs decompressed, her heart flattened. She felt no pain as her body became still, quiet, and cold.

The last vestiges of Darla Hardy's consciousness ebbed away. There was only a mild, distant buzzing sound, like a fly caught against a closed window, yearning for a world beyond the pane:

*Ba*zzzzzzzzzzzzzzzzzzzzzzzzz....

*　　*　　*

CHAPTER FORTY-TWO

Morgan Creek was a small wisp of a town located in the foothills of Arizona's Superstition Mountains. Like all mining towns, Morgan Creek had fallen into disrepair when crematoriums replaced coal as the country's viable energy source. What set Morgan Creek apart, however, was a nineteenth-century mining accident. Known locally as the Superstition Uprising, the plight of 68 trapped undead miners would eventually lead to the first Cold War. Hardy was no stranger to Morgan Creek or its storied past. Indeed, he was a minor celebrity in these parts, for people who knew anything about dowsing.

The bright desert sun was beating down on the dusty Mustang as Hardy rolled into town. He had driven nearly non-stop since leaving Indiana and was now running on fumes and little else. Jesse Bettenay was still foremost in his mind, and yet he couldn't get Darla out of his head. He promised himself to do right by her, but first he had to stock up on essentials before the next leg of his journey. Which led him to Jerky's Pawn Shoppe, a monkey's fart of an establishment in a forgotten, sun-scorched corner of Arizona.

Morgan Creek, like the rest of the state, was openly anti-undead. Local authorities were known to "accidentally" incarcerate the living simply for being too pale or too gaunt. Luckily for Hardy he was neither of those things. Still, he'd had run-ins with local law enforcement before, and he had no intention of running afoul of them again.

Jerky's was pretty much as he'd remembered it—not much had changed in ten years. Hardy found a strange comfort in the old pawnshop's stagnation, especially since his own life had become so topsy-turvy.

The dry desert air followed Hardy inside the darkened shop. Gerry "Jerky" Pruitt emerged from the back at the sound of the bell. He held a tuna fish sandwich in one hand, and a battered paperback book in the other. He was so surprised to see Hardy he nearly took a bite of the book before setting them both down on the counter.

"Holy crap on a cupcake, look who it is!" he exclaimed over the rattle of an old air conditioner.

Hardy felt like he hadn't smiled in ages. Jerky was just as rail thin and quick-eyed as he ever was. The stubble on Hardy's fleshy cheeks bristled as he broke into a wide smile.

"Jerky. Are you ever a sight for sore eyes."

"You find Atlantis yet, tough guy?"

"Still looking, Jerky. Still looking."

Jerky Pruitt stepped around the counter and flipped the faded OPEN sign in the door to CLOSED. They spent the next thirty minutes sharing the tuna fish sandwich and catching up on the last decade. The discussion ranged from baseball to beer to better halves. And it was here that Hardy suddenly found himself at a loss. But Jerky, a former dowser, could read between the lines of Hardy's careworn face.

"I just want you to know, I heard about you and Darla—"

Hardy was surprised news of his failed marriage had made it this far west. He dismissed the comment with a brusque wave. "It is what it is. This time next week she'll be charm school valedictorian."

Like Hardy, Jerky Pruitt was nobody's fool. But in deference to his friend, he let the subject drop.

"So why are you here?"

Hardy regarded Jerky from the corner of his eye. "You tellin' me your intuition up and quit on you?"

Jerky shrugged his narrow shoulders. "It happens to the best of us."

Just then a man in faded fatigues tried the front door and found it locked. He rapped on the glass and peered inside.

Jerky thrust a crooked finger at the sign in the window. "Closed!" he yelled. He turned to Hardy. "Well, that's not good."

Hardy glanced around the modest shop. The shelves were lined with a selection of merchandise that was both mundane and unexpectedly eclectic. A dusty, dented tuba shared a crowded shelf with burlap voodoo dolls and a stack of Merle Haggard CDs. But Hardy knew there was more to this simple pawnshop than met the eye.

"Don't scare away customers on account of me," he said. "A buck is a buck."

"That was one of Sandy Mellon's boys."

Hardy chuckled as he considered the half-empty can of Burly Brew in his hands. "Sandy Mellon. Great. That guy is a real piece of work."

"He owns half the town now," said Jerky. "And the other half owes him."

Hardy was glad the Mustang was parked out front. Had he been driving the Peugeot, he might not have made it past the Morgan Creek town line. If he didn't get moving, he might not make it out of Dodge, period.

"Time for me to vamoose," said Hardy.

Jerky's pronounced Adam's apple bobbed as he sucked down the last of his beer. "So, really, enlighten me. Why are you really here? It can't be for the sparkling conversation."

Hardy leaned across the table and fixed Jerky with an intense stare. No more beating around the bush—especially if Sandy Mellon knew he was in town. "I need a Reboot Special."

Jerky knew exactly what that meant: a new identity, stat, with no questions asked. "No problem," he said without missing a beat.

Jerky disappeared into the back and returned a few minutes later with a battered shoebox. He slid it across the scuffed Formica counter. "Here you go. Everything the discerning fugitive needs to get his lam on."

Hardy pulled back the lid and pawed through the box's assorted fake IDs and credit cards. He held up a driver's license and pondered his new identity. "'Andrew Kane,' eh? Has a nice ring to it."

"Seemed like a good fit. He even looks like you."

He flipped the license over. The next-life designation was marked DO NOT RESURRECT. "So now I'm a Cremationist?"

Jerky shrugged again. "Less conspicuous."

Hardy never thought of himself as the sort who blended in anywhere. Anonymity wouldn't be so bad for a change of pace.

Jerky removed the cell phone from the box and switched it on. "Burner phone. Fully charged, plus two extra batteries, also fully charged. Comes pre-loaded with 500 minutes. Totally untraceable."

Hardy belched his approval as he fished a wad of sweaty bills from his pocket. "What's the damage?"

Jerky gently pushed the money away. "C'mon, what're you doing? I owe you my life, Barnabas."

"I ain't keeping score," he said gruffly.

"Look, I don't know what's going on but you probably need that cash right now more than I do. We can settle up next time."

"You mean in another ten years?" He turned the phone over in his hands and frowned.

"Something wrong?"

Hardy pushed the phone back across the counter. "Listen, for where I'm headed, I'm gonna need a di-band phone instead."

Jerky Pruitt smirked as he pushed the phone back at Hardy. "Very funny. We both know you're not stupid enough to show your ugly mug in the Havens."

"I showed my ugly mug here, didn't I?" Hardy was struggling to keep his cool as his intuition suddenly went berserk. "Just gimme the di-band, Jerky. And I'm gonna need a HAMR, too."

Jerky stared long and hard at his friend. "I still think you're nuts."

Hardy wiped beads of perspiration from his brow with the back of his wrist. Either the heat was getting to him or he was about to keel over from exhaustion. "I got nothing left to lose."

"You said that last time, and you were wrong then."

"Yeah, well, this time I mean it," snapped Hardy.

Jerky removed a round key from a silver key ring. "So who's the quarry? Must be pretty high-profile if you're willing to risk your life."

Hardy sized up his friend; Jerky Pruitt knew how to take care of himself if trouble ever came knocking. He motioned Jerky closer.

"The corpse whisperer."

Jerky, stunned into silence, could only stare blankly at his old friend. "I think you need a vacation," he said finally. "The longer the better."

Hardy chuckled. He could hardly blame Jerky for being skeptical. "This ain't a joke."

"No, it sounds a lot like a trap, Barnabas. Solomon's probably setting you up. He'll kill you the first chance he gets. A fake ID isn't going to help you waltz past Burly Gate."

"I got a plan, awright? Just...trust me."

Jerky furrowed his brow. "Listen, as your friend—"

"The mines," said Hardy. "I'm going through the mines."

"The *mines*?" Jerky barked with laughter. "Your master plan is to go *under* Burly Gate?" He slapped the counter and laughed again, riotously. "What do you know about those tunnels? If you got such a death wish, I'll drive you over to Sandy Mellon's place myself."

"You know it ain't like that," said Hardy. "I'm locked in. If I don't find this guy soon—"

Jerky raised his hands in protest. "Fine, fine. But at least let me help you, okay? I know a guy who runs a sightseeing tour out of Debtor's Mine. You can probably access the tunnels from there."

Once he gained access, Hardy knew he could navigate the catacombs of the abandoned Railroad Styx blindfolded. "You're a good guy," he said.

Jerky frowned. "For helping you kill yourself?" He shook his head. "Save your compliments for a real friend." He stared long and hard at Hardy, his eyes bright, flinty. "One di-band phone, one HAMR, coming right up."

"Might as well add night vision goggles while you're at it."

"You're lucky if I don't come back out here with a straitjacket instead."

Hardy drummed his fingers impatiently on the counter as Jerky went to the back. But it wasn't finding the corpse whisperer that worried him—it was Darla. He had a nagging feeling that something was wrong. The kernel of doubt had been there all along, he realized now. Were it not for this fool's errand of his, he might have figured it out sooner.

"DeStefano," he muttered as he recalled her witch doctor's name. But even if his hunch was right (and his hunches were always right), what could he do about it now? He swore under his breath as he grabbed the phone from the counter.

"Gimme five, Jerky," he yelled over the rattling air conditioner. "Gotta make a phone call."

The parched earth glittered with a painful incandescence beneath the glare of the Arizona sun. Hardy squinted towards the shimmering horizon and saw nothing but desert and brush. Vengeful posse or no, the sooner he was back on the road, the better. He had no business dallying when his quarry was finally within reach.

Hardy considered the sleek outline of the cell phone in his hand. It was heavy, too heavy; it pinned him down in a way that a pay phone couldn't. Finally, here was a lifeline, a real connection, to a world that was forever reduced to the limited perspective of a rearview mirror.

Hardy leaned against the building and waited as the phone rang. He kept a watchful eye on the road as he forced a weary smirk from his grimy face. Time was running out for the Hardys, that was a fact. The mother of his only child was as good as dead.

"And then there were two." He was about to head back into the air-conditioned refuge of the shop when Darla finally answered the phone.

"Listen, it's me," said Hardy quickly. "I just—"

"Darla's not here," replied a frosty voice he didn't recognize.

"Who's this?"

"This is Lydia. Who the hell is *this*?"

"This is her husband." He smacked his forehead. *You're her* ex-*husband, damn it. You're nothing to her now. Nothing.*

"You're too late. She left for the rebirth clinic hours ago."

Hardy was dumbfounded. "But today's not supposed to be her rebirth-day."

"Well, she decided to move up the big day."

Hardy wanted to smash the phone over his stupid, sorry head. "Then why aren't *you* with her?"

"We're not together anymore, that's why. Not that it's any of your business."

The hell it's not, thought Hardy.

"I'm just here to get my things," she went on. "Again, not like it matters to you."

Hardy white-knuckled the phone in his trembling fist. "She shouldn't be alone. You should be there. It's because of you that she's doing this."

"Wow, she said you were dense, but I didn't think anyone could be this dumb."

The blood rose in Hardy's cheeks. "You better watch yourself, you zombie bitch."

His wife's undead lover laughed. "She was ever only doing it because of you, you idiot. She never cared about me. And all you ever cared about was chasing down corpses." She laughed again, bitterly. "I mean, what better way to get your attention than to become one of us?"

"Bullshit. That's bullshit."

"If you can't beat them, join them, right?"

Hardy was not an emotionally demonstrative man. Never was, never would be. And yet as the line went dead in his ear he was overcome by an earth-shattering sadness.

"Darla," he said, his voice breaking.

His legs buckled, and Barnabas Hardy fell to his knees in the sweltering heat. But only the scorpions heard him weep for his dear, darlin' Darla.

CHAPTER FORTY-THREE

Greenbeard's Tavern was located a few miles from St. Joan's campus in downtown Chillicothe. The bar was a favorite among students and locals alike. The have-not cadavers communed in the dark pub, mainly to play darts and shoot billiards, while those with a pulse, the fleshy, warm-blooded haves, consumed spirits at an unnatural pace.

Sofia Hardy and her friends were hunkered down at their usual rickety table next to the pay phone in the corner. From there they were afforded relatively unobstructed views of both the bar's patrons and of the dusty flea market memorabilia lining the dark-paneled walls. The popular undead reality show *Who Are They Now?* played on an old TV above the bar.

Sofia stared blankly at the program while her roommate and their boyfriends added to the din with their own drunken chattering. More than once her friends tried to draw her into the conversation, but the dowser's daughter found the topic of Professor Forrest's death distasteful.

In the conspicuous absence of media coverage, rampant speculation about Forrest's mysterious demise became a pastime for students and locals alike. Sofia cared only about one death in particular, the sort of glorified suicide masquerading itself as a rebirth.

She glanced up at the TV as the show's studio audience cried out in unison, *"WHERE! ARE! THEY NOW!"* *Good question,* she thought. Her mom could be literally anyone now, her dad anywhere. Sofia, meanwhile, felt listless. She was a nobody going nowhere. "Let's meet today's mystery cadaver!" shouted the leathery host. Sofia was suddenly terrified that her mother might shamble onto the bright stage.

She quickly turned away from the bar and forced herself to enjoy her friends' company. It was obvious that her roommate, Ashley, was worried about her, in a mother hen sort of way. It was intrusive, deliberately so, but Sofia loved her for it anyway.

Are you okay, Ashley mouthed from across the table. Sofia merely shrugged. What was there to say, really? How could she compete with the allure of *Cadabra Rasa?*

"I heard one of the Public Safety guys say Forrest was murdered," said Craig, Ashley's boyfriend. "But that's a real stretch, right? You can't really call it murder if someone doesn't have a pulse."

A brown-haired cadaver at a nearby table glanced up sharply from the newspaper he was reading. Only Sofia noticed the dirty look he gave them over the top of his coke-bottle glasses.

"Guys," she said. "You may want to keep it down."

Ashley playfully swatted Craig on the arm. "You are so bad."

"I'm serious! A heartbeat is a prerequisite for life, isn't it?"

Now the yellow-eyed cadavers at the pool table were glaring at them from across the crowded bar. Sofia did a quick head count and recognized a few familiar faces from around campus. Otherwise, the undead easily outnumbered the living.

"Guys," she said again. "Can we talk about something else?"

Craig cast an unworried glance over his shoulder before sucking down his fourth Ash Ale of the night. "It's a free country," he said loud enough to be heard all the way to the front door. "And I'm a paying customer."

Sofia's boyfriend signaled to their undead waitress for another round of beers. "A janitor in the Cultural Studies building told me there was nothing left but a pile of bones in Forrest's office," said Mark. "And like a million flies."

"Oh, man," said Craig, "don't you hate it when you're talking to a zombie and there are, like maggots and flies and shit all over their face?"

The z-word got the attention of the undead bartender—and the rest of the cadavers.

"Stop being so *gross*," shouted Ashley.

"If you think that's so gross how are you going to do the outreach in the Havens?" asked Craig. "It's gonna be a hundred times worse out there."

Ashley clutched Sofia's hand. "You're still going, right? You haven't changed your mind because of you-know-what, have you?"

"You-know-what?" asked Mark. "What does that mean?" He turned to Sofia. "What is she talking about?"

"Nothing," Sofia snapped. "She's just drunk, okay?"

Craig knocked over the saltshaker as he leaned across the table. "So are you?" he asked Sofia. "Going with us, I mean."

If she'd been asked the same question two weeks ago the answer would have been a no-brainer. But now, the thought of venturing beyond Burly Gate filled her with dread.

"Of course I'm going," said Sofia impatiently. "I won't graduate if I don't." *Besides*, she thought, *it's not like I can go home for winter break.* Where was she going to stay—her dad's tiny apartment?

"You guys," said Ashley with such unexpected earnestness it made Sofia smile. "I hear it's really dangerous out there."

"Well, yeah," said Craig. "I hear they eat people in Charnel Point. Like, they boil the bodies or something to make the bones all soft."

Sofia imagined her mother, blank-eyed and grey, prying open a body to eat the steaming, pulpy mess inside. She tried desperately to banish the thought from her mind. "Can we please talk about something else?" she said.

"You said soft *bones*," said Mark. "That's hilarious."

"Please pass the pancreas," moaned Craig, and pretended to stuff his gaping mouth.

"Can we *please* talk about something *else*," Sofia said, louder this time. "Seriously." She quickly stood up.

Mark playfully tugged at her sleeve. "Hey, where are *you* going?"

Sofia angrily shrugged him off. "Don't. Just...don't." Arms folded across her chest, she stormed off to the bathroom. She locked the door and fought back a sudden onslaught of tears.

You're a Hardy, she told herself. *Act like it.*

Someone knocked on the bathroom door as she splashed cold water on her face. "In here," she yelled into the grimy sink basin. The person knocked again. She straightened up and glared at the closed door. "Someone is *in* here!"

"Sofia, it's me," Mark called through the locked door. "You okay?"

She leaned against one of the freshly painted walls and shook her head. "Would you still care about me if I was undead?"

The silence that followed was the only answer she needed. "Yeah, I didn't think so," she muttered under her breath. She waited until Mark's shadow disappeared from the space under the door before unlocking it. Just as she opened the door she noticed FUCK YOU ZOMBIE scribbled in black marker on one of the walls. Someone had clearly tried to remove the marker with soap and water, causing the thick ink to weep down the fresh coat of paint.

It was the futility of trying to erase such an ugly, pervasive sentiment that finally opened Sofia's eyes to the surprising ugliness in her own life. She threw open the door and was startled to find Mark patiently waiting for her.

"C'mon, Sofe," he said as he swayed unsteadily on his feet. "Just talk to me."

She quickly shoved past him. He was drunk; his flushed complexion and sour breath only made her angrier. "I can't do this right now."

"So when were you going to tell me about your mom? Never?"

She glared at Ashley as her roommate hurried over to her. "I'm so sorry,

Sofia. You were acting so weird. I *had* to say something."

"Whatever, Ashley," said Sofia. "You fucking *promised* me."

"It's not her fault," said Mark. "I made her tell me."

But Sofia wasn't listening. She was watching Craig push back from the table and saunter over to them. "No biggie," he said with a drunken smirk. "You can just pick out a new mom from Charnel Point."

"Jesus Christ, Craig, shut up!" said Ashley.

"Hey, you can even call her Mombie," he guffawed. Sofia quickly laid him out with a quick jab to his nose. He blundered into a nearby table before hitting the floor with a loud thud.

"Hey!" yelled the undead bartender as he stepped from behind the bar. "Take that shit outside before I call the cops!" *Gaw duh cobz.*

"Go ahead, call them," said Sofia as she headed for the door. "But I was defending *you*, too."

"Don't do us any favors, blood bank!" the bartender yelled after her.

The chilly night air felt good on her face. Sofia closed her eyes and savored the unexpected silence of the deserted block. But such bliss was fleeting; she quickly marched up the street before anyone followed her outside. If she was lucky, she'd be able to walk the three miles back to campus in less than an hour.

It was a different experience, witnessing downtown Chillicothe on foot, rather than speeding through it in a locked car. She actually took the time to read the shop names, and to consider the importance of apothecaries and ether reader salons to the locals. How could the living ever hope to understand the undead if they were so consumed with trying to change them?

"Or kill them," she said quietly. She walked for another few minutes before stopping outside an ether reader salon that actually had a catchy name. LEENA'S LOST & FOUND, declared a buzzing, purple neon sign. Below that, a handwritten poster was taped to the window: *First Pronouncement Is Free.*

Ashley confessed she'd once visited an ether reader—on a dare, of course. No self-respecting Cremationist would ever be caught dead talking to one otherwise. But then, Sofia Hardy no longer considered herself a respectable anything—her throbbing right hand was proof enough of that. She studied her reflection in the blackened window and didn't like the beetle-browed girl staring back.

You can't find a memory, her dad said many times of ether readers. *But for a sawbuck, you can make one up, easy.*

"First one's on the house, Dad," she said as she reached for the door.

She was greeted by a large woman in a red silk robe, her long, jet-black hair tied back with a scarf. She was sitting on a rattan love seat, a glossy magazine splayed on her lap. Incense and candles burned and flickered beside her on a glass end table. To her right, a paisley-patterned tapestry covered a doorway. Sofia smiled—she would have been gravely disappointed to find anything less.

The rattan crackled as the woman pushed to her feet. "I'm Sister Leena."

"Yeah, I figured," said Sofia.

Sister Leena's smile was kind. Sofia felt such a nicety was more than she deserved. "And you," said Sister Leena gently, "you must be lost." Her gaze fell to Sofia's right hand, which was beginning to redden and swell. "I'll be right back with some ice." She motioned for Sofia to have a seat while she waited.

"I'd rather stand, thanks." Alone in the small room, Sofia had time to finally gather her thoughts. She knew she had no business being in such a place, yet why did leaving seem so much harder than stepping through the door?

She wandered over to the bookcase in the corner. The first shelf was lined with bundled incense sticks and scented oils in tiny vials. Sandalwood, jasmine, musk—five dollars apiece, two for only eight dollars. "Of course," Sofia said under her breath.

The next shelf contained New Age CDs touting alto clarinet soloists and mountaintop performances—also for sale. Her father's teasing would be relentless if he ever found out about this. But, of course, her father would remain in the dark, as always. *You can't compete with Bigfoot,* she reminded herself.

The bottom shelf was crammed with the sorts of books that were once part of Professor Forrest's syllabus: *Ancient and Medieval Magicks. Spells for Every Occurrence. Tripping the Ether Fantastic.* And, no surprise, she had *Undead Like Me,* by Alistair Moon. Even her mother had owned a copy. She and her dad had laughed at her when she began talking about Resurrectionism. How were they supposed to know it wasn't a joke? When her mother brought home that death coach—that was literally the beginning of the end.

Her attention turned to the window as a boisterous group of students hurried past. None of them gave the salon or its flickering purple neon sign a second look. Sofia was disappointed; part of her wanted to be discovered, wanted to explain to someone how she'd inexplicably been drawn to this particular parlor like a moth to a flame.

Sister Leena reappeared with ice cubes wrapped in a mint-green tea towel. "Here we are." The ice cubes clattered together as she placed the towel on Sofia's aching hand.

"He deserved it," Sofia said with a nervous laugh.

"He was being disrespectful, yes."

Sofia was instantly suspicious. "How would you know that?"

"Motherhood is sacred, a lifelong gift shared by both mother and child."

"Okay, you're really freaking me out." Did she somehow have the tavern bugged? What other explanation could there possibly be—unless she was some sort of witch? Sister Leena clutched her by the wrist as Sofia turned to leave. "Don't—"

The ether reader silenced her with a violent hush. "Not safe," she whispered, and pointed at a black van that slowly cruised past the salon. "Listen with your eyes," she said, and grabbed a leather-bound journal from the end table. The van turned around at the end of the block and headed back down the street. Sister Leena pulled Sofia back from the tinted glass before locking the front door. "Listen with your *eyes*," she said again, and stabbed the blank page with her finger.

Sofia turned her back to the window as the black van drove past the shop. *Don't freak out,* she told herself. *She's not a witch—and that was so not a skeleton driving that van. This is all just part of the show.* "Okay."

"School is obviously very important to you," said Sister Leena. But on the blank page she wrote, *Your father is lost.* She quickly handed the pen to Sofia before she had a chance to respond. "Write." She made the command sound like a question. To anyone eavesdropping, it would sound like *Right?*

"I guess so, sure." Sofia frowned as she wrote, *My father is never lost.*

"And your friends are clearly very important to you," said Sister Leena. *You must help him find his way,* she scribbled in the journal.

"My friends?" How many bridges had she burned with a single punch? "Some of them." The pen scratched across the page. *I have no idea where he is. I never do.*

"Patience is the key for troubling times, my dear." *Find him, and you will find her. She is the key.*

A second black van drove past the salon. "I don't understand," said Sofia.

Sister Leena set aside the journal and quickly took Sofia's hands in hers. "Now you must see with your ears to envision the path." She locked eyes with Sofia and spoke slowly and deliberately. "Your *mission* is clear. Have *faith.* Reach out. *Rekindle.*"

Was she talking about the outreach in Charnel Point? "Do you mean—"

"Believe in your heart that you are meant to save him."

An image of her mother clawing her father's terrified face exploded in her thoughts. Sofia's eyes welled with tears as she tried to think of anything else but the grisly scenario. "So he's really lost? He's in trouble?"

Sister Leena nodded. "And you will find him, child," she whispered. "But first, you must believe that such a thing can be done."

"But how?"

"Picture him in your mind."

She tried to convince herself that her father wasn't injured, wasn't afraid, wasn't as alone as she felt. "I—I really miss him," said Sofia. "So much it hurts."

"Discover the love hiding inside that fear."

Sofia suddenly imagined herself traveling along a ribbon of asphalt that cleaved the land in two. The road became a blur, tugging at her insides, drawing her westward like a rocket, an unstoppable missile bearing down on the implacable face of Burly Gate.

Sister Leena smiled. "Do you see it, child? Do you yet see the way?"

The fountain dowser's daughter smiled, too. The path from Chillicothe to the Charnel Point slums was so bright and so obvious it may as well have been marked upon the very earth itself. Sofia wondered if this was how her father perceived the world—with such unshakeable clarity.

"Then you, too, share the gift."

"But how—?"

Sister Leena squeezed her hand as both vans stopped outside the parlor. "Time for you to leave, dowser's daughter."

Grey-skinned cadavers piled out of the vans. They huddled together in the middle of the road, stoop-shouldered and slack-jawed. Their vacant expressions reminded Sofia of corpses from the old zombie exploitation films she'd watched in her Morbid Media class.

All at once, the cadavers turned as one to face the parlor. They shuffled in unison towards the building.

"What's wrong with them?" asked Sofia. "Why are they acting that way?"

Sister Leena's grip tightened around her hand. "Because they are repossessed by their shaman. He wills them to do so."

The cadavers began pressing themselves against the tinted glass. A third black van screeched to a stop outside the parlor. Five more cadavers spilled into the street and began shuffling towards the building. Spiderweb cracks squeaked across the window as the undead continued to push against the glass. One cadaver, his gaunt face riddled with decomp sores, stared blankly at them as the horde flattened him against the glass. He left behind oily, maggot-streaked smears on the window as he struggled to turn his head.

"Hurt," he moaned through cracked, split lips. "Hurt you."

Sister Leena pulled Sofia through the tapestry-covered doorway into a candlelit hallway. The door on the right led to a kitchenette with a scuffed linoleum floor. A sweating ice cube tray sat on the cluttered countertop. The doorway on the left led to a bedroom with a wrought-iron daybed covered in tasseled, multi-colored cushions. Sister Leena led her past both rooms to a closed door at the end of the hall. Behind the door was nothing but a linen closet.

The moaning from the next room grew louder. Sofia wrenched free of Sister Leena's hand. "Are we supposed to stop them with towels?" she yelled.

"Faith is also a gift, child." She pulled aside a large box to reveal a crawl space at the back of the closet.

The front window shattered with a deafening crash. Sofia didn't hesitate—she dove through the narrow opening in the wall. She turned and quickly held out her hand to Sister Leena. "Hurry!"

Sister Leena merely pursed her lips and slid the heavy box back into place. The closet door slammed shut, plunging the cramped crawl space into total darkness.

This time Sofia did hesitate. Loud footsteps drew nearer. Moans became ragged shrieks. Plaster fell into Sofia's face as something heavy struck the wall.

"This is bullshit," whispered Sofia. There was no way she was going to sit in the dark when someone else was in danger. Her dad would never run from a fight; neither would she. The floorboards creaked beneath her as she crawled back through cobwebs towards the closet. A sharp clang was followed by a loud thud.

"Do it," she whispered.

She took a deep breath and shoved the box to one side just enough to squeeze past. The harder part was pushing the door open from inside—

something heavy was blocking it from the other side.

"No time for this!" she grunted. She ignored the throbbing in her hand and pushed her way out of the closet. A cadaver lay prone by the door, a cast iron skillet embedded in his collapsed forehead. A yolk-like eyeball lolled from its fractured socket. His neck crackled as he slowly turned to face Sofia.

"Hurts," he moaned. Maggots spilled from his mouth onto the scuffed floorboards. Sofia tried not to gag as she wrested the skillet from the wreckage of his rotted skull.

She wielded the cast iron skillet like a tennis racquet as she bounded down the hall. A balding cadaver in a blue suit lunged from the bedroom and grabbed Sofia by the arm. She whirled and struck him with the bottom of the heavy skillet. Maggots and dun-colored shards of jawbone exploded from his head as he stumbled into the wall. He staggered towards her again, his broken bones crunching beneath his feet.

"Unnh," he groaned, his tongue dangling from the top of his exposed esophagus like a giant, shriveled slug.

"Back!" she cried. "Get back!"

He grabbed her again by the arm. His jagged fingernails sliced into her flesh as he tightened his cold grasp. The pain was bright, unexpected; it shot through her body in a blinding flash. She raised the cast iron without thinking and split his skull in two. He lost his footing and crashed to the floor.

Another cadaver leapt from the kitchen and wrapped its gangly, mold-covered arms around her head. Sofia swung blindly until the cast iron found purchase with a dull clang. Her attacker fell back, startled. The cadaver was a woman with black, straw-like hair and pale, deep-set eyes. *She was probably someone's mother in her previous life,* thought Sofia.

The cadaver cupped a hand to her shattered temple. Pickled brain matter oozed between her spindly fingers like rancid oatmeal.

"Doe wandu hurr tew," she moaned. *Don't want to hurt you.* "Cand hell bit." *Can't help it.* She lunged towards Sofia again, her yellow teeth bared, her rheumy eyes wide and fearful. "Um sawr ee."

Sofia swung the cast iron in a wide arc and struck the woman squarely between the eyes, splattering the walls with the contents of her ruined head. She immediately collapsed to the floor in a leathery heap.

Sofia fought back tears as she turned away from the awful carnage. She retrieved the skillet from the undead woman's remains and struggled not to retch. Even in her wildest dreams she would never have envisioned such senseless violence.

"I'm sorry, too," she said quietly.

She ignored the sudden weakness in her legs as she pushed into the parlor. The paisley curtain lay on the floor, covered in splattered blood and shards of glass and neon tubing. In the corner of the room, next to the overturned end table, fallen candles flickered in shiny pools of melted wax. Outside, the vans were gone, as were any remaining cadavers. And gone with them was Sister Leena. All that remained of her was the journal, its pages stained with blood. A ripped page lay beneath the broken coffee table. A single word was written upon the paper: *RECONNECT*.

Sofia dropped the skillet and fled into the empty street. She ran towards the main road, knowing exactly what she'd find there. Mark's Chevette sped towards her and screeched to a stop. Ashley leapt from the car and threw her arms around Sofia.

"The—the tavern!" said Ashley. "They started going crazy! We couldn't find you!"

Craig leaned out the window. His jaw was swollen, his eyes bloodshot. "Is she okay?" he yelled.

Sofia's arms ached, yet she felt an odd numbness inside. Craig repeated the question with a surprising urgency. She managed to nod mutely as Ashley dragged her into the idling car. Down the street, bodies lay in the middle of the road. The tavern door banged open. Several undead patrons stumbled outside wielding pool cues.

"There's still nothing on any of the news channels," Craig said from the front seat. "How is that possible?"

"You're bleeding," Ashley gasped. "Sofia is bleeding!" She quickly removed her sweater and wrapped it around the gashes in Sofia's arm.

Mark glanced at Sofia in the rearview mirror. She had never seen him look so frightened or so lost. "We are so outta here," he said.

Only Sofia paid Leena's Lost & Found any mind as they sped past. Dark smoke billowed from the broken window, smudging the sky with a conflagration's destructive promise of sacrifice, of rebuilding and renewal. But even as she nursed her wounds both seen and unseen, the dowser's daughter did not despair.

Instead Sofia Hardy found comfort in the certainty of the path laid out before her. She would surely stumble in her journey and falter in her convictions. But one thing she knew beyond any doubt was that she couldn't lose her way even if she tried.

CHAPTER FORTY-FOUR

Meanwhile, back in the Havens, Damon had escaped the confines of his small hotel room and was fast becoming comfortably drunk in the Kadabra Estates lounge. Though not normally a drinker, he favored inebriation over the shame he felt from his unexpected falling out with Cornelius. So much so, in fact, that he'd managed to convince the bartender to mix *verboten* Zombies—at $500 a pop. And now, $2,500 later, Damon had finally hit his limit.

"One more for the road?" asked the bartender.

Damon smacked the counter. "Nope. That's enough for me. Gotta be up early tomorrow. That Kenny Kadaver costume's not gonna wear itself."

"Didn't you say you were nominated for a Harpo?"

Damon laughed into his glass. "Yep. Twice."

"So then what're you doing at a Havens theme park? Shouldn't you, you know, be acting on the other side of Burly?"

"Who says I'm not acting now?"

"Right," said the bartender. "I get it. The whole world's a stage."

"Very well then," Damon said with a lopsided grin.

He took a moment to scan the bar for anything out of the ordinary, as

Cornelius was wont to do. While he was at it, he gave his oversized body-guard's equally outsized morality a spin. Would Cornelius have disparaged Damon for bribing the bartender? Without a doubt, yes.

And what of the heavily made-up, redheaded cadaver at the end of the bar, a probably once-comely woman in her previous life? Would it have mattered that she'd clearly hit the Noodle a little too often in this relife? No, probably not. Would Cornelius have viewed her milky-eyed, come-hither glances as an opportunity to strike up an innocent conversation?

Damon decided that his bodyguard most certainly would have been both a gentleman and a scholar, as was also the big man's wont. Cornelius made being a decent person appear deceptively simple.

Damon smiled awkwardly as he inadvertently made eye contact with the redheaded cadaver. She bared her crooked teeth in what he assumed was supposed to be a smile; in the absence of lips, it was hard to tell if she was friendly or hungry—or both.

Damon quickly looked away. Unlike his gregarious bodyguard, he wasn't looking to make new friends on either side of the wall.

The bartender slid another Zombie across the counter. "Compliments of the lady," he said, and chucked his chin in the direction of the undead redhead.

Damon picked up the proffered drink and saluted her with the glass. She took this as her cue to join Damon at the other end of the bar.

Damon could just see the headlines now: *GRAYSON CAUGHT CA-NOODLING WITH CORPSE!* Or worse yet, *STIFFED ACTOR STIFF FOR STIFF!* Damon quickly motioned for her to follow him to one of the booths in a dark corner of the bar. She dutifully tottered after him in three-inch heels.

Up close, her desiccation was more obvious. Damon didn't think there wasn't enough White Away in the world to cover up the exposed skull peeking through her spoiled flesh. He wondered how long she'd rotted underground before her unexpected resurrection. What had she made of her new relife as she emerged from beneath six feet of earth?

"I'm Shara. New in town?" she asked as they settled into the leather benches.

Damon quickly downed half his drink. The rum hit him like a hammer right between the eyes. "Boy is that ever an understatement."

"Got a bones jones, stranger?" *Gaw duh hunnzunn zay zuh?*

Damon smiled. Her Havens accent was thick, but there was no mistaking that question. "You don't know who I am?"

"No. Should I?" Damon shivered as she rested a talon-like claw on his leg "You must be someone big back in the states, I bet. Someone important." *Zunnzun innodend.*

"That's debatable."

"So are you in town for the convention?"

"You really have no idea who I am?" Damon laughed, relieved. "I like you already."

"Give me twenty minutes and I guarantee you'll like me a whole lot more. So what's your name?" *Zowahz yunay?*

He downed the rest of his drink in one, loud gulp. He swiveled and considered the badly decomposed cadaver, her skeleton shrouded in tight, leathery skin. She was someone's daughter once, in another lifetime, centuries ago. Who had cherished her existence when she was young and vital and vigorous, once upon a time? Who had she adored in turn? Whose attention filled her with hope, with happiness? They were all ghosts now, these long-ago relatives, these would-be suitors.

And yet, as Damon stared into her cloudy eyes, he managed to understand that Shara was more beautiful in death than she ever was alive. Such was the Resurrectionist way. Better to be a walking bag of bones than a feast for insects or a pile of ash any day.

Damon smiled at Shara as he mulled over a response to the simple question put before him. "I gotta tell you, Shar, this is not the life I pictured for myself. Not by a long shot."

"That makes two of us," she said with an unexpected twinkle in her rheumy eyes. "Sometimes I like to think I was someone who made a difference in my previous life, you know?"

Damon did know. But he also understood that death was not a prerequisite for becoming a new person. Reinvention was a matter of will and dedication—of never breaking character, no matter what the cost. Even if the world thought you a narrow-minded fool.

He shivered again as she ran a chilly finger down the side of his smooth, pampered face. She bared her teeth in another gruesome, lipless smile.

"You never did tell me your name, handsome."

Damon glanced around the darkened lounge. No one paid them any mind in their corner booth. For just an instant, the actor, revered, reviled, convinced himself that he didn't exist, that his life up until that moment had all been a fantasy lived out by the lonely, heartsick boy he had once been. Her question demanded an honest response—and he was weary of donning the identity of an unrepentant, hurtful necrophobe.

As Damon Grayson spoke, he invoked a name that was as dead to him as the one true love that forever got away.

"Muhnay mizzjed daybedden nuh," he finally confessed in a pitch-perfect Havens accent. *My name is Jesse Bettenay.*

ACKNOWLEDGMENTS

The process of writing a book is simultaneously solitary and collaborative. I received help along the way, from a great many patient, supportive people who believed in what I was doing even when I myself had doubts.

Much thanks to Jose Nario, Evan Goldstein, and Brad Feuer, for their honest input and excitement for *Posthumous* even in its earliest stages. Thanks to Heather Ryan, my would-be publicist and a font of level-headed advice. Much gratitude to Nicole Lunsford, my first reader and my most outspoken critic; your red pen kept this book on the straight and narrow.

Much thanks to my parents, because everyone should take the time to thank their parents, especially in print. Much thanks, too, to my brothers Gabe and Andrew, for their friendship, support and advice in all things, whether book-related or not. Creativity runs in our blood; one brother's accomplishment is nothing if it can't be shared.

A tip of the hat to the twinkling stars of the CALZaR universe.

A dip of the chin to my friends and coworkers, who are all too familiar with this book and its sometimes gory details.

My biggest thanks to my wife, Jade, whose unconditional support of my creative endeavors has meant the world to me. Thank you for keeping me honest, for keeping me sane. Thank you for giving me the room to explore, to fail, and now, to succeed. Thank you for correcting my mistakes, both on the page and in our shared life. You are my champion.

As for my three wonderful children—I did this for me, yes, but, ultimately, your dad did this for you.